GREEN MONSTERS

NICKY SHEARSBY

SRL Publishing Ltd

GREEN MONSTERS

NICKY SHEARSBY

SRL Publishing Ltd
London
www.srlpublishing.co.uk

First published worldwide by SRL Publishing in 2022

ISBN: 978-1915073-07-5

1 3 5 7 9 10 8 6 4 2

A CIP catalogue record for this book is available from the British Library

SRL Publishing is a Climate Positive publisher removing more carbon emissions than it emits.

Envy

/ˈɛnvi/

noun

A feeling of discontented or resentful longing aroused by someone else's possessions, qualities, or luck.

verb

Desire to have a quality, possession, or other desirable thing belonging to (someone else).

1

I perched on the edge of my sister's king-sized bed, staring at her brand-new Gucci dress that hung innocently from the wardrobe door in front of me, my thoughts wandering to places they had no business being, my mind unable to prevent such travesty. I am quite certain that if things had been different between us, our earlier relationship would have fortified the very bond we might have otherwise manifested. However, my existence equated to nothing more now than a one-bedroom flat, shockingly few possessions, and a cat I wasn't entirely certain I liked. As for Emma, we were practically strangers. How that happened, I honestly do not know.

It had been one of those days. One of those horrendous, annoying mid-week days, where I just wanted – no, needed – something to happen. Anything, in fact, that might have the potential to lift me out of the otherwise dull existence I was shocked to admit had seemingly become my life—the last few years of unwitting monotony unable to sustain any kind of contentment I may have found comfort in. A tepid blend of boredom and frustration equating now to a blackened mood that had surreptitiously found its way into my psyche. It wasn't a good feeling.

I am not proud of the fact that I was tempted to do something rather stupid that evening—the blades of a simple pair of scissors slicing together in my clammy palms, cold metal feeling ambivalent between throbbing fingertips, unassuming. Innocent in compound only, yet quite happy to allow unfiltered thoughts that actively created a malignant intention no one could have predicted.

I could have even convinced myself that I did not set out with any preconceived notion of causing mayhem. But that would be a lie. My self-serving existence would be entirely misplaced in such matters anyway, and I dread to think the type of person that would make me – an unfathomable, unbridled hatred for my sister, something I had developed over a considerable period of time. I could do nothing about such matters now, even had I the capacity to change the past.

I glanced at my somewhat worn, overused jacket lying innocently across my lap — nothing more than an item of clothing that should have found its way into the dustbin some time ago had it not held a weird sentiment with relation to a boyfriend whose name I barely recalled. This simple covering was all that protected my thoughts from those around me, from my sister's gaze, from everything I did not wish the world to see in me — a modest pair of scissors hidden on my dithering knee, beneath fake leather and sweat, trembling in the calculating hand that held them. Hidden enough so I could somehow convince myself I was doing no harm. No one could see my speculation, hear undeniably bitter thoughts or condemn not so carefully considered actions. *A single nick.* An accident. That is all it would be — what a shame.

Emma would, of course, curse and mutter profanities. She would wonder how she'd failed to notice such a conspicuous slash mark in the overly expensive material purchased that very day. She may even blame the poor shop assistant for folding her garment so carelessly inside the same bag as the new shoes that had hastened her indulgence. What an unexpected occurrence, her otherwise prestigious shopping trip now unfathomable, my unrefuted mix of shock and drama adding further chaos to the equation.

From my perfect vantage point on this bed, a savoury smile would linger behind my weary eyes, hidden from view — hidden from my sister's incorrect assumptions and outrage. I would be glad to have caused such sudden suffering, satisfied even for the briefest of moments to have brought forth an unexpected pain to her day. A pain I was destined to endure most days, my suffering burrowing a hole into my brain every bloody time I looked at her. I might even relish the satisfaction that I'd stopped her wearing the sodding thing. It didn't suit her anyway. Such bliss I would feel. Such pride I would glean from my impromptu accomplishment.

I could, of course, convince myself that it was for my sister's own sake that I was considering such an appalling act of sabotage. I could pretend to my brain and anyone interested, should they ask, that I hated the dress, that it looked ridiculous on her, that it didn't suit her figure in the slightest. I could even tell myself that I was merely trying to help, to save her from total embarrassment — to save us all. But the simple truth was, it did suit her. Actually, it looked incredible. And I am sickened to admit that she looked incredible wearing it. The way it hugged her slim frame, dancing from curvaceous hips that, even after childbirth, bore no resemblance to the ones owned by little old despondent, childless me.

No. The simple truth was, if I had to place an actual word to my emotions, I am slightly ashamed to admit that I was probably a tad envious. How can my sister indulge in such lavish items when I struggle to afford the simplest of clothing from my local charity shop? Envy isn't the nicest of sentiments, I know. Yet, forming such an emotion inside the privacy of my own head doesn't feel altogether inappropriate because I can privately justify my innermost thoughts unknown to anyone else. Emma has, after all, made me the way I am. She has no one to blame but herself for the way things have turned out between us, so my distressed emotions are entirely understandable.

'Come on, Stace. Better get a move on if you don't want us to be late.' Emma shoved her overinflated head around the bedroom door, offering a smile that appeared to me as fake as her overbearing lipstick. *That bloody smile.* I swear if I were ever able to summon the guts, I'd knock the thing clean off her shoulders. Why was everything always about my goddamned perfect sister?

4

'Sure thing, sis,' I chimed in, unable to help the sarcasm that left my lips unchecked, a sigh involuntarily escaping my throat. I was quite shocked that I attempted to return a smile of my own, probably failing in my quest, and utterly unsurprised it went unnoticed, as usual, by the woman who only ever saw her own reflection in the mirror. I certainly did not wish to be inside my sister's head or experience any emotional response that might mean I had to pretend, even for a moment, that I cared about her wellbeing. I was here now purely because our mother had insisted I share in her good fortune. Good fortune? Why could she not send some of that my way?

'You okay?' Emma absently muttered what sounded like a molecule of concern as she rounded the bed, searching for an elusive tube of mascara.

It wasn't genuine. Emma was never genuine. Had I been fortunate enough to have noticed the discarded plastic wand sitting forgotten on her bedside cabinet, I probably would have dipped it, entirely by accident of course, into the toilet bowl before reuniting it with its ignorant owner. Conjunctivitis would have been, in my opinion, a far better look for my sister than the smoky eye shadow that hid her true malignant identity. An unexpected eye infection would stand out against any makeup she attempted to cover it with, the perfect opportunity to make me smile and raise my otherwise subjacent spirits. She would actually appear the very demon I knew her to be. Heinous. Shocking to those who looked at her. *Ever so slightly ugly*. She wasn't asking about my welfare out of genuine concern for my state of mind. She merely did not want me ruining her otherwise perfect evening. How should I react to such a throwaway question? *No, Emma. I'm not bloody okay if you must know. I could think of around a million things I'd rather be doing with my evening than accompany you to your pathetic flaming book celebration dinner.*

'Sure,' I replied, offering nothing more than a single grunting syllable, detached from her gaze, congratulating myself on the ability to keep my offhand opinions to myself. 'I'm good.'

I dropped the scissors, that were beginning to dig into my palm, carefully into my inside jacket pocket as Emma snatched her mascara from the bedside cabinet and floated towards the bathroom, humming. She unhooked her new dress from the coat-hanger, not even bothering to grace my disgruntled response with any kind of acknowledgement. I sat and stared at the back of her head, recalling how many times I'd trailed behind her as a toddler, then as a teenager. Gazing in awe at the world in which she lived, compelled to remain forever invisible to her, no matter what I did. I wasn't surprised that my sister failed to notice my low mood tonight. She hardly ever notices me. Why should I assume she might see my emotions now? To care how I'm feeling or express honest concern for me? I was kidding myself with my silent musing that my sister actually gave a shit.

I considered racing into the bathroom and expressing every thought that swam in my head, telling her what I was thinking, what I truly wanted. I wished I had the courage to divulge those little secrets my precious sister didn't know. Secrets I'd kept firmly hidden, telling myself too often not to ponder over them, yet failing in a mission that had become all-consuming. I wanted to stand on this bed and scream at the top of my lungs that I hated her so much. That I wished she would–

'Stacey, for crying out loud, will you please hurry up?' Emma's irritated tone reached my ears, her words no less annoying than a cat scratching at a closed door.

I'd done nothing to warrant such arrogant interaction, hovering on this stupidly comfortable bed for the last hour, mouth welded shut for fear of what I might say. I had been forced to watch while she flitted around me like a headless pig, the apparent centre of everyone's attention, expecting the entire world to stop simply because she now declared herself some fantastic, entrepreneurial, newly acquired author. *Brilliant. Well flaming done, Emma.*

I didn't want to, but I got to my feet, smoothed scissors that now felt as if they were laughing at me against the frayed inside lining of my jacket pocket, and wandered into the bathroom. 'So? How do I look?' she asked, spinning around in the mirror several times, gleaning attention she assumed I would provide without question. *You look bloody shit. Seriously, Emma. SHIT.*

'You look great,' I offered, my own less than perfect image standing mockingly behind her. I wished I could disappear. At least until the end of this unbearable evening. I wondered if I could get away with shoving her head through the mirror. Would that count as an innocent accident? Maybe I could convince Jason that his wife had simply spun around too fast in deluded pursuit of perfection? I sighed under my breath, suppressing an urge to scoff. Don't be stupid, Stacey. *Play nice.*

2

'Just, *great?*' Emma was beside herself with my irrefutable and lamentable response. I was still staring blankly at her, my thoughts lost in transit somewhere far away. Yes, of course, she would require over-exuberant praise for the fact that she could afford such an expensive garment and a tonne of make-up to complete the façade. Who knew such a simple act warranted so much astonished approval? I felt like clapping my hands together in forced congratulations, a twisted grin imprinted onto a less than impressed face, probably appearing slightly deranged, demonic even. But I thought better of it.

Instead, I attempted a smile I didn't feel like offering, pulling my jacket over my somewhat less expensive, several-year-old sage green all-in-one trouser suit, scissors still mockingly lying in a pocket that now felt slightly heavy and encumbered. I hoped it wouldn't burst a seam, revealing my hidden intentions, my sister's glossy bathroom tiles bearing witness to a savage act not yet complete. I wasn't sure what might offend her the most: the appalling reasons behind the presence of scissors or the unfortunate crack the impending fall from my pocket would certainly create on her bathroom floor? She would probably expect me to pay for a new one.

'What else do you want me to say, Emma? You look beautiful. You always look beautiful.' I hoped she wouldn't notice my irritability, the roll of my eyes behind her head, trying hard not to automatically shake my head with over-enthused sarcasm. I honestly just wanted this evening over and done with.

She had a weird knack of making me feel inadequate, ghastly, sometimes to the point of nausea. It was exhausting and far more than I could contend with right then. I couldn't bring myself to look in the mirror. Next to my sister, I always appeared slightly less than acceptable — less than perfect. I sighed. I had made as much effort as I could with my own appearance, but nothing in my wardrobe would ever contend with Emma's. I could wrack up a credit card bill to end all credit card bills and still be unable to afford the luxury brands indulged by my sister. We both knew that truth.

'Oh, I get it.' Emma turned to face me then, probably for the first time that day. It unnerved me.

'Get what?' I was in no mood for games.

'Time of the month? Am I right?' Emma gave me one of her knowing laughs, nudging me on the shoulder much harder than I would have liked. In her deluded mind, she probably meant it as a playful action, but I wanted to push her straight out of the goddamned window and be done with it.

'Seriously?' It was the only rational thing I could

think to say. At this moment, it was all that stood between the two of us and complete fury. I was staring at her, my face blank, glad she didn't notice the seething look behind my now offended eyes. If I said much more, we would end up in a fight — and not a verbal one. I couldn't believe my sister's callous attitude towards a sibling so obviously unhappy.

I held my breath, allowing unhealthy thoughts to dissipate before daring to open my mouth again. How dare she assume my low mood would be due to anything other than the fact that she was acting like a total bitch? Yet, saying that, Emma always acted like a bitch, totally unable to see her own reality. She assumed she was perfect, convinced that everyone else could see how perfect she was too. Seriously, what more could I expect from the woman?

'Well, you've had a face on you for the last hour, sis. What am I meant to think?' Emma was applying dark red lipstick that made her look cheap. If she applied any more make-up, someone would have to carry her to the car because she would never get her inflated head out of the bloody door.

This is the only face I have, bitch. Besides, I'd much rather have my face than to be forced to stare at yours all night, thank you very much. I stared at her, wishing I could express exactly how I felt at this moment, suffocating in the overbearing heat of the room. Yet, I knew to keep my opinions to myself. I didn't need the stress they would have provoked, the argument we would have ended up having.

'I seriously hope you're not going to have that wasp-

11

like look on your face all evening,' Emma said, totally oblivious to my emotions as she continued to enjoy her reflection in the mirror.

'I have a headache, if you must know.' It was only a half-lie, so it didn't count. Emma was enough to give anyone a headache. 'I'll be alright once I've taken something.' I smoothed fingertips across my now throbbing temples, wishing I had the guts to use the scissors Emma was unaware I had in my possession. I needed to get out of this room before I did something regrettable.

'Oh poor baby.' Emma's berating voice merely increased my impending nausea. 'Jason will show you where the paracetamol is, if that'll help?'

'Okay, whatever,' I muttered, needing to get away from her now in case I accidentally threw up, threw something at her, or stabbed her to death with my scissors.

She didn't even turn my way as I staggered back into the bedroom, the mere mention of her husband's name enough to send my head into a complete spin along with the swirling image of my sister's Gucci dress.

I didn't want her to notice the look in my eyes right then, her condescending tone already too much. I swallowed. The unadulterated thoughts of this woman's husband were something I'd spent many evenings alone with. I smiled slyly as I ventured onto the landing.

As much as I hated to admit it, I could never endure my sister's company for long. She was overbearing, and any extended time with her provoked dark thoughts no sane person should experience. I often wondered what

Jason saw in her.

I was now actually developing the very headache I'd only moments ago invented. Typical.

***

'Is everything okay up there?' Jason's alluring voice filtered from the kitchen as I plodded barefoot towards an inviting aroma of coffee. I was unable to dissipate my lustful thoughts as I walked into the room, slumping onto a barstool in front of him and picking up one of my niece's discarded dolls from the countertop to distract myself from his gaze. Emma had drained me, my energies now so low I feared I might not be able to converse with the very man I'd secretly fantasised over for several years.

'Mm,' I groaned, the reality of my invented headache kicking in. I rubbed my temples for a moment, desperate for Emma's sickly perfume to leave my nostrils, her words still ringing in my ears. 'She's in the bathroom.'

Jason laughed then, forcing me to open eyes I hadn't realised I'd closed.

'What?' I asked, not meaning to sound so irritated yet unable to unravel my now twisted emotions. Emma had a way of bringing out the worst in me. It wasn't ideal.

'I take it you've spent the last thirty minutes enduring endless wardrobe options that have all ended up discarded on the bed?' Jason was pouring coffee, his back to me. I visualised his cheeky grin by the way his shoulders juddered in response to his words, the flush of his cheeks, the tightness of his buttocks. I allowed a genuine smile then, feeling momentarily glad to have been given such a provocative distraction. Jason had a way of doing that to me. He didn't know it, of course. It was an unfortunate truth.

'Nope. She picked her outfit hours ago.' It indeed felt as if I had been in that room for hours. Metal blades sat silent in my pocket, unused, my breath as unsteady as the hand that quivered in misspent anticipation. Eva's doll mocked me, smiling behind vacant eyes that appeared to know my sinister intentions.

'Oh yeah,' Jason turned around, handing me a large mug of steaming black coffee. He sat on the stool next to mine, our knees almost touching, oblivious to the thoughts that swam in my aching head. He sipped his drink. An overwhelming scent of aftershave added to the headache I had unwittingly bought forth. 'I forgot about today's *big* purchase.' He emphasised the word big, as if it had cost a fortune. It made what I wanted to do to the thing all the more enticing — my grievous missed opportunity unforgiving.

I picked up my mug and took a sip. 'Thank you,' I offered, feeling able to relax a little now I was away from that bitch's glare. 'I don't suppose you have any painkillers, do you? I'm developing a bit of a headache.' The irony of my words was not lost on me. Shit.

'Yeah, sure.' Jason rose to his feet and popped open a cupboard, handing me a small box of paracetamol. 'Are you okay? You seem a little tense.'

I gave my sister's husband a genuine glance then, a much-needed moment to catch my breath. I smiled. 'Yeah, sorry. It's just that she can be a bit –'

'Intense?'

I laughed. Intense was indeed an excellent word. 'Yes. She can be a little highly strung, can't she?' I tried to sound diplomatic, yet a wayward thought popped into my head: how good it would be to have her strung up high from somewhere desolate. And cold. Somewhere very cold.

Jason laughed, my casual, throwaway words hitting their mark, despite secret thoughts hidden from a world I didn't anticipate would possibly understand. I was impressed he had agreed with me on the uncomfortable subject of my sister. It was a rare occurrence, an exuberant moment in time that I wished I had the power to bottle. I would have made a fortune. I liked Jason. No, that's not entirely true. I fancied him like crazy. He was so very different from my sister. Normal. Sane. Although they had been together a decade, married four years, he was the polar opposite of Emma. Relaxed, easy-going. I often wondered what the hell he saw in –

'So? How do I look?' That oh so annoying voice filtered into the kitchen behind us, breaking our relaxed moment, forcing my head to throb again, my stomach to churn.

'Oh my God, honey, you look incredible. Doesn't she look stunning, Stacey?' Jason walked across the kitchen to his wife who twirled around in the doorway as if she was the Queen of bloody Sheba, a smile on her face that I wanted to slap clean off her shoulders. Oh, how I hated that woman.

'Yep, she looks terrific.' I took a swig of coffee, dropping two, no, three, chalky paracetamol tablets into the liquid, allowing them to fizz and bubble in pursuit of swift dissolution. I didn't dare look at my sister again until a distinct sound of kissing reached me — a harsh, discordant mixing of oral fluids that made me want to vomit.

'Urgh. Get a room, you two,' I snapped, suddenly feeling as if my coffee might accidentally end up all over my sister's inflated head. But Jason looked nice. He had made a genuine effort. He always did. I didn't wish to ruin his freshly ironed shirt with unfortunate splashes of coffee that probably wouldn't wash out. Those crisp, tight trousers. Those alluring butt cheeks.

I allowed a cheeky glance in his direction as he engrossed himself with the sister I wished would disappear into thin air and be gone forever. I'd hardly hidden the fact that I found him good-looking. Most people did, to be fair. I wasn't proud of myself for the thoughts that swam through my mind as he slid his hand across Emma's waist, wishing it were my waist he was wrapping his arms around.

I sighed. 'Are you guys ready?' I was unsure how much of their unrestrained affection I could stomach.

I picked up my still half-full mug, hovering for a moment, contemplating. *Be careful, Jason,* I wanted to say. *You'll smudge her make-up, and it will take another goddamned twenty minutes before we can leave this house.* But, by some miracle, I remained calm enough to simply place my mug in the sink, paracetamol bubbles still frothing to the surface of liquid that was now going cold.

Emma laughed, unapologetically forgetting for a moment that I was actually in the room. The irony wasn't lost on me. She pulled away from the eager hands of her husband, glancing my way, cheeks now flush, make-up threatening to melt. 'Oops. Someone isn't very happy with me today,' she said, implying that I appeared oddly pissed off with something she'd done yet she couldn't possibly imagine what it could have been. *As if.*

'I could do without the sarcasm, please, Emma,' I replied, smoothing my jacket, wondering if Jason would at all mind if I plunged these scissors – that were beginning to feel quite heavy in my pocket – straight into her bloody eye socket.

'Come on, you two, let's not start any unpleasantness tonight.' Jason always had a way of calming my shredded nerves. He knew us well. And he, of course, knew that my sister usually instigated any argument we had. He unhooked an Armani jacket from the stand in the hall, slipping his feet into freshly shined shoes that didn't look as if they had ever left the soft pile of the rug on which he stood. He genuinely looked handsome. I wondered if I should say so. I gave Emma a fleeting glance. Maybe not.

My sister whispered something into his ear, and he laughed, a quiet, muffled chuckle that made me wish I could be a party to what she'd said. Was it something sarcastic uttered to dislodge any wrongly formed opinion of me? Or had she simply made him a promise he couldn't refuse? A promise he'd no doubt need to wait all evening before she gave it to him. I would most definitely give it to him. *I'd give it to him good and proper.*

3

As much as I hate to admit it, the restaurant Jason had chosen for his wife's celebratory meal was actually quite a pleasant location. Five-star luxury, full table waiter service, candlelit atmosphere. Nothing had been left unconsidered. Only the very best would be good enough for Emma. Yet again, Jason had impeccable taste. He was hardly going to choose a venue of substandard quality. The idea of my sister agreeing to eat a meal at *Milly Mac's Burger Bar* or *Dr Friendly's Fried Food Emporium* was ever so slightly inconceivable.

I suppressed a sudden urge to smile as inappropriate thoughts washed over my brain, the likes of which would have potentially made Jason smile too had I included him in my wayward thinking. It wasn't that I believed Emma to be a snob. She simply considered herself better than everyone else. Actually, that ultimately makes her a snob. It also made Jason's marriage to her all the more confusing because he, of course, was anything but.

With a bit of forced persuasion, I ensured that I was

seated next to him that evening. My sister offered questioning glances when I swiftly bagged a seat by the window, but Jason was already in position next to me, unconcerned. My excuse? That I merely needed to see out of the thing, my headache still lingering, and I did not, of course, wish to be a burden. Emma seemed to believe me, thankfully.

Prolonged endurance of this woman's company was something I had zero tolerance for. My thoughts now happily wandering to a place they had no business being. I had no issues telling myself that, as long as my capricious ideas stayed firmly within the confines of my head, I was causing no harm. I could not, after all, help the way I felt. It was not my fault that, whenever I was around Jason, my thoughts wandered to dark locations, the likes of which I could never have expressed to anyone.

The fact that I hadn't eaten much that day did nothing for my churning belly either. My decision to save my stomach for the luxury feast my sister's money would be purchasing mocked my intention to ensure she spent well above an acceptable level. My gut twisted as we took our places at the table, yet whether it was from hunger or desire for a man that wasn't mine, I simply could not tell.

The restaurant was awash with low voices and soft background music that oddly made me sleepy until, ever the devoted husband, Jason rose to his feet, this occasion calling for an important speech. Emma's face stretched into a neat little grin in anticipation of her man expressing to the room the pride he felt for a wife who seemingly could do no wrong. I wanted to wipe that smile clean off her face, along with the gleaming cutlery that lay on the table in front of me.

Picking up a butter knife from the freshly pressed tablecloth, Jason gently tapped the edge of his wine glass before clearing his throat with a casual abandonment that made me want to stick my tongue down his throat. I even had to look away, convinced the entire room would uncover my secret thoughts.

'I would like to make a toast to my beautiful wife, Emma,' he declared, raising his glass to my sister. Everyone around the table muttered half-hearted confirmations, raising half-empty glasses in response to what I believed to be lukewarm words. I wanted to smash my own glass straight into her smug face. She wouldn't be so beautiful then, would she?

'Emma has worked so hard over this last year,' Jason continued, unaware of the dark ideas that swam in private thoughts, glancing around at the glazed faces of their mutual friends, hoping to convince them all of how incredible his wife was in a few unrehearsed words. *Oh, I think they already know precisely what Emma is, Jason.* 'And I'm so proud that her debut book will be available in bookstores near you very soon.' Everyone cheered, laughed, applauded, congratulating my sister on her apparently incredible achievement. I raised my glass in response to everyone else's cheering, allowing it to hover mid-air for longer than necessary, staring through crystal at the distorted image of my nemesis. *Well, bloody done, you.*

There are photographs in existence of my sister and

me. Plenty of them, in fact. My parents were seemingly unable to stop themselves from producing photo albums whenever the occasion called for it. Images that, to any stranger, might even look agreeable, adorable. Two fading, chubby-cheeked sisters, frozen in time, my once prodigious protector gazing lovingly into a pram that housed a peculiar-looking baby, happily chewing a toe. My toothless smile set against thick, fiery red hair that had turned a dull, mousy brown many years ago, Emma's recognisable grin spread across rosy cheeks that I had learned to love during those early years. Even back then, she was beautiful, and I am convinced we must have been close at one point. I simply cannot allow myself to think anything else. My childhood depends on it.

I have vague recollections of following her everywhere she went, hovering behind her, nothing more than a misplaced possession, wanting desperately to share her world that to me, seemed wondrous, astonishing. But not anymore. Now, irrationally, without warning, I hated her with everything I had inside. It was not a pleasant feeling. Somehow, I had been scorned, yet I had no idea when it had occurred.

I'm not entirely proud of the way my relationship with Emma has turned out. I would have loved to perpetuate our earlier close-knit relationship bubble. The type of sisterly togetherness I often sickeningly witness on television and in the world around me. A togetherness I am convinced we must have shared once but now seems forever elusive. For my sister and I, that existence is no longer our reality. No. For reasons that

21

have evaded me for quite some time, we genuinely do not like each other. It is just the way of things.

We tolerate each other for the sake of our family name and those we wish to appease but, other than that, our lives now could not be more different. Actually no. That is a wrong assumption entirely. It is I who tolerate her. A tolerance I'm steadily becoming tired of maintaining, these scissors in my jacket proof of that fact. I am utterly indifferent to what she thinks of me, and I did not want to be here tonight, this entire evening all about Emma's needs, Emma's success, Emma, Emma, Emma.

'Is everything okay there, Stacey?' I turned to see Sophia, Emma's oldest friend, leaning across the table towards me. *What was it with all the bloody questions tonight?* My glass was still hovering mid-air, my glare set across the table, unseeing, unkind thoughts unrelenting.

I nodded, unsure what else I was meant to do. 'Sure. Why shouldn't I be?' I didn't want to be here. I couldn't have sounded less enthusiastic had I tried.

Sophia smiled. 'You just seem a little distracted, that's all.'

Yeah, well, maybe that's because I'd rather be at home drowning myself in a bath of boiling water. Why none of you can see Emma for the spiteful cow she is, seems beyond rational logic. Perhaps, if you all open your eyes just a tiny bit, you'd be able to see her for the monster she really is.

'Nope,' I answered blankly, swilling expensive dry white wine around my already half-empty glass, the hefty price tag doing nothing to lift my wavering mood, the idea of disappearing into the carpet beneath my feet

22

somewhat inviting. 'I'm good. I have a headache, that's all.' I offered Sophia a thin smile, hoping she'd take the hint and leave me alone.

I had no capacity for polite conversation, Emma's earlier intrusion wholly ensuring I had few reserves left for anyone else. I realised that tonight my headache excuse was following me around, growing tiresome with each retelling. The only genuine thing I wanted to do right then was to go to bed. I glanced towards Jason, my eyes resting on the open, top button of his shirt. I would like to say he had caught my attention at that moment for no particular reason, but I would be telling absolute whopping great big lies. Going to bed would indeed be fantastic. I simply didn't mean it had to be by myself.

'She's worked so hard, hasn't she?' Sophia again.

Bloody hell, I get it. Yes, you all think my sister is some fantastic person who can't do a goddamned thing wrong. How she has managed to delude you all for so long is beyond me.

'I guess,' I managed to say, unable to hide the irritation that lingered behind my weary voice. I coughed. 'Forgive me, Sophia,' I muttered, realising that tonight it was me who was acting rude and out of place. Not unlike Emma, in fact — the idea that we were more alike than I would have dared contemplate not entirely sitting right with my rational thinking. 'It's been one of those days.' That wasn't a lie. I had spent the entire day mulling over this very evening, hunger pangs unrelenting, not at all looking forward to the forced prolonged company of my sister whose cumbersome personality had a nasty side effect of rubbing off on me.

Sophia scoffed. 'Christ, tell me about it,' she chuckled, taking an overly large swig of wine before pouring us both another glass from the open bottle in the middle of the table. 'They all feel like that for me at the moment, if I'm honest.'

'Oh?' I asked absently, not needing any, lengthy or otherwise, yet also not wishing to appear as uninterested as I felt.

'Yeah, between work, the kids and John, I'm frazzled.' She gulped down yet another mouthful of wine, nodding a casual head towards her husband who had been busy chatting to Jason for the last few minutes. *Lucky sod.*

It genuinely never fails to amaze me how married women seem to have so much to complain about. What is it about having a man in your life, someone to share the burden of life, someone to cuddle, to share your bed, to keep you warm at night, that makes these women so goddamned cranky? *Poor them.* I wished I had a man to cuddle up to in the dead of night. I glanced at Jason again, wishing I wouldn't. It was hardly appropriate. But none of these people could have known of my lustful thoughts right then, so who cared?

'Stacey, come on, join the fun?' It was Emma. I shuddered. *Fun? Seriously? You call this fun?* You need to live a little, girl. Get out more. Hardly a party animal, are you?

I watched my older sister, perpetually oblivious to my emotions, laughing, enjoying some private joke with John, Jason, and Lloyd, *her editor*, that the rest of us had been uninvited to comment on. Oh, how my sister loved

24

to be the centre of everyone's attention. How she gleaned the adoration of those around her. Just once, I would like to experience a normal, sane conversation with someone — preferably Jason, preferably in private. I knew that would not happen any time soon, but I would have settled for the occasional, knowing wink. He was the only person around this table who understood me, completely, utterly. It wasn't fair.

'I'm ok on this side of the table, thank you,' I called out, appearing as cheerful as I was able to muster the strength for. I turned to Sophia, rolling my eyes at my sister's developing drunken loudness I was happy for her to believe I was merely joking around. What good would the truth do, anyway?

'Oh, come on, sis.' Emma clambered to her feet, stumbling around the table towards me, her pretentiously created grandeur slipping away, along with the copious amount of alcohol being consumed. 'As my favourite sister…' Emma slurred. I shook my head in disgust, unable to hide my expression and threatening to display my irritation to the whole group. *I am your only sister, you stupid bitch.* I wished I wouldn't keep rolling my eyes. 'You are my guest of honour this evening,' she concluded, leaning over, placing a clammy hand on my shoulder from behind. She stunk of booze and too much perfume. It made me want to gag, completely unable to hide my disdain for the woman calling herself *family.* And those awful talon-shaped nails did not suit her at all. She looked like a whore.

Oh, sorry, yes, I forgot. Emma was indeed a whore. I should have mentioned that earlier.

25

4

It would have been impossible to explain the truth to anyone unless, by some spectacular miracle, I was able to uncover the painful dynamics of our relationship. But the repulsed hatred I had developed for my big sister had not occurred overnight. It had taken several years before I snapped, the bitter poison she had dripped into the minds of everyone around her going unnoticed until one day something inside of me revolted, making me realise that every time we were in the same room together I literally wanted to –

'Stacey, are you okay?' Jason's quiet, brooding voice bought me sharply out of my inappropriate daydream. I glanced at him. Although Emma's hand was still burning a metaphorical hole into my shoulder blade, I was glad her attention was now filtering back towards the other guests, my apparent disinterest of no concern to her whatsoever — her only focus being to snatch as much attention for herself as she could muster, the approval of fake friends more important than my welfare ever would be.

I smiled, nodding. I really wanted to shake my head and scream. I hoped he could see straight through me - see that I wasn't happy here tonight - and be willing to rescue me from the certain catastrophic destruction I did not know how to avoid.

'You look a bit pale, honey.' Jason was touching my arm. I sighed, allowing my guard to drop slightly, only noticing then just how tight my shoulders were beginning to feel. Tense, aching, throbbing. Not unlike another part of my body as Jason's touch lingered a little too long.

'I'm so sorry,' I whispered into his ear, my sister remaining oblivious behind me. She was unapologetically drunk, hovering above my head like a wasp I wished I had the strength to squash. 'My headache isn't clearing up.' I was oddly beginning to enjoy my newly discovered headache. It helped me disappear into private considerations without appearing as ignorant as I felt. It was just a shame the bloody thing was now actually a reality.

'Need some air?' Jason smiled, a secret wink that expressed far more to me than my brother-in-law had probably intended. Yes. Absolutely, yes, I most definitely needed air — anything to remove me from this unbearable situation. In fact, if Jason was offering, I would go anywhere in the world with him and never look back.

I nodded, attempting to remain calm and unaffected by such an innocent request that actually made my heart pound and my lips feel dry. 'Would you mind taking me outside for a moment?' I relished the idea of getting

Jason alone. Alone we could talk, laugh, enjoy a few moments of peace. Together. Just the two of us. Sheer bliss.

Jason nodded a silent understanding, winking again as he rose from the table. 'Sorry darling, but would you mind if I take your sister outside for some fresh air?' He turned to his wife and promptly unpeeled her sticky clamp from my aching shoulder blade. I have no idea if she realised she had been digging her nails into my skin, laughing among the group, seemingly oblivious to any harm caused. Jason could take me outside for far more than fresh air if he so desired.

'Oh!' Emma sounded slightly taken aback by her husband's unexpected interruption. She patted me patronisingly on the arm with a grin. 'Sorry, sis, are you still feeling icky?'

Icky? Seriously, Emma? How old are we?

I smiled, a fake smile I no longer had the strength to hide behind, which presumably didn't go unnoticed by the others. Yet, at this point, I was genuinely past caring. I was hot. The headache I had earlier invented now threatened to make me faint. I was being slowly suffocated by a lack of stimulating conversation, and expensive food was no longer critical to my immediate requirements.

'I'll be okay. I just need a bit of air, that's all,' I replied, patting her a little too forcefully on her own shoulder, purely so she would know how annoying it felt. I couldn't help it. She had a way of turning me into something I wasn't. Something dark. Something sinister.

I shuddered as Jason slipped his arm around me and

we squeezed past the crowded table towards the door. Fresh air and Jason's undivided attention would be perfect right then. I had entirely underestimated how stifling Emma's prolonged company could be. Besides, I craved rational conversation, the sane company of someone who didn't drive me to distraction, no matter how much time we were given.

I wanted my sister to notice her husband's hand cupped gently around my waist, my one-piece trouser suit hugging my curves in all the right places. But she didn't seem to, instead remaining focused on the confirmed attention of those around her. Shit.

***

'I'm so sorry to drag you out like that,' I said, as Jason and I stepped into the refreshing evening air. The restaurant was violently buzzing in my ears, along with a few lingering birds who now joined the commotion in my head. It was warm out. Stars in a clear sky were lighting our way as we wandered across the car park in pursuit of escape. I leaned in to Jason, pretending that I was feeling slightly chilled. It was naughty, silly even, but I couldn't help it. When I was with him, I felt like a dizzy schoolgirl. He had a way of doing that to me.

'Hey, don't worry about it,' he replied, pulling an unopened packet of cigarettes from his pocket before slipping his jacket off and draping it around my shoulders. I thought of my own, much cheaper jacket, a pair of innocent scissors still tucked inside its unassuming pocket, currently on the back of a restaurant

29

chair, waiting to be discovered at any moment, uncovering my true purpose and the twisted motives I could never adequately explain.

I shivered. 'Thank you,' I said, breathing in his aftershave and hoping I wasn't making myself look too obvious. It had been a while since any man had showered me with this kind of attention. Being in Jason's company tonight was a welcome relief.

'To be honest with you, Stace, I was glad of the distraction.'

My God, did I sense trouble in paradise? Oh, how I could hope and dream. 'Oh?' I asked, wanting to hear more — desperate to hear more – yet trying to remain as neutral and relaxed as my uncontrolled brain would allow. I tried to suppress a smile.

'Emma has talked of nothing but this bloody book launch for weeks.' He lit his cigarette, handing the freshly unwrapped packet to me. I shook my head. When did Jason start smoking? I wondered if Emma was driving him to distraction in such a way that smoking helped calm his nerves. I could hope. I could dream. Maybe he needed saving from her? I certainly knew I did.

'You know I love her, don't you?' He allowed a laugh that, in my limited experience, sounded as if he was hiding something. Something he didn't yet feel he could share with me. I sensed a *but*. Maybe he didn't love her after all, and their entire marriage was a charade? If only. I smiled, trying to appear relaxed, wanting him to open up, to talk about Emma to slag her off and tell me he secretly hated her guts. I needed him to tell me everything without giving away my position entirely. I hoped he'd consumed a sufficient amount of wine to be comfortable divulging every one of my sister's annoying habits.

'But, Jesus, Stacey, she's been hard to live with recently.' Only recently? Seriously? When was my sister anything *but* hard to live with?

I laughed. 'My sister? Hard to live with? Never.' Shit, I hoped I didn't sound too bitchy. Yet, the words had left my mouth before I had given myself time to check such unhinged emotions, so I couldn't overthink any of it now. All I could do was hope that Jason had been hiding his true feelings for my sister behind a façade of perfection she had created, and he was about to unravel it all. Their apparently perfect life. Perfect house. All that money in the bank. Flashy cars on the drive. Holidays to luxurious, far-off destinations. My sister's ideal man. Actually, yes, that last assumption was undoubtedly valid. He was indeed ideal. Perfect, in fact. And, to top it off, she now had a bloody book deal that would no doubt net her millions. *God, how I loathed that smug bitch.*

Jason took a drag of his cigarette and breathed out deeply; too deeply, as if he needed some well-deserved time out. 'It's hard, sometimes, you know. Living in her shadow.'

I knew exactly what he meant. I had lived in my sister's shadow my entire life; our parents far more interested in Emma's achievements than my own. I wondered for a moment if I should divulge a little more of what I knew about my sister but thought better of it. I hadn't drunk nearly enough alcohol to warrant that kind of chatter, and, I assumed, Jason had drunk far too much.

'You're telling *me.*' I allowed the words to slip unchecked. I pressed my lips together. Did I seriously wish to open Pandora's box tonight? 'You must put up with a lot from my sister,' I added. *Shit, Stacey, stop with the confessions. Soon you'll be professing your unwavering devotion to the man.* I swallowed, realising my hidden feelings might be more than I'd initially assumed. *Devotion?* Was that what this was? Maybe it was the reason I had been spending so much time at the house recently? It certainly wasn't for my sister's sake. Perhaps I wanted to protect Jason from her overbearing, spiteful ways.

'Are you feeling any better?' he asked, utterly oblivious to my previous statement. Either that or he had chosen to ignore it. He stubbed out his half-smoked cigarette against the lid of a litterbin and turned to me. 'Please don't tell Emma I started smoking again. She's spent so much time and money getting me to quit.' *Again?* I had no idea he ever smoked at all.

I smiled. I wanted to set aside the persistent negative feelings I had for my sister. I wanted to allow myself the opportunity to feel normal, even for a second. She seemed to consume my days now. It wasn't pleasant. Being with Jason was all I needed to be me again. 'I'm good, thank you. And no, of course, I won't say a word.'

'Good to hear it.' Jason took a deep breath and absorbed the evening air along with lingering cigarette smoke that threatened to choke me. 'It's pleasant out, don't you think?'

I smiled, relaxing a little. Away from the hassle and

expectation of tonight's meal, I was able to unwind. I could be myself around Jason. I didn't have to pretend to be anyone other than who I was. It was a nice feeling. 'Yes, it is nice out. It's a shame we have to go back in there, really,' I laughed, motioning a free hand to the heaving restaurant while tucking my other beneath Jason's elbow.

I could already feel the place closing in around me again. I did not wish to go back inside, despite the fact that we hadn't even ordered our food yet, and I was starving, bread rolls and copious amounts of alcohol notwithstanding. 'Maybe we could sneak off while no one's watching and grab a cheeky takeaway?' It wasn't the only cheeky thing I wanted to grab.

Jason laughed then, uninhibited by the earlier stiffness of the evening's expectations. 'Yeah, I'm sure Emma would love that,' he chided as he nudged me playfully on the arm. I am not sure why, but in Jason's company, I always feel relaxed. It is as if he genuinely gets who I am and what I am about. An impossible thought popped into my mind that he only endured my sister in order to get close to me. I could wish. 'Come on, you.' He clasped my hand under his arm casually and led me back towards the oppressive restaurant door. 'Best not keep her ladyship waiting.'

We both laughed. It was as if he could read my mind. I wondered if this might be the perfect opportunity to tell him how I felt, to open up to him about the emotions and thoughts I secretly harboured about him? The mere idea made my legs weak, my private parts exude a slightly damp sensation and my mind jolt in eager anticipation. *Shit, Stacey, get a grip.* How was I going to eat a three-course meal with my lady parts throbbing and these unrelenting thoughts racing? It might be quite funny to watch my sister's face while I sat and fantasised about what I want her husband to do to me. It might make the evening pass a little faster, if nothing else.

5

By the time the taxi had dropped me at my flat, Jason
and Emma casually heading off to collect their daughter
Eva from the sitter, my emotions were in shreds. I had
endured an uncomfortable ride in the back of a taxi that
smelled of the putrid sick the poor driver had failed to
dislodge from some previous perilous journey. I could
have done without that.

I'd pressed my clenched buttocks as close to the rear
passenger door as I could get, avoiding the antics of my
sister and her husband, who, seemingly still on the
promise she'd made him earlier, giggled into her ear,
alcohol apparently having the desired effect. I wondered
why I hadn't chosen to sit in the front seat with the
driver, as my presence was unwanted. I awkwardly
folded my arms across my crushed chest in a futile
attempt to evade the occasional touching of sweaty skin
against my own while they giggled sweet nothings into
each other's drunken earlobes, unaware of my existence,
Emma nibbling his neck, Jason's hand blatantly between
her legs.

It wasn't lost on me that there were several occasions where he seemed to brush his wandering fingertips against my thigh, lingering a little too long, a simple action that made me want him all the more. But maybe that was wishful thinking on my part. I still had those god-awful scissors tucked inside my jacket pocket. I closed my eyes. What would happen if I were to stab her to death with them right now? Would Jason feel aroused enough to accompany me back to my place, unaffected by his wife's sudden and unexpected demise? Would the taxi driver understand that, due to the unbearable behaviour of the woman sitting next to me, I merely did what needed to be done? Would he acknowledge my actions, go on with his evening unaffected? He might even congratulate me on such a prompt act of mercy — a nod of his head, a single, knowing wink.

I thwarted a sudden inappropriate urge to laugh, the driver noticing my private amusement as he glanced at me in his rear-view mirror. A toothy smile was offered behind flustered cheeks, eyes that did not entirely know where else to look. He clearly felt my embarrassment, offering the very wink I'd only moments earlier imagined. It forced me to glance swiftly out of the window, my volatile moment of ill-considered madness seemingly determined to leave its mark. I smiled into my lap, this evening turning into a somewhat exuberant affair, the driver offering an impromptu grin of his own.

It wasn't as if I hadn't enjoyed this evening's meal. On the contrary, God knows I had ensured that Emma paid enough for my share. Who knew so many bread rolls and sharing platters could be consumed in a single evening? My part of the bill already exceeded normality as Sophia and I gorged haplessly on side dishes, tiny herby garlic mushrooms, caviar canapés, something with uncooked smoked salmon. I ensured I ordered the most expensive items on the menu, our impromptu bottle of Kit's Coty Coeur de Cuvée, not entirely going unnoticed by my sister. Yet, tonight was a celebration, so we knew she would happily let it go. I did notice the look on her face, though. *Priceless.*

I offered a swift goodnight as the taxi drove away, my sister's face pressed unapologetically against her husband's, tongues exploring, the poor taxi driver aware of the wandering hands behind him — none of them aware of me at all. And then it was silent. I was left alone outside the front door of my first floor, one-bedroomed flat on the side of Newbury I wished I didn't reside, desperate to trade places with my sister for, oh, say around an hour or so — less than that, even. That would be all the time I needed to –

As if to bring me out of my fiendishly wicked thoughts, my over-enthusiastic cat, Sylvester, came bounding around the corner towards me, and nuzzled his body firmly against my leg, purring loudly. It brought me sharply back to reality, back to the life I often wondered how I'd managed to acquire. I would have, at one time, expressed a firm belief that my life wasn't that bad, but now, amid everything that was happening around me, that would be a complete lie. In fact, I hated my life. I hated the way things had turned out for me.

Single for over three years and counting, I was an assistant in a temping agency office in the busy town centre of Newbury. A career I hated, in a town I hated, with people I hated even more. Of course, I could delude myself that I was merely having a bad day — a bad week. A lousy week made worse by an overbearing sister who seemed to want everything her way, all the time. But that would have been a lie. My life was exhausting. My sister was exhausting.

The simple truth was, I genuinely didn't feel as attractive or as good as my sister at anything I did. With stunning looks, thick glossy hair, and a slim figure she never seemed to have to work hard to maintain, Emma did not have any trouble finding good-looking men. She had an annoying ability to make money easily, drawing the very attention I wished I could find. It was infuriating how she only had to flutter her bloody eyelashes to get precisely what she wanted. What might it be like to emerge from my sister's shadow? To finally stand in the light of my own success after almost thirty years of total oblivion, hiding behind a woman I could never truly contend with?

I shook my head at such a preposterous idea, bending to stroke Sylvester, cat fur now attached to my ageing, and slightly threadbare in places, trouser suit. A suit that I was pleased to note at least still fitted me. That was some accomplishment. Who needed designer brands anyway? I closed the apartment door behind me, my cat pestering for the food I'd forgotten to provide him earlier this evening. *Me, actually. I did.*

***

Why I slammed the fridge door so hard, I have no idea. I'm honestly not usually such an incensed person, despite how I may have come across tonight. Being around Emma for longer than five minutes tends to tip me over the edge, that's all. It isn't pleasant. She doesn't even have to do anything in particular for my temper to tip violently into overdrive. She simply needs to exist. Tonight has made me unbelievably irritated. She's impossible. The way they both ignored me in the taxi like that, our journey home producing visions of Jason I didn't want in my head right then. Who does she think she is, anyway? Jason must have known I would feel uncomfortable watching them together like that.

Yet, in fairness, he had consumed a lot of alcohol by then, and he did touch my leg several times. Of that much, I was confident. Maybe he simply didn't wish to arouse Emma's jealousy. He was on a promise. An argument was the last thing he needed. I could tell that he wanted to include me in his hidden thoughts. For that, I was grateful.

I grabbed a chilled bottle of Lambrini from the countertop, slightly ashamed I'd be drinking alone, as I unscrewed a lid that did not create any sudden rush of bubbles—no popping of corks, no posh, expensive Coeur de Cuvée for me now. I didn't even bother with a glass, opting instead to take a rather unladylike swig straight from the bottle. I'd had enough of restaurant etiquette for one night anyway, which was probably just as well in my current drunken state. Sylvester swirled around my legs, waiting for a meal I was too tired to provide. How I managed to pour kibble into his bowl is beyond me.

It's not as if I have a shitty life — just a very shitty sister. I scoffed as I flopped onto a sofa that had seen better days, kicking stilettos across the floor, only just missing Sylvester's hind leg in the process. He flinched, offering a moment of irritation before skulking into the kitchen in search of sustenance. I took a long swig of my cheap supermarket wine and sighed. Emma, Emma, Emma. How the hell do you manage it all? Miss Prim-And-Bloody-Proper with the perfect life and perfect man.

I wondered if Jason was currently making love to her, the urge to drink my wine momentarily turning to nausea. It made me want to throw the bottle straight through the window and be done with it entirely. What the hell did he see in her anyway? The question sounded stupid even as it formed in my mind. What wasn't there to like about Emma? She was rich, successful, beautiful, slim. She could cook — annoyingly well, if my memory served me correctly. She'd given him his first child already while still, may I add, maintaining that bloody figure intact.

I have to admit that my hatred for my sister is far more profound than a mere jealous tendency for a life not my own. It runs far deeper than the life she currently has or the man she allows into her bed each night. As kids, Emma and I had been close. I could often be found following her around, waiting for her to notice her younger sister in tow, trailing behind like a lost soul. At four years her junior, I had wanted to be just like her. I wanted the long dark hair and the breasts that transformed her once childlike figure into a blossoming beauty long before mine had resembled anything close.

At sixteen, Emma was already out all night partying, while poor Stacey was left at home. I had not yet encountered my first period, and an actual real-life snog was something I could only dream of. I'd often copy my sister's make-up techniques, sneaking into her room when she wasn't around to steal her mascara, lipstick, or anything I could get my hands on, purely to feel as she did. To feel close to her.

Emma's first serious boyfriend actually had the nerve to try it on with me in the back row of the cinema once. I was thirteen. Emma had gone to buy us popcorn, our parent's having expressed a desire for my sister to take me out that evening, to cheer me up, or so they said. The truth was they wanted me out of the way for a few hours, fed up with witnessing their youngest daughter's miserable face ambling around, cluttering up the place. I wasn't miserable, but I went anyway, glad to be in the company of my big sister.

When I told her what had happened, she, of course, did not believe a word I said. She told me I was jealous and didn't speak to me for two whole months. She later discovered that her boyfriend was seeing other girls behind her back. *Shocker.* However, she did not apologise to me about that night or express any concern for her underage sister's potentially compromised wellbeing. Not once.

To be honest, we hadn't been close since we were young enough to think Barbie dolls were an acceptable part of our day. And I guess, after that, I simply grew tired of living in her shadow. She was always our parents' favourite anyway; always the one to lead the way, show me how things are meant to be done. The eldest. The role model. *You should take a leaf out of your sister's book, Stacey*, my dad was fond of saying. Yeah, right. Cheers Dad. Here's to Emma — such a vision of perfection.

I sauntered into the kitchen, my bare feet slapping against floor tiles sticky from something I must have spilt earlier. I ignored the strange smell that lingered around the vicinity of the draining board as I grabbed a second bottle of wine from the fridge, shocked to discover that my first had seemingly evaporated. I actually glanced around to check I'd not accidentally spilt some of the precious liquid onto the floor, convinced in my drunken stupor that I couldn't have consumed the entire bottle already.

I wouldn't usually class myself as a messy person. Yet, over the last few months, I'd slipped into a random pattern of self-delusion, my disjointed emotions overtaking practical requirements, meaning that my flat now often remained uncleaned. I blamed Emma for that too, of course. Her needs seemed to outweigh my own these days, her constant requirement for attention factoring higher than anything I might have needed. Being single didn't help, either. I'd somehow managed to convince myself that, if I had a man to help around the flat, we could share the cleaning and the cooking, halving the amount of work I had to do each day.

It was stupid. Many people live alone without resorting to acts of wanton and unashamed filthiness. I thought of Jason again then, visualising him in a skimpy kitchen apron, naked from the waist down (if I had anything to do with it) cooking delicious food for my selfish, ungrateful sister. I'd never actually witnessed him cooking much at all, so where my vision had come from I have no idea. Probably nothing more than the idea of him waiting on me, naked, my very own slave, serving me food from his fingertips and other places.

I sighed, retreating to the front room, curling onto my sofa with a second bottle of wine tucked under my elbow. Tonight, this would be my best friend. The only one I'd need. This unassuming bottle would understand my needs when no one else possibly could. I even wondered what I might do with its empty twin brother, now lying unattended at my feet on the rug, but didn't entirely feel I had the energy for such exuberance. I flicked through my mobile and put on some music that might help take my mind off my annoying sister, curling my feet into Sylvester's warm body, who had joined me on the sofa. Together we sat, two forsaken and forgotten creatures, nothing between us but endless boredom, time rolling into the early hours and beyond.

I don't exactly remember when I began to cry. Still, without warning, I found myself sobbing into my cheap wine bottle and make-up-stained cushions. Sylvester moved to the opposite side of the room so he wouldn't have to in any way console me. When would amazing things happen to me? When would I have the chance to feel what Emma felt every day when she opened her eyes to see her husband's sleeping face next to hers? Their large master bedroom, en-suite king-sized bloody bathtub staring back at her, its sheer size outperforming my entire flat. I would have given anything to wake up next to Jason. To feel his warm, engaging arms around my body as he whispered good morning, offering much more than a wake-up kiss. Instead, all I had in the world was this flaming cat who only seemed to notice me at feeding time. Typical.

6

I couldn't help myself. I guess I'd consumed far too much alcohol. I certainly didn't remember dialling his number, but when Jason's smooth voice filtered into my ear, I couldn't help smiling.

'Hey, you,' I tried to sound as innocent as I was able, failing to control the slur that arose from the back of my throat, a tiny belch making its way into the room before I could stop it. It was probably a tad sadistic of me to call my brother-in-law at this hour. Something had happened inside my brain, and I wasn't able to control my actions. Maybe the devil made me do it. Whatever it was, I liked it.

'I am so sorry it's late, Jason, but I heard a noise outside, and I'm terrified someone is trying to get into the flat.' *Wow, where did that come from?* I assumed I'd dialled his number because I was feeling horny — I mean, melancholy. I don't even recall knowing what I wanted to say to him until faced with his undivided attention.

'Stace, are you okay?' I loved it when Jason showed

genuine concern for me.

'I'm not sure, to be honest, mate. I think I saw something or someone lurking around outside, but I'm too scared to go out and take a better look.' *Mate?* Why was I acting so casual? He was undoubtedly no mate of mine. I wanted so much more than friendship from Jason.

'Have you called the police?' Jason asked the question innocently, obviously concerned for my safety. *Of course, I bloody hadn't.* That would imply that I had an actual intruder — which I most certainly did not.

'Yes, of course I did,' I lied. 'Ten minutes ago. But they haven't shown up yet, and I can still hear something creeping around outside. Even Sylvester seems on edge.' He wasn't on edge at all. In fact, my unassuming cat had drifted to sleep some time ago, his belly fattened and content from eating too many biscuits I'd accidentally poured into his bowl an hour earlier. 'Jason, I'm petrified.' God, I was good at laying it on thick.

'Don't worry. I'm sure the police won't be too long.' Shit. No. This was not how I wanted this thing to go.

'Can't you pop over and check outside for me?' I had adopted my innocent, frightened feminine voice, ensuring I trembled in all the right places, appearing weak. Emma had the same voice whenever she wanted to get her own way. I guess it was a family trait.

Jason hesitated. We both knew he had Emma and Eva to consider at such a late hour. 'It's gone two o'clock in the morning, honey,' he said. Was it? *Bollocks.* I had to get up for work in a few hours. 'Plus, I've been drinking. I'm not sure it would be a good idea.'

'Oh, please. I promise that, if you can't see anyone outside, I'll wait for the police, and try and get some sleep. I'll make you a coffee while you're here. To help sober you up.' I was practically begging now, even pouting into the mobile though I knew he couldn't see. I didn't care that he would be driving his car over the legal drink-drive limit. I simply needed to see him. What the hell I expected to achieve from getting Jason to my flat at such a late hour, I had no idea. I smiled. Apart from the obvious, of course.

'Okay,' Jason breathed. He almost sounded irritated by the idea of driving across town in the middle of the night. I wanted to promise I'd make it worth his while but thought better of it.

'Oh, Jason, you're a superstar. Thank you so much.' I was practically jumping up and down, inability to contain my excitement thankfully confined to the inside of my flat.

'See you in fifteen minutes,' he said. 'Stay inside and keep the door locked. I'll text you when I'm outside, so you know I'm on my way up.'

'Bless you, Jason, thank you. You will literally be saving my life. Seriously.' I was ecstatic. I knew he wouldn't let me down. Jason was amazing like that.

As soon as he hung up, I raced into the bathroom to check that I looked presentable. Please don't judge a girl for trying her best. Emma most certainly did not deserve him. It was a fact that did not sit well with me. My only intention was to show my brother-in-law what he was missing. That's all. Nothing more than that, I swear. I was mortified to discover that I'd smudged most of my make-up in my drunken despondence and tear-filled self-indulgence. It had taken me well over an hour to apply it, too. And my hair now looked as if I'd just got out of bed. *Bugger.*

I dragged a brush through my tresses, glad at least the waves had stayed in place. They looked quite sultry, actually. Maybe this was the perfect look to impress Jason with? I wiped a face cloth swiftly across both eye sockets, careful to leave a lingering trace of eyeliner before applying a fresh coat of mascara, pinching my cheeks to appear slightly flushed, anxious. I was going for the *Oh Jason, I'm so flustered* look. But I was probably creating more of an, *Oh shit, I think I might have drunk too much, and now I might throw up* look. However, I couldn't overthink it.

I undid the top two buttons of the trouser suit I hadn't bothered to remove before embarking on my evening of self-absorbed contemplation, allowing the push-up bra I'd worn especially for the evening to spill, accidentally, over the top. It was red lace with a silken padded layer beneath. I'd purposely worn my red underwear tonight, top and tail, the perfect match. Not for this moment, obviously. That would be too weird. How could even my devious brain have preconceived the possibility of getting to this point in the evening? No. The reason behind my red underwear choice was that my outfit's material was relatively thin, probably washed too many times. In a particular light, you could see straight through it. It was the very reason I had made sure I'd seated myself next to my brother-in-law in front of a window that allowed natural light from behind.

It was an unfortunate fact that he hadn't seemed to notice. I would most definitely ensure he noticed when he got here. I looked in the mirror. Maybe I should remove my outfit altogether? Yes. Perfect. I slipped the thing off as quickly as I could, catching my foot in the bottom of it in my haste and hearing a slight tearing sound that I tried not to overthink. Underwear alone would have looked too much. But I owned a bathrobe. I could simply leave it undone — by mistake. Yes. *Perfect.* I had just got out of bed, after all, and was rather frightened. What did he expect?

I paced my flat for too long, checking my appearance too many times until I no longer felt satisfied with what was greeting me in the mirror. I most certainly couldn't compete with Emma or her perfect features. *Where the hell was he?* I pressed my breasts together, adjusting my bra too many times, almost losing my balance through the volume of alcohol I'd unashamedly consumed. I actually felt a bit sick, truth be known. When my phone pinged, I almost threw up over my neatly tidied bed linen.

'Just outside now, honey. I'm coming up.' The text message read.

God, I wish he would. Shaking off my ludicrous thoughts, I unlocked the front door, knowing full well that no potential intruder would suddenly make an entrance. I could relax because I was in no actual danger. I checked my breath to ensure I didn't smell like some old brewery, mortified to realise that actually I did. *Why the hell hadn't I cleaned my teeth?*

Footsteps. Taking my outside steps two at a time.

Jason was obviously worried. I knew he would be. When he appeared, he was still wearing the same shirt and trousers he'd worn for dinner. I hoped he hadn't been to bed yet. The idea of him lying next to that *witch* threatened to make my dinner reappear. Maybe she had been too intoxicated to fulfil her promise to him after all?

'Hey.' He reached the top of the landing, out of breath, looking dishevelled and rather sexy, as always. 'You okay?' He glanced around, ushering us into the flat quickly, before closing the door behind him. I loved his masterful commands.

I was standing in my underwear, covered only by a thin black bathrobe that had been left untied. I waited until he noticed my perfectly displayed body before pulling it around me as if I'd been forced out of bed not long ago. I should have been an actress.

'I am, now you're here,' I said. It wasn't even a lie.

'Come, sit down,' he said, guiding me into the front room expertly. I realised I'd forgotten to clear away my now empty bottles of wine in frantic pursuit of physical perfection, trying to disguise an unkempt flat that had taken longer than a day to create. Maybe I could blame the cat. My robe "accidentally" flopped open again, revealing my lace bra and levitating breasts beneath. Perfect timing, girls.

'Oh, thank God you came,' I sighed, allowing Jason to place me onto a cushion, my breasts still perfectly on display, for his eyes only, of course. 'I was terrified that someone was going to hurt me.' Damn, I was good at this lying thing.

'Let me get you a drink. You look as if you need one.'

Jason went to busy himself in the kitchen. I'd forgotten about the pile of washing up in the sink that had been there for three days. Shit. That must be where the smell was coming from. 'I can't see anyone outside now,' he called from the other room, unconcerned, I hoped, by the mess surrounding him or horrendous stench in his nostrils. 'The police should be here by now, though, shouldn't they?'

'Oh, you know what the police are like,' I laughed, knowing damned well that no police officer would show up to a property they hadn't been called out to.

Jason returned moments later. 'The kettle's on.' He hovered in the doorway as if he wasn't entirely sure what he should do next.

'Thank you,' I replied, feeling slightly more relaxed now that he was actually here. 'Come and sit down for a moment.' I patted the cushion next to me, brushing several unread magazines to one side.

'I'd feel better if I go and have a proper look outside.' He stepped past me, and peered through my curtains as if he was on a mission. He really was my knight in shining armour.

'No rush. Now that you're here, I feel safer already.' That wasn't a lie.

'What did you actually hear?' It was a good question. The simple truth was that I had heard absolutely nothing at all.

I shook my head. 'Some kind of weird banging.' Seriously? Was that the best I could offer?

'Could it have been a neighbour?'

'Well, I definitely saw a dark shape out by the bins.'

51

That part was genuine. I had witnessed next door's dog out for his last ablutions of the evening, attached to his rather sleepy owner.

Jason was still standing by the window. 'I can't see anything now. Maybe I scared them away.'

'Probably. Hopefully.' I smiled. 'Why don't you sit down? Just until I catch my breath?'

'I'll make that coffee.' Jason disappeared into the kitchen, and I followed, embarrassed by the state of the place I called home.

'I didn't have a chance to clean up today.'

'Oh, don't worry about it, honey. I hadn't noticed.' God, he really was amazing. *Fuck me. Fuck me now.* I coughed then. I couldn't help it. Something felt as if it was trying to get out of my throat and throttle me for the unconscionable thoughts I was having.

As I knew he would, Jason came running and rubbed a well-placed hand across my back. 'Jesus, I'm only making you a coffee. Don't keel over on me.' He was laughing, but all I could think of was his hot hand against the thin material of my robe, glad I'd chosen to remove my trouser suit and wishing I'd had the guts to remove it all. Maybe I could pretend I was overheating and take my robe off right now? He was patting my back, trying to dislodge a lump in my throat along with my inappropriate thoughts. 'Are you okay?'

I took a breath, nodding, not daring to look into his eyes in case I accidentally leaned in for a kiss. I wasn't sure either of us had drunk enough for that. 'I am now,' I said, thanking him with a mouth I wanted to wrap around his –

'Good. Go and sit down, and I'll bring your drink in to you.' Jason was oblivious to my thinking. *Calm down, Stacey, for God's sake, calm down.* I did as I was told. I literally could do nothing else. My brain was beginning to display unwanted side effects of the wine I'd been drinking all evening. The room was spinning. As much as I would have loved my sister's husband to ravage me right there and then on my sticky kitchen floor, I don't think either of us would have found it amusing once the cold light of the following day kicked in. I needed to relax a little. To uncover (excuse the pun) a little more about the actual state of my sister's marriage. If only Jason would allow such intrusion, that is.

7

We sat together on my sofa for almost an hour, waiting for police officers I knew would never arrive, consuming several cups of coffee I knew would keep me awake for the rest of the night. 'Are you sure they told you they were sending someone?' Jason sounded slightly irritated as he got to his feet to look out of the window.

'Well, they did say they were understaffed.' Another complete lie. 'But they promised they would send an officer at some point.' I assumed they would probably send someone if the need arose. This area of town hardly had the best reputation for crime statistics. The only thing I needed right then was Jason by my side. My mission was complete. I no longer wanted to discuss fake news. I leaned across my coffee table to pick up a bottle of brandy I'd accidentally left in full view of him, unscrewing the cap without apology.

'Woah, what are you doing?' Jason grabbed the bottle as if it was a poison that might devour us at any second.

'My nerves are shredded,' I answered, feeling somewhat chastised.

'I think you've had more than enough to drink tonight, Stacey,' he scolded, getting to his feet and placing the bottle onto a chest of drawers behind him. 'I didn't even know you drank that stuff.'

'I don't really,' I said. I always slipped a tiny drop of brandy into Jason's coffee mug whenever he came over. It seemed to relax him. He always assumed my coffee was simply overly strong, a distinct taste of something he couldn't quite place. Tonight, Jason had made the coffee, so had ruined my plan.

'I should let you get some sleep.'

'No. Please, don't leave me.' I sounded far more desperate than I had intended. Maybe I could blame it on fear. Or the booze. 'What if the prowler comes back?'

'Maybe I should call the police again –'

'No!' *Shit, Stacey, quit with the aggression already.* I laughed. The nervous kind of giggles I often get when I've accidentally cornered myself and have no idea how to emerge unscathed. 'The police are probably too busy to deal with my silly little wobble.' I forced back a sudden urge to vomit. Maybe I had drunk too much after all. Jason stood in my front room looking as if he didn't know exactly what I wanted him to do next. I thought for a moment about telling him exactly what I wanted him to do. *To me.* 'It isn't like I was actually burgled anyway,' I added, realising I'd inadvertently told Jason that I was okay. Shit, shit, shit.

'Drink your coffee before it gets cold,' Jason said then, handing me a steaming mug that I took without question. *He truly is fantastic.* He perched on the sofa next to me and glanced at his watch.

'She knows you're here, doesn't she?' I asked, slightly irritated, black coffee and dark thoughts threatening to drown me.

'Of course,' Jason smiled. 'Don't worry. I won't leave until I know you're okay.' He was genuinely concerned about me. I loved it when he showed honest affection. He picked up his mug and together we sat enjoying an innocent late-night drink, my thoughts anything but. If only Emma knew I was currently fantasising about her husband. If only Jason knew. I gulped, taking in too much coffee and almost choking in the process. Jason came to my aid for the second time that evening, patting my back in the way he had earlier. I was not getting any sleep tonight, of that much, I was certain.

'Maybe I have had a little too much to drink,' I whispered, utterly exhausted, the effects of alcohol finally kicking in, hoping Jason would take me to bed. A girl could dream.

'Oh, you think?' he laughed, placing my now half-empty mug onto the table with a shake of his head. 'Come on, you. Let's get you into bed.'

Oh God, I thought he'd never offer. 'Seriously?' I stared at him, not entirely sure I was managing to hide my excitement.

'Unless you are planning on sleeping out here all night,' he scolded, pulling my now trembling body from the sofa into a standing position.

Oh yeah. Shit. *Sleep.* I sighed, offering some random groaning I'd not intended. 'But I don't wanna go to sleep.' Jesus, I sounded five years old. I wanted him to reach inside my robe and touch my breasts, along with other things. I leaned towards his mouth with the full intention of kissing him.

'Steady there, girl,' he laughed, assuming I'd simply stumbled, my drunken stupor no longer agreeable to my composure.

'Nooo,' I was still groaning as Jason steered me towards the bedroom. I wanted to rip off his shirt and stick my tongue down his throat. I wanted to –

'Come on, in you go,' Jason folded back the duvet, helping my now limp body to flop beneath the sheets. I reached out to him and pulled him on top of me, hoping to land a full-on kiss as I groped with trembling fingertips between his shirt buttons, his warm skin welcome against my rampaging hands. At that stage, I didn't care if I tore them all off.

'Stacey, calm down,' he laughed, still way too calm and understanding of the drunken state he assumed was making me act so out of character. I wanted to tell him that I wanted him. *Desperately.* He pulled himself free from my grip, not in any way upset or shocked by the fact I'd tried to land an impromptu snog. Instead, he looked me straight in the eyes with a simple wink. 'You're drunk. Get some sleep.'

He pulled the duvet over my body, seemingly unaffected by the fact that my robe was now fully open, revealing the red lacy underwear I'd worn just for him. I liked lying on my back. My belly looked flatter, my hips wider, curvy. And this bra was brilliant at making my girls stand to attention when otherwise they would have been in a somewhat less than perky state about now. When the duvet covered my attempts to impress my brother-in-law, I sighed.

'Jason, stay with me,' I was fully mumbling now. I may have even pulled a pouting face.

He was laughing. God, I was probably making a complete fool of myself. 'Get some sleep, you.' He made sure I was lying on my side, just in case I threw up in my sleep. Such a wonderful image I'd provided for him. 'I'll leave your mobile by the side of the bed, and I'll have a quick tidy round before I leave.' Jason glanced around my bedroom. 'I'll check outside too, but I'll make sure the front door is locked, and I'll pop the key through the letterbox on my way out.'

I faded out after that, not precisely catching his following words, my bed suddenly feeling too comfortable and appealing, thoughts of Jason swimming inside my head. I didn't even hear him leave, instead falling asleep to images of his naked body on top of mine, forever entwined in my imagination. I woke up around five o'clock with a terrible headache, realising I'd made a full-on pass at my sister's husband. This would need addressing promptly before things totally got out of control: shit, shit, shittery shit.

***

It wasn't the hangover that made me feel so terrible. It was the snippets of information from the previous evening that kept leaving imprints on my brain, providing memories I hoped were not real, my remembered actions now giving me the biggest headache. How much did I have to drink? I genuinely couldn't remember. I leaned across the bed, staring too long at my mobile phone, unable for a moment to focus on what I was looking at, the screen in front of me seemingly hazy, blurred. Two missed calls from Emma. Yuk. *What the hell did she want?*

I shot upright in bed then, remembering my drunken lunges at her unsuspecting husband at three o'clock this very morning. Shit. Maybe Jason had already told her what I'd done — what I tried to do. How the hell did I assume I could get away with such brazen acts of selfish abandonment? I almost vomited. She would no doubt be gunning for me about now, unable to comprehend such unspeakable acts of wanton debauchery in her absence.

I considered messaging Jason to check if I had accidentally done anything stupid, apologise if necessary, beg even, should the need arise. But, after holding my mobile in trembling fingers for several minutes, I eventually thought better of it. I would be utterly mortified if he refused to speak to me, my sudden urge to get him into bed now making me somewhat uncomfortable and anxious.

The very last thing I wanted was for Jason to consider me some kind of deluded, easy, wayward tart. It didn't matter how much I fancied him, how amazing I thought he was or how undeserving Emma was of him. I had probably gone too far. I sighed, lifting my body unhurriedly out of bed, my legs feeling like lead as I stumbled into the bathroom to pee and investigate the state of myself. Shit. I looked worse than I'd imagined. I hoped to God I didn't look this blotchy and hungover last night. No wonder Jason didn't want to –

Just then, my phone pinged. Jason. With my heart racing and hands clammy, I grabbed my mobile and opened his message, unsure I even wanted to know what I was about to read. 'Hope you're feeling better this morning, you little minx?'

I sat on the toilet, knickers around my ankles, bathrobe hanging around my shoulders as if I had totally lost the plot, last night's bra digging into places it had no business digging. 'Sorry about last night,' I replied, too eagerly. Which part was I was apologising for? And why was he calling me a minx? I couldn't recall us doing anything that would warrant such a cheeky new pet name. And I am confident I would have remembered, savouring every detail, utterly unable to believe my luck.

'Hey, don't worry about it. I was happy to help,' he replied.

No, Jason, I meant about the sudden urge to snog your face off that I vaguely remember, unfortunately. Unless I had dreamt the entire thing, of course, and then I might just about get away with it.

'I hope Emma wasn't too mad at you,' I messaged. Actually, I wished Emma had been utterly livid by the sight of her husband returning home after three in the morning, hopefully smelling of my perfume and cherry-flavoured lipstick Emma would know wasn't hers. I hoped it had caused a catastrophic argument that had resulted in Jason sleeping on the sofa.

'She was asleep when I got home, so nothing to report on that front. Did you get any sleep?'

I visualised him sitting alone in his front room, thinking of my underwear and unexpected pouting lips heading his way. *Yes, I dreamt of your* – 'Eventually. Thank you. I think I drank a bit too much, though,' I replied. I needed to confirm that my actions were in no way indicative of my usual characteristics. I wasn't a cheap slut. No matter what conclusion my dreams had already reached.

A laughing face emoji came back to me then, making me smile and forget my sorry state. 'Headache pills, plenty of water, and don't overdo it.' God, Jason had such a beautiful way with words.

'I will.' I hovered for a moment with my thumb over the send button, adding, 'Thank you again for last night,' before pressing send quickly in case I changed my mind. I stared at the words in front of me for quite some time, as if I believed they might leap off the screen and bite me. I desperately wanted to ask him why Emma had found the need to call me twice before five o'clock this morning.

Had she awoken alone, fuming with her selfish sister's attempt to take her husband's attention from her? Did she fully intend to chastise me keenly and unapologetically for getting blind drunk and throwing myself at her man? I wondered then if she had indeed started a fight that Jason had been polite enough to avoid sharing with me? I could only hope. I closed my eyes, head pounding, not entirely wanting an explanation right then. No doubt I'd find out soon enough.

8

An hour later, I was standing in my kitchen staring at a piece of toast I could barely stomach the idea of swallowing, apparently ready for work, yet not exactly in the mood for a long day locked inside a humid office. The last thing I needed was to spend any length of time with the overbearing people I worked with, their equally domineering lives more than my brain could take today, or any other, truth be known. I considered throwing a sickie, unashamedly hiding beneath a duvet that now weirdly smelled of Jason, my growing embarrassment blending with this bloody hangover to create a sludgy mix of turmoil I didn't want anyone to witness. I also looked horrendous. Maybe that could work in my favour?

My hair had, however, amazingly maintained a slight kink from hours of bending and shaping into a seductive style I hoped would impress Jason, yet now realised he'd barely noticed at all. Unfortunately, probably due to the way I'd lain in bed, it was slightly sticking up in places that made me look rather odd. It took a further fifteen

minutes for my straighteners to perform miracles —
several times creating commotion from my mouth that
might have made Sylvester blush had he understood the
English language. I had no time to wash it this morning,
so it would have to do. At least my panda eyes had been
eliminated, as was the lipstick that had oddly found its
way to my cheekbone.

As usual, Sylvester swirled around my ankles,
brushing against my leg for the breakfast I almost forgot
to provide him. I had accidentally inherited this cat from
the elderly lady in the flat below mine, so I could almost
forgive myself for the occasional lapse in animal welfare.
Jason had noticed the indigent thing hovering on the
landing for several days until we realised the poor
woman in the ground floor flat had sadly passed away.
If it hadn't been for Jason's swooning over the animal for
a full hour, Sylvester's purrs mixing with Jason's soft
coos that made me act somewhat impulsively, I probably
wouldn't have taken him in at all. I had merely wished
to impress Jason — as usual. Still, here we are. Stacey
Adams. Proud cat owner. It fitted perfectly with the
spinster status I had recently adopted. *Crazy cat lady seeks
night of lust with man of dreams. Will do practically anything
for attention. Willing to travel.* Bridget Bloody Jones had
nothing on me.

***

I stood at the bus stop trying not to vomit, still
wondering if I should simply call in sick and spend the
day with my head beneath the duvet. The same duvet

that, only hours earlier, Jason had carefully placed over my vulnerably exposed, half-naked body. I was quite impressed that he hadn't taken advantage of me, to be honest. Things could have been so very different this morning had he reciprocated, ripping off his shirt along with my bra and pants. I shuddered, pulling my jacket around my seriously hungover frame. It wasn't even cold out, yet the after-effects of the alcohol I'd failed to avoid made me shudder anyway. Any sane person might have vowed there and then never to touch the stuff again, but I wasn't going to lie to myself or anyone else about such things. I wasn't wholly deluded.

I boarded the bus dreaming about the would-be look on my sister's face, had Jason taken a different route and chosen to place his manhood inside me last night. It would have been a total dream come true for me, of course, yet I do not believe my sister would quite see it that way. I thought about how he'd casually brushed his hand against my leg in the taxi. Then again, if he had intended to express his desire for me, he probably would have done so last night when we were alone with no one to disturb us or witness our antics. We'd certainly had enough time to ignite any potential enflamed passion, invented intruder or not. And I had done a damned good job of displaying my potential requirements, potential assets.

As I paid my bus fare, I concluded with a scowl that my unfortunate drunken state was no doubt the actual reason behind Jason's hesitancy. Shit. *Christ, Stacey, had you simply remained sober and lucid, things might have been very different.* After all, Jason is a gentleman. And true gentleman certainly do not take advantage of pathetic-looking, drunken sisters-in-law. No matter how *up for it* they appear to be. I tried to ignore the damp patch that had formed in my underwear as I boarded the bus, thoughts of Jason and what might have been causing my head to throb intensely.

The bus driver offered me a sideways glance as I cursed under my breath. I screwed my brow into a knot that must have made me look ten years older, and unashamedly slumped onto a chewing gum-stained seat, feeling as if I might at any moment vomit into the aisle, completing my loutish image entirely. I wished I could rewind time and leave those bottles of Lambrini safely inside my goddamned fridge, untouched. Yet, we had all been drinking last night. I wasn't the only one. The fact that Jason drove those three miles to my flat after he had clearly consumed more than legally allowed meant that maybe he had wanted to see me after all, willing to risk his license to do so.

I closed my eyes, realising my drunken state had tipped the balance between what could have been an incredible, consensual sex-filled evening and a regrettable *what the hell happened last night?* moment. With a sharp intake of breath, I concluded that Jason wouldn't have wanted me to regret opening my legs for him in such a desperate, drunken way. He liked me. He most definitely thought better of me than that. I swore then, making some poor old woman sitting on the seat in front jolt forwards in a futile attempt to get out of my way. She could probably still smell the booze on my breath, assuming I was some cheap lush. I certainly felt like one at that point — a cheap lush who hadn't even got her man.

Such distasteful thoughts about my sister's husband may not have sounded rational to an unconcerned outsider, but I genuinely couldn't help the way I felt. Whenever Jason was around, I wanted to rip his clothes off with my teeth and, when he wasn't around, I still wanted to rip his clothes off with my teeth. It was utterly insane. I'd recently joined a dating website with little to no luck. My dates mainly consisted of desperate thirty-somethings who realised they were heading towards forty with nothing more concrete in life than a mountain of debt they'd seemingly developed without notice, and now keen to settle down before life passed them by completely. Whenever I dropped my guard, allowing myself to enjoy a meal with a potential new man, I simply compared him to Jason. It wasn't fair.

I thought of discussing my feelings with Emma, yet I knew that would go down like a bloody lead weight in a boatload of feathers. I could, of course, choose to leave out the fact that my male obsession was her husband. Still, I fully anticipated the only advice she might provide would be a selection of patronising and overbearing comments I honestly had no desire to hear. I couldn't help thinking of her would-be words as I stared out of the condensation-dripping bus window, its dewy appearance not too dissimilar to how my underwear felt. *Oh, Stacey, you have to get out in the world and try different things*, she would most definitely advise me, sounding just like Dad.

I would have loved to divulge details to Jason about

the number of boyfriends Emma has had over the years. To see the look on his face when he realises his wife isn't the sweet little innocent she would have everyone believe. My bed notches, on the other hand, consist of merely four — a measly four men in twenty-nine years of life on a planet housing billions of potential husbands. Four, compared to Emma's double-figured liaisons: triple maybe, if she had encountered any one-night stands I wasn't aware of. I wondered how many women Jason had slept with. I closed my eyes. Lucky bitches, whoever they were.

I tried to think back to when Jason had met Emma, and I struggled. I stared at the town passing by, its morning commuter traffic now out in force along with its residents, already angry and frustrated. What the hell was I doing to myself, creating such self-fulfilling torture that came at me in the form of a man I couldn't have? I shook my head. I couldn't endure eight mind-numbing hours of work. Not today. I would probably spend the entire day with my head stuffed inside the toilet anyway, meetings and deadlines remaining unachieved, my boss remaining unimpressed.

Unable to sit with my wayward thinking unchecked any longer, I got to my feet and pressed the bell three times in swift succession, getting off at whatever stop happened to be next and not bothering to thank the driver as I practically fell out of the bus onto the pavement. I ignored the shake of his head as the door closed behind me, the sound of the front end rising swiftly as he drove off far too loud in my ears. I was left hovering by the side of the road, appearing more demonic than demure. It didn't matter that I happened to be a mere two streets from Jason's place of work. I hadn't noticed. *Honest.*

9

I must have stood outside Jason's work for at least fifteen minutes, looking to the entire world as if I had completely lost my mind. I hovered like a wounded bee, phone in hand, only remembering to text my line manager at the very last moment, offering some pathetic excuse that I was currently in bed with a violent bout of sickness so would not be at work today. It was only a half-lie. I did indeed feel I might vomit at some point. It wasn't entirely my fault that the precise reason had been exaggerated. I knew Jason always arrived for work early, his job as an automotive designer something I'd secretly admired for years. Him coming home, needing a shower, covered in unavoidable perspiration that I just wanted to lick off –

'Can I help you, miss?'

I flinched, almost dropping my mobile into a nearby drain. 'Oh, sorry. I'm just –' What the hell was I *just* doing? 'I'm just waiting for someone.' *Really? Is that the best you can come up with? You look like a weird stalker.*

'Anyone I know?' he asked, making his way slowly

towards me, unsure of my motives, questioning eyes piercing mine. It was none of his goddamned business. I offered him a scowl I hadn't intended, failing to diffuse his apparent suspicions.

'Jason Cole,' I replied too fast. Shit. I'd done it now. Now I couldn't back out, slink away, avoiding seeing him this morning, after all. I hoped this guy hadn't noticed the green tinge my cheeks had acquired. Alcohol, it seems, does not care how you look.

'May I ask what you need with Mr Cole?' My invented lies were not being well met by this guy, the folding of arms across a broad chest confirming he thought he had seen it all. Who the hell was this guy? He could probably already tell I was up to no good, my motives anything but innocent.

'I'm sorry. He's my brother-in-law.' Why was I apologising to a complete stranger? I placed my now unwanted phone casually inside my handbag as if my appearance here was normal, offering a smile I didn't feel like providing. I simply needed to appear sane, rational. It was none of his business what I wanted from my brother-in-law. It was, in fact, nobody's business. 'I was on my way to work and forgot that I needed to give him a message.' I could have, of course, simply messaged or called him, my mobile phone only moments earlier in my hand. I had to think fast. 'My phone's playing up,' I added casually, offering this guy a shrug that made me appear slightly moronic, foolhardy. *Why the hell do I find it so easy to lie these days?* I hoped the thing wouldn't suddenly decide to ring and give away my idiocy entirely. I felt stupid enough as it was.

'Okay. Hang on. I'll see if he's in.' The guy disappeared into the building, leaving me standing on my own once again, unsure what it was I actually thought I was doing. I already knew Jason was at work. His car was parked behind me. I wondered if this guy even knew him at all.

'No problem,' I nodded, more to myself than anything, feeling suddenly nervous by the idea of seeing him this morning, in the flesh. I giggled under my breath. *I wish.* I smothered this sudden urge to laugh. This guy was obviously some kind of security staff, probably already wondering, like most people today, if I'd completely lost my marbles. He reappeared a few moments later, heading off towards some location he didn't feel the need to share with me, glancing in my direction with a nod that I wasn't entirely sure meant anything good.

So what was happening now? Was Jason coming out to see me? Had he even been told of my arrival? Was I meant to simply stand here looking deranged and forgotten? Jason appeared a few seconds later, relieving my tattered emotions, the security guy becoming nothing more than a frustrating moment in my already disappointing morning.

'Hey, you,' Jason said, a friendly smile spread across rosy cheeks that made me cross my legs in lustful anticipation, his freshly ironed designer clothing and freshly showered features making him look heavenly in the early morning haze. 'I assumed you'd be pulling a sickie this morning,' he joked, casually crossing the car park towards me, hair flopping in the breeze, biceps rippling. He smelled amazing. Not a hint of last night's drunken disposition in sight. How the hell did he manage to pull that off so effortlessly when I struggled to get out of bed?

'I am, to be honest,' I breathed, drinking in his presence. 'I was on the bus, on my way to work, when I suddenly felt ill and needed some air. I didn't notice I'd got off the bus near here.' Now that most definitely was a lie.

'Bless you, honey.' Jason leaned towards me, placing a warm hand on my shoulder. I shuddered. 'Do you want to come in for a moment?' It was an innocent question, yet it made me want to burst into tears. How could he be so nice to me when I was having such distasteful thoughts about him?

I nodded graciously, suddenly needing to be carried in his arms, my legs wobbling beneath his touch. 'Actually, if you don't mind. I could do with a glass of water.' And a 'hair of the dog' too, perhaps. Or a sledgehammer. Whichever came first.

'Sure thing. Step this way, mademoiselle,' Jason grinned and stretched out an arm for me to take, gesturing me to follow him inside a building I realised I'd never visited until today. I wished he would wrap his arms around me and scoop me up — preferably before I fainted from overthinking. He didn't do that, unfortunately. Instead, we walked side by side, mere acquaintances, into Jason's place of work, my mind racing with thoughts of what Emma might do if she knew I was having such ideas about her man at such an ungodly hour of the day. Anyone might think I was unable to get the guy out of my mind!

Thankfully, we reached his office in one piece — any inappropriate urge to pounce on him in the hallway kept well and truly under control. *Thank Christ.* 'Take a seat,' he said as he closed the door behind us. The room smelled like new leather with a random faint lemon after-tone that reminded me of the cheap air fresheners overly enthusiastic car sales assistants give away to make you believe you've had a good deal. 'Is water alright for you, or would you prefer something a little warmer?'

'I wouldn't say no to a cup of tea, actually,' I muttered, realising that tea would take longer to make and would therefore ensure I remained in Jason's company a little longer. I rarely drank tea, the beverage something only my mum made me when I visited her house. Nevertheless, it seemed appropriate in this moment, the thought of coffee no more appealing than alcohol. I still wasn't entirely sure what I was doing here. I perched on the edge of a leather sofa that looked as if it had never been sat on, making me feel as if I was imposing slightly. It had that distinct new car smell and something that reminded me of bondage equipment. Not that I know what bondage equipment smells like, of course.

'Tea it is, ma'am.' Jason offered a swift salute and a sharp click of his heels. He was funny. He always made me laugh. He could be my action man any day. 'Jen?' Jason called from the doorway, drumming expectant fingertips against its frame. 'Grab me a coffee and a tea for my guest, would you please, love?' I loved the way he commanded attention from those around him. He closed the door again and walked directly over to sit next to me, not at all unnerved by our previous close encounter. 'So how are you, really? And I'm not just talking about the amount you drank last night?' He offered me a cheeky wink.

I didn't entirely know how to respond. What exactly did he mean? Shit. Was I about to be chastised for coming onto him so unapologetically? It wasn't like me to be stuck for words. I had come here to test how the land lay between us, so to speak, to apologise for my actions if needed, pretend I was sorry.

'Did the police ever show up? You looked so shaken. I almost didn't want to leave you alone.' Jason didn't wait for my response as he brushed a casual hand across my leg, holding it there for longer than he might have intended

Oh, *that*. Was he deliberately trying to avoid the elephant in the room? I wondered what was going through his mind right then.

'They didn't turn up in the end.' I'd forgotten about my pretend intruder. *Shit, Stacey, you really must learn to remember your own lies.* How drunk was I?

'Why am I not surprised? The police never fail to bloody amaze me these days.' He got to his feet with a roll of his eyes, utterly oblivious to the fact that he'd patted my thigh twice before standing up. I wanted to open my legs for him there and then. No apology or explanation needed. He hadn't even mentioned the kiss I'd offered.

'Do they ever?' I muttered with a laugh, squirming in discomfort at the ache that was developing somewhere rather delicate. I seriously needed to get a grip.

'If I'd realised they weren't going to show up at all, I'd have stayed with you.'

Christ, now he tells me.

'You would?' My words emerged delicate, slightly despondent, sounding as if I'd retreated into the mind of a fourteen-year-old schoolgirl. All I needed now was to add a smile, a nervous giggle, perhaps a slight tilt of my head, an eyelash flutter, and I'd be all set.

'Of course. Why wouldn't I?' I had to look away, fear of what I might unexpectedly blurt out too much for my brain to consider. Just then, the door opened – *damn it* – and a young woman walked in carrying a tray of mugs, milk, sugar. No biscuits.

'Thank you, Jen, you're a lifesaver,' Jason smiled at the girl who looked as if she had recently joined the company, judging by the nervous glance she gave him, the tray in her grip seemingly too heavy for her tiny hands. 'This is Stacey. My sister-in-law.' Jason gestured a casual hand towards me to confirm I was merely an innocent family member. But my not-so-innocent wet knickers hidden between crossed legs told a different story. I feared I might slide right off the leather sofa at any second.

I nodded, offering a smile I didn't feel. The girl returned an equally half-hearted grin that simply stretched pale lips towards flustered cheeks for a split-second, before returning her attention to Jason. 'Mr Cole, your meeting has been moved to ten-thirty. I hope that's okay.'

She left the room without needing a response, but

Jason thanked her anyway and closed the door behind her. For a moment, I was glad. Glad I would have Jason's undivided attention for a while longer. Glad of warm tea that might soothe my throbbing brain and other pulsating areas of my anatomy. I was even glad that Jason was acting normal around me. Yet, I felt somewhat stupid sitting here now. What had I expected to happen this morning? Fireworks?

'Emma called me this morning.' I have no idea why I brought that up. It just seemed to fit the mood of the moment.

'Yeah, I know. She was worried about you.' Jason was busy turning on his computer, strange, noisy equipment springing to life around us.

'Worried?' Did I care?

'She was mad at me for leaving you alone. Told me anything could have happened to you in such a drunken state.' He rolled eyes that I wanted to melt into. Had I heard correctly? Did that mean he actually could have spent the entire night with me? I felt sick again. 'She said I should have called and let her know that I was spending the night at yours and that I could have gone straight to work from there. I wish she had suggested that earlier. I hardly got a wink of sleep thinking about you.'

I sat on Jason's office sofa listening to words that vaguely sounded sane, unable to comprehend the fact that he could have actually spent the entire night in my bed. Or, at the very least, on the sofa in my front room only a few feet away. I might have wandered out of my bedroom, totally naked, accidentally falling over him, legs open—ready for whatever *arose*. Totally in error, of course. Sofas are seemingly easy to trip over, many affairs set against such accidental backdrops.

'Did you hear what I said, Stace?' Jason was still speaking, but I had switched off already, dreaming of things that had no business being in my head. Oh, I heard. *I heard every goddamned word.*

'Please, allow me to make it up to you,' I blurted out. What the hell was I saying now? Jason was pouring tea, his back to me, so I, unfortunately, could not see his reaction.

'Stace, it's fine, honestly. As long as you are okay, Emma and I –'

'Seriously, Jason. I don't know what I would have done last night had you not been there for me.' I was such a liar, although I had been extremely glad of Jason's company. It temporarily took my mind off my otherwise lonely existence. 'Allow me to cook dinner for you. Tonight. My place. No arguing.' I wished I could shut myself up. I had no business making such sudden inappropriate offers. Why was I even here?

'Dinner?'

'Mm,' *Stacey, you idiot. What did you have to say that for? Now he's probably going to become uncomfortable and kick you out.* I waved my hands with a dismissive air I didn't enjoy the feel of. I would never dismiss Jason. Ever. 'Just my way of showing gratitude.'

Jason smiled then, a broad smile that displayed teeth I wanted to stick my tongue between and lick. 'Sure, why not. Shall we say around eight o'clock?' He placed a mug of hot tea onto the table in front of me and picked up his diary, obviously to check he didn't have any prior arrangement with anyone else, my sister included.

'Eight sounds perfect,' I confirmed. I almost couldn't breathe, unable to absorb the concept that he had actually agreed to have dinner with me. How was he going to explain tonight's disappearance to his wife?

'Fantastic. We will see you tonight.' He closed his diary with a confirmational thud, a nod of his head.

We? Shit. Oh my God, of course. He assumed Emma would be coming too. Why wouldn't he? Why would Jason believe that I had intended to cook a romantic, candlelit dinner for two instead of an innocent "thank you" meal for three? My smile slipped a little, forcing me to form a grin that made my face ache. I hoped Jason hadn't noticed. *Stacey, what the hell have you done? No one needs a bloody gooseberry.* Yet, I would now, in fact, be the gooseberry. I couldn't even back out. My forceful nature once again creating plans I wished I could change. Still, I would be able to spend time with Jason. That had to count for something.

I left my brother-in-law's office feeling sicker than when I'd arrived, tea I couldn't bring myself to swallow still warm on his desk, untouched, my nausea more now to do with the meal I had accidentally offered to cook than the alcohol swilling around my gut. A lump had formed in the back of my throat, threatening to make me vomit over the receptionist as Jason, ever the gentleman, saw me out of the building and into the morning air. I wished he wouldn't keep placing his hand on my back in the way he seemed to have developed a taste for. Who was I kidding? I loved it. I loved every single touch he afforded me.

'Will you be okay getting home by yourself?' he asked. We were strolling across the car park, my hand so close to his, it was almost painful.

'Sure. I have a few things to collect from town anyway.' It wasn't a lie. I now had an entire three-course dinner to prepare for, my inability to keep my mouth shut creating a panic I hadn't expected. I also had a flat to clean from top to bottom, all so Emma wouldn't pass judgement. *Genius.* I hated spending time with my sister — a sister who I would now have to entertain for an entire evening — a second evening in a row, in fact. *Just perfect.* 'I'll head into town. Then I can go home and vomit in peace.' I literally meant that for what it was. No pun intended. I felt such an idiot. Luckily Jason had no idea. Oblivion was bliss.

He laughed, my apparent joke creating a moment of amusement, unaware that I was secretly seething at the idea of accidentally inviting my bitch of a sister to my house. I suppressed an urge to groan.

'Okay, see you at eight,' Jason leaned in and planted a gentle kiss on my cheek.

I sucked in too much air – I didn't mean to – holding my breath at the proximity of his cheek against mine. *Fuck me.* No. Literally. *Jason. Fuck. Me. Now.*

I have no idea how I made it out of the car park alive — or, at the very least, without fainting. If only he knew how I felt about him. I bit into my lip absently. If only Emma knew. Jason waved as he headed back inside the building, leaving me standing in the morning air, the security guy offering the occasional sideways stare that made my skin crawl. The idea of spending any length of time with my sister made me want to scream. I would now have to endure an entire evening of fake laughter, fake tan, and fake bloody conversation. *Just perfect, Stacey.* Well done. Well done indeed.

10

An unfocused, unprecedented panic saw me hurrying from shop to shop, scouring the town centre for what I hoped might, by some incredible miracle, impress Emma. I had no idea what Jason would even enjoy eating, my limited cooking abilities threatening to make me appear wholly inadequate — failure something I could not bring myself to consider.

I was fully aware that I should be at work by now, and the hastily contrived text message to my boss remained unread, unnoticed, creating a spike in body temperature I had no idea how to dissipate. No matter. I would face whatever they cast my way tomorrow. My job was factoring worryingly way down on my list of current priorities. For now, I had more important things on my mind.

By the time I arrived home, arms aching with bags of food I'd purchased in a hurry, my mind was already racing with ideas above my station about murder — my sister's murder, to be exact.

I am certainly not confirming that the idea of

murdering my sister actually popped into my head at that moment, although, to be honest, the more I thought about it, the more appealing it sounded. It was merely a throwaway idea, a concept beyond normality, my hangover probably to blame for such ill-conceived thoughts. In my post-drunken state, I allowed myself the notion that I was being nothing more than a facetious cow, nasty, slightly unhinged, experiencing a moment of deluded ridiculous fantasy.

It was only in my head. It wasn't real, therefore it didn't count. After all, my sister rarely needed an excuse to act like a total bitch, able to perpetrate unrehearsed actions without consequence. Why should I not now take a moment for personal self-fulfilling gratification? Did I not deserve a little villainous consideration of my own? I stood in my kitchen, forcefully chopping vegetables for a lasagne I had no genuine idea how to make, hoping the frozen chocolate pudding thawing in the sink behind me would disguise any misguided wrongdoing. I then remembered that Emma was a vegetarian. Shit. Or was she a vegan? *Bloody hell, Stacey.*

Not wishing to overthink, I popped my hastily purchased packet of cheap beef mince into the bottom tray of my fridge before searching online for 'veggie lasagne'. I was extremely grateful to discover that it was pretty much the same thing, just without the mince, and with extra chopped mushrooms for an apparently meaty texture. I could do that. I thought.

If cheese, butter, and milk were going to be a problem for my bloody *health freak* of a sister, then it would leave all the more for Jason and me to enjoy. Besides, the way to a man's heart begins in his belly, and all that. Emma could shut up and eat breadsticks. Everyone loves a breadstick. She would have plenty of wine to swill them down with. What more did she want? Maybe they'd choke her, preventing unwanted chatter that may otherwise escape her mouth? Bliss.

I had no idea what I should wear. I couldn't wear the same outfit I'd worn last night, and I most certainly wouldn't be wearing my favourite red underwear again. Even if, by some bizarre miracle, Jason happened to see my matching set again this evening, I could not delude myself that it would be appropriate to wear the same items two nights in a row. He might even assume I hadn't washed them, which I certainly would be doing, should I have chosen to wear them again this evening. It wouldn't offer a good impression at all. He might assume I had little in the way of quality underwear to impress him with, and, although that might be true, I was in no mood for Jason to discover this fact so promptly. I allowed my mind to ponder Emma's probably brimming underwear drawer as I left a heavily seasoned pot of mushrooms, tomatoes, and finely chopped onions, bubbling and blipping on the stove behind me and headed into my bedroom to swiftly dissect the contents of my wardrobe in a panic.

***

By eight o'clock, my nerves were completely shredded. Sylvester had been fed. Amazingly without much prompting from him, I am thrilled to confirm. The meal was in the oven (it didn't look too bad, even if I do say so myself) and two bottles of Cava were chilling in the fridge. No matter how many times I checked my appearance, I felt like screaming. What the hell was I thinking, inviting them for dinner at such short notice? *Although, technically, I hadn't meant to invite my sister anywhere.*

I must have stared out of the window a dozen times before I finally forced myself to sit down and take a breath. I then stood up again, applying yet more lipstick that I instantly wiped away, only to reapply moments later. I knew I needed to calm down. My head was going into overdrive, my heart potentially exploding along with the food in the oven behind me, my inability to relax threatening to dislodge my fake composure entirely. *Calm down, Stacey, please.* How many times have you shared a meal with these people? Anyone would think they were total strangers I'd pre-ordered from some online dating app.

The doorbell rang then, allowing no time to check that the blue wrap dress I was wearing even suited me, or that the hastily chosen underwear wasn't unexpectedly leaving indentations in my otherwise fairly acceptable curves. Did I have cat fur on me? Another buzz. *For Christ's sake Stacey, answer the goddamned door.* I planted a smile on my face and opened the front door, unable to do anything further about my appearance now. However I looked, it would have to do.

Wow. Jason stood in front of me, a delicious bottle of Pinot Grigio in one hand, shirt undone to reveal the tiniest hint of chest hair below, freshly washed hair in urgent need of my wandering fingers, his entire body in need of my wandering hands. I wanted to melt. Or vomit. Either would do. At that point, I wasn't entirely fussed.

'Wow, sis, you look amazing.' Emma's patronising voice hit my ears as she stepped forward, kissing me firmly on the cheek, leaving behind a lipstick impression that Jason kindly wiped away. He winked. I lingered too long with his warm fingertip against my cheek, not even noticing my sister standing next to her husband. She was dressed top to toe, as always, in designer clothes, her hair and make-up looking as if she had stepped out of a magazine. *Bitch.*

'So do you.' I was unable to take my eyes off her husband, hoping I didn't look too obvious, not entirely caring what Emma thought. After all, I couldn't help it. It was utterly beyond my control. Emma leaned in, handing me a bunch of flowers that I wanted to shove in her face. She smelled good, as did the flowers I was now holding in my trembling hands. I wanted to spray her in the face with bleach — or tip cat litter over her head. Anything, that would remove her existence from this otherwise perfect moment. I didn't dare mention that I'd purchased the same fragrance my sister always wore, only this very day, our aromas now blending in a futile attempt to confuse Jason's senses. *Lady Demure* smelled far better on me anyway, in my opinion.

Emma bowed her head, assuming that, of course, she always looked good, as she wafted into my flat, silky red dress whipping across her legs like a free-flying flag to expose her perfectly tanned skin beneath. I screamed in silence, wanting to rip the thing from her shoulders and claw her eyes out of her head. I hoped Jason would provide a little better company. *God, how I needed an escape.* I wondered for a moment if I could grab his hand and race screaming into the night with him in tow? Would he leave without a fight? I smoothed my dress, hoping I looked sexy, glancing down in disgust at my bulging waistline. I breathed in, felt suffocated, breathed out, my dismay threatening to surface unrelenting.

'You do look good, actually,' Jason handed me his gift, gently kissing me on the cheek as I allowed them to step inside. He brushed his hand across my waist as he stepped into my hallway. I smiled. Had I heard that correctly? Does Jason genuinely think I look good? Emma hadn't noticed. She was far too busy assessing the current state of my flat, hoping, no doubt, that it looked a mess so she could once again proclaim unwavering superiority. Jason and I exchanged glances. For a moment, I thought I noticed something in his eyes –

'I wanted Jason to wear this gorgeous new shirt I bought him yesterday, but he insisted on wearing that old thing.' Emma turned with a slight roll of her eyes to her husband's chosen attire.

'I thought I'd save it for another time,' Jason said, winking at me as he closed the front door with a click. I wondered what the hell was wrong with my sister. He looked fantastic. He always looked fantastic. Everything he wore looked fantastic. He could wear a bin liner and still impress me — nothing but a bin liner. Completely naked below.

'Leave him alone, for God's sake, Emma,' I spat,

unintentionally vocalising irritated disdain for my sister's throwaway attitude. 'He looks great.' I smiled at Jason, unable to take my eyes off his escaping chest hair. Jason nodded, mouthing a thank you in my direction.

'This place is looking great too, Stace,' Emma's irritating vocals were now in my front room, where she had already settled her bony backside onto my sofa without a second thought for the pointed words she had already aimed at her husband, ignoring my comment entirely. I thought I noticed a hint of sarcasm in her tone, yet such a tone was her default mode, so I ignored it. I was too busy giving Jason a lingering stare, hoping the moment between us hadn't simply been in my head, the flowers and wine bottle in my hands now rendering me incapable of anything else.

'Thanks,' I answered, half-listening, half-wishing I could drag Jason into my bedroom and slam the door behind us. I almost rolled agitated eyes towards my sister's husband but thought better of it. I didn't entirely know at that point how far I could push things between them. I had to play this right.

'Need help?' Jason had a way of making me want him so badly. It was all-consuming — irrational thoughts already tipping the balance between normality and fantasy.

'You can pour the wine if you like,' I giggled, offering him the bottle he'd handed me only moments earlier. When the hell had I developed a tendency for giggling? How old was I? Unaware of my silent musing, he followed me into the kitchen. My inappropriate attempt to pretend it was just the two of us here tonight, slightly missed its mark, yet remained in my head all the same. I secretly hoped he was staring at my bottom, my dress undoubtedly tight enough, curves wrapped as carefully as my limited options allowed, displaying breasts I hoped Jason would approve of. Nothing left to the imagination — of that, I had made damned sure.

I discarded Emma's flowers onto the countertop, adjusting my dress so it would display a little extra cleavage as I bent over, apparently looking in the cupboard for wine glasses that had eluded my attention — glad I had chosen a lacy pair of black underwear that had been lying in the back of my sock drawer for too long, forgotten, providing a moment of considered glee upon their unexpected discovery. *Oh, Stacey, you naughty minx.* I liked that word now. Ever since Jason had called it me this very morning, in fact. It was a phrase I would be using more often.

11

'I like your dress.' Jason walked up behind me in the kitchen and leaned forward. He brushed his leg against mine as he took the wine glasses from my hands. I swear he did it on purpose.

'What, this old thing?' I said, knowing full well that I'd sobbed into a large pile of clothing this very afternoon after realising my wardrobe resembled an underprivileged charity shop storeroom. It was a miracle I even found the time to cook the meal that I was about to serve, because this dress was hiding forgotten at the bottom of my wardrobe, along with a ragged old pair of jeans, smelling like old socks and in urgent need of attention. Thankfully, a steam iron and a generous spritz of perfume meant it was good enough for this occasion, albeit a little tight in places and threatening to break the occasional seam if I breathed out too much.

I must have sounded like a complete idiot — a desperate, despondent female with absolutely nothing decent to wear. *Calm the hell down, Stacey, for Christ's sake.* I smiled, and checked that my lasagne was still bubbling happily in the oven, cheese browning nicely, unexpected lumpy sauce making a desperate escape into the bottom of the oven tray. My nerves were shredded. I considered vomiting into the oven dish, and was glad my stomach lining remained intact.

'Stacey, I simply love what you've done with the place,' Emma's annoying voice filtered in from the other room as she popped her head around the kitchen door. I wanted to tell her not to be so damned patronising. I was fully aware that my meagre one-bedroom flat was nothing compared to her five-bedroomed, detached, executive property with bloody en-suite facilities in seemingly every room and double garage that Jason used as his home gym.

I was impressed I had found the time to tidy up, though. I couldn't recall becoming such a messy person. Most of the possessions I owned were now stuffed precariously inside cupboards and under my bed. I tried not to think too long about the volume of cat fur and crumbs currently residing under my living room rug. I hoped she wouldn't suddenly become nosy. She might become buried under a pile of discarded crap. Actually, that was not such a bad idea …

'Are you taking the piss?' I snapped, realising my error as Jason shot me a look.

'No. Sis, seriously, this place is genuinely really nice.' I'm sure what she meant to say was, *this place is really small*. Compact. Bijou. *Ugly*. Probably exactly what she thought of me.

'Thank you,' I said weakly, wondering how my sister always managed to make me feel like shit even when, apparently, she was being nice. I wished I could open the window and throw her out of it. Or myself. That would work too.

'Something smells nice,' she continued, oblivious to how she had made me feel, tracing judgemental eyes across my unkempt work surfaces. I dared not look at Jason now for fear of what he might think of my offhand outburst. Everything that escaped Emma's mouth sounded like a dig in the chest, aimed at me with the intention of making me look bad.

In my opinion, the phrase, 'something smells nice', could well have been translated into, *God, what the hell are you cooking, Stacey?* or *what on earth is that terrible smell?* I knew I would never be as attractive, wealthy, charming or successful as my sister, and her cooking ability far outweighed mine. But *it is what it is*, as they say. She received the best genes. I made do with what was left.

'How's the book stuff coming?' I asked as I pulled my now crispy lasagne from the oven, not realising it would burn so quickly and hoping neither of them would notice. I didn't give a shit about her bloody book. It simply seemed the perfect opportunity to turn my sister's attention back to herself for a moment while I dealt with this dodgy offering in front of me. I wondered if I could peel away the burnt bits without detection.

Emma scoffed, seemingly overworked by the entire concept. 'Oh my God. Slow,' she breathed, tipping her head back to display a long slim neck that I just wanted to throttle. 'Who knew this publishing thing took so long?' She was laughing now, but I honestly didn't give a damn. I had merely asked the question to divert unwanted attention from my terrible cooking for the amount of time I would need to serve something that might pass for reasonable consumption. What had I done to deserve such punishment?

I glanced towards Jason, already busying himself pouring three glasses of wine. He handed one to me with a wink. If I didn't know better, I might have assumed he wanted her to shut up as much as I did. It was as if we had shared a private moment I wished I could savour forever. I smiled, taking a sip of my delicious, crisp white wine, its soothing texture a welcome distraction, the back of my throat easing with momentary relief. If Emma had continued her rant, I was no longer listening. My attention now turned firmly back to this incredible male in my kitchen.

***

Dinner was quite tasty if I do say so myself. I was impressed by culinary abilities that I didn't even realise I possessed. The crispy parts of the lasagne Jason ate without incident, actually asking for a second helping. I ensured that Emma was seated on the opposite side of the table, alone, far away from me. Jason was free to enjoy my company unhindered, our knees able to brush together, hands lingering, should such a moment occur. She would, of course, overlook the hidden reasons behind my deceit, unaware of the dark thoughts that swam in my mind unchecked, unspoken lustful ideas about her husband unknown to them both. After all, Emma only ever noticed Emma. It was a perfect scenario.

We chatted for a couple of hours about anything that might keep my sister happy, entertained, away from our otherwise unsustainable attention. The fact that my previously promised three courses accidentally became two when I forgot to cook the prawns, thankfully went unnoticed by my guests. I could always offer cheese and biscuits if things became too desperate: my chocolate pudding had only just made it to the fridge before collapsing into a melted mess. And coffee. Coffee was always a perfect way to end any sophisticated evening.

I swear, if I didn't know better, Jason occasionally positioned his leg against mine as he leaned across the table for salt he didn't need, reaching for wine bottles that stood open in front of us. My sister chatted away to herself, unaware of the secret moments happening in front of her eyes. Or maybe it was all in my head. Naturally, I chose to pretend not.

'That was yummy,' Emma said, scooping down a second helping of chocolate tart as if her diet mattered little to her at all. 'It was genuinely nice of you to do this for us, Stace.' For a moment, she sounded sincere. It threw me off balance, creating havoc inside my head that I didn't quite know what to do with.

'More wine, anyone?' I offered, feeling suddenly embarrassed and unsure how to respond.

No one declined as I headed to the fridge for our third bottle of the evening. Emma took too long in the loo, while Jason leaned back in his chair, seemingly full, content. Although I didn't plan what happened next (my thoughts merely on how I could get Jason alone for a bit) I would be lying if I said I hadn't fantasied about this exact scenario for quite some time. As I pulled the wine from the fridge, a devious idea crept into my mind. It would be such a simple act — all I would need to achieve my ultimate ambition, this timing never better.

By the time I returned to my guests, Emma was giggling next to her husband, their lips touching, his hand stroking hers. I wanted to scream. My momentary removal from the room had prompted a change in Jason's attention from myself to my sister. How did she manage that so swiftly? I hadn't been gone that long. I placed two bottles of wine on the table, one red, one white, with a loud thud. Shocked by my own sudden and incredible mischief, I couldn't help the smile that appeared on my lips as Jason's eyes averted from Emma to me, my heaving cleavage a mere two feet from his eyes.

'Em, darling.' *Shit, I was laying this on a bit thick.* I never called her Em: she made me sick. The last thing I would ever do is give her an affectionate pet name. I needed to take a step back. 'I got this for you because I know how much you love Cabernet Sauvignon.' It was a total lie. I had actually won the bottle in a raffle at work some months earlier, forgetting that it had sat at the back of my fridge ever since because I didn't like red wine. I handed my sister the entire bottle, cork already popped. Her face displayed enthusiasm that didn't go unnoticed by her husband. The critical thing to remember about my sister was that the more she drank, the easier it was to get her to drink. Jason and I, of course, would be enjoying our own private bottle of Cava, I hoped. In a different room entirely.

'This is all for me?' Emma hugged the bottle as if I'd given her an entire box of chocolates, tied with a pink bow, covered in sprinkles and marshmallows.

'No way,' Jason chipped in then, shaking his head. 'I'll never get you home.'

'Oh, leave her alone,' I laughed, not in any way wanting him to take the bottle away from her. 'We don't get the chance to spend much quality time with each other all that often. And she's still celebrating her book stuff.' I wanted my sister to drink the entire bottle, and I would not be taking no for an answer. I poured myself and Jason a glass from our own bottle, handing my sister a freshly washed wine glass, the biggest I could find in my flat, watching with delight as she took it from my hand keenly. 'All for you, Sis,' I said with a knowing wink I hoped wouldn't give me away.

Emma poured herself a glass of red wine, glugging it down in one go, seemingly savouring the texture and enjoying the moment I had afforded her. It was as if she had just found herself standing inside a giant chocolate shop. 'God, I love it when I can let my hair down,' she sighed, kicking back in her chair with a laugh. 'Mum is so good, having Eva for us on such short notice.'

'You're getting drunk,' Jason pitched in.

'Oh, she's okay,' I chimed in, clinking my glass against his. 'It's not as if she's got to get up for work in the morning, is it?' We both knew this was true. Emma ran her own business. She could choose her hours. If she decided to stay in bed an extra hour or two, who would dock her wages?

Jason laughed. 'She's impossible when she's drunk.'

'Oh, so am I,' I taunted, watching my sister absorb herself in a private red wine moment. I laughed then, *accidentally* brushing my foot across Jason's leg. 'Oops,' I giggled. 'See what I mean? If you're not careful, you'll have your hands full by the end of the evening.' I poked him playfully in the arm, testing the water. I wasn't even drunk. Tipsy, yes. Drunk, definitely not. I wanted to remember every detail about this evening. I couldn't leave anything to chance. The sleeping pills I'd crushed into my sister's bottle of wine must not go to waste.

12

It didn't take much for me to persuade my sister to keep drinking. I ensured the compliments flowed, just how she liked it, her glass topped up every few minutes, much to Jason's unwitting despair. Fairly soon, she was giggling like a teenager, offering her body unapologetically to her now embarrassed husband as he tried to manhandle her to my sofa for, in his opinion, some well-needed time out. I suppressed an urge to laugh as my perfect sister stumbled around my flat like a common tramp. I should have taken a photograph and posted it on social media.

'I am so sorry about this.' Jason was utterly mortified.

'Oh, don't worry, it's not the first time we've seen her in this state, is it?' I giggled, unable to contain myself, my infectious laughter filling the room. I was unable to control my pent-up emotions that had been held inside for so long.

'I've never seen her this drunk before,' he said as he laid his almost comatose wife on my sofa. She was in a world of her own, muttering strange words we couldn't understand, but sleep offered itself to her swiftly and without remorse the moment she rested her head against my cushions.

'Oh, I have,' I lied. 'She was always getting blind drunk when we were kids. This is tame for her, actually.' It was a complete and utter load of crap. My sister enjoyed a drink, of course. We all did. But she knew her limits, and I knew Jason knew this too. 'We used to call her Emma Problema.' That was a lie too. No one had ever called her Emma Problema. I had, in fact, invented the nickname on the spot, impulsively, impressively. *Well done me.*

'Has she *never* told you the stories?' I continued, totally absorbed in this moment of triumph over my big sister, a roll of my eyes not going unnoticed by her man. Jason shook his head, his confusion apparent. Poor sod. He had no idea of the number of sleeping pills his wife had inadvertently swallowed along with her delicious bottle of wine. I should have thought of this idea long ago. Maybe I should perform such wondrous acts of charity more often — anything that would give Jason a break from her overbearing presence. He deserved it. We both did.

Jason offered me a blank look, so I continued. 'She probably didn't tell you because she was embarrassed, but she had a drink problem a few years ago.' *Oh my God, Stacey, you total liar.*

'A drink problem?'

'I shouldn't be telling you this. It's not my place.' I shook my head, totally glad to have rattled my sister's devoted husband. I merely wanted to show him a glimpse of the real Emma. The Emma, that for reasons still eluding me, only I seemed able to see. He deserved so much more than the cheap slut that currently lay dribbling on my fur-infested cushions. I glanced towards her for a moment, hoping I hadn't accidentally given her too many crushed pills. Had I crushed two, or three? Maybe four?

'Maybe I should get her home,' Jason said.

'Oh, leave her for a while,' I waved my hand casually towards the snoring sofa, unconcerned by the idea that I might have accidentally overdosed the woman, alcohol adding to the possibility of her demise. 'She'll be okay once she's slept it off.' I allowed a second glance towards her, trying to convince myself that I meant what I had said.

Jason looked at his wife with a shrug. 'You're probably right.'

I was glad he didn't look too concerned either.

'Fancy a coffee?' I asked, needing to sober up a little myself now that the evening could finally resume in peace. Jason nodded and together we cleared away the dinner plates. We headed into the kitchen together, the night suddenly feeling a little more excitable, enticing. 'I'm surprised Emma never told you about her alcoholism,' I pitched in casually as I waited for the kettle to boil.

'She drinks wine *all* the time,' he confirmed. 'But I never knew she had any issues.' He genuinely looked confused, concerned.

'She was trying to save face, I guess.' What did I assume he would do about my unexpected revelation?

Throw himself into my waiting arms? 'Probably best not bring it up, actually, or mention I said anything.' The last thing I needed was for Jason to discover I had lied to his face. 'Come on, let's sit outside for a moment and take in some air.' I unlocked the double French doors in my kitchen that led onto a rear balcony. I hardly used the space, but it was a pleasant evening, and I couldn't bear the idea of listening to my snoring sister while attempting to seduce her husband.

Jason nodded, heading out onto the balcony ahead of me. 'It's nice out here,' he called as I poured boiling water into two mugs of instant coffee.

I joined Jason surveying my neighbourhood. This place was rich in the town's history, yet I rarely stopped to notice. It was too overlooked for my taste, too crowded, not like Emma's suburban home with its views of fields and trees beyond. I handed him a hot mug, allowing the split in my dress to separate as I sat down on an old rattan sofa that I had earlier brushed dead leaves and dead bugs from. Anyone might assume I had this whole evening planned. *As if.*

'Sit down for a while. Relax. You look overworked.' I wanted to bring his focus back to us. *To me.* His wife was of little concern to either of us now.

Jason sat down and took a sip of his coffee. 'Sorry, it's instant.' I was embarrassed I had forgotten, in today's haste, to purchase the posh Italian coffee beans I knew he drank.

Jason shook his head. 'This is perfect.' I knew he was lying to me, but it was sweet of him to protect my feelings. 'The meal was also delicious, Stacey,' he said between sips of coffee and breaths of familiar perfume I knew he couldn't quite place. I couldn't help smiling. 'I didn't realise you were such a good cook.'

I blushed, yet in the darkness of my rear balcony, I hoped Jason wouldn't notice. 'I try,' I giggled. Why the hell was I giggling so much tonight? We sat together enjoying the peace of the late evening air along with seemingly passable coffee. I shivered then, not altogether unintentionally.

'You cold, honey?'

'A bit,' I lied, allowing my dress to unravel a little further.

Jason reached forward and grabbed a throw blanket from the edge of the sofa that I'd placed there earlier that day, just in case. He draped it across my knees, tucking it beneath my legs. 'Better?' he asked.

'A bit, thanks,' I replied, cupping my hands under his arms and snuggling against him. He didn't pull away. 'This is nice,' I said, feeling a little sleepy yet fully awake, the magnitude of the moment too crucial for me to forget. 'Just the two of us.' I sighed. 'I don't believe my sister knows how lucky she is to have you.' I realised my error too late, my words escaping my lips too swiftly. 'I'm so sorry.' I sat upright, pulling myself free from Jason's arms, my breasts now entirely on display beneath a thin black bra that didn't hide nipples standing to attention in the inviting evening air. My wrap dress was slowly – weirdly – unravelling itself. Anyone would think I had untied the thing. 'I have had *way* too much to drink.' I casually attempted to pull my dress together, failing, as it loosened more. 'What must you think of me?' Such damsel-in-distress acting skills I had acquired.

'Don't worry about it.' Jason didn't pull away. He cupped the blanket across my breasts, lingering his hand a little too long over the thin fabric that covered them.

'Can I ask you a serious question?' I muttered then, completely unable to control myself. *Shit Stacey, be careful.*

'Sure. You can ask me anything you like.' Jason placed his mug onto my dusty makeshift tabletop that was actually nothing more than a pile of wooden planks I'd stacked together in an attempt to appear trendy. He turned to face me, expectant, unconcerned.

'What do you see in my sister?' I couldn't believe I had asked the question. It came out of my mouth with no remorse whatsoever. I held my breath.

'Where did that come from?' he asked with a smile that didn't entirely turn into the casual laugh I might have expected. However, he wasn't laughing off my query at all, instead choosing to stare intently into my eyes, searching for an answer to a serious question.

'Because you can have the pick of the crop.' I continued, my quest for truth something I could no longer hide. 'So why pick Emma Problema?' I loved the new name I'd invented for my sister. I had a feeling it would stick.

'Hey, that's my wife you're talking about,' Jason was laughing now, although he didn't appear the slightest bit irritated by my words. More intrigued, surprised.

'And?' I couldn't help it when I leaned towards him and kissed his lips. I expected he would pull away and that I would be forced to blame the booze once again.

But he didn't pull away. Instead, he brought his hands to my face and pulled me to him, embracing me in a passionate, open-mouthed kiss I wasn't expecting. Shit. What the hell was happening?

After wishing for so long for Jason to kiss me in such a way, was this actually happening or was I simply dreaming? It would be entirely ironic if I had fallen victim to my own drunken slumber, not unlike Emma's current state. Maybe Jason was, in fact, currently in the kitchen washing dishes instead of exactly where I wanted him to be. I pulled away a little, allowing his hand to linger against my cheek. My breathing was shallow, anticipating. 'Is this what you want?' I asked him, still unsure whether I was actually awake or had fallen asleep in his arms.

'Is it what *you* want?' he breathed, his breath warm against my ear.

'God yes,' I replied, no longer able to prevent the emotions that swam through my mind. We kissed then — a fully absorbed, passionate embrace. I allowed myself to fall to his whim, allowing his hands to explore my body, glad I looked hot enough tonight to draw his attention. I had known for a long time that there was lingering chemistry between us. I could tell. A woman knows these things. Emma had obviously been unable to provide her husband with what I now hoped I would. It was nice. No. It was bloody fantastic. To be wanted by Jason, my needs outweighing my sister's. Jason's lips searched my skin as his hot breath united with mine, a heady mix of coffee and alcohol awakening our unfathomed senses. He was pulling at my dress now, the

103

wrap tie coming undone quickly as his warm hands searched my body, the blanket falling to the floor, discarded, no longer required. Jesus Christ, was this seriously happening?

'I want you,' he whispered as he pushed my legs apart with his knees.

'The feeling's mutual,' I answered, grabbing his shirt and pulling it free from his trousers. His skin felt so warm against mine. I literally couldn't get his buttons undone fast enough.

Jason momentarily glanced towards my open kitchen doors. 'What if she wakes up?'

'She won't,' I said. I was confident we would not be disturbed, pills and alcohol firmly in her system. My plan couldn't have worked any better, and I'd only thought of it less than an hour earlier. *Well bloody done, me.* I kissed his lips, willing him to shut up and focus on me. He didn't argue. He confidently undid my front fastening bra, allowing his hands to cup my breasts expertly. I almost orgasmed there and then within his willing grasp.

13

The sex was fast, our fumbling too rampant, yet the feeling of Jason's body against mine as he slid himself frantically inside me was something I was never going to forget. He opened me up to him, his keen desire thrusting deep into my body along with wild thoughts I'd only ever dreamed of. He groaned his orgasm unapologetically into the evening air, my body at his total unwavering mercy. I loved every moment of it.

He lay on top of me for a moment after our frantic act was over, his manhood still throbbing between my legs. *No condom. Shit.* Still, at that moment, neither of us gave a damn. If he got me pregnant, that might be the best thing that had ever happened to me. It would mean that Jason could genuinely become mine — the perfect excuse for him to leave his wife. I pulled my sister's husband towards me and kissed him, my body still throbbing and desperate for the orgasm I hadn't yet experienced.

'Touch me,' I breathed, pushing his hand between my legs. I was in heaven, lying in full view of any unsuspecting neighbour who should happen to venture outside, Jason's fingers touching places I'd only ever dreamt he would discover. Finally, we were both spent, the evening washing over us unapologetically.

'That was unexpected,' Jason whispered into my ear. Then he kissed me, his tongue searching mine for proof that this moment had happened.

'Totally,' I replied, pulling him close, his fingers and private parts telling of an act forbidden. I smiled then, no shame or embarrassment for me. I had wanted this for so long. I didn't care that our passion had been swift, the coffee in our mugs still warm. I wondered what might happen if Emma were to wake up, my measurements incorrect, the sleeping pills wearing off too quickly. I wrapped my legs around my sister's husband's bare bottom and sighed. To be honest, I would love it if she discovered us out here. The sight of his exposed buttocks, trousers around his ankles, my legs set on either side of his. What would my perfect sister have to say about that?

Jason's breath was shallow against my skin, the moment passed, our passion receding. 'You okay?' he asked. It was so kind of him to care.

'Never better, actually.' I allowed the first honest words to escape my lips in quite some time. When I was with Jason, I felt that I could genuinely be myself. No older sister hovering for compliments, my feelings rating higher than hers, for a change. He rose to his feet and buttoned his trousers, allowing me a brief glimpse of his now shiny member as he slipped it back inside his clothing. I sat up, closing legs that didn't want to be closed, still throbbing, excitement unable to contain itself. I stood up, my dress open, my bra undone, my knickers *God* knows where. He could see everything I was. He pulled me close to him, my semi-naked flesh pressed against the warmth of his body.

'Stacey, I –'

'Shush.' I most certainly did not need excuses. I did not care about the reasons why this had never happened to him before or the fact that he would never, under normal circumstances, cheat on his wife. I knew he was a good man. We both knew this was a mutual thing. Something I'd secretly believed we had both wanted for quite some time. It was understandable, of course, that he should want me. Physically, mentally, everything in between. God knows this evening's passion had lingered between us for a while. Now I'd felt him inside me, I wasn't about to let go of what I knew could become amazing between us. 'We have a lot to talk about, I know,' I breathed against his ear, a sudden desire for another session building between my naked legs. 'Touch me,' I nibbled his neck for a moment, pulling his hand towards my –

'Stacey, stop,' Jason backed away, unable to stop himself kissing me, yet, for some reason, not entirely willing to repeat our brief performance. The more I thought about it, the more it made sense. Tonight had been hurried, unexpected, our time together fleeting, my sister a mere few feet from our exposed position. The next time we made love, he would want to take his time. No algae-ridden rattan furniture jammed against bare skin, that creaked violently beneath the weight of frantically moving bodies. No uncomfortable, six-foot-wide balconies overlooked and underused. My bed. That was what was needed next time.

I giggled. Giggling had oddly become my thing now, and I was embracing the concept. 'Come on, you,' I pulled him roughly towards the French door of my kitchen that had been purposefully left ajar, my passed-out sister in full view of everything we had just done together, creating a heightened sense of achievement in my mind. My spine tingled, adrenaline pumping through every inch of my body. My full intention was to get him into my bed, strip him naked and do the most unspeakable things to him.

'No, Stacey, stop it.' Jason pulled his hand away from my warm place, hurrying to button his jeans, to straighten his shirt.

'Oh, shit.' I stood in the doorway of my kitchen, my body on display.

'What?'

'You regret that?' I hadn't contemplated such a concept. In my mind, Jason would never hurt me in such a way. I imagined that once we opened the floodgates, our love would blossom in an instant.

'No. Of course not, Stacey. I don't regret anything.' He walked those couple of steps towards me that now felt like a vast cavern and kissed me, sliding a hand around my bare bottom. I sucked in the heated air, the warmth of his hands too much for my fragile mind. What the hell was he doing to my senses tonight? 'It's just that I want our next time to be a bit more –'

'Me too,' I giggled again realising, of course, he

fancied me far too much to want this moment to end so abruptly. Obviously, he, like me, would want our next time to be perfect. We had crossed the threshold. We could do nothing about that now. 'Come on then,' I pulled him towards my bedroom, ignoring the fact that we would have to slip right past my unsuspecting unconscious sister in the process.

'No. Stop it,' he was laughing, playfully touching my breasts and bottom as we fumbled around together in my kitchen like a couple of teenagers. He glanced into the front room. 'I can't with her lying in that room.' It was true. *And very off-putting — if I took the time to think about it.*

'It didn't stop you a moment ago,' I whispered, nibbling his ear and allowing my tongue to slide momentarily inside.

'Well, that was your fault for looking so goddamned hot.' I was thrilled to hear such words. I had known he fancied me for a while. I concluded it was because he preferred his women to be a little curvier. Emma was too thin, too brittle. I shuddered. How did he not break her?

'You seemed to enjoy brushing my leg in the taxi last night, too,' I laughed, his arms firmly around my waist now. He didn't want to let me go. I didn't give a shit where my knickers had gone.

'You noticed?'

'I always notice you, Jason,' It was true. I couldn't hold it in anymore. I wanted him to fully appreciate that I did not regret what we had just experienced and that I would be happy for him to fuck me every morning, noon and evening, for the rest of my life. I could tell he wanted the same thing.

We kissed again, his hands touching my body in a way no man ever had. I was lost within this moment, oblivious and uncaring that my sister was lying just feet away, unconscious, scorned by her sister and cheated on by the man she assumed loved her.

'I have to get her home,' Jason said then, freeing his body from my willing grip, sounding as irritated by the concept of leaving me as I was.

'She'll be okay if you want to join me in the bedroom for a few moments.' I groaned. I was deadly serious. I honestly did not want this moment to end.

'I would love to. Really, I would, but –' he glanced over his shoulder. The fact that my sister was even in my flat now was something I detested. It brought slight nausea to the back of my throat. I wanted to tell him to throw her in the back of the car and be done with it, preferably knocking her over the head in the process. But I refrained. I pulled my dress around my body, covering my modesty and this moment, temporarily relieving Jason of my wandering hands and his wandering gaze.

'Jesus Christ,' I couldn't help sounding so pissed off. I was in the zone, and now the moment was over.

Jason laughed then, embracing me in a full-on French kiss. I just wanted to melt. It was as if I'd fallen in love with him, and he'd only just decided to reciprocate my feelings.

'Call me when you get home,' I wanted him to talk dirty to me all night long. He laughed, scooped his half-dead wife from my sofa and carried her out to the car, allowing a moment's lingering look as he left my flat.

Then he was gone, leaving a throbbing sensation between my legs where he had been inside me only a short time earlier and nowhere for me now to place that emotion. Shit.

14

I literally could not believe it. I can't even recall tidying the flat, dirty dishes lying untouched in my sink, along with dirty thoughts I couldn't get out of my mind. Jason had actually made love to me. It had really happened. I was in a daze as I floated around the flat, my dress still smelling of him, my underwear still on the balcony somewhere, discarded, forgotten. I had to pinch myself, to tell myself that I hadn't dreamt the entire thing. More to the point, I was thrilled he hadn't retreated in disgust afterwards, confessing that it had been a terrible mistake and could never happen again. I actually got a distinct feeling that it would indeed be happening again. And a lot more often if I had anything to do with it.

I climbed into bed, satisfied, naked, remembering the feel of his urgent hands over my body, needing him to repeat his performance, although a little slower next time, if at all possible, less manic, less forceful. I smiled, recalling the moment he had orgasmed inside me. *Shit.* I'd forgotten about that. Yet, I could do nothing about that now. I hated condoms anyway. They got in the way, halting an otherwise perfect moment, creating a distraction neither of us needed, our urgency knowing no bounds.

A deeply rooted part of me desperately wanted to share this wonderful news with my sister. To tell her that, unfortunately – and as upsetting as it might be for her to contemplate – her husband now preferred me to her. Actually, the more I thought about it, the angrier I became. I hoped he wouldn't go home and have sex with her simply because he felt guilty, unable to repeat his performance with me merely because I wasn't there. The idea sounded stupid. Emma was unconscious. Surely he wouldn't have sex with a half-dead woman? I laughed, such foolish thoughts ringing pitifully in my head.

Although Jason and Emma had a child together, I assumed he would love it if we had our own, one day. I pressed a trembling hand over my belly. I might already be pregnant if Jason's urgency tonight had anything to do with it. Emma might be upset for a while, her cheating husband unable to control himself, our unconstrained lust unable to hide in shadows forever. I fully intended that she would not remain in our lives, her presence no longer needed. Eva would be offered the freedom to spend time with her father on alternate weekends, so Emma would be unrequired for anything other than a handover every fourteen days or so. That is, at least, what would happen if I had anything to do with it. He would be far too busy with our little family for anything else.

I sat upright. *Christ, slow down, Stacey.* It was one fumbled – agreeably urgent – sex act. Not a proposal of marriage. Yet, I could not allow myself the concept of anything other than embarking upon a proper relationship now that our feelings were finally out in the open. It had, after all, taken us long enough to embrace the inevitable.

The longer I lay in my lonely bed with thoughts of deluded romance, the more everything made sense. The way Jason offered knowing sideways glances in my direction. The fact that he called me honey when no one else could hear his words. Those little winks he gave me when no one else saw. It all made complete sense. I had no idea how long he had been secretly in love with me, such a simple thought causing my belly to bubble as I stared at the ceiling, contemplating the very idea that we could have been fucking this entire time had I simply been more observant of his needs. Wayward thoughts washed over me then, unable to subdue unfettered ideas of Jason becoming my man.

I leaned across the bed, picking up my mobile. No messages yet. *Jesus, Stacey. Take a breath.* He would need time to get my sister into bed, the very thought of that creating a discomfort I couldn't ignore. I shook my head. I didn't anticipate that manhandling Emma upstairs would be a fun use of his time, as caring and thoughtful as he was. She might even vomit over him. I shuddered, glad that Eva was with our parents, unable to witness her mother's current pathetic state. My mum was utterly devoted to her granddaughter, overnight stays meaning she could spoil the child without consequence. Jason would have plenty of time to message me once things were more settled, his house falling silent, Emma no longer an issue. I wondered how my mum might feel about having a second grandchild someday to dote upon? Maybe a third?

Unable to wait a minute longer, I sent him a message. 'You guys okay?' I needed to keep it casual in case Emma was, by some miracle, awake, witnessing words intended only for the lustful imagination of her husband. I needed to pick my moment carefully before I told her the truth. A few moments passed, my belly churning over the evening's event, words yet to be spoken, actions yet to be taken. My phone pinged. I practically jumped out of my skin.

'Yeah, all good this end,' the message read. 'She's having a glass of water.'

I felt sick. How was she awake? *Bitch.* I wished I could scoop Jason up, safely wrapping him in my protective arms forever. Away from her poisonous clutches.

'Is she okay?' I didn't give a shit. I wanted him to dispose of her emaciated corpse and turn his attention back to me. I wasn't even glad I hadn't accidentally killed her. It might have worked in my favour.

'Yeah, I think so. A bit hungover, obviously.'

Why the hell were we talking about my sister? 'Let me know when you are free,' I replied, not expecting the long silence afterwards and hoping Emma hadn't accidentally read my message. I felt sick. What if she had questioned its content? What if it had created an unwanted scene I was unable to witness? After all, why would she think Jason would need to message me at all? Our three-mile separation wholly prevented any influence I was unwilling to relinquish.

Around twenty minutes later, my phone rang. 'Sorry about that, honey.' Jason's flustered voice: he had called me honey. I lay back, naked, stroking my stomach at the sound of his voice, remembering his fingertips against my skin.

'Is everything okay?' I asked, adopting my most sultry voice for him, hoping it would have the desired effect.

'Yeah, she's finally gone to bed. So, I guess, I'm all yours.' I heard a spring somewhere as if he'd sat down. Or lay down. I smiled. I wondered if he was naked too.

'Where are you?'

'My office. I told her I'd be up in a bit. The truth is, I wanted to talk to you.'

I could have melted into my bed linen right then in a pool of desire. I licked my lips, curling around my pillowcase as if it was his throbbing body. 'Ditto,' I giggled, entirely unable to prevent my indulgent outburst.

'What are you doing?'

'You need to ask?'

'Stacey, you're so naughty,' I heard a shuffle as if he'd leaned back against something soft.

'You don't regret what happened, do you?' I held my breath for a moment, not entirely convinced I wanted the answer.

'Never.' I heard a low breath as if he was reliving our incredible time this evening, unable to believe it had actually happened. I know I most certainly couldn't. 'But, for now, this must stay between us.'

Why? Why did I need to keep quiet? I wanted to shout it from the rooftops. I wanted to race into the street right then, screaming that I was in love with Jason Cole and that I did not care who knew it. I licked my lips, my throat suddenly dry, the moment darkening. 'Sure,' I replied, not entirely believing my own words yet needing Jason to absorb them anyway. 'Jason?' I wanted to tell him that I loved him.

'Yeah?'

I hesitated. I couldn't simply blurt it out. Not over the phone. It would have been entirely inappropriate. 'You made me happy tonight.' It was the truth. I'd never been happier. I would gladly save my declarations of love for another time — a time when I was lying in his outstretched arms. I wanted to tell him that he was amazing, but the truth was the whole thing had been far too rushed for any genuinely considered, accurate performance-level assessment. For that, I would require a repeat performance. And soon.

'Likewise,' I heard him suck in air as if remembering the feel of my –

'When can I see you again?' I needed him to say that he would gladly drive straight over, unable to wait another second.

'I'll pop by tomorrow after work.'

Shit. That long? 'Promise?' Why did I sound so disappointed?

'Where else would I rather be?'

I slept like a baby that night —dribbling, lying on damp sheets, unable to find a comfortable position in which to curl up and disappear into my thoughts.

***

The following morning came slowly, the entire night dragging in a haze of isolation and self-delusion, thoughts of Jason lying next to *her* making my skin itch and my brain boil. I was fully aware that I had promised him – rather casually – that this would stay between us. But what the hell did that even mean? If he assumed he could have us both, he was sorely mistaken. I even got out of bed in a bad mood, my restless night mixed with feelings of Jason inside me, hot skin against mine, words I wished I had the guts to say out loud. I didn't dare consider calling in sick again today. I needed this job, for now at least. Once Jason and I were together, officially, I would reassess my life and needs. Emma was running her own business and taking care of a two-year-old. I had no reason to believe my own life with Jason might be anything other than perfect, no matter what career path I chose.

I patted my belly expectantly as I took a shower, recalling we hadn't used protection, secretly hoping I was pregnant already. It would, of course, help speed things up considerably if I was. It would make the truth of our relationship obvious, our feelings out in the open, free, unhindered, unapologetic. I wasn't concerned about how our sudden change in relationship status might look to everyone else. Jason and I had known each other for over a decade. Surely that was long enough to discover how we felt about each other? *If other people didn't like it, too bad!*

I wanted to text him, ask how he was and tell him to have a good day. But I thought better of it. Jason would undoubtedly need time to explain to his wife that he was leaving her for me, the understanding that such a conversation would not be an easy one for him, lingering in my mind. It was, however, weirdly something my brain struggled to contend with. I assumed she would be the one to move out of the house, her presence no longer required, taking Eva with her hopefully. At least, that is how things would be if I had my way. It would all come as a great shock to my perfect sister. But as Jason's money had paid for their home, she could bloody well do one.

15

I almost missed my stop, staring out of the bus window, thinking of my man. *My man. Wow.* What a concept. After being single for over three years, I was beginning to forget what an actual relationship felt like. A *relationship*. Could I be so bold as to call it such a thing so early in our developing status? Yes. Of course, I could. Jason was fully aware of how I felt about him. He must have been. My urgency for him last night was something I had not kept secret. The looks I gave him, the way I had literally opened up to him, physically, offering myself to him wholly, would have surely told him how I felt. I certainly knew how *he* felt. It was as if, in his utter desperation to be with me, he had penetrated me so urgently because he could hold it in no longer. Metaphorically speaking, of course.

I grinned too widely as I stepped off the bus, waving a cheerful farewell to the driver, who probably assumed me mad. The throbbing sensation between my legs was something I wouldn't be able to do a damned thing about until I saw Jason again tonight. My heart performed a little dance beneath my jacket as I skipped along the street into work. Even an overly industrious air-conditioned office building couldn't dampen my mood today. Unlike my underwear: that was a different matter entirely. I stifled an urge to laugh aloud, my face already aching from too much grinning.

I have to admit that I didn't give my sister much thought in this potentially impossible situation we were about to create for ourselves. Jason and I would have to be honest with everyone about how we felt. Come clean, if you like, get things out in the open. But I wasn't completely deluded that our honesty wouldn't come without consequence. I knew we would have to sit down properly, discuss what would happen next, and soon, I hoped.

I wasn't great at keeping secrets. Christmas was always a complete nightmare in our house, back in the days before Emma turned into an evil freak. She was still a terrible person, and as far as I was concerned, deserving of everything coming to her now. Always putting herself before anyone else, it was about time she had a wake-up call. I felt quite sorry for Jason, always having to put on a brave face every time he was in the company of our friends and family members, my parents especially.

As happy as Jason had made me, I did feel quite sorry for my niece. She was only two years old. Losing her dad so abruptly would be potentially quite horrible for her. But, at two, she wouldn't have a clue what was even happening, surely. By the time she was old enough to understand that her parents did not love each other, she would be used to the new dynamics, the way her parents' lives now were. Of course, Jason and I would see her every other weekend when she visited the house for dinner and a well needed play session. That would be perfect for Jason. He loved his daughter. More importantly, we wouldn't have to see Emma all that often. Perhaps even, as Eva grew up, we wouldn't have to see her at all. She could take the bus to the house. Maybe we could get her a dog? Eva that is. Not Emma.

I practically skipped into work, my sickness bug thankfully now well and truly forgotten. Or, at least, as far as my boss was concerned, it was — my actual hangover still smarted slightly whenever a bright light caught my attention, my thoughts anywhere else but on the work I was required to undertake. I was grateful I wouldn't have to endure this mind-numbing place for much longer, Jason earning enough for me to relax a little, take some time off to consider my next focal point in life. It felt as if I'd won the bloody lottery. Maybe I could quit my job? To see the look on everyone's faces when I told them I was moving up in the world? Priceless. *No. Not yet. Keep your head, Stacey, and keep your goddamned thoughts to yourself. You still have this month's rent to cover.*

Needless to say, my day dragged. Every second ticked by as if it was mocking my existence, taunting the very fact that Jason wasn't here. I wondered how he was, if he had spoken to Emma yet. I concluded that he would probably need my help to explain things adequately, our feelings for each other unable to hide any longer. We needed to express how we both felt so she would understand exactly how much we loved each other. I stopped mid-email to a client, leaning back in my chair, my mind uninterested in the task at hand. Love? Was it not a little early to be thinking of such matters?

'You okay, Stacey?' Helen, a colleague, was leaning across her desk in front of me, her ever-keen senses pressing into my private affairs, her nose as imposing as the brightly rimmed spectacles on her face.

'Never better,' I replied, continuing my email with little interest, simply needing to message Jason while he was fresh in my mind.

She grinned. 'You look like the cat who got the cream. So, who's the lucky man?'

I smiled, allowing a wink I wasn't expecting to provide so readily. *Was it that obvious?* 'Let's just say it's been on the cards for some time, Helen.' It was true, although I had only just realised. Our urgency last night told me everything I needed to know. Jason was desperate to make love to me. He couldn't get my knickers off fast enough. The way he called me honey when Emma wasn't in the room, brushing his hand several times against my leg in the back of the taxi the other night. He had even driven across town in the middle of the night to rescue me from a potential intruder, the effort he'd made testimony to the fact that he cared more than I had realised. Even the copious amount of alcohol in his bloodstream last night hadn't affected his performance. My deluded sister didn't have a clue what was about to hit her. I grinned then, wide, content. Not unlike how I had felt after Jason had ravaged me so wildly.

'Things are about to change,' I said as I stood up, picking up my coffee mug that had sat on my desk for two days and now had a weird ring of mouldy coffee skin around its rim. 'Things are about to change.'

***

I invented some ridiculous excuse about needing a coffee and a couple of headache pills, venturing into the kitchen to make Helen and me a drink. My mobile was tucked inside my waistband so no one would notice I was sneaking off to text Jason in private. I hoped Helen wasn't thirsty. I might be some time.

'How are you today, lover?' I pressed the send button, sitting on the loo in the ladies, waiting expectantly, demandingly, wanting an immediate response that wasn't forthcoming. I needed instant gratification for my time spent alone with my phone and runaway thoughts.

A few moments later, my eagerly awaited reply arrived. 'Thinking of you.'

Those were the exact words I needed to hear. I licked my lips slowly, anticipation growing. 'Did not get a minute of sleep last night,' I replied, feeling that familiar throb that now seemed to control my existence.

'Neither did I. Stayed in my office, in the end. Emma was out cold, snoring like an express train. I spent the entire night wishing I was inside you.'

Jesus, Jason, tell me like it is, why don't you. Please. I beg you. I grinned, crossing my legs in an automatic response to the ache that was bubbling uncomfortably in my underwear, wishing I wasn't sitting inside an often used toilet cubicle, wanting to do something about the throbbing sensation I couldn't dissipate. 'Talk dirty to me.' I needed sexual gratification right then, at work, in the middle of this ordinary morning, unapologetic, unseen behind a closed door with a lock that probably wouldn't hide my shame.

'I can't. I'm in the middle of a meeting.'

I laughed, too loudly, realising it was inappropriate while sitting in the ladies toilets, pretending to pee. No one found urinating funny. Unless, of course, the person in question was suffering from a urinary tract infection, and then peeing might indeed feel entirely exhilarating. 'So you're *sexting* me while in a meeting?' I was super excited by the idea that Jason couldn't get me out of his mind, placing my needs before his work duties. I was all too aware that the buzz of a new relationship can be thrilling, but I'd honestly never felt anything as real as this. This was true and honest love. Genuine, incredible.

'Don't tell anyone,' he replied, followed by a winking face and aubergine emoji. *Cheeky boy.*

'Are you nursing a semi?' My face felt as if it was going to split open with the magnitude of my own amusement, silent visions of Jason's potential erection, something I couldn't get out of my head.

'Let's just say, I'm glad I'm sitting down.'

I giggled again, but then someone banged the cubicle door, jolting me out of unfettered private thoughts.

'Stacey, I thought you were getting coffee? If Peter finds out you're skiving again, he won't be impressed.' It was Tori, the office gossip, probably already aware of my previous evening's conquest that was none of her goddamned business anyway. I knew Helen would have been wholly unable to stop herself from spreading such freshly acquired office gossip. I also knew, of course, she was merely jealous, but I needed this job, for now. I unclicked the door, popping my head out, offering a weak smile and a little wink I hoped would do the trick.

'Have you never been caught in the excitement of a new relationship before?' I asked coyly, holding my phone aloft while giggling. I genuinely could not stop doing that now. 'Give me two minutes, and I'll make you a coffee too.' How could she resist?

Tori wrinkled her brow, folding her arms as if considering my offer. 'Two minutes. Hurry up.' She walked out of the ladies, leaving me alone, the thought of someone else making her a coffee too much for her to turn down. Who the hell did she think she was anyway? Just because she was my supervisor, it didn't give her the right to determine my day. Oh, wait. Yes, actually, it did.

My phone pinged twice as I pretended to wash my hands, taking too long over such a simple task that I seemingly found too amusing. 'Gotta go. This semi won't shrink while you keep talking to me.' His message was followed by a second aubergine emoji and a love heart. *A love heart? Wow.* He seriously had it bad. But, of course, he did. I was irresistible, after all.

16

I was unable to get home fast enough that evening. I raced through the front door, tripped over Sylvester, swore, took a misplaced breath. I was finally able to begin the ritual I had spent my day neglecting work tasks in favour of, having planned the entire evening in the smallest of detail, nothing left to chance.

Number one. I would arrive home, feed the cat. Check. Sylvester glared at me as if three days of dry kibble and nothing more was beginning to wear slightly thin. I promised him I would get some tinned tuna at the weekend. He deserved it.

Number two. I would tidy the flat. To be honest, it wasn't too bad, yesterday's efforts remaining somewhat intact. I might even get away with fluffing cushions, straightening the rug, picking up escaped dust and debris from around the edges. Did I need to run a vacuum across it? Maybe. No, sod it. Jason would not be looking at the rug — at least, not the one on my living room floor. I suppressed a giggle as I headed into the bathroom to treat myself to a long soak in a hot bath before choosing the most seductive outfit in my arsenal, which technically was *Number three* on my list and probably the most important.

Number four was to order a takeaway — because the last thing I needed was any distraction tonight. I was done slaving in the kitchen for one week. It made too much mess that I would then be required to tidy away. I couldn't expect Jason to help. He had other requirements that I needed him to fulfil. So, for this evening, there would be no cooking for me, thank you very much.

I ran my bath, accidentally pouring in too much bubble bath, having to scoop a considerable amount of foam from the top of the water before I could get into the thing. Yet, I needed to feel squeaky clean and perfect for my man, so, bring on the overkill. The very concept made me shudder — *my man*. Could I now officially call Jason my boyfriend? My partner? My lover? I assumed I would be able to. I didn't imagine for one moment that he would mind being labelled as such. It would merely be a matter of time before we could go public anyway, declaring our feelings to the world — or, at least, to our immediate friends and family. No one else mattered. No one else factored on my radar. My sister included.

I lay in the bath, dreaming of what I wanted him to do to me and what, in turn, I planned to do to him. We had all night. Alone. No distractions. We could take our time — no bloody *Emma Problema* to mess things up, taking Jason's undivided attention away from me. I giggled at the fitting name I'd created for my sister, proud of myself for inventing such a befitting title so swiftly and with relatively little thought. I messaged

Jason three times to check he was still coming round, to which he replied the first two times with *can't wait*, and the third with a simple winking face. I suspected his curt response probably meant that my endless questions were wearing a little thin, but I was excited. He would understand my frivolity, surely.

Every time I was due to see Jason in the flesh, my heart threatened to leap out of my throat and into my lap. It was difficult enough seeing him before he had performed unspeakable things with me. Now, my head was an utter mess. I played sickly love songs on my iPod on repeat until they became too much. I put the lights on low and dressed top to toe in the most killer outfit I could find in the shops during my lunch break. I could not have contemplated searching my paltry clothing pile again, so my dreaded credit card statement was something I would have to deal with when it arrived. I had no time to consider such nonsense anyway. Maybe Jason could clear my balance? After all, this outfit was for his benefit.

It wasn't my fault that a local Ann Summers outlet was a mere couple of streets from my workplace. The momentary detour had happened hurriedly and without total rational awareness. *Give a girl a break.* I hadn't needed to impress a man for quite some time, and I was panicking. I most certainly was not going to take any chances tonight, and the current contents of my wardrobe were highly embarrassing.

I still hadn't found last night's knickers. I had visions of them falling over the edge of my balcony during Jason's urgent discovery of my private parts, potentially now recovered by an unsuspecting neighbour or dog walker whose animal would no doubt emerge with them between gritted teeth, tail wagging. It was funny to think of my discarded underwear in the mouth of some poor unsuspecting dog, its owner shocked by the appearance of such an unsavoury garment. Although, it probably wouldn't feel so funny if anyone was to knock on my door with them in hand. *Are these yours, miss? I found them beneath your balcony.* Oops!

I stared at my reflection for ten minutes, dressed in fake leather underwear that looked far nicer from a distance than it did up close, to be honest. My breasts looked incredible, though. I tried not to concern myself that my new faux leather bra was padded beyond anything I could have imagined physically possible. The fact that the padding equated to a bigger bust size than my actual breasts was immaterial. My girls looked bloody fantastic, sitting to attention, practically levitating.

I was adorned with a matching thong that disappeared between my cheeks with absolutely no remorse whatsoever. Thin, carefully placed faux leather straps rose in places that would probably make a prostitute blush, disappearing slightly too impressively amidst wayward curves, as if my body was eating the thing by mistake. High heels and hold up fishnet stockings completed the outfit, along with make-up and hair looking hotter than a firestorm in a volcano. I knew Jason would take one look at me and ravage me on the doorstep. Or at least, that was the plan. I was content. *Nervous as hell.* But content.

I relieved Sylvester of the claustrophobic atmosphere within my flat, his urgency to escape the volume of perfume I'd sprayed myself with, not entirely going unnoticed. I opened a window. I might have slightly overdone it. I equally did not wish for him to disturb us with incessant moaning for his favourite cat food that I'd forgotten to buy, again — the poor cat factored low on my consideration list right now. I am ashamed to admit that I actually scooped him into my arms, practically throwing him outside, slamming the front door in a hurry so he wouldn't race straight back inside. It wasn't my fault it was raining.

I thought about messaging – or calling – Jason again to confirm the precise time of his arrival, but I'd asked three times already and had been given the same answer: 6:30. I assumed that he was coming straight from work. Maybe he could shower here. We could shower together. The thought made my nipples stand to attention. I did, however, begin to feel a tad silly hovering in my flat wearing nothing but underwear that might have looked more at home on a porn shoot, so I relented, pulling on my black bathrobe, mortified to discover it had developed an odd-looking stain, the previous evening eagerly recounted in my mind. I glanced at the clock. It was 6:38. He was late.

I took a breath, folding trembling arms across my overstuffed bra. I needed to relax. *What the hell is wrong with you, woman?* Seriously, anyone would assume I'd never dated a man before in my life. I peered out of my closed curtains to check if his car was outside. Not yet. Maybe he had changed his mind about us? Maybe Emma had discovered his sneaky plan, inventing some unwanted chaos he could not escape from? I closed my eyes. *Jason was eight minutes late, for God's sake, not eight hours.*

I slipped off my shoes, my feet already aching, quickly slipping them back on again for fear of looking anything but flawlessly seductive. I needed to be ready. I couldn't be seen barefoot wearing an outfit of this magnificence. I have no idea what it is about killer heels that make sexy underwear so bloody irresistible to men. Maybe it completes the illusion of apparent perfection?

I stared out of the window for longer than I probably should have, unaware for a moment that I was accidentally providing a complete, unfiltered, uncensored view of myself to the entire street. *Amsterdam, here I come.* I retreated swiftly behind the safety of curtains that Sylvester enjoyed climbing, too stressed to laugh at my momentary madness, but shocked to notice the curtains needed updating to something with fewer claw marks and holes in them. Bloody cat.

My feet were already beginning to burn in the six-inch patent leather stilettos I only ever kept for special occasions. In truth, they usually sat in a box at the back of my wardrobe, a previous impromptu purchase. Until this very evening, they did, in fact, still have tags on the bottom. They must be at least ten years old. Never worn outside, to be honest. I could barely stand up in them in the comfort of my flat.

Eventually, the sound of a car outside pulled me from my irrational considerations, back into reality. Jason's car came to a stop, and he climbed out, looking hot, flustered, as if he had raced from work, his urgency to get to me as quickly as possible almost as impressive as mine. I took a breath, holding it for too long, nausea building in my throat. This was it. *My first, fundamentally important, private moment with my newly acquired, slightly incredible, if not unfathomably irresistible, man.*

I straightened, realising I hadn't checked my appearance in the mirror for at least two and a half minutes, wondering if my lipstick and hair had retained perfection. The doorbell rang. Shit. Too late now. *Do I remove my robe now or wait until I open the door?* I didn't wish to provide any unsuspecting neighbour with an accidental eye full. The bell rang again. Shit. Anyone would think I was deliberately keeping him waiting. Playing hard to get. Nope. Not me. Never in a million years could I ever be so casual.

17

I hobbled somewhat less than seductively into the hallway, heart pounding, bra heaving, thong threatening to disembowel me at any moment, feeling rather uncomfortable and almost regretting today's purchase. I was glad Jason couldn't see this moment of displeasure. I placed my hand on the door handle, trembling fingers I could do nothing about, licking lips I hoped hadn't lost their earlier glossy sheen, before opening the door with the most seductive smile I could muster.

'Jesus Christ.' Jason's jaw fell to his chest as he stared at me unapologetically. He traced my face, unable to prevent his eyes from dropping to the cleavage spilling over the top of my robe. I was glad he noticed how carefully I'd applied my make-up, freshly washed hair smoothed and straightened, just for him. I was even more impressed that he hadn't failed to notice my girls. He couldn't take his eyes off them. 'Stacey, you look incredible,' he muttered, chin hanging low, eyes popping from his magnificent head. *We have lift off. Oh, yes!*

'You haven't seen anything yet,' I giggled, untying

my now unwanted robe, allowing it to fall from my shoulders to the floor in what, I hoped, was a flawless motion. I had practised several times in front of the mirror, needing to create the ultimate impact upon his arrival.

'Shit,' he gasped, a bunch of roses in his hands threatening to wither at the sight of my hot throbbing body standing in front of him expectantly. I'm saying hot. I literally was hot. I had decided in a random move to turn on my heating. It was a futile attempt to keep my ageing, rather draughty flat warm. My default outfits consisted of thick woollen socks, jogging bottoms and comfortable oversized jumpers, even in the summer months. The last thing I needed tonight was goosebumps on the overly prepped shaved skin that had taken more than an hour to produce and was now clad in faux leather and itchy lace stockings that threatened to fall to my knees mockingly at any moment. I had been sucking in my stomach for the last hour. I needed to breathe at some point. I certainly did not need to look like an overstuffed, freshly plucked chicken that had just been removed from the fridge.

'Stacey, I don't know what to say,' Jason was still standing, mouth agape as he closed the door behind him. 'I never realised just how fucking gorgeous you are.'

I laughed, knowing, of course, I'd never be like Emma, yet wanting desperately to make an effort all the same. I assumed I could have a tummy tuck and breast implants later on, should I deem such procedures necessary. I was, after all, dating a rich guy now. He could afford to indulge me a little, surely. Maybe that is how Emma stays in such a well-preserved state? For now, however, I needed all the help I could bloody get.

I walked as seductively as I could manage towards my awaiting man, keeping my steps slow so as not to ruin the illusion that heels and I were actually friends. I kissed his mouth hungrily, keen to avoid any acknowledgement by him that I couldn't exactly walk straight, my need to be penetrated as urgent as I needed these shoes anywhere else but on my feet. He returned my eager kiss, his hands searching my body, touching my brand new underwear and things that lay beneath. I shuddered.

'I want you,' I whispered, Jason following me into the flat, allowing unfiltered words to reach his ears, desperate to say things to him I could no longer hold back. He didn't argue. Together we drifted towards my bedroom, the freshly ironed sheets on my bed ready for the wild action I'd anticipated, a gentle scent of lavender and jasmine making me as horny as a rabbit on steroids.

We were kissing each other, desperate for a repeat performance of the previous evening, as we tore at each other's clothing in frantic pursuit of sexual relief. When Jason penetrated me, I felt the entire world fall away, nothing else existing but the two of us. We hadn't even made it to my bed, Jason's urgency too much, my appearance too distracting. To say that I was in ecstasy would have been an understatement. We lay together on my bedroom floor after our act was complete, the two of us naked, hungrily sharing bodily fluids, laughter and urgency in a way I had never before thought possible.

I wanted to do things to him that would make him

groan with pleasure. I wanted him to return the favour, kissing places reserved only for that particular person in life I thought I might never find. Unfortunately, my newly acquired faux underwear didn't stand up to our thrashing; two broken straps later discarded on the floor beside me, ready now for the nearest dustbin, the force of Jason's touch too much, his urgency more inviting to my senses than it had been the night before.

I am no idiot. I know that sex isn't designed to last long. But we seemed to be on an obsessive mission to break all records. It was almost as if we had waited so long to rip each other's clothes off that when we were finally able to do so freely, with no distraction, orgasms came swiftly — for Jason, at least. Once again, we had failed to provide any protection for our lovemaking, our frantic pursuit of each other too inviting. Condoms were something that didn't factor into our urgent misadventures.

We eventually made it onto my bed, my newly acquired underwear in a heap on the floor, entirely forgotten, the stockings I'd bought only a few hours earlier now peppered in rips and ladders that would probably have looked more comfortable on a board game. Yet, I was in Jason's arms, a place I'd dreamt of being for so long, and I was happy. Nothing beyond this moment mattered. For me, nothing else existed.

'So, where does she think you are tonight?' I asked, breathless, content, my own orgasm still waiting to be brought forward, yet thankfully in no hurry, my man's peaceful slumber suspending me in otherwise perfect bliss.

'I told her I had a work thing.' Jason kissed me on the top of the head, making no attempt to move or cover his now flaccid length as he lay naked on my bed in full view of my wandering eyes.

I smiled, kissing his shoulder, then his chest, my insatiable need for sex, something that took us both by surprise. I sat upright, straddling him, grinding my open legs against him until he began to swell again. We had sex again, this time Jason unable to orgasm since he was still recovering from his last one. I enjoyed grinding against him, the springs in my bed groaning as I thrust myself wildly onto his erection without remorse. When I finally orgasmed, I assumed Jason would be pleased, yet he looked at me as if he was merely relieved, exhausted by my lasting performance. I had no idea why it took me so long. Maybe I was overly excited?

'Wow,' he told me as I lay next to him, my moment of intense rampage over. 'You're a complete nymphomaniac.' It wasn't true. I'd only ever slept with four men in my life — five now, officially. It was simply that I couldn't get enough of this new and unique thing that had happened to me. Secretly I had spent the evening visualising my sister's face as I allowed her husband to penetrate me without apology. It was exhilarating. It made me so incredibly turned on. My life was about to change most spectacularly. How was I expected to react?

I giggled, feeling more like a teenager than a twenty-nine-year-old woman. 'What do you think Emma would say if she could see what we've been up to?' I had a cheeky look on my face. I couldn't help it.

Jason pulled away from me then, sitting upright, swinging clammy legs over the side of my bed. 'I don't want to think about her tonight if you don't mind.'

I felt for a moment that I had hurt his feelings, broken this otherwise perfect moment. Shit. I crawled across the bed towards him, wrapping my still trembling arms around his shoulders. I knew he worked out, his muscles firm beneath my touch. He did, in fact, spend most evenings at the gym before heading home to his so-called family. Maybe that was purely to avoid being around my sister. I gulped at the concept of Jason having anyone else in his life apart from me. It was a problem I would need to rectify swiftly.

'I'm sorry,' I whispered, kissing his neck in an attempt to bring his now distracted attention back to me. The last thing I needed was to accidentally bring thoughts of that bitch into my bed. Into our bed. Yuk. The very idea made me nauseous.

Jason reached around and kissed me. It was heartfelt, genuine. I'd never felt so safe and protected in the arms of any man before. Doubting Jason would yet be ready for a fourth session, I stroked his neck, my breasts pressed gently against the back of his arm. I would try to refrain from jumping on him again — for an hour, at least. It felt so incredible, having him see me completely naked like this. I didn't want him to go home. Ever. I thought of the movie, *Misery*, and how that mad woman had brutally broken both of her captive's ankles to keep him secured inside her home. I doubted I could get away with such an inconceivable act. Jason needed his mobility to take me to dinner, to manoeuvre his body flawlessly on top of mine. This was the only thing I had ever wanted. Honestly, I was in heaven.

18

I did not see Jason again for two days. His work apparently required his attention due to a deadline that loomed for some new concept vehicle his company was working on that he probably told me about, but which had escaped my notice because I honestly wasn't listening. The only thing concerning me was that he would be unavailable for our lovemaking to my utmost horror and dismay.

I did not give a shit about deadlines, concept vehicles or urgent employment requirements. How dare Jason's bosses take him away from me when we were barely days into our relationship? However, I most definitely cared about the money he earned, so I guessed I would have to suck it up and shut the hell up. We would need his income more than ever once our baby arrived and Emma was finally out of the picture.

We messaged each other every few hours, the sex talk he provided more than adequate to keep me satisfied during those forty-eight gruelling hours of Jason-free existence. I had never fantasied so much about any man before, my thoughts fixated on what lay inside his trousers, my private parts numb with a need unfulfilled. The one thing that helped me through my trial was the simple fact that, while he neglected me, he also would not have any time for his wife. For that, I was eternally grateful.

By the time Friday afternoon came around, I was desperate for some Jason time, my weekend diary packed full of ideas for what we could do together. It did not enter my mind that he might have made other plans with Emma, Eva, or them both. On the contrary, I was convinced I would become his utmost important priority from now on, and I was determined to make damned sure he had no time for anything else. If I had my way, he would have no energy left inside him to go home and engage in any activity with Emma, sexual or otherwise.

I usually finished work early on Fridays. It was one perk of my job that made an otherwise intolerable forty-hour week bearable; Friday afternoons left free for shopping, personal indulgence and whatever else I might wish to focus my time on. Which, now, it seemed, was Jason. When my doorbell rang, the flat was in complete disarray, my mind elsewhere, Sylvester AWOL. I flinched, unable to consider that Jason had arrived early.

We had arranged, of course, to spend our afternoon together. Emma was luckily distracted by something Eva required, some mother and toddler group I wasn't exactly bothered by and wasn't entirely listening when Jason explained her absence. Jason's work priorities were now becoming an everyday existence for my unsuspectingly stupid sister. Shit. I wasn't even dressed, my freshly showered, make-up-free appearance and damp hair not entirely the look I was going for.

I peered hastily through the peephole in my front door, slightly exasperated to see that it wasn't Jason at all but my bloody, goddamned sister. *What the hell did she want?* I opened the door to the sight of her tear-stained face staring at my freshly flushed version. *Jesus Christ.* Had Jason come clean about the two of us already? I almost smiled yet managed to subdue it swiftly before Emma noticed. It would have been highly inappropriate, judging by the look on her face. My heart skipped a beat, all the same. Is that terrible of me to feel so elated by the idea of my sister's undoing?

'Emma?' I gasped, pretending in my most gentle of sisterly voices that I actually gave a shit. 'What's wrong? Is it Eva? Is she okay?' I knew, of course, that my sister's unexpected visit had nothing to do with my niece – or at least I presumed – but I needed to remain neutral at that moment. What did I care what was wrong with her? I couldn't simply assume that Jason had confessed his undying love for me, no matter how hard I wished for such an exuberant action.

'Can I come in, Sis?' she was sobbing, her tears threatening to drip onto my freshly washed skin as she leaned in for a hug. 'I need someone to talk to.' I stepped back, allowing my sister entry, hoping I'd left nothing on display that might give away my recent and rather rampant affair with her husband, knowing full well this visit did not conform to social etiquette. She would never usually come here uninvited. Heaven forbid she should willingly associate herself with this part of town without just cause — Maple Gardens offering so much more in the way of affluent circles than my back street location ever would. *How dare she act such a snob?*

'You okay?' I asked again, still unsure why she was here and not entirely wanting the answer. I was desperate to know that Jason had come clean, and that finally I could tell her the truth about the two of us. My dislike for keeping secrets didn't fare well with my brain at all. However, she would have probably scratched my face to pieces by now if she actually knew the truth. Emma stepped into my flat, make-up running, her usual perfectly kept hair now an untidy collection of strands, not unlike a disused birds' nest. It wasn't like my sister to present anything but perfection to anyone, especially me. I almost held my breath with expectation.

'I didn't know where else to go,' she whispered, wiping a make-up-streaked tear across the back of her hand, taking some foundation with it and not appearing to care. 'Mum has taken Eva to the zoo for the day, and I just needed someone to talk to.'

'Emma, what's happened?' My heart was in my mouth now. A terrifying idea jumped into my thoughts that something might have happened to my beloved Jason: nothing else made sense and a sudden urge to scream made its way into my mouth.

My sister stumbled into my messy kitchen and lowered herself at my somewhat untidy kitchen table, not even bothering to remove a pile of fur-covered cat blankets that she sat on without concern. This place most certainly did not resemble the image of perfection I had painstakingly created for our previous evening meal, that's for sure. But, of course, I had wanted to make a good impression then. For Jason.

Now, my previously perfectly-laid table was covered in laundry I had forgotten to place inside the washing machine, this morning's breakfast dishes I had been just about to clear away, and several pregnancy and wedding magazines that I promptly sat on, leaning into Emma as if she was the most crucial person in the world right then.

'I think Jason is having an affair,' Emma blurted out, still sobbing, allowing pained words to escape her mouth as if they might actually burn her.

I gasped in horror, a moment of unrehearsed pretence that I was shocked to hear such a distasteful possibility. How could she believe that her loving husband was even capable of such a travesty?

'Really?' I asked, unsure if I sounded either concerned or convincing in my response. With a sudden rush of anger and rather unimpressively resisting an impulsive urge to swear, I realised Jason hadn't told her yet about us. *What the hell was he waiting for?* Surely he was as keen to leave that toxic relationship as I was to get Emma out of our lives? I considered telling my sister now and saving him the trouble entirely. After all, we were already on the subject of infidelity, and she was already upset. I couldn't possibly make it worse. Could I? What did I have to lose? 'What gives you the idea he's having an affair?' Yes, Stacey, for the moment, remain neutral. And calm. *For Christ's sake, stay calm.*

Emma scoffed then as if my question was ridiculous.

'I know the signs, Stace,' she breathed, shaking her head as if she couldn't believe I didn't know any better, more tears falling, her hair needing a brush that I oddly wanted to provide her.

You know the signs? Bloody hell Emma, anyone would think he'd done this before. 'What do you mean, sweetheart?' Shit, I was laying it on a bit thick. *Sweetheart? Seriously?* When did I ever use that term to describe my sister? Take a breath and slow down, Stacey. *Please.* I sucked in a mouthful of air.

'He's been distant ever since the night of my book celebration dinner. Which, by the way, is going well.' Jesus Christ, did she seriously have to take this moment to talk about herself? Yes. This was Emma. Of course, she did. No wonder Jason wanted out.

'He did mention something about being manic with work. Maybe he's just tired. He works so hard, you know, Em. You should be proud of him.' *Stacey, seriously. Stop trying to get your sister to fall in love with her own husband all over again. Everyone knows he's amazing. You DO NOT have to rub it in her face.*

Emma shook her head, unaware of my duplicitous thinking. 'He's been cagey, acting weird. It seemed to worsen after we came round to yours for our meal.' I swallowed, knowing the reason why. 'You didn't notice anything unusual that night, did you?'

I did, if you must know. I noticed him on top of me, underpants around his ankles, ripping off my knickers in a blind fury while you were out cold in my front room — our first, incredible night together, in fact. Of course he's acting weird. He can't wait to fuck my brains out most days now, and the feeling is entirely mutual. *He knows what I can offer him and what you can't.* I took an ill-timed breath, my inner musing something my sister did not need to speculate over, for now at least.

'Cagey?' I was trying to keep my words soft, sympathetic. I sounded pathetic. Fake.

'Every time his phone goes off, he disappears into another room. I swear I heard him giggling the other night, Stacey. Jason? *Giggling?*' She muttered the words as if the very concept of her husband actually being happy and able to laugh was ridiculous. Of course he was giggling. He was sexting me. Giggling had become our thing.

'Have you asked him about it?' I was now curious about what Jason had actually divulged and why I had become this considerable secret he didn't feel capable of sharing.

'Of course I did. He told me it was work stuff. But how can it be his work? Who from his workplace would be texting him at eleven o'clock at night unless he's sleeping with one of his colleagues?' She shook her head. 'That bloody new girl Jenny has been sniffing around him.'

'Maybe it's his boss?' I offered. 'I know he had some important concept meeting thing this week.' The idea of Jason sleeping with any of his work colleagues gave me a shudder, especially that tiny young thing I'd already met and who could barely carry a tea tray. Jason wouldn't go near someone like that. I was actually impressed that I'd listened long enough to recall him mentioning such a meeting. It gave my words a sprinkling of credibility, at the very least.

Emma shook her head. 'I know Jason's boss, Stacey. *He's* five feet tall with a balding head and a huge complex about it. So unless Jason has suddenly turned gay in some unexpected turn of events, I very much doubt it would have been him making him giggle in secret at such a late hour.'

'But an affair?' I piped up. *Why the hell was I trying to convince my sister she had it all wrong?* I should have been shouting from the rooftop, screaming aloud at the top of my lungs that yes, actually, Jason *is* having an affair. He is, in fact, fucking me. We love each other. *Get over yourself, and get the hell out of my flat, bitch.* But, of course, I did not lower myself to such an unexpected and loathsome announcement, no matter how much I wanted to. The only thing confirmed today was that we urgently needed to sit Emma down and explain what was happening. She deserved that much, at least. My nerves couldn't take many more of these surreptitious lies.

'He's been acting sneaky, Stace. I don't like it. I don't like it one bit.'

For the first time since Jason and I had got together, I considered what Emma would actually do when she eventually found out about us. It shocked me. I hadn't thought much about my sister's feelings until now, because as far as I was concerned, it genuinely didn't matter. She would, of course, find out soon enough, and I had visualised the removal of her from my life for so long, I enjoyed the idea immensely. It had kept me going during those long nights alone. But, judging by the look on her face now, the truth was going to break her heart.

19

Was I so callous that I didn't care about my sister's feelings? If I was honest with myself, probably, yes. Emma was a horrible person. She thought only of herself, of her own needs, no one else factoring in her life at all. She deserved what was coming to her; whereas my thoughts were always for the wellbeing and happiness of her husband. *My* husband one day, I assumed with a smile I tried and failed to suppress.

'What now?' she asked, rising to her feet at my sudden smirk, quite ready for me to divulge information she had not yet uncovered.

I had to think fast. 'Emma, you're overthinking it. Jason would never cheat on you.' What was I even saying? 'He adores you,' I added. *Again, Stacey, stop with the random declarations.* Jason did not love Emma. Jason was in love with me. There was literally nothing more to say about that.

'You think?' she was sobbing again now. Do I comfort her? Pat her on the back or something?

'Of course, I do.' I reached out and placed a fakely

sympathetic hand on my sister's bony shoulder. *God, when had she lost so much weight?* 'If Jason says he's been distracted with work, then that must be the truth. When was the last time you guys were intimate?' *Jesus Christ, Stacey, what the hell did you have to say that for?* Did I care? Yes, actually, I bloody well did. I did not want Jason anywhere near my sister's private parts with the same tool he used to poke me with; so suddenly, yes, I cared a lot.

Emma looked puzzled, probably wondering why I'd asked such a random question. She shook her head. 'I don't know. A couple of nights ago, I guess.' It was a throwaway comment, a response she probably didn't consider any of my business.

I shook my head, unable to prevent the bile that was rising in my throat. *What the hell did she mean? A couple of nights ago?* What in God's name was he doing still putting his cock into this bony bitch? I had spent this entire week thinking of nothing but him, and he was still going home to his wife to... I took a breath, unable for a moment to stabilise my thinking.

'Actual sex?' I questioned, the words leaving my mouth as if they had caught between my teeth. Shit, I sounded like the girlfriend scorned. It felt as if he was cheating on me, not his actual wife.

'Stacey, what does that matter? I'm telling you my husband is seeing another woman, and you're only interested in what he does with me?' I could see she wasn't yet able to add up the numbers to the calculation that would answer all the questions racing around her head. *Two plus two, sister dearest. I was not able to hide my emotions. She knew that. Surely she could see what was happening here?*

'All I meant was that if he wasn't interested in you anymore, he wouldn't have –' I had to stop, unable to bring myself to say the words. 'You know,' I added.

'I appreciate that you only want to help, Sis.' She offered a smile that made her look washed out, exhausted. I wished she would keep her acts of apparent kindness to herself. I didn't need her emotions or her sentiments. It was cringeworthy, and I wasn't used to it. 'But I think I know my own husband,' she added with a sigh.

You don't know him that well, or he wouldn't have come to me for the affection you obviously can't give him. 'Sis, please. Try and keep calm.' I needed her to keep calm before I blurted out the entire affair and probably made things worse for everyone. I made us a pot of tea. I should have been awarded an Oscar for my performance in comforting my sister. I was quite proud of myself, in fact, for my debut performance as a caring sister. 'I'm sure there will be a rational explanation.' There was indeed. He was sleeping with me. Job done. What more needed to be said about that?

***

By the time Emma had left my flat, my nerves were in shreds. Even as she descended the stairwell with my eyes pressed firmly into her back, the first thing I did was give Jason a call. I cared nothing that he was at work or might be in a bloody meeting, unavailable to experience the rant I was about to launch. He needed to know what his wife had done and what she had told me only moments earlier. How *dare* he have sex with me, then go home to her and repeat such a lustful performance.

'Where are you?' I spat into my mobile as I watched Emma's fragile limbs climb into her car outside. Her mug wasn't even cold. Lipstick still wet around the rim.

'Why? What's happened?' Jason sounded genuinely concerned.

'Emma has just been round to my flat, in tears,' I scoffed. 'Bloody woman thinks you're having an affair.' It was ironic, the way I almost convinced myself of the absurdity. It genuinely felt as if she had told me that I'd been the woman scorned, not the other way around.

'What? What the hell is she burdening you with our personal life for?' he sounded almost as irritated as I was.

'Indeed. Why would she need to burden me, Jason? Why haven't you told her the truth about us yet?' I didn't think I could cope with much more sneaking around. My request wasn't negotiable. The last thing I needed was random visits from Emma whenever she felt the urge to unload onto someone. I could barely stand her company when she was in a *good* mood.

'I will. It's just with Emma, things aren't that easy.'

What the hell was he saying? 'Why? It's simple. Like ripping off a plaster. Fast. The pain only lasts a second, and then it's done. Easy.' Jason laughed then as if my words had amused him. 'Funny, am I?' I scolded into the phone, in no mood for games.

'No, you just sound so cute when you're mad.' His sultry tone created a wobble in my pants I wasn't expecting. He had a knack of doing that to me.

'Stop it, Jason, this is serious.'

'I'm not doing anything.' As angry as I was with him, I couldn't help but laugh at his cheekiness. I wondered if this was what had drawn Emma to him initially, too. I visualised his facial expressions. That cute, lopsided smile. The way he held himself, proud but not cocky. Not arrogant. Not like other men I'd dated.

'She has to be told.' I had nothing else to say on the matter.

'I know.' I wished I could see his face. Read what was going through his mind. He had been with my sister for almost a decade. I expected he would be as desperate to get away from her as I was to get her away from him, my prompt timing meaning we would be free soon enough. Free to be together. Free. The very word gave me shudders. How incredible would it be to no longer feel held back by lies that had caged my emotions for so long? It was simply the way of things, the way it was always meant to be.

'She has this book thing coming up next week. She'll be away from Monday to Wednesday.' Jason said. 'Some signing event that Lloyd wants her to attend. A marketing thing.' I wondered for a moment about Eva and how my sister seemed to think nothing about dumping her only child onto our mum and dad whenever she felt like it. I know they loved having their granddaughter stay with them, but my sister should seriously take more responsibility for her child. *Bitch.*

153

'So you'll tell her when, exactly?' I knew Jason was due to come to mine within the next hour. Our afternoon would be engaged in the most disgusting sex, watching corny movies while stuffing our faces with pizza and chocolate. Lots of chocolate. I'd planned the entire weekend. Tomorrow we would lie in bed until around lunchtime, feed Sylvester at some point when his whining became too much, have yet more hot passionate sex, eat takeaway food until we were sick. Jason would have already told Emma he was away with work until Sunday morning at the very earliest. At least next week would be easier. I could spend a couple of nights at his house for a change. I smiled, allowing the thought of rolling around in my sister's bed to swim freely in my mind. I would change the sheets first, though, obviously.

'I will tell her when she gets back on Wednesday. Promise.'

I fell silent for a moment. 'I can live with that, I guess.' It was a lie, of course. I hated sneaking around. I wanted to shout it from my flat window right then that Jason was my man, that he absolutely loved me. I hoped Emma would hear my screams as she drove away. I wanted to shout it directly into her face. 'So, when are you coming round?' My excitement was growing again.

It was Jason's turn to fall silent now. 'Actually, honey, I'm going to have to take a rain check on our weekend, unfortunately,' he sighed.

What? 'Why?' I wanted to cry. Seriously. I'd never felt so let down.

'If she came round to talk to you about it, then she's already suspicious. If I disappear again, we'll end up having a huge row,' he said, utterly oblivious to my feelings. *Good.* I wanted them to have a gigantic argument — an argument to end all arguments. I wanted them to split up this very day so that we could get on with our lives in peace. Just the two of us. Oh, and Sylvester and Eva, obviously. 'Stacey?'

'I was looking forward to seeing you,' I paused. *Fucking you,* were the words I wanted to say. But *seeing you* was what I managed to mutter, under my breath, sounding more nine than twenty-nine. I held back a tear.

'Missing me already?' Jason's cheeky tone had returned.

'Can't we just have tonight together? Even if you pretend to work late and go home after midnight.' I knew damned well that I wouldn't allow him to leave if I actually got him here. Not tonight. I'd chain him to my bed if I had to. I kept that to myself, of course.

'I can't, honey. Eva is going to be staying with your mum and dad until Thursday next week, and I've got to drop her off tomorrow morning.'

I thought about the last time Emma and Jason had slept together, seriously wanting to confront Jason about it. But I bit my lip, a jealous rage steadily building in my gut. I wanted to see his face when I asked him about it. 'Can't *Emma bloody Problema* drop her off?' I didn't mean for that to sound so pointed, bitchy.

'She'll be with Lloyd tomorrow for a meeting, then with me until Monday because we won't see each other for a few days. I have to make an effort. Keep up appearances.' I wanted to smack Jason in the face for daring to say such things. Why did he need to make any effort with Emma while seemingly unable to spend one single bloody hour with me? We wouldn't be seeing each other at all now for a few more days. *Who the hell is your priority here, Jason?* 'Stacey, you keep going quiet on me.' He sounded slightly nervous, spooked by my untimely pauses.

'We need to talk. About quite a lot of important things that I don't want to say over the phone.' *Such as the fact that you should no longer be sleeping with my goddamned sister.* My tone had darkened. I couldn't hold this in much longer. Emma needed to know the truth, and I needed to understand why my boyfriend was more interested in spending time with his wife than with me. Even as I thought the words, the irony wasn't lost on me. He wasn't mine. Not really. He still belonged to her. Still wore her bloody wedding ring. Still slept in her *fucking* bed.

'We can talk, I promise. Give me this weekend to sort everything out, and I'll pick you up on Monday. You can stay here with me. I'll cook us something amazing. I'll look after you.' Jason sounded sincere, something in his tone that made me want him all the more. It made a lump form in my throat and a damp patch form in my pants. What the hell was I going to do for an entire weekend without him? I doubted Sylvester would be good company. I closed my eyes, dreaming of his body against mine.

'But I haven't seen you since Wednesday,' I wasn't even aware I was sulking. Had it been that long? Why did I sound like a child?

Jason laughed softly. 'Then it will be all the more

incredible when we see each other on Monday.'

'Okay,' I whispered as a tear fell to my cheek. I could wish. *Bollocks*.

20

I have no idea how I made it through that weekend with my senses intact. I'd gone from deluded elation to terrified silence, unable to dare look at the clock, thoughts of my evanescent lover in bed with that woman overpowering my seemingly inadequate brain capacity. It was crazy, irrational. Yet, the more I thought of him lying naked with that skinny cow, the more I hated my sister beyond rational thinking. I couldn't eat. I couldn't think. Even when my mum called, requesting I join them for Sunday lunch, my mind swam with visions of Jason pumping wildly into my sister's bony backside, unconcerned by my isolated presence, alone, unwanted, unsatisfied.

I didn't want to, but I endured the company of my parents that Sunday afternoon for as long as I was physically able, listening with diffused aggravation to *Humpty Dumpty* on repeat, as Eva bounced happily on my dad's proud knee, her unfiltered and somewhat infectious laugh filling the room, nausea filling my belly, irritation growing with every glance I afforded her. It wasn't Eva's fault, of course. She was merely a child, and I honestly loved my niece. But she was Emma and Jason's child. It was a concept that had hardly bothered me until now. Now I wished with everything I had inside that I were already pregnant. I wanted my parents to swoon over my child in that way; their attention focused on me and my unappreciated needs for a change. Oh, how I longed for that day.

I had secretly hoped that Jason might come round to check that his daughter was okay, my invitation acceptance partly in anticipation of seeing his smiling face, the wink I knew he would offer when no one was looking, his smile, unfiltered, thoughts that nobody knew about, hiding behind greedy, eager eyes. But he didn't, and I was momentarily glad that I didn't have to cook for myself today, the entire meal potentially ending up against my kitchen wall. I'd already endured an isolated weekend, hiding beneath my duvet pretending sleep was something I craved, and unashamedly masturbating from time to time when thoughts of Jason became too much for my senses. My belly occasionally growled from a hunger I could barely bring myself to gratify, so I was grateful for my mum's liberating invitation today.

A couple of girls from work had called to ask if I wanted to join them for a drink. I declined. It was unlike me, they said. But their carefully planned evening of abandoned indiscretion oddly did not interest me at all. I did not wish to indulge in male attention that did not answer to the name of Jason Cole. My usual grandiose need to be admired and adored by otherwise complete strangers who, for a few hours, I could pretend saw only me in the world, now made my stomach churn. It was as if I had become a different person. Overnight, Jason's uncontrolled penis had created a monster I had no idea how to sedate. It was unhealthy, they told me, to stay indoors, alone, pining over some man who obviously had better things to do. *How dare they assume to know my emotions? How dare they presume to know Jason?*

When my mum asked if I was okay, noticing perhaps a despondent look behind silent eyes, it all became too much. I left the house practically in tears, my poor mum wondering what the hell was wrong. I hated lying to her. She was usually the one person I could turn to when I needed support, and I desperately wanted to share my new relationship with her now. But how could I? How could I tell her that Jason and I were together before he'd grown a set of balls and told my sister the plan? Our plan.

***

I practically sprinted along the street away from my parents' house, its proximity to mine luckily within walking distance. My lack of a car was something my dad often commented on, yet it had hardly bothered me until now. Tears threatened to spill with a pain I hadn't expected to experience. My mum's thoughtful words had been too much. My friend's berating tone had been too intense. Jason and I were in the throes of first passion. Our desire for each other unrestrained, no boundaries to hold us back, no fear, no regret for what our touch had created. *So what the hell was wrong with me?* A week ago, I would have given anything to be with Jason. I hardly classified myself as a jealous or obsessive person, the crazy sentiments swimming through my cluttered mind now feeling alien, disjointed.

I made my way across town to my sister's house, needing to get this thing out of me and in the open, once and for all, freeing my mind from the discomposure that had engulfed my recent turbulent emotions. Who knew being in love could create such a chaotic rebound and induce the power to turn otherwise sane, rational thoughts into demonic obstructions? I couldn't allow any further deception to lie unaddressed between us. Emma needed to know the truth before I was carted away in a strait jacket, my brain imploding with thoughts I had no place for. I needed to be with Jason. It was as simple as that. I knew that once I saw my lover's face, everything would be alright. I would calm down a little, relax, unwind the tightly coiled spring that had become my brain. He knew how to make me feel good. I needed that right now. Anything else was simply not an option.

I reached my sister's house looking and feeling slightly more dishevelled than I had intended. It had started to rain, and my hair was now a dampened mess along with my mood that had darkened considerably since I'd last had the pleasure of my beloved's company. I knew he was missing me because I had texted him several times in quick succession and he had replied each time within a few minutes, unable, I assumed, to go long without imagining the sound of my voice.

He wouldn't mind my sudden intrusion now. We

needed to do this thing together. It was for the best. Emma's house was set within a modern, new-build estate of six large properties. Neighbouring homes possessed flashy cars that looked equally expensive on driveways sweeping around front doors hiding riches I could only dream of experiencing. I needed to remain calm, the idea that I could one day live here was one I did not wish to dislodge. I certainly could not afford to create a wrong impression, disturb my potential new neighbours with my untidy and unapologetic appearance now.

I hesitated when I arrived outside my sister's front door, unsure if my carefully considered actions were so well planned after all. I visualised her inside right then, snuggled into her husband's chest on their overstuffed sofa, eating bloody avocado, poached quinoa, and God knows what else she deemed healthy enough for permitted consumption. Why she had become so obsessed with healthy eating lately, I had no idea. What was wrong with good old-fashioned pizza? She had no problems putting away the entire bottle of wine I gave her a few nights ago. I afforded a glance at my less than athletic stomach muscles, hidden beneath several layers of clothing, unable to concern myself with excuses for not eating healthily at this precise moment in time.

I hovered a trembling index finger against the doorbell, wondering, if I were to sneak around the side of the house and take a look through the window, would my unwanted suspicions be confirmed? I took a breath and shook my head. It didn't matter what they were doing in there. It wouldn't change my opinion as to the importance of this event. This thing needed dealing with. But I was kidding no one. If they were having sex in there right now, I might not be able to prevent myself from committing murder with no remorse or concern for my actions whatsoever.

I rang the bell and stood, strands of hair slowly gluing themselves to my now soaked scalp, face contorted, thoughts racing. I have no idea how long it took for the door to open, but when Jason appeared in front of me, his face looked as if he had been caught stealing chocolate bars from the fridge, melted confectionery still on his lips.

'What the hell are you doing here?' he snapped, pulling me to one side and closing the door behind him. Why did he need to sound so agitated with me? Was he not pleased to see me?

'I came to see you.' I strained my neck to see over his shoulder towards the slightly ajar front door. 'What are you doing in there?' *What business was it of mine?*

'Nothing. Jesus, Stacey, I told you I'd pick you up on Monday.'

'But I needed to see you now.' I was actually quite desperate. It was pathetic. Jason was standing barefoot in front of me, wearing little more than jogging bottoms and t-shirt, looking casual and relaxed. I, on the other hand, stood in front of him soaked to the skin, dressed in clothing that had seen much better days, ill-applied make-up mixing with tears I'd been unable to prevent, appearing wholly deranged and damaged.

163

21

Jason placed warm hands over my frozen shoulders and looked into my eyes. 'Have you been crying?'

'No,' I answered too quickly, forgetting the blotchy red tinge my eyes had probably developed on my self-absorbed, self-defeating journey here. I was hovering by his front door. It now seemed entirely stupid.

'Talk to me. What's happened, honey? Are you alright?' Jason's tone was calm. Soothing. *God, how I needed him right then.* I leaned in for a kiss. Just one. That's all I wanted. 'Stacey, not here,' Jason glanced around as if, at any moment, a neighbour might see. Or Emma. *God forbid Emma should witness our unbridled passion.*

'What's wrong with you? No one's looking,' I chided, feeling suddenly sneaky, sexy, standing soaked to my underwear in the cool rain, damp in places Jason would have loved to explore. 'Come on, just a quickie, right here,' I was giggling then, looking and sounding as if I'd had far too much to drink. I hadn't touched a drop. I was completely sober. It was not a pleasant realisation.

'Stacey, stop it,' Jason was peeling me off his skin as if I was a leech that needed dealing with before it sucked dry the very blood that was keeping him alive.

'Jason? Who's at the door, babe?' Emma's annoyingly whiny voice filtered from the hallway behind us then, bringing me swiftly out of my horny deliberations. *Damn it.* I dropped my arms to my side as Jason turned to face the half-closed door. Why the hell was she still calling him babe? Surely, by now, she would be packing a suitcase?

'No one, Em. Just a salesperson,' he lied. *Why the hell was he lying to her?* My mood darkened further, this moment threatening to become far more than a confession, a declaration of love.

'May I come in?' I asked, suddenly needing to speed this thing up a bit, trying to force my way past Jason in an unplanned futile attempt to confront my sister with facts we both knew he was in no mood to disclose.

'No way. Not in this mood, you're not,' he replied. 'Stacey, I told you that I would tell her in my own time.' He was deadly serious. I could see it in his eyes, feel it in the way he held my upper arms within his now unkind grip.

I shrugged. 'Let's tell her now and get it over and done with. We can then enjoy the rest of the weekend together. No. Actually, the rest of our lives.' I laughed then, too loudly, bringing Jason close to me and forcing him to plant a kiss on my lips in an attempt to shut me up. He placed his tongue inside my mouth, searching, probing. It had the desired effect. I was putty in his hands. I'd have done anything for him at that moment —

anything he desired.

'Jason, are you coming back in? Your dinner is getting cold.' I baulked at the idea of my sister gleefully cooking her husband a meal when I had been forced to endure overcooked vegetables and tinned steak pie, cooked by a mum I loved yet who wasn't exactly the person I wanted to be with at that moment. *Fitting.* I suppressed an urge to shut Emma up, once and for all, to march inside the house and slam her face straight into the nearest wall. The mere sound of her voice was becoming too much for my brain to contend with.

'Yeah, just coming, honey,' Jason called out to the space between our unfettered passion and his wife, a woman who knew nothing of our relationship or events unfolding on the doorstep behind her. *Honey?* What the hell was he doing calling her honey? I glared at him. 'What's wrong now?' he asked, unaware of the pain he had just callously inflicted on me. He may as well have punched me in the gut.

I shook my head, unable to hide my despondency. 'It doesn't matter,' But it did. It mattered more than I could have expressed. I felt as if I was about to vomit all over him, words unsaid festering inside my rancid mind.

'Let me take you home,' Jason offered, the sight of me standing in the rain, body trembling, lip quivering, obviously too much for him.

'And what about bitch face?' I couldn't help my spiteful words. I hated her. I wanted to kill the bitch. To watch as the life drained from her body forever.

Jason brushed my cheek with his fingertips, causing an automatic throbbing sensation in my underwear.

166

Shit. *How did he have such power over me?* He turned to face the front door for a moment, unaware of the darkness growing in my thoughts. 'Em, I'm popping into the garage for a second.' Jesus, Jason was as good a liar as I was. He didn't stop to listen to any response his wife might have offered. She was no doubt wondering what the hell her husband was up to, leaving his lovingly prepared meal untouched. He ushered me out of the dry porch into the rain, unconcerned by his bare feet, shuffling me unceremoniously around the side of the driveway to the garage where he knew we would be out of view, out of earshot.. He was quite forceful. I liked it.

'What are you doing, Stacey?' It was a simple question, yet one that sounded irritated, annoyed.

'I'm sorry,' I breathed, allowing a moment of reflection. I wasn't sorry at all. 'I was missing you.' That part was true. 'And I just – '

'Just what?' Why did he have to sound so furious with me?

'I just wanted things out in the open. You don't know what all this secrecy is doing to me,' I pouted, hoping my feminine and weakened appearance might make him want me all the more.

He sighed then, noticing the pleading look in my eyes. 'I know, my darling.' He stroked my wet hair, wiping a rogue raindrop from my forehead. 'It's killing me, too.' I believed him. I believed everything he told me. 'I only agreed to spend this weekend with Emma because she has it in her head that I am having an affair, and I need things to remain neutral for the next couple of days while we sort things out.' I smiled then, licking my lips at the thought of Jason's infidelity. Yes, indeed, an affair was true. *With me.*

I leaned towards him, wrapping my soaked arms around his warm body. We kissed, our hidden position keeping us from prying eyes, away from neighbours and Emma alike. Jason held me close, his breath warm against my cooling skin, oddly astonishing to my senses. God, how I wished he would shove me against the side of his car right now and have me. He cupped my face in his hands.

'I'll drive you home. Then I'll pick you up after work tomorrow, and I'll cook that meal I promised you.' He kissed my nose with a smile. 'Okay?'

I nodded, feeling I would do anything if Jason beckoned. He disappeared into the house, returning moments later, a car key in hand, with boots untied, and a jacket which he handed to me. He genuinely knew how to take care of me. I did not care at that moment if he had not yet told Emma about us. I cared even less about his excuses for leaving the house in such a hurry, his dinner left to go cold. The fact that I had him all to myself for a few moments was all I needed. Yet, we were silent as he drove me home, my actions today ensuring I felt as stupid as I looked.

'Are you still fucking her?' I had no idea why I'd asked the question so abruptly. Was it any of my business? She was his wife. Was he not entitled to act accordingly? I bit my bottom lip hard, knowing I did not have the right to ask such a question, yet not wishing to contemplate such vile actions. He was mine now. In my mind, my question was entirely valid.

'What?' Jason had pulled up outside my flat. I could see Sylvester swirling around the front door as if his life depended on it, scratching at a closed door, unaware that no one was inside to realise his needs, desperate for attention. I knew exactly how he felt.

'I said, are you fucking her?' I repeated my question, firmer, louder, turning to look at the man I'd fallen completely and utterly in love with, terrified of the answer I knew was coming.

'No.' I didn't believe him. He sounded cagey, as if he had been placed on the spot too quickly.

'She says you fucked her.' *Why couldn't I stop saying fuck?*

'When?'

'Friday. When she was sobbing at my kitchen table at the thought of her husband's pathetic cheating ways.' Anyone would think I was the one being cheated on. It certainly felt as if I was. As if I was the woman scorned.

Jason fell silent, obviously trying to recall such a disgusting act. 'She's my *wife*, Stacey. I think it might look odd if I didn't.'

Wow. I could not believe what I was hearing. 'But you're with *me* now,' I said, fresh tears welling, unable to hide my shock and sudden upset. 'Why would you want to be anywhere near her?' It was a fair assumption. Why, indeed, would he ever need my sister again, now that he had me?

'I don't want her,' he answered too fast, almost making me assume he was playing me for the fool I was beginning to feel. He sighed, turning off the car engine and positioning himself to face me. 'I want *you*.'

'Prove it.'

'How?'

'Fuck me and tell me you love me.' *Wow. Shit, I'd accidentally bought the L word into the equation.*

'I'm not doing this now, Stacey.'

'Fuck me, or I'll make a phone call to Emma after you leave so that when you arrive home, she will know everything.' I left out the love part this time. I hoped I hadn't overstepped the mark. Love was a big thing — a thing we hadn't yet discussed. I was oblivious to the fact that I was coming across as slightly psychotic.

'Why are you being like this?' He looked hurt. I wanted to believe that I had no idea why I was acting like such a hideous cow right then, but if I was sincere, I knew exactly why my mood had taken such a turn: I was falling in love with the man. His apparent inability to tell his wife that he was leaving her was something I couldn't fathom. Was this what real love felt like? Pure, unadulterated jealous envy that bombarded me from nowhere? It was a sickening emotion that I had never felt before.

'I'm not being like anything,' I whispered, unable to stop the tears that fell freely, consolidating my blotchy appearance: red nose, bloated eye sockets, snot everywhere.

Jason leaned over the central console, pulling my head towards him with one hand, cupping my chin with the other. 'Tomorrow night, you're not going to know what's hit you, Stacey Adams. Do you understand my meaning?' I couldn't help adoring the cheeky look in his eyes.

I giggled, pressing my lips together in eager anticipation, my wayward thinking already diffusing beneath the promise of his touch. 'Promise?'

'Promise,' he kissed me then, gentle, tender. It was all I'd ever wanted. To feel this way, forever, with Jason. Just the two of us. He'd enchanted me for years, and my need now for us to be together was so strong, it was becoming all-consuming. 'We can talk properly tomorrow. I'll pick you up after work. Now go, and bloody get dry before you end up with hypothermia. Or worse.' I shivered, feeling the cold of the rain for the first time, the potency of his words having the desired effect.

'Okay,' I whispered as I climbed out of his car. 'I love you,' I called into the late afternoon air. But he had already started the engine and was driving away. I had no idea if he heard me at all.

22

Luckily for me, the following day came swiftly after fielding calls and messages from my mum.

'I'm worried about you.'

'I'm fine, Mum.'

'You didn't look fine yesterday.'

'Really. You don't need to worry about me.'

'I'll always worry about you, Stacey. I'm your mum.'

Although I was trying hard to listen to my mum's concerned words and to assure her that my oddly timed outburst wasn't as important now as I'd made it appear during that moment, the only thing I could think about was my impending time with Jason and the next two blissful days that we would be together. I even considered crying off work, my thinly spread position at the temping agency of no consequence to me now — my boss's voice a mere moaning sound I was forced to endure from time to time.

We could spend those days and evenings together, the debaucherous weekend I'd planned merely postponed until today. I didn't want Emma to come home. Ever. I wanted her to get into her car and disappear. By the time Jason's car pulled up outside my place of work, I'd several times reapplied lipstick I now worried made me look clownish, cheap.

'There she is,' Jason's soft voice filtered through his open car window as I ran around the side and jumped into the passenger seat. I leaned in and kissed him forcefully on the lips, ensuring two of my co-workers noticed, not at all concerned that I had transferred lipstick to Jason's face. We could look like clowns together. 'Steady on, girl,' he laughed as we pulled out of the car park. 'What's the urgency?'

He had no idea how much I wanted him. 'I'll let you know when we get back to yours,' I breathed, acting and feeling intoxicated, yet having touched no alcohol for days. Jason laughed, and took me the short drive across town to his place. Without Emma there, I could pretend that their house was mine, that I was Jason's, and Jason's alone. Bliss.

***

I stepped through my sister's front door to the sight of a large bouquet of flowers sitting on the dresser in the hallway. For a moment, I felt sick. When had he begun buying Emma flowers? Was that even a thing? Jason hurried through the door ahead of me, stopping me in my tracks, his obvious anxiety something I couldn't ignore.

'Close your eyes,' he said, apparently dizzy with an excitement that made my tummy churn and my throat

173

tighten. I did as I was instructed. His hands were warm as they slipped around my waist, guiding me forward. 'And keep them closed.'

'Jason, what are you doing?' I asked, not entirely sure what was happening or convinced I liked it. When he released me, I heard a scuffle — the sound of tissue paper, a distinct rustle of plastic wrapping.

'Hang on.' More rustling. 'Okay, open your eyes,' he said. I opened my eyes to the sight of Jason's grinning features, the bouquet I'd only seconds earlier wanted to shred to pieces, held in his outstretched arms. I gasped.

'For me?' I couldn't believe it. No one had bought me flowers before. Not ever.

'You are the best thing that has happened to me in a very long time,' he whispered, handing the bouquet to me, leaning in for a kiss. 'I might even go as far as to say that you have actually saved my life, Stacey Adams.'

I knew it. I knew he hadn't been happy with Emma for quite a while. And now I knew it was because he had probably secretly been in love with me for a considerable amount of time. I knew I hadn't imagined the entire concept. I held the flowers in my hands, a mixture of red roses and other species I couldn't name, complimenting the arrangement beautifully. A heady variety of red, pink, tiny white buds and soft greenery that made me want to cry with joy. They were simply heavenly.

The first thing I wanted to do was post a picture of them on every social media account I had, boasting about my newly acquired *in a relationship* status, but knew that would be a terrible idea seeing as Emma regularly commented on my posts. It would have been funny, though: my sister's enthusiasm for the flowers she couldn't have known in a million years were actually from her husband. I wondered if she would even recognise her own hallway in the background, practically laughing at her.

Jason pulled me to him, my beautiful flowers threatening to disintegrate beneath the weight of our passionate embrace. 'I was so upset to see you in such a state yesterday. I never want to see tears in your eyes again.' His words were music to my ears. We kissed, pulling at each other's clothing as our passions once again ignited. The flowers dropped to the floor as we lunged at each other, hands reaching out, clothes tearing, the sound of laughter and snapping of flower stems creating a heady mix of desire and gratitude neither of us could escape.

When we were spent, our exhausted semi-naked bodies lying across a flattened pathway of devoured flower heads and what would have once been a neatly tied bow, we lay together giggling, the aroma of my sister's recently treated hallway floor doing nothing to hide the heavy flavour of body fluids as our anatomies connected, our frantic lovemaking complete — Emma's clock ticking behind us as if time itself might actually stop.

Starving, we headed to the kitchen, my once incredible flowers now looking somewhat less so, scattered in the hallway behind us, discarded, no longer important. The moment passed, our urgency eased. I was dressed in nothing now but what was left of a pair of cotton knickers that I wished I'd taken better time choosing. My sister's kitchen provided post-sexual sustenance I would have, at one time, never dared contemplate. I wondered what she would think if she was to see us now, standing in her kitchen like this, me in my shredded pants, her husband standing with arms wrapped around my naked torso, fingertips brushing firm nipples, nothing but boxer shorts to cover a continually expanding body part, that, to be honest, I'd grown quite obsessed with.

I glanced around the house, carefully scanning nooks and corners as if I were seeing the place truly for the first time with eyes that hungrily absorbed everything that represented their life together. Shelves of books that didn't look read. Cushions, pebbles, scented candles I assumed she had purchased to make this place feel more like home — photographs of a seemingly *happy* family. I smiled to myself. If Jason were so happy with Emma, he'd have kept his cock in his pants, keeping his lustful urgency for his wife's attention only.

'What are you grinning about?' Jason asked as he wrapped searching hands around my waist, kissing my neck, making me feel complete. I could smell beef mince cooking in the background, garlic and thyme.

I tilted my head back and kissed his cheek, breathing in his aroma, his presence all I would ever need. 'I'm just happy.' It was true. I had probably never been so happy in my life. Everything I had ever wanted was right here in front of me, in this moment, in this very space. I allowed a deep breath, absorbing everything that I believed Jason to be. In his arms, my body submitted effortlessly to his will. Beneath his body, my mind was introduced to endless possibilities. I am fully aware that new relationships can be far too focused on sex, but this was different. I could see myself with Jason for the rest of my life, in his protection forever, no one and nothing to deter our exciting life journey.

He turned me around, cupping my cheeks in hands that smelled like chopped carrot and parsley. 'Hungry?'

'Starving,' I breathed, feeling a strange urge to fill my belly with something other than his frantic love juice for a change. It was a surprising realisation. I smiled, licking my lips, kissing the tip of his nose, utterly unable to curb such wanton acts of lust, my exaggerated demureness and mock-bashfulness quite unforgiving, encouraging Jason's continued keen desire. I had enchanted him as much as he had enthralled me. 'Something smells delicious.'

'Dinner will be around fifteen minutes. Why don't you go up and have a shower? Change into something more comfortable,' he squeezed my bottom, making me jump and giggle like a naughty schoolgirl. No one had ever made me feel so giddy before, no previous boyfriends holding such power. 'Preferably try something with fewer holes,' he chided, jamming a rogue finger inside a large hole in my underwear that he had made a short while earlier in desperate pursuit of what lay beneath, a fresh ripping sound momentarily making me chuckle.

'Well, if you would be so kind as to refrain from tearing the damned things off my body whenever you want to fuck me, I might stand a chance of keeping my underwear in better condition.'

'You love it.'

'I do.'

He tapped my backside cheekily as I left the kitchen, whistling in his boxer shorts, tea towel over his shoulder, tomato sauce in his hair, still laughing to himself at the sight of my once acceptable-looking underwear now trailing from my bottom as I walked away. This was the life I wanted. My man cooking for me, needing nothing in life other than to feel the touch of my naked skin against his. *What more to life is there? Really?*

This might sound slightly selfish. No, it probably sounds highly narcissistic. But the more time I spent with Jason, the more I needed it to be just the two of us. Emma was a distraction I couldn't allow to continue. Not anymore. Not now that Jason and I were developing a bond that no one else would ever possibly understand. Not my parents. Not Eva. Certainly not Emma. She would have to go, and go soon before I did something utterly unforgivable.

I climbed the stairs of my sister's expensive home, dreaming of the day when this would all be mine, not at all concerned by the fact that I was walking around semi-naked, looking more caged animal than sexy siren. I even had the scratches on my skin to complete the image, welts and all; some even streaked with blood. I stood staring at photographs lining my sister's landing walls, unsurprised that there were more of Emma than Jason or Eva. The sight of her smiling features wrapped around my boyfriend's frame made me shudder.

I stared at an image of the two of them on some holiday I couldn't entirely recall. Beach-bronzed bodies draped around each other unapologetically, my sister's smug smile filling the void of an otherwise beautiful photo frame. I wanted to grab the thing and smash it to pieces. I unhooked it from the wall, residual marks left behind from gathered dust she probably hadn't noticed. If I dropped it, it would be an accident. Nothing more. I could pretend it had merely fallen from my grasp. I had suddenly felt faint, our lovemaking too much — an innocent event. Jason would come running.

A loud crash then broken glass, splintered wood.

'Stacey?' Jason's incredibly caring tone filtered into the hallway below, footsteps hurrying towards me. 'Is everything okay, honey?'

'Oh babe, help,' I called out, not entirely sure what had happened. My hand was bleeding, glass shards lying in mocking surprise on the mock-wooden floor beneath my bare feet.

Jason raced up the stairs. 'Oh my God,' he gasped, seeing my bloodied hand dripping red liquid on the floor around us. 'Are you alright?' He could have no idea what had happened. For a moment, neither did I.

I glanced around me. Several once beautifully framed photographs were now on the floor, the wall showing signs of slight damage where screws had been tugged from their raw-plugged security — broken glass, wood, and torn glossy photo paper everywhere.

'I'm so sorry,' I breathed, glad when he reached out, taking me in his arms. 'I felt faint for a moment.' It was true. I had felt faint at the sight of my sister's disgusting face glaring at me from walls that were not yet my own.

23

Jason guided me expertly into the bathroom, sitting me on the edge of the bath and running the hot tap in order to clean my wounds. 'Here,' he offered me a towel that I wrapped around my injured hand.

'Ouch,' it was painful, glass possibly still embedded inside.

Skilfully, my man grabbed a first-aid kit from the bathroom cabinet and set about cleaning and dressing my wound. He should have been a surgeon. His steady hands wiped away angry blood, removing pieces of glass from beneath damaged skin, pressing a bandage over the area and wrapping it tightly.

'There,' he said, kissing the tips of my fingers. 'All better.'

I stared into his eyes, my moment of madness passed. 'I don't know what happened,' I told him, believing my own words as I uttered them, still unable to comprehend the unimaginable moment between hidden twisted thoughts and unforgiving actions.

'Don't worry about it. Those stairs can be a bit on the

slippy side. I tell Emma not to polish the bloody things, but will she listen?' He laughed then, and I knew my sudden, unexpected *slip*, now perfectly masked my somewhat unhinged wall-swiping performance.

'I need to clean up the mess. Before Emma sees,' I said. My intentions were genuine, yet I wanted to vomit into the bath even as I spoke my sister's name.

'I'll do it,' Jason offered, putting away the first-aid items and washing his hands. 'Will you be alright to have that shower by yourself?'

I nodded, needing to cleanse myself of impure thoughts of my sister's demise. 'I'll be fine. I'm just so sorry about all those lovely photos.' I wasn't sorry. I hated every single one of them.

Jason kissed the top of my head, offering me a smile with a brush of his fingertips against my cheek. It was something I would have at one point only ever dreamed of experiencing. He left me alone in the bathroom, utterly unaware of the poisonous ideas that raced through my wild demonic mind. I wondered what he would think of me if he knew. I shuddered. I could not allow myself the thought that he might hate me for them. I showered, ensuring I kept my bandaged hand as dry as possible, letting images of Emma's face wash away with the hot water that ran down my spine, wishing the water was Jason's exploring fingers, tickling across my skin, tracing the lines of my body, top to toe and back again.

I met him in the kitchen. Dinner was almost ready. The only evidence of my performance on the stairs was the absence of several photographs, the landing wall looking bare, uninviting, cold, stained with surface damage and outlines of gathered dust where my sister's prized family portraits had once hung. I was wearing Emma's bathrobe. Cream silk, large floral print, nothing beneath. Jason looked at me and smiled.

'I hope she doesn't mind me borrowing this?' I asked, swirling around the kitchen doorway, allowing the light to catch the curves of my freshly showered skin, loving how it made me feel. Rich, successful. *Exactly how it should be.*

'You look amazing in it.' Jason licked tomato sauce from his fingers.

Better than she does, no doubt, I mused with a smile of my own.

***

We ate dinner, laughed and relaxed to the soft sound of background music I couldn't place my finger on, yet enjoyed anyway. Classical notes, piano, violin, the occasional sway of a woman's voice, not English, often not actual words. I couldn't have been happier than I was right then. I would have made a bloody fortune if I could have bottled the emotions that swam through my body. People lapped up this stuff. We talked and chatted about life, what we wanted to achieve out of it, Jason's skin glowing with a calm happiness I'd never seen before. I could tell that I made him happier than my sister ever had. We discussed in private future plans that I couldn't wait to set in motion.

'Who was that weird guy Emma was hugging, and, may I add, looking very cosy with, last week at dinner?' I asked. That evening now felt so long ago as we sipped coffee that Jason had topped with cream and marshmallows purely because we thought it would taste nice, our childish mannerisms knowing no bounds.

'What weird guy?' Jason was tidying the plates, scraping uneaten salad into the bin. How perfect. My very own sex slave. A sex slave with a sexy bum.

'I don't know who he was,' I replied absently, swilling liquid around my mug. Jason looked at me, waiting for me to say more. 'Some guy in the restaurant,' I added.

'Lloyd?'

'No. Some other guy.' I was lying, of course. Emma had only spent time with the five of us, but I wanted to see if Jason would show any signs of jealousy at the idea of his wife's potential cheating. I was testing the water, if you like, absorbing the resulting response in order to understand how much Jason truly loved me. I needed to know his true thoughts on his wife while he was in such a relaxed state of mind. 'I saw them at the bar together after you and I had headed outside for some air.' *Jesus, Stacey, how do you think this shit up so fast?*

'Oh, she's always talking to someone,' he laughed, not at all sounding bothered. 'I'm used to it, to be honest. I don't take much notice.' I resisted an urge to smile. *Good.* I didn't ever want him to take notice of anything that bitch might do. Not ever.

'They looked cosy, that's all,' I persisted. I didn't have anything else to say on the matter. He'd passed the test. I was content. Wholly satisfied it was most definitely me he wanted now. *Not her.* I jammed an index finger inside the rim of my now empty mug, dragging it around the warm edges, scooping up what was left of frothed cream and melted marshmallows before bringing it to my mouth, savouring the moment. I imagined that my finger was a part of Jason as I brought it to my lips. *A vital part of Jason.* It made me smile. 'So, what's the plan?' I asked, marshmallow and cream tasting delicious on the finger I'd turned into Jason's penis.

'Plan?' Jason had finished loading the dishwasher. Our open bottle of wine was resting on the kitchen table, ready for us to take to bed. He looked innocent, standing in simple domestic surroundings, a phallic symbol of everything I wanted from life.

'With her?' Why did I have to say it so venomously?

Jason glanced towards me, this conversation something we both knew we would be having at some point, inevitable, obvious. I wasn't going to let it go, no matter how uncomfortable it might be.

'Stacey,' he groaned, an unfathomable sound emerging from his throat. 'Are you not enjoying our time together?' He wiped damp hands on a tea towel and leaned against the sink. He was wearing a pair of jogging bottoms, grey t-shirt, no socks. I preferred him naked. He needed a shave.

'You know I am,' I whispered, my voice adopting its usual throaty husk. It was my newly acquired *fuck-me* voice. A voice I had developed in order to get precisely what I wanted. Right now, I wanted Jason to promise me the world, to thrust into me with screams of wedding proposals and divorce agreements — tossing a set of house keys my way along with a credit card with which I would have no problem making Jason's eyes bulge at the sheer level of spending I would manage on his behalf.

'Then why do we have to talk about Emma tonight? Can't we just be happy enjoying each other for a few hours? No distractions, please.' Jason walked over to me and kissed my mouth, sliding my lips open with his tongue. I knew what he was doing. He was trying to change the subject. To get me to invest in a sexual act that would momentarily force me to forget such a pointed question.

I pulled away. *Not yet, my darling. I'm not finished speaking.* 'I am happy enjoying your company, Jason,' I breathed, slightly irritated that my questioning needs now came ahead of his desires. 'That's why we need to talk about this. You promised.' He had indeed promised that we would discuss this thing in detail. I was pouting again, although my nipples had hardened to the feel of his tongue inside my mouth, the anticipation of what he was offering. In Emma's thin silk gown, nothing about me was left secret. He slid a warm hand across my covered left breast, gently stroking me over fabric we were both very much aware left nothing of my reciprocated desires hidden.

'Jason, please,' I whispered, rising to my feet and backing away from him, the taste of marshmallow now mingled with Jason's uncontrolled arousal. It was the last thing I wanted to do. I wanted him more than I wanted rational thinking. But, at that moment, I needed to discuss my sister more. It made my skin crawl to consider the idea that I would rather talk about Emma than have sex with Jason. *Was I completely mad?*

Jason sighed and breathed out a little too firmly. He was irritated, I could tell. 'Fine. What do you want to know?'

He knew precisely what I needed to hear. 'When exactly are you going to tell my sister about the two of us?' It was a simple question — simple enough to warrant a reasonably simple response.

'I have already tried to explain to you, Stacey. I'm hoping to tell her when she gets home, but with Emma things are not as easy as you might think.'

What the hell was he talking about? I furrowed my brow. 'What do you mean, you're *hoping* to talk to her? I don't understand. You want to be with me, don't you? I want to be with you. So what's the problem?'

'No problem at all. You know I'd love nothing more than to be with you every day for the rest of my life.' That was more like it. 'But,' *here we go.* 'Emma is a complicated person. She needs —'

'She needs telling.' I couldn't have said it any clearer. I folded my arms across my chest. I looked like Eva during one of her many tantrums.

'She will be told. You do trust me, don't you honey?' God, I wished he wasn't so bloody good at twisting me around his fingers. He was stroking my hair.

'You know I do.' I was pouting again, unashamedly licking my lips in response to his probing tone.

'Then trust that I have this.' Jason reached forward, pulling me to him, kissing me, no more words required, searching his tongue inside my lips, opening my mouth to his desires. I couldn't argue. I allowed him to reach under his wife's bathrobe to a body that wasn't hers, touching places she didn't know he was touching, searching for solace we both desperately needed.

Damn you, Jason Cole. Damn the fact that in your arms, I cannot resist you. I allowed him inside me, unapologetically, his fingers and penis doing the talking that he seemed otherwise unable to provide. Emma could wait. For now.

24

When I woke up, I was in my sister's bed, expensive sheets riddled with bodily fluids that I just wanted to rub her nose in and laugh while doing so. Events of the previous evening were hazy, my comfortable slumber still fresh in my mind, as was the sex that had filled our entire evening — both of us exhausted, content, the occasional knowing glance never far away. We had spent our first real night together in our actual, proper home. Not the flat I hated, with a cat that got in the way. But a home I would make my own as soon as my sister's belongings were a thing of the past.

I glanced around me, Jason asleep to my right, my sister's perfume lingering on air that was now unashamedly mixed with forcefully needed sex, urgent panting. I fought the desire to open a window and throw my sister's belongings onto the driveway below, the feeling of Jason's soft breath next to mine, the only thing helping me retain a calm persona.

It was Tuesday morning. I would usually be waking up to the sight of Sylvester on my pillow, his face against mine in an attempt to get me out of bed, to feed him, to notice he existed. I sat upright, my mind still awash with thoughts of Jason's infectious touch.

'You okay?' he groaned next to me, turning over and placing a hand on my leg.

'Sylvester,' I muttered.

'What about him?'

'I forgot to feed him.' I had a habit of doing that.

With all the emotions and passion that had filled my brain over the last week or so, my poor cat had factored far down my list of priorities, my only reason for his obligatory care due purely to Jason's supposed affection towards him and my insatiable need to impress. We raced around the house together, grabbing clothing and each other, laughing at the incredible fog that had become my brain as we headed out in pursuit of feline nourishment. By the time we had returned to the house, we were both exhausted, starving, in need of sustenance we could not deny ourselves.

'Don't go to work today,' I begged as Jason busied himself with coffee and toast. He was staring out of the kitchen window, shirt undone, my hand casually across his buttocks.

'I can't take the day off.'

'You can.' It was true. He could.

He smiled. 'Well, only if you do.' He didn't have to ask me twice. By the time lunchtime had come and gone, we had christened practically every room in my sister's house, making sure I soiled everything that belonged to her with my naked, eager body. I wanted Jason to walk into any room of his home and think about what we had done together, my womanly parts the only thing I ever wanted on his mind. We had even ruined her expensive sofa, the stains left behind something we both found amusing. Even the kitchen sink had seen the underside of my bottom, twice.

Our sex wasn't always passionate, however. We were not living in a romance novel, and I wasn't deluded. No. Mostly Jason's thrusts were urgent, needy, somehow tied to emotions I felt he couldn't otherwise express. He usually lasted a minute or two, seconds sometimes, if I had to put an actual timeframe to his frantic orgasms. I surmised it was purely because he had been unhappy with my sister for so long that he was now wholly desperate for the release that came in the form of my willing body, the promise that lay ahead.

I had firmly familiarised myself with almost every room in this house, my attention on Jason and surroundings I'd become somewhat obsessed with. When I opened the closed door of Eva's room, Jason took my hand to stop me.

'Not in there,' he muttered, as if his daughter's room was sacred, off-limits.

'What do you take me for?' I asked, tilting my head as if he had hurt my feelings. He hadn't. I would have had sex with Jason inside Eva's cot if it meant he would think only of me whenever he looked at the thing. 'I just want to have a peek. I love Eva.' That was true. I did indeed love my niece. Not that I had ever tried to bond with her before now. Toddlers could be a little snotty, irritating, somewhat absorbing of your time and attention.

Jason allowed me entry to his little girl's room, the

door opening to a bright pale pink space that smelled of candy floss and freshly washed towels. For a moment, I hesitated. The idea of becoming a mother myself one day was something that had played on my mind for several years. I was, after all, almost thirty. I couldn't wait forever.

'It's a beautiful room,' I sighed, brushing my hand across a teddy bear that sat on a chair by the door.

'It is,' Jason breathed, something in his voice making me turn to face him.

'It will be okay, you know,' I said, reaching my arms under his. 'We will make everything okay for Eva.' I wanted that more than anything. I honestly did. Snotty noses, the lot. I would have loved a ready-made family. *Jason's ready-made family.* Just him, Eva, and me, with possibly another little one on the way to complete our perfect foursome. Yet, what I actually wanted to say was, we will make everything okay for *me*. It was, after all, everything I had ever wanted. To be in this house, with Jason, with Eva. Emma gone. I would become Jason's much-needed replacement for a sister who didn't deserve any of it anyway. She didn't deserve him. The sudden change in dynamics was something everyone else would have to get used to or shut the hell up.

Jason kissed me, allowing a moment between us as I ran my hand over his crotch, for a second forgetting his need to keep this room purely for his little girl. A mere innocent child. He could have had me on the floor in a heartbeat had he simply requested it, bending me over her playpen, flipping me like a pancake. He laughed, pulling away, the moment passed, Jason needing us out of this room. He knew what I was like when left to my own devices.

'Sorry,' I groaned, bringing his attention back to our innocent chat.

There is a little-known fact about me that, for as long as I can remember, I have been able to bring forth fake tears on cue if ever the need arises for me to glean attention from those who might not otherwise freely offer it. I have always been able to display false upset and turmoil — my parents, teachers, even friends often becoming embroiled in my selfish attempts for attention. I chose to bring about such emotion at that moment, allowing effortless tears to fall to my unsuspecting cheeks. It had the desired effect.

'Honey, what's wrong?' Jason asked, cupping my face in hands that had a way of melting my soul. I loved it.

I sighed, blinking away fake tears that looked too real. *God, I was good.* 'I'm sorry, babe,' I replied, my need, unforgiving, unprovoked, for Jason's affection threatening to devour me whole. 'This is all too much.' It wasn't entirely a lie.

'What is?'

'You. Emma. Eva. I'm –' I paused for effect. I didn't want to say *I'm Jealous* – although I was – merely adding, 'I'm feeling left out.'

'Why?' Jason laughed, rubbing salty tears from my skin.

'Because I want this. I want this all so much.' I was at least speaking some truth within the falsity I'd created.

'Want what?' He wasn't getting it.

192

'You. This home. Our own child.' I was probably unintentionally telling more that I should have offered, our relationship new, our love for each other not yet openly declared. Yet, I was never going to let any man fuck me with such force and potential maleficence as I'd allowed Jason to do, without some clarification of a future secured.

'You want a baby?' he asked, sounding quite taken aback.

I nodded. 'I want *your* baby, Jason. One day.' I replied, feeling suddenly dizzy, secretly hoping I was pregnant already. If the sheer number of unapologetic sex acts he had performed on me without a condom had anything do to with it, it was certainly possible. I pulled him close, not entirely wishing to see his face right then. 'Tell me you want the same things as I do.' I was desperate for answers I knew only Jason could provide.

He hesitated for a moment. I wavered. Had I said too much? Then he smiled and laughed. Our moment eased. 'Of course. I'd love nothing more.'

'Oh, thank God,' I breathed, releasing a giggle I'd kept hidden behind an inhaled breath. 'Now, all we need to do is get rid of Emma.' My words probably sounded worse aloud than they had in my head, yet we did indeed need to get rid of my sister. There wasn't any other option. Luckily for me, Jason failed to appreciate the magnitude of my thoughts, simply kissing me on the top of my head with a sigh. He did not need to know that my mind raced with ideas I could not share with him. They simply were not sane. Not even to me.

25

I returned home to my flat that Wednesday morning feeling that someone had stabbed me to death with a pair of blunt scissors. *The irony was not lost on me.* I knew I couldn't stay with Jason indefinitely, two blissful days spent mostly in bed, oblivious to the world, our honeymoon period firmly in motion, crying off work, our unfettered passion knowing no end.

Sylvester was pleased to see me, Jason having offered to feed him in my unavoidable absence. Now I hated that cat. I hated that he stood for my single, lonely life. A life without the man I couldn't live without. Emma would be home today. She would wonder what those odd, intrusive stains on her precious furniture were, and she would wonder about the smell of sex in bedding I deliberately hadn't changed. It offered me a moment of contentment. A moment in time that linked me to a future I couldn't wait to hold in my hands.

I rubbed my belly as Sylvester rubbed himself against my leg, his purr adding to the sickly feeling building inside me. Maybe I was pregnant, and my nausea was morning sickness? Yet, I had been sleeping with Jason for little over a week, although it felt much longer. It would be impossible to know at this early stage; morning sickness couldn't possibly manifest in such a short space of time. I deduced that my sickly feeling had more to do with Emma's return than anything else, unfortunately.

I didn't feel like going to work, but I wanted the sack even less – I needed to hold onto my job for a while longer. Thoughts of becoming a stay-at-home mum with Eva and my new baby dislodged all rational thinking. Jason was already working hard to give me the life I deserved. The life we couldn't wait to start together.

I messaged him three times before I made it into work, all three texts going unread. *What the hell was he doing?* I called. The phone went to voicemail. By the time I arrived at the office, my nerves threatened to tip me over the edge, my face probably displaying the bad mood I could not hide. I hovered outside the building for too long, knowing full well I was late yet unable to start my day without confirmation that Jason loved me and that everything was alright. I called again, leaving a message that this time sounded a little irrational, slightly *bunny-boiler-in-the-making:*

Hey, you. I hope you're not ignoring me. You can't just fuck me and leave, you know. (A little nervous laugh). Call me when you get this. PLEASE. I need to know you're okay... I love you.

I hung up, realising I'd dropped the L bomb again. Shit. Should I call back and leave a second, less intrusive message? Apologising for such a declaration? No. *Don't be stupid.* That would make me sound crazy. Yet, I probably already sounded crazy. But the truth was, I did love him. I loved him with everything I had inside me. I think I always had. I entered work with a scowl on my face, in no mood for a lecture over three unplanned days off work within the last two weeks. I didn't care. In fact, I didn't give a shit.

***

I didn't hear a thing from Jason that entire day or the following one. My L-word confession seemed hell-bent on burning a hole into the depths of my brain and terrifying thoughts swarmed around a mind I struggled to cope with. What if I'd said too much, too soon? What if I'd scared him away? What if Emma had her claws into my man again?

I felt I might actually burst something as I paced my flat alone. She would be home by now, yet neither of them had contacted me. Had Jason told her about our affair yet? He had promised to do so, the very moment of her return. I thought about our desire for each other, the way he held me, the things he did to me when no one else could see. There was no way that wasn't real. We both felt it in our bones, to our very core. I still had the bruises and scratch marks to prove that his love for me was real.

Thursday came and went in a haze, my only focus now on Jason and the current state of our relationship. I called him several times, holding my phone in my hand for so long I felt it might become a part of me and need to be prised from my angered grip. I almost threw it across the room, he would indeed contact me soon enough.

I even allowed myself the assumption that Emma was simply keeping him busy, yet it had never stopped him before. We were rampant until I had uttered that bloody word. Unable to stand it any longer, I redialled his number, my thumb practically breaking beneath the forcefulness of my urgency, fully expecting to hear yet another voice message recording.

'Stacey, I can't talk now,' Jason answered on the second ring as if he had been waiting for my unwanted intrusion.

'What are you talking about?' I asked, unable to fathom what the hell was going on. 'Why haven't you contacted me? I miss you.' I did not mention my earlier declaration of love. That could wait for now.

'Stacey, I have to go. Don't keep calling me.' He sounded as if he was biting his lip. As if my phone calls were ruining his day.

'What's going on, Jason?' I could sense something in his tone — an unfathomable distance, a simmering pain he couldn't share with me.

'Emma's home. We've been talking things through.'

My heart lunged. 'Seriously? My God, that's amazing.' My feet did a little skip on my living room rug at the thought that my man had finally come clean, confessed his uncontrollable love. I smiled.

'Stacey, listen to me –'

'Jason, hurry up,' Emma's distinctive flat tone filtered from somewhere in the background, her slippery voice slicing my eardrums to pieces.

'She doesn't sound as if she's all that upset by what you have told her, Jason.' My own words cut into me now, my smile slipping away.

Jason fell silent. 'We are trying to work things out. Things were different when she came home, Stace. She seemed calmer, better.'

What the hell was I listening to? 'I beg your pardon?' I questioned, my teeth gripping my jaw as if it had been stuffed into a vice. Was he trying to tell me that they were giving their relationship another go? 'Did you tell her about me?' I needed the truth. *Now.*

'Stacey, I can't talk to you about this now.' He was desperate to get off the phone. To leave me hanging like some old used sock, no longer wanted. *No fucking way was he getting off that lightly.* 'I'll call you tonight.' He hung up, leaving the dialling tone in my ear. I couldn't believe it. Jason – my man – had dared to hang up on me. I didn't know what to do. I couldn't breathe. My flat seemed to close in and squeeze the life out of me. *I was nobody's bitch.* He couldn't do this to me. No way. Not Jason. I grabbed my keys and headed out of the door.

***

I made my way like a madwoman scorned across town to my sister's house. It was only three miles, yet my feet throbbed with each step I was forced to take. It was as if each stride pointed me towards a doomed state I wasn't yet able to see, a place I couldn't bring myself to acknowledge existed. If I had a knife, I seriously do not think I would have been responsible for my actions.

I arrived at the house, early evening prompting lights that shone against this expensive neighbourhood like Harrod's shop window at Christmas. Banging on the door, I hoped to break the thing down, my emotions no longer rational, my thoughts no longer sane. When Emma opened the door, she did not appear shocked to see me. In fact, she had a look of a woman ready for what was coming her way. There was no way I could keep quiet any longer.

'Where is he?' I demanded, probably looking as if I had lost my mind completely, eyes cold, features unhinged.

'He's in the shower,' Emma replied, a flat tone telling me she knew more than she was letting on. I wondered if he had fucked her, and now needed a shower in order to remove her unspeakable stench.

'Do you know what your husband did?' I didn't care how menacing or deranged I sounded.

'I do, Stacey, yes.' Emma sounded depressed, as if my forthcoming revelations were already addressed, no longer new. She simply stood and stared at me. It was unnerving. I had been quite ready for the firing squad. Prepared to feel my hair being torn out at the root, Jason coming to my aid, protecting me from the bitch of a sister I had despised for years. I expected yelling, angry outbursts, pain. Instead, there was now a looming silence between us that disturbed me.

'So you already know he's been fucking me for the last couple of weeks?' I wanted my words to shock my sister, to have her reel in horror at the mere thought of us together.

She nodded. 'We talked things through when I came home.' Emma sounded as if she had already forgiven him for an affair I had not yet confirmed. No. This was not how this thing was meant to go.

'About?'

'About us. About *you*. About how sorry he feels for cheating on me.'

I couldn't believe what I was hearing. I felt my legs slide away from me and had to grab onto something for fear of looking weak in front of this bitch I hated. I chose to grab flesh. Her flesh.

'He's been fucking me and loving every second of it, and you stand there in your designer bullshit and tell me you're talking things through?' I laughed directly into her face. She didn't flinch. In fact, she looked as if she had played this all out in her mind already, waiting for this very reaction.

'I know, Stacey. I know it all.' Emma appeared pleased with herself for a moment. Pleased that my plan to get her husband had failed. She hung her head. I couldn't read what she was feeling.

'Jason!?' I screamed, releasing my sister and heading for the staircase, unable to comprehend that he would have told her about our love affair with any other intention than to leave her behind. Visions of our recent heady sex now threatened to explode me with every glance I took around the place. The staircase. The hallway floor. The kitchen sink. The lounge sofa. The bedroom. I ran upstairs, my sister attempting to grab onto my clothes as she tried to prevent the inevitable.

'Jason!?' I yelled again, uncontrolled anger pulsing through my lungs.

He emerged onto the landing, towel around his middle, hair wet, shock on an uncertain, unreadable face. 'Stacey? What are you doing here?'

What the hell did he think I was doing here? How the hell did he assume I would react? 'What's going on, Jason?' I breathed, reaching the top of the stairs with little interference from the scorned sister behind me.

'I tried to stop her.' Emma was wrestling with my jacket, yet quite unable to stop my purposeful mission.

'Jason? Are you going to explain why your wife seems to think that you guys are giving your relationship another go when only days ago we were practically destroying every room in this goddamned house?' My words were as bitter as I felt.

Jason swallowed, conversations I wasn't a party to already shared with a wife I thought he detested. 'Stacey, calm down. I can explain everything.'

I wished he would. I wished he would hurry up and explain. None of this made a shred of sense. 'Well?' I spat, looking from Jason to my out-of-breath sister. Eva was in her room, chatting to herself, content, unaware.

'Tell her, Jason,' she berated, heading into Eva's room to check on her vulnerable daughter.

Jason glanced at me, wholly unable to bring his full gaze to my face. I stepped forward, the sight of my glistening man wrapped in a towel more than my faint heart could take.

'When I collected Emma from the airport, she seemed different. Happy, even.' *How the hell did he assume that would in any way change a damned thing?* 'We came home. We ate dinner –'

'You had sex.' It wasn't a question. I was shocked at how angry I sounded. *How could he do that to me?*

He glanced away, his eyes unable to confirm or deny my allegation. 'She saw some of your underwear. In our bed.' He paused. I knew what that meant. *After they had made love.* After he tried to make up for events that could never be undone. 'We argued. I denied everything. But I couldn't lie to her, Stace, and in the end, the whole thing came out.'

'But that is exactly what we wanted, wasn't it? So what's the problem?' I still wasn't grasping this.

'She cried. I cried. We have a fucking kid together, for Christ's sake.' Jason stormed into their bedroom, a sudden need to protect his child's innocent ears from anything he had to say not lost on either of us. He stood with his back to me, his rippling shoulders still bearing the nail marks I'd passionately given him only two days earlier. 'In the end, we talked. We talked for the first time in a long time, actually.' I wanted to punch him in the face. 'We have decided to give things another go, Stacey.'

I stood, hovering between Jason and his *other* family, my feet on shaky ground in more ways than one. It was as if I was the injured party.

'No...' I let out the word as if I was a scolded child. 'Please, don't do this to me.'

'I'm sorry, honey. I have to.' Jason looked as if he had been caught stealing sweets from his daughter's Christmas stocking. *How dare he call me honey!*

Emma appeared on the landing behind me, Eva in

her arms, her daughter happily playing with the tresses of her mother's hair, unaware, oblivious. 'You forgave him?' I asked my sister, tears in my eyes now, my emotions and ego broken.

'I did,' she whispered. They had spoken words to each other in private that I was not a party to and could not have contemplated.

'But you were so angry that day at my house,' I spat, unable now to comprehend the notion that I had failed to tell her everything when I had the chance. When I could have created a different outcome.

Emma nodded. 'I thought I could trust my sister.' She was whispering still, unwilling to upset the child in her arms with words we both knew she wanted to express. She could barely look at me.

I stared at Jason, unable to understand what had gone so wrong in such a short space of time. 'But I love you,' I said, unable to stop myself. No one spoke. It was as if my words had been uttered in a foreign language, of no concern to anyone now.

Feeling suddenly weak and pathetic, I screamed, racing down the staircase, out of the front door, taking out a vase of freshly picked flowers in the hallway with a wave of my outstretched hand as I left. The thing smashed, Eva's sudden cries of fear hitting my ears along with the realisation that I had been dumped by the one man I had allowed into my heart in a long time. For the first time ever, in fact. I ran along the street, a light rain now dusting my skin, absorbing tears that ran freely down abandoned cheeks. *What the hell was happening?* How could I possibly comprehend anything that had happened here today?

26

I got back to my flat in a daze, unable to think straight or figure out what I was going to do next. My life had literally turned upside down, the man of my dreams daring to choose the sister I despised over me. I left Sylvester swirling frantically on the landing as I slammed the front door behind me, the sound of cracking glass in an ageing frame triggering a feast of emotions that created anger I'd never experienced in my life. I stood in the middle of my front room, unable to prevent the fury that bubbled inside my chest.

Allowing the appearance of emotions I had no other place for, I didn't stop until my entire flat lay in tatters, the sound of smashing ceramics, glass, and electrical goods not enough to sedate my increasing pain. It was overwhelming. I stood surrounded by carnage I had willingly created, memories of Jason in my bed causing secret suffering that rocked my world, mocking the very essence of my existence. *He couldn't do this to me.* He loved me. I knew it in my heart to be true.

I had cut my hand on a piece of glass, a recent wound

reopened, reminding me of a previous act not yet confessed. Fresh blood dripped onto the ageing rug. I allowed it to soak in along with my unfettered embarrassment. I had allowed him willingly into my life, into my bed, into my underwear. It was not something that I had undertaken lightly. My previous relationships had consisted of little more than a fumbling, acne-covered boyfriend in high school, a one-year on-off relationship in college before the guy had unexpectedly headed off to Australia to live with his parents, and two short-lived dating app encounters in my mid-twenties whose names I could not recall. Two guys, in fact, that I most certainly did not wish to think about.

I had secretly been waiting for Jason to notice me for an entire decade. He had been the one male I'd genuinely connected to and been able to feel confident and comfortable allowing into my life. He could do what he wanted to me, when he wanted, because I had willingly given myself to him wholly, without regret or remorse. Now what the hell was I meant to do?

I slumped to the floor and sobbed, pain erupting from me in the moment it had taken me to realise my unwarranted shame. Did our time together mean so little to him? Did *I* mean so little to him? I picked up the mobile I'd already slammed into a wall and now displayed a broken screen, cracked case, and dislodged battery casing, and with hands trembling, dialled his number, glad the thing still worked. I should not have been surprised that it went to voicemail, but it made me scream into the room wildly, unhinged, as if I had, along with Sylvester, turned feral overnight.

I dialled again. Voicemail. I endured seventeen agonising redials, his sultry voice chiming in each time, inviting me to leave a message, too upbeat for the magnitude of this moment. I kept redialling, over and over, unable stop until he caved in and picked up. He would have to pick up at some point. I wasn't going to let this lie. I didn't care if it took all night.

Eventually, I heard a click. 'What?' Jason wasn't happy. He wasn't the only one.

'We need to talk about this,' I sobbed, my attempts to remain calm failing completely, the broken mobile clutched in trembling hands witness to my wrath.

'I can't, Stacey.'

'Meet me. Please. We need to talk about what's happening.' I was deadly serious. I wasn't about to let him say no.

'No, I really can't –'

'I'm pregnant.' I had no idea what the hell I was thinking, stating such a thing aloud, no confirmation or proof whatsoever. I could think of no other way to get him to change his mind about us. I was clutching at straws. Besides, it might be true.

Silence, followed by what sounded like Jason taking in oxygen too quickly, his breath unsteady. 'What?'

'I'm pregnant,' I repeated, louder this time, allowing more confidence than I had the right to express. 'I did one of those early test thingies.' Did they even exist? I assumed they must do. Jason didn't question it.

Silence again. 'I'll come over.'

'No.' I glanced around my ramshackle flat. That most certainly would not be a good idea. I did not wish to appear entirely deranged to the man I wanted only to adore me. 'Meet me by the old train line over by Wingrove. In an hour.' I offered, not entirely sure why I'd chosen such an abandoned location, merely desperate for us not to be disturbed. I most certainly didn't think Emma would want us to meet. The less she knew, the better.

Wingrove wasn't actually a street, but an old disused factory the railway had once used to repair locomotive engines. The ageing rail track still ran through the town, leading out to the abandoned place. No one ever went there, the old track long abandoned, disused, misused on many occasions. Only dog-walkers ventured there now. And druggies. We wouldn't be disturbed.

'One hour,' Jason confirmed, hanging up before I had a chance to question him further or proclaim anything else that might have upset his otherwise perfectly balanced mindset.

I stood in the middle of carnage that I'd created, musing over damage I'd caused, unable to fathom what was real over what I'd accidentally invented. I could hear Sylvester outside, yet couldn't bring myself to let him in, his presence in my life directly linked to the man I adored. A man who was about to scorn me, it seemed.

***

An hour later, I found myself standing amidst overgrown bushes and weeds, next to a dilapidated building, rotting fly-tipped furniture and a disused rail line I could barely make out in the evening haze. Jason would show up. He wouldn't leave me hanging like this. We had enjoyed such perfect moments together. It had to mean something. I hung around for ten unbearable minutes, fearing he had indeed stood me up, feeling pure relief when his car came around the corner and stopped some feet ahead of me. It had, at least, stopped raining now, yet my hair was still damp from my earlier walk home. My clothes were dirty, my mood in tatters, and a fresh bandage covered my earlier rampage. He climbed out of his car, a look on his face I couldn't read.

'I don't have long,' he stated, tone flat, expressionless, his usual caring side unwilling to show itself to me now.

I shook my head, tears falling. 'What are you doing to me?' I asked, sobbing as if he'd broken me into tiny pieces. I was trembling, nothing more than a broken child, forgotten, mistreated, left alone to suffer in silence.

'I never meant for things to turn out like this, Stace,' he said, holding his hands in the air as if everything had happened without his consent and, for the most part, without his knowledge. I walked towards him, needing comfort I feared might not be forthcoming. 'Get in,' he said. 'You look terrible.'

I got into the car and closed the door. Jason climbed into the driver's seat with a deep sigh. 'What happened?' I asked, still unable to comprehend the events of the last few hours.

'Emma was talking of making a fresh start. Her book launch is going well. She was so much brighter than she has been in a while,' I felt he was leaving something out, something he dared not express aloud, but I didn't want to hear about Emma at that moment. I wanted to talk about us — our future. 'I never meant for her to find your underwear. I fully intended on ending things with her. Honestly, I did. But she looked so lost. So frightened.' Jason glanced my way, hanging his head as he closed his eyes. 'I felt sorry for her.'

I scoffed. *He felt sorry for her?* 'And what about me? What was that all about?' The only thing I needed was the truth. 'Don't you feel something for me?'

'Of course I do.' He turned to me, reaching for my trembling hands, noticing the fresh bandage on one. 'You were never a mistake. I want you to know that.' I knew it. I hadn't imagined it after all.

'You can still leave her, Jason. We can still do this thing.' I leaned towards him, grasping my man's hands in mine, noticing how hot they felt against my cool skin.

He shook his head. 'You don't realise how fragile she is,' he told me firmly. 'I can't leave her just yet.'

'Why?' My words sounded as irritated as I felt.

'It's hard to explain,' he muttered.

'Try me?'

'Emma has issues. She doesn't like to talk about it. I guess I still love her. I need to help her.' I couldn't believe what I was hearing. *What the fuck was he saying to me?* I did not hear a thing about any problems my sister might have. All I heard was Jason telling me that he was still in love with his wife.

'But I love you.' I was crying again now, unable to contain emotions so strong, unable to contain the L-word a second longer.

Jason stared at me, reaching a hand to my face in the way he always did. It made me so hot for him. He knew

210

exactly what I liked, what I needed. 'I hope you understand that I don't love her in the way I love you. I can't love her the way I am allowed to love you. I want you to know that, Stacey. I need you to understand. Emma is just so fragile at the moment. I can't explain why.' He was making no sense. The only thing I heard was a declaration of his faithful and genuine feelings for me. He had told me he loved me, confirming everything I needed to hear. He loved *me* more than my sister. I knew it. I knew that he loved me. *So what in Christ's name was holding him back?*

'If you truly love me, leave her, and let's start our life together,' I stated firmly, grabbing his hand from my cheek, remembering I'd told him I was pregnant and not wanting to ignore such an important proclamation now. I pulled his hand to my stomach, pressing his fingers against my probably empty vessel.

'Our baby needs you.' What the hell was I saying? I needed to think fast, and our lack of protection provided this perfect opportunity for me to tell him what I needed him to hear. I hoped it would be enough for him to want me again. To need me. To need *only* me.

Jason breathed out, remembering my recent words as if, in his haste, he'd completely forgotten. He began to cry, tears falling onto unforgiving cheeks, nose wet with snot and regret he did not otherwise know how to dissipate. I leaned over and embraced him, our emotions entwined, our passion unguided. His kiss felt hot, frantic. He pulled at my clothes, and I reached between his legs, feeling his arousal, needing him inside me, past moments forgotten, already forgiven.

Together we slid into perfect union, our sex as chaotic as ever, demanding, angry, slightly uncomfortable yet Jason's needs igniting my own infectious, hidden fury. He pulled at my jeans, tearing my underwear, leaving nothing of my dignity behind as he grabbed my body, forcing me into the backseat of the car. Eva's car seat was tossed to one side as if it meant nothing to him, the tearing of clothing and frantic grunting the only thing we needed to focus on.

He fucked me harder than he had done before, his thrusts angry, almost violent. I allowed him to flip me over, to use my body, parting eager legs as he forced himself inside me from behind, his lunging bitter, probing, ramming himself into me like a rampant beast. I loved every second of it. Not the sex act itself. That was actually quite uncomfortable, painful even. My knees were crushed against hard seatbelt slots, his body heavy against mine, his thrusts too eager. No. I simply loved the way he needed me. With every desperate thrust of his penis, I could feel how much he wanted to release a pain he had nowhere else to place. It was why I knew we could never be apart for long. *I assumed this was love.*

I was undoubtedly providing something Emma could never give him. I wondered if he was even able to use her in this way? She was so thin, so delicate. She would probably break beneath his urgency. I had never known anything like it, Jason appearing in my life from some other place entirely, some infectious disease I could not live without. *Love.* What did I know of such things anyway? Passion and slow sex were not for us. We were needy, urgent, angry, often violent, it seemed, unforgiving.

When he finished, we lay slumped together in the back of the car, spooning and spent, a light rain tapping the glass as if we had been caught in all our splendour. He was inside me still, his erection throbbing, becoming flaccid with each shallow breath he took. I could feel sticky liquid between my thighs as I tightened my grip around him. I needed that liquid. It may just save our relationship.

***

I wanted to fall asleep in Jason's arms as I had done previously at his house and my flat. I stroked his hair, kissed his skin, not for a second wanting this moment to end. I knew he found me irresistible. If he had genuinely wanted to be with his wife, he wouldn't be with me now. He wouldn't have done what he'd just done to me, our urgent lovemaking the only thing I needed to know about the man I truly felt understood me, my needs, my desires. My sister might have been able to convince him she needed him, that she loved him and wanted to work things out, but we both knew we wouldn't be able to stay away from each other. Not ever. Our needs were too strong.

He lifted his head, sweat dripping from his now unkempt hair, skin glowing hot with the unbridled passion he seemed desperate to reserve only for me. He turned me over, kissing breasts that had been torn from my wrecked bra, suckling hardened nipples keenly, breathing heavily. He didn't say a word. Neither of us

213

needed to express anything of what we felt at that moment. His actions had confirmed it all. Placing his head on my chest, he closed his eyes. We were spent, everything about us entwined into one person, our need for each other strong, unrelenting.

I lost track of time for a while, Jason's presence all I would ever need to feel secure in a life I did not entirely understand. I didn't wish to face our everyday lives. This was our life now. Together, naked, Jason inside me, declaring his love with each angry burst of emotion. I knew my man was merely playing out obligations to a wife he didn't want. He had agreed to stay with her, to work things out, because that was what husbands did. I even admired him for such a committed act of sacrifice.

It was simply a question of how we released him from this new, challenging situation. It was what we did next that counted. As we lay together in the backseat of his car, condensation dripping from windows so that I was reminded of a scene from *Titanic*, I hatched a plan. It wasn't any elaborate plan. Not initially. But with each breath of the man I adored on top of me, my impossible idea grew.

Jason drove me home, cried in my arms, told me he loved me. It was music to my ears. I wanted to let him inside, to join me in a bath, to warm him with my unwavering passion and womanly parts, but my flat looked as if someone had exploded a bomb inside, and my earlier overreactive state was too mortifying to acknowledge. For now, it was enough that we had been given this time together. Time to reflect and connect in a way I knew he could never connect with anyone else. He wanted me, and I wanted him. We loved each other. That was all that mattered. Whatever happened now, we would support each other. From this day forward, nothing would ever be the same again.

As Jason left me that afternoon outside my flat, I promised him we would find a way to figure this out, my mind swimming with poison no one should have been left alone with. If he'd had any notion of the ideas allowed to fester inside my brain, I am not entirely certain how he would have reacted.

I carefully tidied my discarded belongings, glad

nothing of actual value had been broken in my ridiculous, unrehearsed state of turmoil, and gleaning satisfaction from a nagging thought I couldn't dislodge. I needed to save Jason. I was shocked by such a simple moment of clarity that hit me the moment he drove away. I needed to protect him from that monster who came in the form of a sister we both secretly hated. He knew as well as I did that she would never release her grip on him. Her claws were sunk firmly into my man's perfectly toned flesh. But he was mine, not hers. She had merely borrowed him, and now I wanted him back. My anger grew with every shard of glass I emptied into my already brimming wheelie bin.

***

I allowed a smile as I dialled Emma's number the following morning, knowing she would not resist the urge to rub salt into what she assumed would by now be my excruciatingly painful wounds. The sound of the phone ringing against my earlobe mocked my already shredded mood, creating inside me a piercing disdain that I could not dislodge.

I would deal with this. I would make everything better.

But what if Emma chose to ignore my call? What if she had already deleted my number, vowing never to speak to me again? Blocked me from her life, from her world? Her hate for me was as strong as mine was for her. I held my breath, a broken phone pressed against my face, my heart in my throat, vomit threatening. When she answered her phone, I wasn't ready.

'Emma?' I released a loud sob into the mouthpiece, fake tears surfacing perfectly on cue. I was quite proud of my uncanny ability to form tears precisely when the moment called for it. I had grown up not always proud of such a strange ability, yet I was now delighted by it, my desperate need to sound as sincere as I was able, something I could not have explained to a living soul.

'Stacey, please. I don't want to speak to you right now,' Emma muttered, sounding hurt. But she'd answered her phone anyway. I knew the reason would be nothing more than an insane curiosity to see me squirm. My downfall had been brought about because of a discovery she knew I had not intended. Still, it had gone in my favour.

'I know, darling, I know. I really do not know what to say to you.' I was laying it on as thick as I possibly could. I had to. I had no other choice. I simply couldn't take the risk that my plan might not work, that she might somehow see straight through my lies. 'Please, don't hang up on me. I need to tell you how sorry I am. For everything.' I held my breath, waiting, my mind racing with thoughts I shouldn't have possessed.

'Stacey, what the hell do you want me to say? You slept with my husband. How can I ever forgive that?'

Yes, Emma, your husband was inside me only last night, actually. How do you feel about that, bitch? I took a breath, careful, calculated. I closed my eyes. 'I know. I honestly can't tell you how bad I feel for doing such a terrible thing to you, sweetheart.' I had no idea I could lie so effortlessly. I never called her sweetheart, either. Calling her by such an affectionate name implied she actually meant something to me. She didn't. She made my skin crawl and my bones ache.

'I was weak. *Stupid.* Please, Emma. Let's meet up. I need to see you face to face. I need to explain properly. I feel so ashamed. So embarrassed.' There was nothing I felt embarrassed about at all, but hey, needs must. I was glad Emma couldn't see my face. That was something, at least. She would have probably seen right through me. If my eyes weren't currently squeezed shut, *I* might have seen right through me.

My sister sighed. 'I don't think that's such a good idea.' She sounded mortified. If I'd felt anything at all for her other than repulsion, I might have felt sorry for her. As it was, she deserved everything that was coming to her.

'Please,' I was begging now, my sobs echoing loudly along a crackling phone line to ears I knew wouldn't be able to resist seeing my raw, exposed pain, face to face, one on one. I hoped my performance would be enough to convince her that, if nothing else, she would at least experience the satisfaction of seeing me in turmoil, devastated by what she assumed I could have avoided.

Emma took a breath. A clear inhale behind despondent emotions I struggled to ignore. 'Okay, Stacey. We can meet. But I don't think it will do either of us any good.'

It was all I needed to hear. I couldn't help it when I breathed out in sheer relief, allowing light to flood my eye sockets again, blood to flood my seemingly narrowing veins. 'Thank you, Emma. Oh my goodness, thank you, my darling.' I allowed another sob, louder this time, my breathing shallow, frail, needing to appear as broken as I wanted Emma to believe me to be. As broken as I wanted my sister to become. 'Meet me at Bailey's Coffee Shop, around three o'clock.' We used to go there as teens. Back when we were sisters. Back when I thought she loved me.

'Okay. Three it is. But I'm so angry with you, Stacey. I can't bear what you've done to me.' For a moment, I wavered. Emma's words sounded honest, heartfelt. As if she genuinely could have never comprehended that her own flesh and blood would do such a thing.

I hesitated. 'I know,' I breathed, surprised at how easy she was to manipulate, and feeling slightly sorry for her, despite my discomfort. 'I'm so sorry, Emma. Three o'clock it is.'

***

Emma was waiting for me outside Bailey's by the time I had made my way via taxi to the coffee shop, my mind filled with thoughts of Jason, the future that awaited us, my sister's upcoming downfall. I was impressed by her promptness. Her need to verbally tear me to shreds showed on her face as I walked towards her, the scowl she offered creating a heady mix of adrenalin and satisfaction I worried might give me away.

It was raining harder now, the earlier light rain that had seemed to dominate this week giving way to a heavy blend of dust and sludge. This summer afternoon was slipping away along with the relationship I knew we could never have. We stood looking at each other for a moment, my plan forming perfectly with each breath my sister took. She wouldn't have that problem for much longer.

'Can we talk?' I asked, my face giving nothing away, my thoughts kept secret, as I let fake tears fall without apology.

Emma was holding an umbrella, trembling slightly, looking lost, broken. She glanced towards the ground. 'I have no idea what you think you might be able to say to me, Stacey, that would make any difference at all to what you have done.'

I glanced around. 'We can't talk here. Let's take a drive. Somewhere private. I need to explain.' I was bloody good at this lying thing. But I was sick of getting wet, rain something I was growing tired of, English summers becoming loathsome to me. Maybe we could emigrate to Spain once all this shit was over.

Emma hesitated, contemplating her next move. 'We can talk well enough here.'

No. That was not how this thing was going to go. 'Look. I know I said to meet here, but I couldn't think of anywhere else. I don't want the whole town to know our private business. And I didn't think you would want me turning up at your place.' Yes, Stacey. *Perfect.* Use emotional blackmail. Emma hates looking anything but perfect in front of other people.

Emma nodded. 'Okay,' she said, unaware of the actual reasons behind my request, the motive, the twisted dark thoughts. 'But I really don't know what you will be able to say that could make me –'

'Let me try.' I cut in, needing her to shut the hell up so we could get out of the rain. She nodded, heading towards the car she'd parked in the next street. I have no idea how she could remain so calm. If Jason had done anything like that to me, I probably would have stabbed him to death, then gladly murdered whatever woman had thought she could possibly take him away from me in the first place. Luckily, I knew Jason better than that. I was lucky that he only wanted me. Emma just happened to get to him first. It was a shame. Yet, I could hardly blame her for that.

We climbed into my sister's brand new, top-of-the-range Mercedes GLC, the smell of new leather not yet affected by Eva or life, and blending effortlessly now with Emma's overbearing perfume. A box of Jimmy Choos lay in the footwell by my feet, mocking me, laughing at me. I hated how Emma always seemed to come out on top. On top of her game. *On top of my man.* I clenched my fists and my teeth tightly, thinking of Jason pumping into this bitch. Thoughts of his penis anywhere else but firmly inside me, something I could no longer accept.

'Where exactly do you expect me to drive us to, Stacey?' Emma asked. She sounded angry, bitter. She had every right to. I'd committed the ultimate betrayal. Sleeping with her husband was not acceptable. No sister should ever willingly do such a thing. Jason was not a stranger. He was not some random guy I'd picked up at a bar. But my sister's very own man. My brother-in-law. My niece's dad.

She smoothed hair that had seen too much hairspray

221

from eyes that had felt the sting of too many tears, checking make-up in a mirror I wanted to ram down her throat. Why the hell did she always look so well presented? *So neat and bloody tidy.* Even with her apparent distress on show, she still retained an air of mystique. I dreaded to think what I must look like at that moment. Hair glued to my face, mascara sliding down my cheeks. Still, it mattered little. This journey would be swift enough. I wouldn't have to endure her company for long.

28

I wasn't entirely certain of my plan initially. I wasn't such a calculating bitch that I had the whole thing mapped out in my head. No. For me, it was more a *take it one step at a time* kind of plan; an, *I'll see what happens next, and just go with it* type of plan. I certainly had no intention of actually speaking to my sister about anything, least of all, Jason or my feelings. Still, I had to keep up this pretence long enough for her to feel comfortable driving into the afternoon rain with a potentially deranged woman in her passenger seat. It was exhausting, pulling off a flawless, impromptu crying act, sobbing into her silken headscarf and wanting to vomit over the thing as I pretended, in my most convincing voice, to be devastated by what I had done. Ashamed, disgusted, terribly sorry.

We hadn't driven far when, convinced by my apparent devastation and needing to unburden herself of thoughts that were no doubt consuming her, Emma pulled over to the side of the road. Her plan was probably to simply turn her attention to me for a moment. To talk. To see what I could possibly have to say for myself that might in any way deserve her undivided and potentially forgiving contemplation. After all, that is what I had expressed an explicit desire for.

'Stacey,' she began to speak. I didn't need to hear it.

'I'm okay. Honestly,' I breathed, every inch of my body screaming to commit murder. I wanted to lean over and throttle her with the very thing I was holding in my hands, to feel her life dissolve beneath the grip of my fingers. 'Let's go to our special place.' I was impressed that, in the midst of everything that had happened, I'd remembered we even had a so-called special place, my earlier memories of Emma, something I no longer wanted in my head. 'We can talk better there.'

I offered a smile I didn't feel like providing. Sleeping with Jason behind Emma's back was one thing. The thoughts that engulfed my mind now were something else entirely. 'I just want us to have some space,' I lied, glad when she pulled away from the kerb, driving again now, unable to see the deceitful smile that had accidentally planted itself across my mouth. 'So we can talk properly,' I added. I had stopped crying. She hadn't noticed.

***

Emma knew where I meant. The old railway line on Wingrove. It fitted that I had asked Jason to meet me there only the previous evening. A place he had rammed into me with such intense emotion, I felt my insides might accidentally pop beneath the force of his passionate thrusts. I swear I could still feel him inside me now. I smiled, forgetting my role, already accidentally giving away my disposition. Emma should not trust a word I said. I stared out of the window, the summer rain fogging the inside of the car, creating a haze that, under different circumstances, might have looked quite beautiful. I couldn't allow Emma to see the satisfaction in my wild eyes. Thoughts of her husband inside –

'Down here,' I instructed, pointing towards a road I knew few people took.

Emma, being as stupid as she assumed I was, did not argue. It was quite pathetic how easy she was to manipulate, to mould like putty. I wondered if that was how Jason had managed to get her to forgive him so swiftly. She was gullible. I sucked in air, unable to believe that Jason would have even desired forgiveness. It was me he wanted, not Emma.

We turned left onto Hell Junction, a fitting name given to this narrow road due to its uncanny knack of causing sudden accidents. I savoured the one about to happen shortly. Today's rain added to the unstable conditions of this unassuming, forgotten old road, nothing more than a dilapidated track. Here was a shameful incident in the making. Emma's perfect car jolted along, hitting bumps every few feet, my nerves tingling, my sister clueless. I glanced at her, wondering what thoughts were swimming through her mind, wondering if she hated me as much as I hated her. I swallowed, took my chance and grabbed the steering wheel, forcing it out of Emma's hands into mine.

225

'What the hell are you doing?' she screamed as the car swerved violently across the bumpy road, into the overgrowth ahead, towards certain death and triumph beyond. It was too late for me to change my mind, too late to develop a sudden conscience, too late to realise my error in the making.

'Saying goodbye,' I spat, glaring into her terrified face. Every inch of venom that had grown in my belly over the last few years was finally allowed to escape before my sister's contorted face. With poisonous intent I forced the car across the track, into an open ditched area that lay adjacent to the road, our sustained speed enough to crash my sister's car with ease. The old disused railway line was some ten feet below us as we sped forward, hidden by tree roots and brambles, rotting vegetation soon to join my sister's rotting corpse.

With perfect timing, I unclipped Emma's seatbelt, absorbing her cries in pure ecstasy as the car trundled towards inevitable catastrophe. It did not matter that she had already applied the brake. It was too late to prevent the inevitable. We tipped violently sideways, my seatbelt secured, yet barely enough to keep my jolting body upright, and I braced for the upcoming impact. I smiled as Emma's body flopped and jolted into the exploding airbags and crushing metal surrounding us.

We came to a halt, tipped sideways, the rail track now entangled with my sister's once prized car, destroying her once prized body, screeching in recoil, rearing in pain I'd callously inflicted onto it. Emma was moaning. Her head was covered in blood, her body twisted, bones broken. *Yet, still very much alive.* Shit. No.

This was not the outcome I needed. Without hesitating, I unclipped my seat belt and lunged forward, grabbing my sister's skull and slamming it against the crumpled side of the driver doorframe as hard as I could. I felt no remorse, no regret, as I plunged my brutish hands into her bloodied crop of hair, tearing out clumps in frantic haste.

I lifted her head again, slamming it hard against the steering wheel that had a deflating airbag attached to it. She let out a single groan, a shudder, nothing more, falling silent beneath the weight of my immeasurable wrath. I hesitated for a moment, allowing this event to consume me. Silence. The feeling of bliss was almost too much, my unstable breath the only sound in my ear.

I pushed my sister's body against the crumpled remains of her door. Her head dangled, her blood fresh and angry against the broken glass beyond. Was she dead? Was it over? Were Jason and I free? I checked for a pulse. Nothing. I held my own breath, the bruising I had sustained perfectly adding to the devastating story I would shortly invent. There were no CCTV cameras here, no witnesses to my actions. Even the birds had retreated to safety. It was the very reason I had chosen this location to play out my sister's last minutes on earth. I smiled, breathing heavy. All was good in Stacey's world.

Turning attention to my own needs, I wiped Emma's sickening blood from my palms, purposefully smearing it across my thumping chest and apparently heartbroken face already covered in tears and snot. It would confirm my story that I had done everything in my power to save my older sister — unable, of course, to do anything more than I had the limited capacity to achieve.

As far as anyone else was concerned with desperation and fear taking hold, I had held her tight, grabbing her blood-soaked hair, shaking her awake, willing her with every breath I had inside my own body, to live. To any outsider, it would look as if Emma had failed to wear her seatbelt, my warnings remaining unheeded, unwanted. There was no way to uncover the truth — the rain disguised many falsities, like a conversation hidden, bitter anger now dissolved.

I had not intended it, but before I left the vehicle, I kicked my sister in the chest, my feet dangling and exposed between discarded words and Emma's now thankfully lifeless body. *Nothing.* No grunt. No groan. No release of held breath. Nothing more than a wobble of flesh, a tiny thud. If any bruising should appear on her ribcage, it would be put down to the impact, the force of the incoming steering wheel. Nothing more.

Once totally satisfied that she was indeed dead, I clambered forwards, my legs feeling a little tender, my heart pumping with adrenaline. I climbed out of the car through the thankfully unaffected passenger door window, ensuring I looked to any potential passer-by as if I'd endured the most horrific day of my life. Listless, devastated, my sister dead, nothing more now to be done about that.

Staggering onto the grass verge, away from the wreckage, away from my evil deed, I allowed my legs to falter, sending me sprawling into the dampened, overgrown grass around me, my body no longer able to sustain my unhinged demonic emotions. Emma had not moved, her still and bloodied body now looking as pathetic as I'd ever seen it. I smiled. It was quite unexpected. Finally, we were free.

29

I stood on shaking legs next to the car that had become my sister's tomb, pressing buttons on a mobile with the strange knowledge that, within the next few seconds, this single call was going to change the course of so many lives, forever.

'Stacey, hey. How are you?' Jason's husky voice reached my ears. He sounded tired. He had no idea of my earlier call to his wife, the fact that I had forced her unwitting to this place, taking her life along with any sanity I might have, at one time, convinced myself I possessed. 'I was just thinking about you,' he sounded cheerful, relaxed, our earlier rampant sex act something neither of us would forget in a hurry.

I gulped, breathing in as much air as I could muster, the need strong in me to sound out of breath, flustered, unable – as far as he was concerned – to comprehend what had happened here only moments earlier.

'Jason!' I screamed, louder than intended, taking myself by surprise. 'You have to help me. Something terrible has happened.' I was impressed by my impish sincerity. I should have been an actress.

'Stacey, shit, what the hell is wrong?' His urgent voice now matched the pace of mine, our thoughts twisting. Frantic words as eager as the sex I couldn't imagine him not providing me, the rest of our lives now lying ahead in keen anticipation.

'Oh my god, Jason, I need you,' I sobbed into innocent ears that could not have possibly known what had occurred in this place, how events had unfolded, how my actions were utterly unforgivable. For all he knew, I simply needed the feel of him inside me again, and urgently, my body unable to survive without his lustful attention.

'Calm down, Stacey, you're not making sense.' He sounded terrified, my disturbing tone doing nothing for his sense of wellbeing or my tattered nerves.

I was glad I sounded deranged. I did not want to make any sense at all in my unhinged rambling, this moment needing to be drawn out for as long as possible. I wanted to ensure it remained inside our heads, locked forever within this instance, this day, a moment that neither of us would ever forget. It also helped my cause that the longer my sister lay in the crumpled car a few feet away, the less chance anyone would have of saving her life, restarting her cold, blackened heart, bringing her back to this world.

'Sorry. I'm so sorry. Jason, oh my god. *Oh my god.*' I was crying now, jumping up and down in order to sound even further out of breath, pretending I couldn't speak properly into my trembling, already broken mobile phone — my distressing lies not yet spoken, but this no longer just another average day.

'Stacey, for Christ's sake, talk to me.' I listened intently to his distraught tone, the wobble in his voice. 'What on earth has happened?'

I took a breath, panting into my mobile as if I couldn't quite believe what had happened. *Oh, the horror*. I honestly should have won an award for my performance. It was flawless.

'It's Emma,' I managed to gasp between desperate gulps for air before *accidentally* dropping my phone into the long grass at my feet. A frantic moment of silence ensued while I pretended to search in the undergrowth, offering no further explanation to my now desperate man. Oh, dear, where was my poor phone?

'Talk to me.' I could hear Jason struggling to understand why I wasn't answering his questions. 'What about her?' I could hear his voice at my feet, yet I could not comprehend the panic and concern behind his quivering tone. Emma was the mother of his child, I guess. He would have held some deep-rooted emotion for the woman, even if it had been merely offhanded nausea. 'Shit, Stacey, say something.'

I took a breath, my plan unfolding, the need to focus now more critical than ever. I had *found* my phone again. I picked it up. 'She called me. She wanted to see me. She was so angry with me, Jason. I couldn't say no. I couldn't leave things the way they were between us. I needed to explain about us. I felt terrible for bursting into your home like that. Upsetting Eva. Acting all agitated and out of character.' It was the performance of a lifetime. Jason absorbed every single, ear-shattering word. 'She asked to meet me. Said she needed to ask me to my face why I would ever hurt her in such a vile way.' My unfiltered words weirdly managed a sudden impact I wasn't expecting. I had indeed hurt her. Killed her, in fact. Ended it all.

'Where is she?' Jason was screaming now, his composure failing.

'We met outside Bailey's Coffee Shop,' I replied, still not forthcoming in any actual details. 'She told me she needed to look me in the eyes while I explained what I'd done to her. I just wanted to explain. I promise. To tell her how much I'd fallen in love with you. That it wasn't my fault.' That was indeed the ultimate truth. No acting ability required. 'It wasn't my fault!' I repeated, screaming into the air around me for effect.

'Where is Emma now, Stacey? And where are you?'

'She told me she wanted us to go for a drive. That we needed some privacy. She was my sister, Jason. I had no reason to believe her motives were anything but sincere. You should have seen the look in her eyes.' I was sobbing again, my throat so dry I almost choked on my own lying words. I still hadn't divulged a damned thing. 'She hated me. She wanted to hurt me.' I remembered my bruises, my aching leg, crying in pain I wasn't exactly feeling, muttering words that told a devastating story. I hated Emma. I was the one who had wanted to hurt her. I was now speaking of my sister in the past tense. Jason hadn't noticed.

'Will you please tell me what the hell has happened?' I could no longer keep the truth from the desperate voice screaming at me from the other side of town.

I slowed my breathing, ready, anticipating Jason's reaction to my following words. Words he couldn't possibly have expected to hear on such an average summer day as this.

'She's dead, Jason. She crashed the car. She wasn't wearing a seatbelt.' I paused, waiting for the revelation to hit home, to hear his response to such algid words.

'What?' I couldn't tell how Jason was taking this unexpected news. I couldn't see his face, look into his eyes.

'I don't think she intended for any of it to happen. She was just so angry with me.' I was laying this on with a trowel. If I were icing a cake, it would have been several inches thick in frosting already.

'Where are you?' Jason was crying now. I could almost hear his hand trembling so much he could barely hold the phone steady, the sound of his wedding ring tapping his mobile conclusively, shocked, devastated.

'Along Hell Junction. Next to the old railway track on Wingrove.' I held my breath, remembering how Jason and I had been here recently, our time in this place so very different. 'I've called an ambulance.' I had done nothing of the sort. I wasn't completely stupid. I needed to ensure my sister had been dead too long, nothing for them to do but place her body in a bag and take it away.

'Stay exactly where you are. I'm on my way,' Jason hung up before I could say anything further. Yet, I didn't need to. I'd said it all.

***

I stood next to Emma's wrecked car, waiting for Jason to arrive, scoop me into his arms and take me home. Home. The very idea created a weird warmth inside my brain that helped ease the otherwise unimaginable magnitude of this day. We had all the time in the world now. No more distractions, nothing to ever take him away again from my willing, open arms. Emma's death had been an accident. Too angry to remember her seatbelt. Too bitter to carefully watch the road ahead.

I allowed a few more moments to pass before I dialled 999, carrying out a flawless and emotional account of what had happened to the kind operator who took my call, knowing my voice was being recorded, the poor woman believing she was keeping me calm while swiftly dispatching a crew of emergency workers to our location. I hoped Jason would not arrive ahead of the ambulance. I needed this to appear convincing, everything unfolding naturally. I literally could not have planned it any better.

By the time the ambulance arrived, the police were already at the scene, and Emma was now well and truly dead. I was elated, amazed at how I was able to keep my unchecked emotions to myself, unable to fathom how I wasn't giving myself away to these strangers. My parents would be devastated. It was an unfortunate side effect of my flawlessly performed efforts. Eva would now grow up without her mother. That, too, equally unfortunate, unavoidable. But I'd had to do it — for all our sakes.

My parents would never again suffer their selfish daughter's demands for a constant babysitter. Jason would never again feel obliged to stay with a wife we both knew he hated. Eva was only two. She didn't yet really know her mother. I would take care of her now, and of course, any brothers and sisters who should happen along the way. We would be a family, strong, supportive of one another's needs.

The ambulance crew brought my sister's body out from the wreckage, laying it carefully on a stretcher, covering her from view, away from my prying eyes. Jason arrived moments later, his car displaying obvious signs of speeding, mud splattered against the side panels, his mind in pieces, his nerves shattered. In the rain, I had feared for his safety. I had only just secured our incredible future together. It certainly wouldn't do for him to leave me now, so quickly and with such poor timing.

He raced towards me, already wrapped in a tin-foil blanket. I must have looked a picture, my arms and face showing angry signs that I had been involved in a severe crash, blood that wasn't my own set against a trembling tear-stained backdrop. I knew Jason would never be angry with me. It wasn't my fault we had fallen in love. The accident wasn't my fault. It had ultimately done us a favour. Our lives would no longer be infused with that woman's constant need for attention.

'Stacey,' Jason yelled as he ran, the police momentarily preventing his approach before he told them who he was. He hugged me. I hugged him, allowing every inch of pent-up emotion to dissolve in his arms. I was crying again. This time it was real. He kissed my head, witnessing his wife's blood smeared across my dampened skin.

'I did everything I could to help her,' I sobbed into his chest. 'But I couldn't get her out. I couldn't help her, Jason. I couldn't do a thing.' I was emotional, trembling, my body releasing adrenaline that now threatened to make me vomit where I stood, but such a reaction they would have innocently mistaken for shock. Jason stroked my hair, his own body trembling in the late afternoon haze. Everyone understood that it had been an accident. Tragic, unbelievable, devastating. 'Why didn't I make her wear a seatbelt?' I chastised myself over and over, needing Jason to fully believe that I blamed myself for this wholly avoidable tragedy.

'None of this is your fault, honey,' Jason muttered, his voice wobbling, emotions unstable. He couldn't bring himself to look at the covered body, already in the back of the ambulance, nothing further to be done.

'I only wanted to explain,' I sobbed. That part was genuine, at least.

'I know, I know.' I'm not sure which of us he was trying to convince. Me or himself? I knew he hadn't always hated Emma. He must have even loved her once. I leaned over and vomited on the ground. I could do without those kinds of images in my head, thank you very much.

***

We arrived at the house in a daze. Eva was still at the local nursery, Emma meant to have collected her by now, her unexpected non-arrival not yet explained, Jason not able to absorb the fact that his daughter remained forgotten somewhere in the caring hands of strangers. He unlocked the front door, allowing me entry to a home that was now mine. My flat would soon be forgotten and free of my possessions, my suffering, my isolation. I stepped inside, taking a breath, scents of fresh flowers and plastic air freshener pure ecstasy to my senses. *My home.* Mine and Jason's. I smiled, realising my error before promptly changing it to a sob.

'I can't go in,' I lied, reeling backwards into my lover's awaiting arms.

'It's okay, Stacey,' he soothed, his own pain thankfully lost to my needs. 'I'm here.' We stepped inside the house together, my hand in his, Jason closing the door behind him, tears perched ready. That simple act was a symbol of our future. A door had closed on his relationship with Emma, opening now to a brand new future with me. It was absolutely perfect. I turned around in a hallway where we had once laid naked and exhausted, not entirely able to stop myself grabbing onto Jason tightly for fear I might lose my footing completely, this moment too much.

My trembling was real, at least. I didn't have to fake that. Call it adrenaline if you like. Whatever it was, it helped cement my position and my apparent tragic mourning for a sister I seemingly felt terrible at having scorned so severely. I wanted him inside me then but didn't dare assume my advances would have been appropriate under the circumstances. That could wait until later, my vulnerabilities in my man's arms something I knew he could never resist.

We headed to the kitchen where, instead of making love, we made tea and phone calls to friends and family — our news creating havoc and devastation, anyone unfortunate enough to hear our pained words becoming overcome with instant grief. I remained calm, my performance outstanding, but the prospect of my parents' muffled screams along a phone line I couldn't hide behind forever was too much for me. Jason phoned them. I didn't have the strength to tell them what had happened, what I had willingly created. I genuinely loved my parents. I couldn't lie to them in such a cruel way. They came to the house swiftly, collecting Eva on their way.

When Jason opened the front door, my mother's unfiltered cries echoed in my ears, forcing my brain to recede from the events unfolding. I told myself constantly that I had done the right thing, the only thing, in fact, that needed to be done, but my mother's sobs were entirely unable to silence my unhinged brain.

30

When the house had once again fallen silent, the afternoon drifting into evening, I allowed myself a moment to catch my breath. The police had arrived to officially confirm my sister's death and take a statement from me. My parents' grief was undeniable. My mother's intense need to protect her granddaughter meant she insisted that Eva stay with them for a day or two. To allow Jason to reflect upon the day's event with no distraction, to grieve in peace, or so she said. The reality was that my parents simply needed a way to retain a piece of their eldest daughter — a way to keep her close, now that she was no longer with us. I dared not spend too long considering their desperate turmoil.

The day had unfolded in a way no one could have expected, myself included. Had I seriously wanted my sister dead? If I thought about it honestly, yes, I had thought of the idea on many occasions. Was I glad she was now actually dead? Yes. Yes, I was. Because now Jason was one hundred per cent mine. And she could never come between us again, no matter what. I, of course, would need to be strong now for my man. Strong for my parents. I could do that. It was the least I could do for the people I loved.

'Are you okay, honey?' Jason kissed me on the head as he placed two coffee mugs on the kitchen table. I had been absently enjoying the moment of silence, our home now peaceful, grief and sorrow temporarily gone from these walls, Jason's quiet manner and bloodshot eyes not requiring my immediate attention.

I nodded. 'Just tired,' I replied honestly, needing nothing more now than to curl up in a warm bed with Jason by my side, the security of our relationship complete. I yawned, hoping he would take the hint, whisking me off to bed. Our bed. In our beautiful home.

'What a day?' he offered, sitting down next to me, coffee mug in one hand, packet of cigarettes in the other. He must have thought he could now smoke freely with Emma no longer here to tell him otherwise. I didn't look at him. I didn't want to see the constant tremor in the corner of his mouth, the way he struggled to take a sip of his coffee without spilling it to the floor, his eyes that now appeared black, darkened by a feeling of sorrow I had bought about.

I leaned into his shoulder, a heady mix of adrenaline and aftershave swirling around my mind, along with thoughts of bashing my sister's head against an unforgiving door panel. I closed my eyes and shuddered. I couldn't believe it had been so simple. So perfect. I didn't wish to give away my position, to accidentally let slip that I was beyond happy in my moment of planned bliss. I was meant to be grieving, after all, not dancing on the ceiling because I finally had my man all to myself, free from the woman I hated. I sighed.

'I might go up,' I whispered, not even touching my coffee. I needed only one thing now to complete this perfect day, and it certainly wasn't coffee. 'Coming?' I ran my hand gently along Jason's spine, hoping I would need to say nothing more for him to rise, take me upstairs and ravage my body until I could no longer move a single muscle. Sleep would come swiftly once Jason had come swiftly. *Heaven.*

'In a minute.' He glanced at me as I got to my feet, his cup gently trembling in his hand me, an unlit cigarette sitting on the table in front of him.

Shit. No. 'Jason, come on. I'm so tired.' *Take the fucking hint, man.*

'I said I'll be up in a second, Stace. I'll just drink this first.' I tried not to notice that he was on the verge of breaking down in tears, the tightness behind his words, the shortness of his response.

I sighed. Jesus Christ. When had coffee and tears become more important than what I could offer him? 'Okay,' I whispered, slightly irritated, unable to resist the urge to run my hand across his chest, down towards his —

'Stacey, come on,' Jason pulled away, a look on his face I hadn't seen before. Was it stress? 'I'm not in the mood right now. Please.'

How the hell could he not want me? Jason always wanted me. I was irresistible to him. We both knew this. And today, I had done what needed to be done in order to prove my love for him. Performed the ultimate sacrifice. Surely he could return the favour and focus on what *I* now needed?

'I can get you in the mood,' I whispered, kissing his forehead, his ears, forgetting the grief I was meant to be experiencing in the giggle I allowed to emerge unapologetically.

He got to his feet, making his way over to the sink, taking his barely touched coffee and pouring it straight into the plughole, allowing liquid to slosh around the sides of an otherwise perfectly sparkling sink unit. *Yes. That's more like it.*

'You go on ahead. I'll be right behind you. I'll just tidy up a bit first.' Jason didn't sound his usual happy, eager, desperate-for-sex self. I sighed. *Well, he has just lost his wife. I guess it was bound to have some kind of impact. As long as it wasn't an all-night impact.* I had an impact of my own to make on him.

'Okay, babe,' I said with a smile I was glad he didn't notice, leaving him to clear away plastic cartons from our earlier take-out meal, along with cups of half-drunk tea left by the grieving relatives I'd endured in silence, still dotted around the kitchen, an unwanted reminder of the day. I headed swiftly upstairs for what I had hoped would be the best sex we had ever experienced. With no more Emma Problema to distract him, we were now free to enjoy each other like never before.

He wouldn't have to worry about answering unwanted text messages or inappropriate calls from her that arose, all too often, in the middle of our urgent lovemaking. And, more importantly, I would now never have to return to that bloody flat. Life literally couldn't be more perfect. Yes, we had the funeral to get through. But after that there would be no stopping us.

I lay in bed for forty-five mind-numbing minutes, my freshly showered naked skin waiting patiently beneath sheets I had changed a mere hour earlier. I did not want the stench of that woman anywhere near us ever again. I lay with thoughts in my mind as to what I was going to do to him. Maybe take another shower with him. Maybe just rip off his clothes. When he didn't come to bed, I climbed out and slipped on Emma's silk robe that I secretly loved and would now become mine, along with every designer outfit in her wardrobe. I sprayed it with perfume so that I smelled divine, irresistible, not dwelling on the fact that most of Emma's clothes would be too small for my frame, including shoes that would probably remain in boxes for the next ten years untouched. It was all immaterial at that stage.

I ventured downstairs to find Jason sitting on the sofa, in the dark, staring into space. 'Hey, you?' I said, flicking a light switch and plunging the room into soft focus. 'I thought you were coming to bed?' I tried to hide my irritation at the fact that I'd waited for him to no avail. I hated waiting, especially when I was gagging for a Jason session. He turned towards me, tears in his eyes. *Oh my god. Was he crying?* My tone darkened. 'What's going on?' I no longer sounded fragile. I didn't care.

'Sorry,' he whispered. 'Just been a long day.'

I walked up to him, untying my freshly perfumed robe, allowing it to drop to the floor. I could do that now quite confidently. No one was going to walk through the front door and disturb us. *My* front door, now actually. I didn't care about Jason's feelings at that point. The only emotions requiring attention were mine. I stood naked and wet in front of him. Waiting.

'I was waiting for you,' I said, my sultry tone returning, my body throbbing. I felt my legs open slightly, anticipation growing along with what I hoped would be Jason's willing penis.

'Not now, Stacey,' Jason closed his eyes, not even looking at me. *What the fuck?*

'Jason, come on.' I seriously hoped I wouldn't have to ask twice.

'Stacey, please.' He clearly wasn't in the mood, yet I wasn't about to let that stop me. I needed the release that came only with what my man could offer me. The day was buzzing inside my mind, and I needed it to stop. I lowered my body onto his, opening my legs, giving him a full, uncensored view. I straddled him, pressing my breasts against his face.

'Please, stop it,' he snapped, grabbing my arms, pushing me away roughly. The backs of my legs caught the coffee table behind me. It only egged me on all the more.

I laughed, kissing his nose, probing my tongue into his mouth. 'Come on. You love it when I'm naughty,' I breathed, needing him inside me now more than ever, requiring his urgency, his desire. This day needed a satisfying completion.

Jason glared at me then. A cold stare telling me he thought I'd completely lost my mind. 'Are you mad?' he asked, quite seriously. 'Emma died today, and all you can think of is sex?'

Yes. Actually, sex with you is all I will ever need. I pouted, touching my breasts in expectation, an aggrieved smile appearing on my face, lips parting, tongue protruding. 'Don't you want me?' I sounded like a sulky teenager instead of a grieving sister.

'You know I do, but –'

'Then just *fuck* me.'

It was as if I had flicked a switch inside Jason's mind because, without speaking another word, he grabbed me firmly, dragging me to the floor and spreading my legs. He unzipped his trousers, jamming his still flaccid member against the closed skin of my vagina, stabbing at me hurriedly as if he wanted this whole thing over and done with as quickly as possible. I felt a sharp pain as he forced entry, ramming me with hard thrusts that hurt. I cried out in a muffled pain, not expecting such a violent reaction to such an innocent request. He usually at least found my opening with a free, if not slightly clumsy, hand first.

Jason thrust and grunted on top of me, grabbing my face and neck as he pressed his palm over my mouth and eyes, unable to look at me. There was no love in his actions as he pounded heavily against me, my body at his mercy, my hands unable to appease him. I lay still while he emptied himself into me, quick lunges and cries of frustration the only emotions I was offered. Then he simply pulled out of me, stood up, zipped up his trousers and left me, legs spread wide on the floor, unsatisfied and in shock. *What the hell was that?*

***

Trembling, I got to my feet, my body throbbing with a sex act that felt more like rape. I usually enjoyed it rough. We both did. His unrelenting urgency was something my brain had developed a need for, not unlike the very air we breathed. But this wasn't love. This wasn't right. Jason's hands were usually all over me, not around my throat, over my face, closing my mouth as if he wanted to suffocate me. I pulled on my robe, hands trembling, body aching as I went into the kitchen to find him, head in hands, leaning against the sink.

'What the fuck was that?' I snapped, unable to fully appreciate what had just happened. I was used to Jason's eagerness, his limited sustainability, swift thrusts of keen passion. But this felt different. This felt painful, angry, as if he wasn't really there at all.

'You got what you wanted, didn't you?' he spat back, unable to look me in the face.

'Not like that, no.' It was an honest reply. I had wanted so much from him. I had sacrificed everything for him. I thought he wanted the same.

He turned to look at me, tears in his eyes. 'I tried to tell you I wasn't in the mood.' He allowed himself the freedom to cry as tears fell to his cheeks unrelenting. I felt sorry for him then. He was standing, quivering in front of me, looking more schoolboy than seductive male. I walked over and hugged him. He hugged me back. It had been a moment of madness. I knew how much he loved me, how much I usually turned him on. This wasn't the Jason I knew and adored. Emma had done this to him. Even in her absence, my sister had taken this moment, turning it bitter, just like everything else she touched.

'I'm so sorry, honey,' he sobbed into my shoulder as we stood holding each other. He was trembling. I could tell how sorry he was. I loved him. And that was all that mattered.

31

We lay together in bed that night, Jason's head against my shoulder. I didn't ask for sex again. I didn't dare. I knew, when things settled down, he would once again become his usual passionate self. For now, I could wait. I congratulated myself on achieving such an incredible thing. I had my man. I had my perfect home. Now all I needed was to confirm my pregnancy and life would be complete.

I was fully aware that I had lied to Jason about being pregnant, yet I didn't assume that would be an issue. Judging by the number of times he had relentlessly pumped into me, I merely needed to wait for the due date of my next period to confirm the baby was real. I fell asleep listening to his gentle breathing, the house quiet, my body aching from an earlier sex act I couldn't get out of my mind. This was the first official day of our lives together. We had all the time in the world to create perfection.

The following morning, I awoke with a renewed sense of vigour that seemed to rub off on my man. Jason leaned over and kissed my cheek, apologising for his actions the previous evening, rising to take a shower without attempting to ravage me. I presumed he felt embarrassed. I considered joining him in the bathroom, wet bodies creating a connection neither of us could deny. I walked up behind him, kissing his shoulder playfully. He turned, pulled me close, stroked my hair. We were both naked. This was only ever going one way. I smiled, and we spent the next fifteen minutes in that bathroom; the only indication that would have told a soul we were in there were the constant moans, giggles and grunts from behind a firmly closed door. It was as if Emma had never existed at all. Bliss.

***

I was glad it was Saturday. There was always something about the weekends that made me happy, especially now, with Jason, in my new home, my new life beginning in earnest. I needed to retain my subtle grief, of course, my sister's body not yet cold. But, secretly, inside, I wanted to race through the entire house, cleaning everything in sight, clearing out cupboards, moving boxes of belongings from my old flat to my new home, throwing out everything that once belonged to Emma. Although we hadn't openly discussed the idea of moving in together, it was something I knew didn't need addressing. Of course I would be moving into the house. Where else would I rather be? Where else would Jason rather I be? He needed me. And I needed him.

We made toast and coffee, and I turned on the radio,

hoping to lighten the heavy atmosphere that this place had developed with simple, unbiased background noise that I hoped might, for a moment, settle a lingering unease. Although we had enjoyed a morning of lustful abandonment, Jason remained subdued, and, as much as I tried hard to match his quiet tone, I knew I wouldn't be able to keep up this pretence forever.

I acted the perfect, adoring, understanding girlfriend. Compassionate, gentle, yet secretly angry that none of our friends or family even knew we were together, already a couple. It was a charade, a fake. I was fully aware that I had to maintain my grieving act, convincing everyone that I was as devastated by Emma's demise as they were. It was a difficult time for everyone.

We had visitors that morning in the shape of Jason's parents, who had driven from Scotland to be with their son at this tragic time, and my own parents, who had brought Eva home to spend some meaningful time with her daddy. She was missing him, apparently, unsettled, spending most of the night crying. It's strange what kids pick up on, although I secretly assumed it had been my mum up all night crying. She looked as if she hadn't slept.

I hated the house being so full. When it was just the two of us, we could walk around in next to nothing, acting out any fantasy we might choose to invent. I loved to play games. It was my thing. Jason was my sex slave, and I was his bitch, a whore who loved it hard, fast, and as often as I could get it.

The house was now, however, full of saddened faces and words that didn't mean a damned thing to me, conversations about Emma I wanted to race screaming away from in terror. Yes, it is an unfortunate thing that has happened. *Boo bloody hoo for everyone. Now please, can you all fuck off out of my house and leave us alone?* I painted on the most impressive, aggrieved face, behaving traumatised by the previous day's unprecedented and oh, so tragic event. I even went as far as dulling my complexion with Emma's face makeup, rubbing my eye sockets to make them appear as if I'd spent the entire night in tears. I was lucky that Emma's skin tone was a couple of shades paler than mine. I had no problem achieving the devastated sister look.

'Do you want any help in arranging the funeral, Jason?' My mum choked out her words as we stood in the kitchen drinking tea, barely able to contemplate the fact that she was even uttering such nonsensical questions. The back door was open as my mum quietly watched Eva with her other grandparents in the garden beyond, their own grief momentarily relieved by a child they rarely saw. She had the look of a woman whose entire world had collapsed.

Jason sighed. 'I hadn't thought that far ahead, to be honest, Nancy,' he replied, unable to even look at her. She placed an understanding hand on his arm.

'I don't think any of us ever expected to –' My mum couldn't finish her sentence as she brought a hand to her mouth, a sob leaving her body unchecked. I felt sorry for her. She had been caught in the middle of all this nastiness. It was unfortunate that I didn't feel an ounce of sorrow for Emma, but I genuinely felt terrible for my parents. I knew Jason and I would be fine. I would make damned sure of that. But Mum would need a little time to adjust. My dad hadn't said much. I think he was trying to keep it together for my mum's sake.

Mum turned to me then, placing trembling hands around my arm. She looked older than I remembered, as if a single twenty-four-hour period could age a person literally overnight.

'And how are you doing, my darling?' she asked, tears in eyes devastated by what her daughters had suffered together, the previous day still burning strong in her thoughts. Although she was experiencing her own incredible pain, I was impressed she still found the time to ask about mine.

I nodded, swallowing a lump that had accidentally formed, the back of my throat suddenly dry and hollow. 'I'm okay, Mum,' I answered. It was true, of course. I was, in fact, ecstatic, elated. Mum didn't need to know such a truth. She didn't need to appreciate the actual cause of the crash, the genuine reason Emma had been so angry with me yesterday, emotions neither of us could ever now change. I certainly hadn't told the police the truth behind our unavoidable incident, our accident merely occurring during a relaxed, sisterly afternoon together. Only Jason was partly aware of my somewhat wayward version of events. It was Emma's fault. It was all Emma's doing. She wasn't wearing a seatbelt. She was angry with me.

As far as the rest of the world was concerned, we had simply decided to take a detour along that old disused road, our afternoon spent in otherwise perfect sisterly bliss, our laughter meaning that neither of us noticed the impending danger. Wingrove was a favourite spot where we used to play as kids, and we were caught out by typical British weather and a hazardous situation neither of us could have predicted. It was entirely coincidental that the weather had worked in my favour. In fact, no one would now ever know anything different.

Unable to partake in our small talk and unwilling to show emotions he struggled to keep hidden, Jason headed outside to spend time with a family he rarely saw, leaving my mum and I to catch up in the kitchen. I didn't know what to say to him, how to make this better.

'I still have no idea why you ran off like you did last weekend, Stacey,' Mum queried as I poured her a fresh cup of tea. At least she had stopped crying. I could tell she was glad that we were alone, troubled words no longer able to remain unspoken. 'I was leaving you messages for ages. What happened?'

She was whispering now, unwilling to share such thoughts with the unsuspecting ears of her son-in-law. She undoubtedly assumed my running out like that had something to do with my sister, possibly about what had happened to her afterwards, questions in her head we both knew she had no place for. So much had happened since last weekend. My life felt like a bloody whirlwind. Last weekend Jason was with Emma. It was driving me crazy. This weekend, Emma was gone. My head was spinning.

'I wasn't feeling very well, Mum, that's all,' I replied, congratulating myself for not having to lie to her. Everything I was saying today was the truth. I was indeed okay. And, I had been feeling ill last weekend. I was sick to the pit of my stomach by the thought of my man with another woman — even his wife.

Mum nodded, something in her manner telling me she didn't entirely believe me but was willing to let it go anyway. She had enough on her mind as it was. 'You look tired,' she added then, her maternal instinct still as strong as ever, despite my sister and I heading into our thirties, no longer the children she would always treat us as.

'I am tired, actually,' I replied, keeping most of my thoughts to myself. I was exhausted, in truth. Jason's sex acts were keeping me fully absorbed. I loved every single moment of it. I wanted to tell her about Jason, about our unwavering devotion for each other, about the baby I knew was already growing in my belly. I wanted to tell her that he hadn't been happy with Emma for quite some time. Yet, where would I begin?

Would she question the truth of my sister's untimely death? My presence with her yesterday was certainly significantly less innocent than I had led my parents and everyone else to believe. Mum might correctly assume we had not enjoyed the simple afternoon drive together that I had painted a colourful picture of, everyone else believing my misplaced words. If she had any idea at all about what Jason did to me when no one else was looking, she would have hit the roof. Even Jason had been told a pack of lies about his wife's death. Lies meant only to protect us all.

Mum drank what was left of her tea, carefully washing her used cup under the tap and leaving it to dry upside down on the draining board. 'Do you want us to drive you home when we leave?' she asked, unaware of dark emotions lingering in the murkiest corners of my mind.

Most definitely not. I live here now, Mum, didn't you know? 'No,' I answered too quickly, realising I'd made myself appear skittish, sly. Mum would not understand why I had moved in with my sister's widower the very day after her death. 'I told Jason I would help with Eva for a few days,' I said, forgetting for a moment that Mum had already confirmed that her granddaughter would be staying with them. 'He's not coping as well as he tells everyone.' I glanced out of the window, not needing Jason to overhear my thoughts on his current fragile state of mind. Wow, I should seriously consider that career change. Hollywood, here I come.

Mum nodded. 'You're a good girl, Stacey,' she sighed, leaning in for a hug that I suddenly needed as much as she did. *A good girl?* It wasn't a name I would call myself. Desperate, maybe. Horny as hell most of the time, definitely. But good? Perhaps now that Emma was gone, I could finally discover who I was. I would no longer have to live in my sister's shadow. That had to be a good thing. Didn't it?

***

Two days later, Jason arrived home after collecting some of my belongings from the flat I no longer wished to be anywhere near. My flat was small, pokey, ugly. Not at all like the open, bright and spacious house I now called mine.

'I couldn't find Sylvester,' he told me, struggling with a suitcase and three boxes from the car.

'Oh?' I answered, not really listening.

'When was the last time you saw him?' he asked, sounding puzzled, worried.

'Mm?' I asked casually, unconcerned. I most certainly did not wish to tell Jason where Sylvester was. I couldn't even bring myself to look at him as he manoeuvred a heavy box across the hallway floor. The last time I saw that cat was the day I'd smashed my flat to pieces. The day I thought Jason was going to leave me forever, choosing my bitch of a sister over me. I assumed he hadn't looked inside the wheelie bin. I don't think he would have understood what I had to do.

'Oh, he'll be okay,' I chided with a half-hearted laugh, unconcerned by the fact that I didn't appear worried. I picked a candlestick out of the now discarded box, placing it next to a vase of dried flowers on the hallway dresser. 'That cat has a way of surviving the craziest of things.' I hadn't thought much about that poor unsuspecting creature until now, Jason consuming my every waking thought. I straightened my candlestick, glad it looked perfect next to a seemingly matching vase, before walking into the kitchen, unable to look at Jason for fear of what he might see behind my silent eyes. I was beginning to feel a little guilty. Thoughts of Sylvester's terrified squeals made their way into my mind as I ran hot water over a dirty mug.

32

The funeral came around swiftly, hardly giving me space to breathe. Even after death, it seemed, my sister still had a way of intruding on my life. Mum had arranged a simple service, her grief unable to bring about the lavish celebration of a life that my sister's money could have actually afforded, Jason unable to think of such matters at all. The house, usually so full of bright colours and fresh air, now felt stifling and dark. Black moods accompanied black outfits. My time spent in front of my sister's designer wardrobe allowing a private thrill I was ashamed to admit I couldn't tell a soul about.

I had ridden Jason like a Texan whorehouse slut three times that morning, ensuring that, no matter what happened today, he would have only one thought in his mind. *My willing vagina.* We had enjoyed frantic sex in bed the moment I had woken him up, once in the bathroom after he had actually managed to get out of bed, then in the kitchen mere moments before the funeral car and grieving family were due to arrive.

Sandwiches thankfully covered in cling film did not

stand up to my bare buttocks as Jason pumped carelessly into me over the kitchen table, his grief released along with the needy emotions I wasn't aware I possessed until now. I laughed a little to myself as I reshaped several crushed cheese and cucumber triangles. People would be ignorantly eating these things later, unaware of what we did over them that very morning.

Irritatingly, Jason's mum had arrived relatively early to ensure her son was looked after, or so she said, busy downstairs arranging the wake buffet while Jason was busy upstairs with me — not that looking after her son seemed to matter to her from the home they had purchased the previous year in Scotland. Jason barely heard from her, and I had not spoken to the woman since his wedding day some four years earlier. Why would I? Looking after her son was now my job. I knew what love was. Love was sex. And I was most definitely going to make Jason love me today. Love me as if his life depended on it.

We stood in the hallway together, my hand sliding inside Jason's when no one was watching, waiting for the funeral director to bring us out to the car. Everyone was suffering their own private grief, experiencing some personal way of dealing with this thing. Because of this, nobody noticed the wink I offered my man, the knowing smile hiding my lustful imagination. Today, my way of helping him through this painful day was to remind him of what was important. *Us.* Just us, our very own baby and what we could provide each other, our future the only genuine thing that mattered. This day was merely an unwelcome requirement before our real lives could begin. More importantly, it signalled the beginning of the fantastic lifestyle Jason could now provide for me.

I was wearing my sister's black Gucci dress, utterly grateful that I hadn't ruined with my scissors, although it was a little tight for me, I admit. Emma was a comfortable size ten. Eight on a good day, although looking at her prior to her death, it seemed she had lost weight. I usually wavered between a UK size twelve and fourteen, a ten if I shopped around, certain outlets allowing a glimmer of hope that I was a slimmer frame than I actually was. Yet, I certainly wasn't going to allow such trivia into this day, or any other, come to think of it.

I hadn't been able to zip the back, opting instead for a couple of safety pins to keep the thing together, pinned hastily to my bra and pants. I covered it with Emma's beautifully tailored black Prada jacket to hide my shame. It was shaped perfectly around the hips, exaggerating my curves, the expensive cut it was designed to achieve adding to the illusion of perfection. I didn't need to button it. Not that I could have achieved such a thing anyway. I was simply grateful it looked incredible left open, displaying the very dress I had pretended fit perfectly well beneath. I hoped everyone would notice how good I looked.

'You look nice, Stacey.' As if on cue, my mum's ashen face greeted me in the hallway, her sullen features forcing me to release the warm trembling hand I needed to hang on to, my man disappearing into the kitchen in haste. She had been crying again.

I smiled and kissed her cheek. She smelled of lavender and salty tears. I couldn't tell her she looked nice. It wouldn't have been true. She looked as if she hadn't slept for a week. 'Thank you, Mum.' It was all I could offer. 'Are you alright?' I needed to sound as if I cared, at least. To come across as if Emma's sudden departure from our lives had made a profound impact on me, too.

Mum shook her head, fresh tears welling. She pulled a handkerchief from her handbag and wiped her nose. Dad walked up behind her. He looked lost, as if he didn't quite know what to do. 'Hey, Dad,' I breathed, giving him a hug and hoping he wouldn't crush my newly acquired outfit.

'Hey darling,' he replied, kissing both cheeks with a loud sigh. 'Odd day.' He glanced towards the ceiling for a moment as if he hoped, by some miracle, that this day might be merely a dream. A nightmare from which he would soon awake.

Odd day indeed. A bizarre day I needed out of the way as quickly as possible. I nodded. 'Won't be long now.' I have no idea who I was trying to convince. Myself or my poor grief-stricken parents? After today, I could finally come clean about Jason. Tell everyone that we had grown much closer due to the sudden and shocking loss of a once-loved sister. We had been relatively fond of each other for years anyway, our closeness merely developing further. We couldn't help it. He had needed me in his hour of pain, and we had fallen in love. It was nothing more than a straightforward next level in the natural progression of our relationship. I could tell them all about the baby, too, once I'd confirmed that there actually was one.

***

I hate funerals. You can't tell people to have a good time or to hope it all goes well. You merely express condolences at the most appropriate time, nod a constantly sustained sad-looking face and hope the entire event passes quickly with little aggravation. If you are lucky, you might even be able to bring forth the occasional lingering tear. I was most definitely blessed with such emotions today, needing to appear the devastated mourner. However, I attempted to avoid eye contact with most people during the actual service — my sister's coffin glaring at me from the front of the church my mum had hastily chosen for the occasion, my bones threatening to dissolve beneath the glare of a god I wasn't even sure existed.

By the time the funeral was over, my house had become packed full of people I didn't want around me, including family, friends, and Emma's work colleagues I didn't know, didn't want to know. The only thing I needed was for them to all go away. Sophia and her husband John came over to greet us, offering words of sympathy that made me feel sick. I wondered if my continued nausea was due to morning sickness, yet it was still too early for such an assumption.

Lloyd and a few people I had never met stood huddled together, subdued, too quiet. I wondered what would happen with Emma's book now. Due to her sudden death, would it become an overnight bestseller, netting her poor widower a tidy sum? I licked my lips at the prospect. I wanted to ask the very question yet dared not draw such distasteful attention to myself. I needed to appear the pained sister, not the calculating money-grabbing bitch they would assume I was.

I couldn't get close to Jason for a while, his friends and family taking much of his time with false condolences and fake sadness. How could any of these people feel genuine sorrow? *Emma was a bitch; cold, evil.* I shuddered. How could such noxious people draw such attention? All I wanted at that moment was to be with him, alone. To hold his hand. To feel his soft breath against my aching neck. I stood in the kitchen staring into a garden filled with cheap chatter and glasses of even cheaper wine, cups of half-drunk tea in the trembling hands of half-drunken strangers, lemonade on the grass that Eva had spilt an hour earlier.

'There you are, Stace.' I turned to see my mum hovering in the doorway, a plate of sandwiches in one hand, a box of tissues in the other. 'Come with me. Uncle Terry wants to say hi.'

I hate the way families only ever seem to congregate at funerals, weddings, or christenings. No one sees anyone until such events, fake greetings meaning nothing to these people at all. Decades could pass without a single meaningful contact from any of them. *Family,* simply a word that implies a passable connection.

'I just want to be alone, Mum,' I sighed, unable to take my eyes off Jason standing in the garden talking to two women I didn't know. It was true. I didn't need to be distracted by nonsense chatter today. A random female seemed quite happy leaning against my man's shoulder, the occasional private giggle leaving her lips unchecked. *What the fuck was she saying to him? Giggling was my thing, not hers.* I wondered what she would do if I were to walk outside now and announce that Jason and I were together, officially.

'I know it's been a difficult day for everyone,' Mum offered a sigh of her own, matching my subdued tone as she placed the sandwich tray on the table and walked up behind me. 'But we have to be strong for each other.' She nudged me gently, making me turn to face her. 'You have been amazing this last week. Jason told me that if it hadn't been for you, he'd have gone completely stir crazy.'

I smiled then. It was probably the first honest expression my face had displayed in days.

'He said that?'

Mum nodded. 'Yes, he did. I don't know how you do it. You are a little superstar.' She stroked my cheek, meaning every word, making me want to cry in her arms, confess to unforgivable deeds. Jason had confided with my mother that he had needed me. It may not have been a full, devoted declaration of his love for me, but it was a start. He had expressed sincere feelings for me, telling my mum I had played an important role, no prompting, no hesitation.

I was elated. I wanted to race outside, grab him, pull down his trousers and suck his cock in full view of the entire unsuspecting gathering. I would happily handle their gasps amid the eager gasps of my man. We could all gasp together, Jason's length in the back of my open mouth, my parents agog, my gagging enjoyed. I smiled at these impossible thoughts racing through my remorseless mind.

'Please, come and say hi to your Uncle Terry,' Mum offered again, unaware of the distasteful images my brain had now created, oblivious to my inner thoughts and inner desires. 'He's driven a long way to be with us today.'

I didn't want to, but I ventured into the lounge to greet an uncle I'd only ever met a handful of times in my life. By the time I had finished hugging and chatting to almost complete strangers, I was exhausted, my own needs drowned by chatter I didn't feel able to endure much longer. My living room was brimming with sagging bodies draped across my now sagging cushions, and discarded buffet plates, cups, and glasses that would no doubt leave behind rings I would have to swiftly remove or forever be reminded of this godforsaken day. When Jason walked into the kitchen to get another bottle of wine from the fridge, I took my chance.

'Hey, you,' I whispered, walking up behind him and slipping my hands around his waist. 'Save me from these people, please.' I hovered a free hand over the zip of his trousers.

'Don't. Not now,' he snapped, glancing around to check no one could see.

'Relax,' I giggled. 'Nobody cares.'

'Stacey, I buried my wife today. I don't think it would be in any way appropriate to showcase our relationship so blatantly.'

He was right, of course, but I didn't want to hear it. I pouted. 'Meet me in the upstairs en-suite in five minutes?' I needed a release. Jason's release. This day was threatening to devour me.

'No. I can't. We have a houseful of people, Stacey. For Christ sake, calm down.' He was deadly serious but retained a playful tone to his voice that told me he wanted me as much as I wanted him.

I smiled. 'I think we should be honest and tell everyone about us while they are all in the same place.' To me, it seemed the most logical, perfect solution, in the most perfect and logical moment.

'Are you mad?' Jason turned to face me. I was still trying to grab his –

'Not mad. Just pregnant.' I patted my belly, still not even at the point where I could have missed my period, let alone taken an actual test to confirm such a condition.

It did, however, make Jason stop and stare at me. *Had he forgotten about the baby already?* He glanced around, making sure that no one could see, then pressed his lips cheekily over mine. 'We have plenty of time. Today is not the right time.'

I pouted, still wanting the feel of him inside me. 'Fine. Just a quickie, then. Upstairs. Two minutes.'

'Stacey, no.' Jason stepped away from my eager grasp just as his mum walked into the kitchen carrying Eva.

'Daddy, we need a plaster,' Grace was carrying a crying toddler, luckily she hadn't noticed that Jason's fly was slightly open. I zipped it swiftly for him. He seemed grateful.

'Oh, poor baby,' I cooed, stepping away from him, not wanting Jason's mum to witness our momentary embrace. I scooped Eva from my future mother-in-law's arms before whisking her over to the sink. I needed a distraction anyway, with Jason unwilling to play my game. I still had visions of him standing in full view of everyone, his trousers around his ankles, my mouth going to work, frantic, keen.

Grace smiled at me, her genuine gratitude for my presence not going unnoticed by any of them. Together Eva and I chatted. I cleaned the cut on her knee and applied a Mickey Mouse sticking plaster with a kiss and tender words that I hoped made me appear the doting stepmother in front of all our friends and family.

'She is good with her,' I could hear Jason's mum say behind us.

I loved Eva. That was the truth. She was Jason's child. She had grown from his seed. What wasn't to love about that? By the time I had finished caring for my newly acquired stepdaughter, I could feel untethered broody instincts bubbling to the surface. I made some random excuse that I needed to leave the house for a moment to pick up some medication for the whiplash condition I hadn't even experienced, and headed out to the nearest shop to purchase a pregnancy test.

***

I sat alone on the loo seat of our en-suite bathroom, plastic wand in hand, underwear around my ankles, a strong smell of urine in my nostrils, waiting for the white panel to display two neat blue lines. I held my breath. *Come on, come on.* Three long minutes passed, chatter and irritating noise from below making me want to scream into the toilet bowl. I stared at this unassuming piece of plastic, willing it with everything I had inside my body to behave itself and tell me what I wanted to know, what I *needed* to know. Two lines appeared. Faint at first, then thick, dark blue, revealing a truth I had known for almost two weeks.

Yes. Oh my God. It worked. I was pregnant. It was a moment I should have shared with Jason, our elation celebrating this joyous occasion in a burst of ecstatic, if not lustful embraces. But I had told Jason I was pregnant already. He had already shown his happiness with the urgent thrusting of his body that very day. This was a moment, it seemed, that I had to enjoy alone.

33

It's funny how time slips by when you are having fun. Once the unbearable silence the funeral had left behind finally wore off, my days were primarily spent in simple bliss with Jason, our evenings predominantly entwined in each other's arms. Eva was spending most of her time with my parents, and it was as if Emma hadn't existed at all. Or at least, I could pretend. My belly could now become our immediate focus of attention which was all I needed to initiate a plan to make Jason my own.

Four weeks after the funeral, I felt I had allowed enough time to pass, the need strong in me to tell my parents that Jason and I had fallen in love. It wasn't intended, I would confirm, but we had shared a common sorrow. He had needed me, and I had been there for him when he was at probably one of the lowest points in his life. He was a good man, and in the loss of his wife and my sister we had shared common suffering. Jason, of course, did not think it was a good idea. Not yet, he'd said. Yet, when would the best time be? *At our child's first birthday party?*

Jason had been forced to return to work after that initial first week of grief had passed. I, too, reluctantly resumed my duties at the temping agency, a job I couldn't wait to leave once the baby was born. I had avoided my parents' prolonged company since the funeral, their emotions more than I was willing to accept responsibility for. Friends, neighbours, family members who we hadn't seen for years had all graced us with endless casserole pots and pre-made frozen meals, so our time in the kitchen was limited to the warming of pre-cooked food and peeling of tin-foiled lids. It was sheer perfection — time off work given freely, and meals cooked by other people, offered kindly.

It was a shame when the generosity of others began to waver as time passed, Emma's death becoming no more than a perturbing moment in history and reason to question Jason on how he was coping, to ask after Eva's wellbeing, to display ongoing sympathy whenever they him. I hadn't entirely realised how difficult it would be to care for someone else's child, either. As much as I loved my niece – my stepdaughter in the making – no one had told me how naughty she could be. Most mornings consisted of a battle between the two of us, her inability to do anything I asked now beginning to wear thin. Everyone assumed it was because she was missing her mother, and initially, I had to agree. Yet it was slowly beginning to drive me insane. This was not what I'd signed up for.

Jason seemed less concerned by his daughter's antics, adopting instead the role of *Fast Dad*, getting up in the morning to offer his daughter a casual kiss on the forehead before heading off to work, playing with Eva on an evening until he grew too tired, happy to let me put her to bed alone. I didn't like Fast Dad. I needed help with his child. I wondered how Emma had coped with her daughter so well, all alone, her husband too busy for such a significant undertaking. She had mentioned nothing to me about her daughter's problematic behaviour, about Jason's non-committal to the cause. Emma and I rarely shared anything of each other's lives. For the first time in my life, I wondered if there was more to my sister's story. It wasn't a good feeling.

***

By the time I arrived at my mum's house a few days later, Eva screaming for something I couldn't understand, her buggy taking the impact of a child's temper, I had the look of a woman about to pass out. Mum greeted us at the door, her distraught grandchild's cries enough to wake the dead.

'Oh, my poor baby girl,' Mum chimed in, lifting Eva from her pram and cradling her in her arms, face red with tears and saliva I'd been unable to appease.

'I have no idea what's wrong with her today, Mum,' I said, feeling faint, morning sickness now firmly taking a grip I couldn't have anticipated. *Oh, the irony.* 'I just can't seem to settle her.'

'What's the matter with my little angel today?' Mum was bouncing Eva in her arms, the sight of her grandmother's gentle affection, enough for the child to calm a little, sobs of exhaustion the only sound we were thankfully left with. 'You look shattered, sweetheart,' Mum said. *How good of her to notice.*

I needed to tell her about Jason and me, about her unborn grandchild, about the fact that I wouldn't be heading back to my old flat anytime soon, the rent already past due, no intention at all for any payment to be made on it now. I should probably hand the keys back to the landlord at some point; my wheelie bin was now thankfully emptied, no drowned cat to uncover. I looked at my mum. How would I begin to explain circumstances now changed? Would she understand? Did I even care?

'How are you?' I asked, after we had finally got into her kitchen, Eva settled now with a carrot stick my mum thankfully found in her fridge. I didn't need to ask the question. I could see it in her eyes.

Mum shrugged, wiping her granddaughter's face with a tea towel. 'As good as I'm ever going to be, I guess.' She attempted a smile that didn't make it to her mouth, involuntarily creating a kind of quivering lip reaction she tried and failed to hide.

I sighed, unable to offer any words that might ease her suffering. 'And Dad?'

Another shrug. It was apparent that she didn't wish to speak about my father, for now. Dad had a way of dealing with things in his own way, privately, needing no help from outsiders, my mum included. 'Have you been following Eva's diet plan, okay?' she asked then, changing the subject entirely.

Diet plan? I looked puzzled. 'What diet plan?' I had no idea what my mum was talking about. I was fully aware that Emma had this healthy eating thing going on. It was part of her business, and she would have needed to keep up appearances by following her own advice. I had no idea she was pushing that crap onto her kid as well. I almost rolled my eyes.

Mum looked skywards for a moment in apparent exasperation at her son-in-law's failure to acknowledge something I wasn't yet a party to, something she could not hide. 'Surely you know about Eva's needs, Stacey? Emma didn't like to talk about it, I know, but Jason certainly would have explained it to you by now, surely?'

Explained what? I continued to look puzzled, offering no response.

Mum sighed. 'Eva is autistic, Stacey. She needs a precise nutrition plan so that her behaviour doesn't get out of control. She used to have regular behavioural and speech therapy guidance sessions to help with her irritability, inattention, and sleep issues before...' Mum trailed off, unable to finish her sentence. 'Surely you know this. Surely Jason has explained.' Mum honestly looked at me as if I had fallen from the back of a passing truck.

This was news to me? *I'd had absolutely no idea.* 'Eva is autistic?' I questioned, wondering if that was why she was so uncontrollable most days. I also wondered if that was what had kick-started my sister's sudden need to bring veganism into their lives. Or vegetarianism. I get confused which is which. They blend into one, to me. I couldn't live without meat, *especially sausage.* I felt slightly guilty that Eva's breakfast that morning had

273

consisted of chocolate, merely because I was tired of hearing her screams. Jason hadn't said a word.

'Yes, Stacey. Your niece has very specific needs.' Mum gave an exasperated shake of her head, taking a chair at her kitchen table, looking frail, older than I remembered. I joined her, my legs suddenly unstable, oddly filled with rushing blood. 'Emma received the diagnosis last year. Oh, my goodness, Stacey, did she not tell you?'

It was my turn now to shake my head, offering a blank shrug. No. Emma and I did not speak about such important things. The welfare of her family was of no concern to me. In fact, I hardly took any notice of Eva at all until I needed to get close to Jason. It wasn't a good feeling. To be honest, we barely spoke about much at all, if I had anything to do with it, my needs far outweighing anyone else's.

'Well, that certainly explains my little angel's grumpy face.' My mum had adopted her baby voice — the one she'd used on us kids and now saved for her doted-upon grandchild.

Why had Jason forgotten to tell me such an important thing? I surmised that he hadn't been given much time to think about it with everything else going on. Maybe he had forgotten himself? This last month had been more than he could have bargained for.

Mum said, 'Emma kept a blue folder in the kitchen drawer. It contains all Eva's doctor's appointments, home therapy activities, diet plans, et cetera. Everything she needs to look after her child and help her development.' Mum paused. 'Everything she *needed*...'

she corrected, trailing off again.

I had indeed noticed a blue folder. I had, in fact, spilt pasta sauce on it only last week. I'd assumed it was something to do with her bloody nutrition business, being housed in the kitchen and all. I felt terrible then for sliding it back into the drawer and forgetting about it.

'Eva is too young to take medication yet. Apparently, kids need to be over five before the doctors can provide drugs to help with the condition.' Mum was rambling a little, but I dared not switch off just yet. Eva was important to me now.

'Why am I only just finding out about any of this now?' I was a little irritated that my mum hadn't chosen to tell me herself about such an important thing.

Mum shook her head. 'Stacey, you can't be responsible for someone else's child. You have taken on a little too much since Emma –' Mum stopped again, tears ready to fall, everything still raw, too painful. 'I'll have a word with Jason. Your sister used to take care of all Eva's needs. He hardly got involved.' I could see that was true. Fast Dad popped into my head again, irritation developing further. 'You'll be wanting to go home to your flat soon anyway, no doubt, won't you, sweetheart? You can't hold Jason's hand forever.'

She meant well. Of course she did. But she didn't yet know that Jason and I were together. I needed to tell her the truth. I opened my mouth to speak, only for her to cut in first: 'Oh, by the way, speaking of folders, I have something for you.' She got to her feet, rummaged around in a side drawer of her kitchen dresser, and pulled out a flat wallet. She handed it to me.

'What's this?' I asked, noticing the blurry logo of a local bank branch through the transparent plastic. I was in no mood to help with my parents' financial issues. Not today.

'This is yours,' she tapped the wallet, and sat down at the table again. Eva was still happily munching on her carrot stick, orange debris now peppering flushed cheeks.

'Mine?' I didn't understand.

Mum sighed. 'I never anticipated giving this to you under such terrible circumstances,' she breathed, sounding saddened suddenly, thoughts inside a head I couldn't read. A tear appeared and she wiped it swiftly on the same tea towel that Eva had previously smeared carrot juice and snot onto. 'In fact, it was Emma who was meant to be giving it to you. Not me.' Mum looked as if she couldn't believe what she was about to do, her face flush with something I couldn't understand.

I picked up the wallet, unclipping the plastic button on the front, sliding out several bank statements, a bank card still attached to a welcome letter, a PIN letter, unopened, still inside a sealed envelope. The bank card had my name on it. The latest bank statement showed that the account had over sixteen thousand pounds in it. £16,750, to be precise. 'What's this?' I asked, completely taken aback and not at all sure what was happening. *How could this be mine?* I was practically broke.

Mum sighed. 'Emma had been saving this for the last two and a half years. For you, Stacey.' She took a breath, completely shocked that her daughter had failed in her mission to present such an extravagant gift to me herself. 'She was hoping to get it topped up to around twenty grand, then give it to you for your thirtieth birthday, as a surprise.'

What? What the hell was I hearing? I shook my head, feeling as if I had been struck by an oncoming bus. 'I have no idea what you are talking about, Mum?' Emma would never do anything like that for me. *She hated me.* The feeling was entirely mutual.

Mum laughed. A dark laugh that emerged sad, hollow, heartbroken. 'Emma knew how much you wanted to get your degree in law. You talked about nothing else for years. It used to make Emma smile. She used some of the profits from her nutrition business, squirrelling away as much as she could each month. She wanted to surprise you. To help make your dreams come true, because... she loved you.'

I hadn't thought about my law degree for well over a year. I did not believe it would ever be possible. I had no money, no way of ever taking on vast student debt that I might never be able to pay off. *Holy shit.*

34

For a moment, I couldn't speak. I couldn't hear this. I could not have correctly heard that Emma, my evil bitch of a sister, had actually saved money for me? *For me?* I opened my mouth to speak, the sudden and utterly avoidable death of my sibling now beginning to sit extremely uncomfortably in my mind.

'Emma did this?' I mumbled, picking up the bank card, still attached by glue to its original letter, never used. The name, Miss Stacey Adams, was printed neatly on its front. I pulled it away from the paper, rolling a dried blob of glue between my fingers for too long.

'She did, yes. Bless her heart. I told her it was too much, but she insisted. She said that she had never been able to do anything truly nice for you when you kids were growing up, and she insisted that you were to know nothing about it until your birthday.'

'My birthday?' I whispered, turning the card over in my hand, noting it was only a few weeks away now. I could barely take in what I was witnessing.

Mum sniffed, her head nodding. It was as if she had

developed a strange *nodding dog* disorder. 'It took her over a week to sneak your driver's license and national insurance card from your purse when you weren't looking so she could open an account online in your name. It wasn't exactly legal, she knew. Identity fraud and all that. But she was never intending on using the money for herself. It was only ever going to be kept in that account for you.' Mum attempted a smile but changed her mind.

'Jason didn't mention anything about this to me at all.' *Why the hell hasn't Jason told me what Emma had planned?*

Mum scoffed. 'Oh, no. He wouldn't, Stace. He doesn't know anything about it.'

I glared at my mum's ashen face. 'Why not?' Surely if they had been saving such a vast amount of money, Jason would know it.

She sighed. 'Because he would have spent the bloody lot, that's why, Stacey.' Mum picked up our now empty teacups and got to her feet, the kettle suddenly needing to be switched on, unspoken words needing to leave my mum's lips while she had the strength inside her to mutter them. Eva had fallen asleep with carrot juice on her chin.

'What?' What the hell was my mum trying to tell me? *Jason wouldn't do that.* He had his own money. He earned a lot of it, too, judging by the size of the house, the cars, the designer goods.

'Don't worry yourself about Jason,' Mum replied, dismissing her comment as if it wasn't any of our business anyway, that she had said too much. But I did worry about Jason. We were having a baby together.

'You may as well fill me in now,' I said with a laugh that I didn't mean. It didn't even sound like a laugh at all. More like a grunt. I didn't want my mum saying anything bad about the man I adored. *He was amazing.*

Mum filled the kettle, and wiped Eva's sticky lips as she laid a blanket over her now peaceful body. I was glad of the quiet, the solitude, my thoughts racing, uncontrolled, nervous. The child had driven me mad all morning, my mind now threatening to take over from where she had left off.

'Jason is not a very nice person,' Mum confirmed, as if I needed to hear the truth before her confidence left her, that previous dealings with him had been merely out of obligation, necessity, and her relationship with her son-in-law had been nothing more than required because of a daughter she loved.

I wrinkled my brow, anger beginning to bubble inside me that I struggled to subdue. 'I beg your pardon?' I didn't understand why she would say such things. How dare she? *Who the hell did she think she was?*

Mum glanced my way, placing two mugs on the table in front of me. 'I know, I know,' she said, noticing the look of shock on my face. 'He seems nice enough, on the surface. But Emma had problems in her marriage that she did not want anyone to know about. Especially the sister she adored. She would have been mortified if ever you learned the truth.' Mum was busy pouring milk into our cups, unaware of my demonic thoughts. The kettle was boiling in the background, closely matching the rising temperature of my brain.

What the hell was she saying to me? Emma hated me, and I hated her. We tolerated each other, but that was where it ended. I squeezed the plastic card in my hand, running uncertain fingertips over the embossed name, my thoughts now taking a bitter twist. How could she have hated me and yet planned to give me close to twenty thousand pounds as a birthday present? That simply did not make any sense in my brain. You don't hand over that kind of cash to a person you dislike. I wouldn't hand over that amount of money to a person I *did* like. Imagine what I could do with twenty grand. Birthday presents usually consist of a card, perhaps a bottle of perfume or a box of chocolates if you're lucky. *Twenty grand? What the hell?*

I was fully aware of the state of my sister's marriage, though. This was nothing new. Jason had secretly wanted *me* for quite some time. It wasn't my fault that he did not want her. How on earth could I explain this to my grieving mum?

'I know they had issues, Mum. With their marriage,' I offered, needing to share a little of what I knew, at least.

'Oh!' Mum sounded surprised. 'So you *do* know about that?' she asked, releasing a loud sigh and shaking her head as if grateful we both now knew of Jason's misdemeanours and that she wasn't coming across as a moaning, rather annoying, gossipy mother-in-law. 'You know all about his cheating?'

I sucked in my breath, sharply — too sharply. I was fully aware that Jason had indeed turned to me in his time of need. No one else could have given Jason what I had to offer him. I wondered how long my mum had known about Jason and me. How was she able to keep so calm about it all? Why was she not just coming out with it and confronting me head on?

'When did Emma tell you?' I hung my head, chewing my bottom lip. I had to assume she was referring to me. I was shocked that my mum hadn't confronted me about this earlier. Her outspoken personality meant she would usually be unable to avoid unprovoked anger in such matters, especially where her precious eldest daughter was concerned. Maybe it was the grief. Everything had become too much for her recently. I wasn't at all surprised that Emma would have already told her all about Jason and me, though. The look on my sister's face that day outside the coffee shop is something I will never forget. I expect she loved every second of it, too. Sharing tales of my woeful infidelity with our mum. Words of my betrayal allowed to trip from bitter tongues, along with the taste of bitter tea.

Mum scoffed again. 'Oh, Stace. When *didn't* your sister tell me about what was going on with Jason? I dread to think how many times that poor girl called your dad and me, late at night, in tears, poor Eva often asleep in her arms, nowhere else to go. That man put her through so much. He had a wife and a child. It wasn't right what she used to let him get away with.'

What? What the hell was I hearing now? Jason and I had literally only begun our relationship a few weeks ago — a mere two weeks, in fact, before my sister's death. How could Emma have possibly told my parents about us before then? Shit. Maybe she suspected something brewing much earlier. Maybe Jason had failed to hide his feelings for me, and Emma had discovered his intentions before we had even got together.

'Sorry, Mum, I don't understand,' I muttered, unsure exactly what my sister had told her.

'I thought you just said that you knew. Jesus Christ, Stacey, where do I start? Jason must have cheated on Emma at least half a dozen times during this last year alone. And I dread to think about the ones Emma didn't tell us about.' I gulped. Mum continued, oblivious. 'The one-night-stands, the fumbled bunk-ups when he was meant to be working late. Those unexpected working weekends away that seemed to happen without any prior notice. Dad even gave him a black eye once for messing her around so much.'

I couldn't breathe. I remembered Jason having a black eye last year. He had joked it had been a skiing accident. Mum continued, unaware that my world was unravelling around my ears. 'If he knew your sister had over sixteen grand in a separate bank account, Stacey, he would have cleared it out in no time.' She poured hot water into our mugs, the milky texture swirling with tea I no longer wished to drink.

I shot her a look. 'Why?' I could barely speak.

'All that bloody designer crap he wears.' I glanced at the Louis Vuitton bag on the floor that he had bought me only last week. 'Emma's money, mostly,' Mum muttered, totally unaware that I was silently dying inside. 'Whenever he finished spending what wages he had on himself, he started on hers — poor bugger. Emma had to work twice as hard just to pay the bills because she knew he wouldn't help. She barely made ends meet most of the time. Your sister was desperate to keep her marriage together. For Eva's sake more than her own.' Mum looked at me. 'How do you not already know all of this?' She simply had no concept that her daughters did not share their experiences and problems in life.

'That can't be true, Mum,' I scoffed, unable to believe such disgusting nonsense. 'That house is huge. Emma had a successful business, and Jason earns a fortune.' *Plus, he was no cheat.* However, the irony of this assertion wasn't entirely lost on me, considering he had been, in fact, cheating on my sister *with me.*

'The house is just a show, Stacey. Haven't you figured that out yet? It's all about making Jason *look* good. Emma was making herself sick with stress over the debts *he* ran up. She had lost so much weight since Eva was born. I dread to think of the state of his finances now she's gone. I worry about this little one.' Mum stroked Eva's hair, carrot juice drying, my mum's trembling hand hovering over her tiny fingers.

I swallowed. I hadn't even asked about his finances. I assumed he had it all under control. Besides, I didn't think it was any of my business, other than what he was spending on me. I touched my belly — my child growing unawares. 'But Emma was a successful author, a businesswoman.' It was true. She had said so herself.

'Emma would never want you to look at her differently, Stacey. She was your big sister. She wanted you to see her only through loving eyes, someone you could look up to. But Emma's business was hanging by a thread. It barely covered the bills. Have you ever tried to get people to understand the true concept of healthy eating?'

I gulped, knowing I often chastised her outlandish viewpoints on the issue of food myself. Food was food, as far as I was concerned. You stuff it in at one end, and it comes out the other. What more to the equation is there?

'Jason would insist she purchase designer clothes that she hated wearing, when her child needed simple things like formula and nappies. It was merely his way of making himself look good in front of other people. Successful. One of the high rollers.' I wanted to hide my expensive Jimmy Choo shoes beneath my mum's table, her words too much. I hoped my Louis Vuitton bag remained unnoticed, forgotten. I resisted the urge to slide it behind my foot. 'The man is a show-off, Stacey. Loves the attention.'

'And her book launch?' I felt sick.

'Oh, that. She was self-publishing her first book as part of her dietary business. She was so excited. It had taken her over four years to write it, too, bless her. As you know, nutrition was her thing, and that book was meant to educate the general public on how to eat healthily on a reasonable budget while enjoying all the foods most people like to consume. But it cost her money that Jason didn't want her spending. The only reason she wanted to do it at all was to generate a little more income for Eva and to keep a roof over their heads.'

'But Lloyd is –'

'Nothing more than a good friend. A very good friend who offered to edit her book when she had no one else to ask. I don't think she was even paying him. The poor guy was helping her out of the kindness of his heart.'

Paying him? Wasn't it meant to be the other way around? I assumed the guy was a part of some giant publishing company. I felt sick, really sick. 'Mum, I have something to tell you.'

'What's wrong, sweetheart?'

'I'm pregnant.' I leaned over and vomited onto my Mum's freshly washed floor.

35

As expected, my mum was appropriately shocked by my revelations, the endless questions that followed about who the father was, quickly becoming too much for my frazzled mind to deal with. When I refused to look her in the eyes, she realised swiftly that Jason and I had done something unforgivable, launching into a lecture I could have done without.

'Stacey, you didn't?'

'Mum, please.'

'What the hell were you thinking?'

'We couldn't help it.'

'By, *we*, I take it, you mean you and *Jason*?'

No response.

'Oh my God, Stacey.'

I had no idea what she assumed I could do about this situation. I swallowed a lump, still unable to form any words.

'And Emma? What did she have to say about it all?' Mum raised her head skyward, shaking it from side to side as if trying to bat away an annoying fly.

My continued silence kick-started a fresh wave of upset, my mum crying about how her baby had been scorned by the sister she thought loved her.

'Was she angry with you? The day she died?'

'No.'

'Did she crash that car because of you?'

'No!'

I felt sick. Everything my mum was saying to me was too much. I couldn't sit and listen to words about my man that I had no idea if they were true or not. I couldn't calmly digest theories about Emma's death or my mum's misplaced thoughts about the entire situation. I felt ill enough as it was. Eva was still unsettled, and the news of her autism created a lump in my throat that had nothing to do with what I'd eaten for breakfast or the baby growing in my belly.

I knew, of course, that Eva wasn't yet able to communicate very well, her young age telling nothing of the hidden condition I'd failed to notice. She was naughty. All kids are. Some days were worse than others. Some nights were virtually impossible. But I simply could not understand why Jason had failed to tell me something so important. I concluded that he assumed Emma already had. I sat in my mum's kitchen, listening to tales of Jason's apparent infidelity, Emma's secret saving of money that I had no idea about, stories of debt, betrayal, and upset, mine included. In the end, it all became too much for me, and I left Eva with my mum, for an hour. I would return shortly. I simply needed some air.

I practically raced along the street, my thoughts

awash with confusion I couldn't get out of my mind. I called Jason, slightly annoyed when his phone went to voicemail, forcing me to leave a relatively short, somewhat curt message before I hung up and swore. By the time I arrived at the house, I had unapologetically vomited several times across several pavements, many strangers asking if I was okay, my response to their kindness slightly less than polite. I stood in my sister's hallway, Mum's words raging through my mind, the thought of Jason with anyone other than me not sitting well in my thoughts at all.

I had assumed this house was bought and paid for. Why, I now had no idea. My ill-considered thoughts now sounded stupid. This house must have been worth well over a million. So why would I assume it was mortgage-free already? I kicked off my Jimmy Choos that I now didn't want anywhere near my feet, scooped up the mail from the mat and raced into the kitchen to search drawers and cupboards that, until today, had held no interest for me whatsoever.

***

When I heard the front door slam, I was already knee-deep in paperwork, most of which I didn't understand, couldn't understand, didn't want to understand.

'Stacey?' Jason's frantic voice filtered through the vast expanse of the property towards my now buzzing ears. He raced into the kitchen to the sight of me sitting on the floor, debt collection letters, unpaid bills, overdue demands, and overdrawn bank statements scattered around my trembling carcass. I looked as if I was throwing some lavish private paper party — my origami tutor would have been so proud. *If I had one.*

'What on Earth is going on?' he asked, not exactly angry — more worried if anything. 'I got your voice message. You sounded upset. Is everything okay? Is something wrong with the baby?' He stood in front of me, confused, hair ruffled, cheeks glowing. How could he possibly be anything other than perfect? I didn't know what to say to him, my thoughts anything but sane.

'Why didn't you tell me about any of this?' I asked, unable to focus on a damned thing other than the volume of red ink lying scattered around me. I grabbed a few sheets of folded paper from the kitchen floor, raising them towards him, hands trembling, mind racing.

'Tell you about what?' It was as if I had asked the most stupid question.

'The debt. The lack of money.' I could see now, for the first time, that they had nothing. This house, the assets, every expensive item in the place, merely an extravagant result of several credit cards, loans they seemed unfazed by — a colossal mortgage that made my eyes water. Emma's bank account was practically empty, as was his. It was as if the rose-tinted glasses I was metaphorically wearing had now been firmly removed from my eyes. *Forcedly. Somewhat painfully.*

'Stacey, you're making no sense.' Jason removed his jacket and slung it over a stool, motioning forward to help me from the floor as if, in my pregnant state, I was having some kind of unfettered nervous breakdown.

'Everyone has debt. It's called life, honey.' He allowed a tiny scoff as he stated this simple fact ever so slightly patronisingly to make me understand how the real world works. He was utterly unable to comprehend that I could, in any way, assume anything different.

Although I disliked how he appeared slightly bemused, standing over me, hands on hips, brow furrowed, I fully understood that my own words did probably sound ever so slightly crazy, unbalanced. In my mind, I had invented a life that simply wasn't true. Of course, everyone has debt. I wasn't stupid. But it was as if the lifestyle I had imagined my sister to have was nothing more than an illusion that I'd invented inside my head. A grandiose projection of the life I had once dreamed of having.

'I just –'

'You *just* found a few simple, stupid debt reminders and thought you would fly off the handle?' Jason was laughing now. Laughing away any fears I may have unnecessarily invented. Batting away my concerns with a free hand as if I were being ridiculous, unreasonable. Daft.

'No. It wasn't like that.' It honestly wasn't like that. My life, it seemed, was a total fallacy. A lie. *Was I really that stupid?*

'Did you think we were rich, Stacey?' His tone darkened for a moment. 'Did you think *I* was? Is this what all this has been about?'

I stared at him. 'What do you mean?'

Jason shook his head. 'Have you not been living in relative luxury these last few weeks? Am I not giving you everything you ever desired? Have I not spent enough money on you?' He pulled me towards him, playfully nibbling my ear, tugging the waistband of my overly expensive maternity jeggings, nudging open buttons with keen fingers, probing body parts with needy intent. He knew how to play me, fully aware of what I wanted from him. I pulled away, my mum's words still strong in my mind.

'Of course not,' I whispered, tears ready to fall. I kissed his cheek, not in any way wanting to be the cause of an unnecessary argument. I couldn't bring myself to look at him.

He tilted his head back, staring at me for a moment, thinking. I could see the cogs in his brain turning at the realisation that my desire for him might have more to do with the money I assumed he could freely give than anything else he might have to offer.

'Jesus, Stacey. Was the only reason you got with me because of the lifestyle you believed I could provide you? Because of all this?' He released me, removing his wandering hand from the inside of the jeggings I was shortly anticipating to expand exponentially. I wasn't looking forward to the resulting stretch marks. Jason glanced around the kitchen, waving his now free hands towards marble kitchen worktops, polished brass light fittings, a coffee machine that had cost over a grand. He shook his head, opening his mouth to say more before I cut him off with a wave of my hands. I was unable to hear such statements emerging from my man's lips. *As if I would ever think such a thing.*

'No. Of course not.' I replied, slightly too firmly,

becoming irritated, irrational. I couldn't divulge that Jason's potential wealth was indeed part of the plan I had created in my head for a new life I had been dreaming of living, probably since I was a little girl. 'It's just that my mum –'

'Your *mum*?' Jason spat the words as if I had accidentally burnt him with a lit cigarette. He looked hurt. 'Jesus, Stacey, I might have guessed Nancy would be involved somewhere.' He shook his head. 'She was exactly the same with Emma. What *is* it with you two and that bloody woman?'

I resisted the urge to yell at him. I had never heard Jason act so distastefully towards my mum before. That *bloody woman* happens to be my mum, thank you very much.

'She was only trying to look out for me,' I spat, unintentionally making myself appear more annoyed than I actually was. She was looking out for both her daughters, it seemed. Probably always would. 'Hang on,' I shook my head, closing my eyes for a moment. 'What do you mean, she was exactly the same with Emma?' I suddenly wondered if, somehow, my mum had overstepped the mark, said too much.

'Where's Eva?' Jason glanced around, ignoring my question, conveniently noticing his daughter wasn't here and entirely refusing my request for information. *Fast Dad* knew exactly how to time his entrance and demands for attention perfectly. He sounded irritated now, his earlier desire for me gone.

'I left her with Mum, so you and I could –'

'So we could what, Stacey? What exactly am I

supposed to have done now?'

Jason was staring at me. To be honest, until this very morning, I hadn't suspected he had done anything. He had given me so much. His love. His time. His money, although credit card based, it appeared. His penis. *What the fuck was I even doing right now?*

'How was my mum exactly the same when it came to Emma?' I repeated, still needing clarification, yet wanting so desperately to retract words I didn't mean to spill so keenly.

'Nothing I ever did was good enough for your parents, Stacey. Emma could do no wrong. I could do nothing right. It was just the way of things for us. Every little argument sent your sister running to Mummy and Daddy. It's a wonder I'm still breathing, the number of times your dad has threatened me for no genuine reason.' Jason stood in the middle of his kitchen, surrounded by a mess I had created, nothing more than a lost little boy slowly beginning to lose his mind with the stress I was putting on him. I recalled Jason's black eye. The one my mum had already confessed that my dad had given him.

'Oh my God, I am so sorry, darling,' I breathed, my hands flying to my mouth, realising with an embarrassed jolt that my mum had placed ideas into my mind that genuinely didn't need to be there.

36

'What has she been saying to you, Stacey?' Jason wasn't backing down, his brow remaining furrowed. I wanted to smooth it down. Kiss it better.

I sighed. 'I didn't know that Eva was autistic. I felt stupid having to hear it from her.'

'*Is that it* Christ, Stacey, what the hell?' Jason walked over to the kitchen sink and placed his hands on the rim, wiping away a stain that wasn't there. 'Eva was diagnosed last year. She wasn't learning to speak normally for a child her age and wasn't achieving her supposed development goals. Emma was worried.' He shook his head. 'Some young kids can be a bit slower to develop, so she left it for probably longer than she felt she should have done. I thought she would have told you ages ago. You've been great with her recently.'

I nodded my head, understanding of what Jason was telling me hitting home rather painfully. *I have been good with Eva recently. I wanted to impress my beautiful man and appear wholly irreplaceable to the cause.* I had, in fact, been looking after Eva almost single-handed for a few weeks.

But Emma and I hated each other. I thought everyone knew that. I thought Jason knew. Why would she ever share with me anything so important as the health and wellbeing of her child? I wasn't worthy of such prized confidentiality. I thought about the bank card sitting in a plastic wallet in the back of my mum's kitchen drawer. Was that really the action of a sister who hated me? I was confused, my head spinning. *What on earth was going on?*

'Mum said that you cheated on Emma?' *Shit, what the hell did I have to say that for?*

'What?' Jason laughed loudly now as if my revelation was utterly ridiculous. 'Just brilliant. And I suppose you believed her?' His eyes seemed to burn a hole straight through mine, penetrating my very soul.

'No,' I yelled too loud, too swiftly, too eager to diffuse this impossible situation. *God no.* I did not want to believe that my beautiful man would ever do such a disgusting thing. I didn't want to imagine him needing anyone other than me now, either. I began to cry. 'Shit, I am so sorry. She was just –'

'Ranting about me,' Jason confirmed, shaking his head, not needing to hear more.

'No.' My mum wasn't trying to be horrible. She was simply being a parent. Caring, loving, worried. 'She wouldn't have even said anything if it hadn't been for –'

'For what?'

Shit. I couldn't tell him about the almost seventeen grand sitting casually in an unused bank account. *My* bank account. I had no idea if Mum was correct about Jason's inability to stop spending. Judging by the amount of debt he and Emma had accrued, I couldn't

296

take the risk of openly telling him about that just yet. I simply didn't, at this stage, have all the answers. I had to think fast.

'If it hadn't been for the fact that I did not know about Eva,' I offered swiftly, impressed with my ability to complete a sentence with an entirely different subject.

'So your mum assumed she could spread shit about me because Emma failed to tell you that *my* daughter has autism?' He couldn't quite believe the spite of my mother, the nerve of the woman. He emphasised the word *my* to confirm that his daughter was indeed his business and no one else's.

'She wasn't being horrible, Jason, I promise.' I had landed my mum in the shit now. It wasn't her fault. *Bloody hell.*

'I told her about us.' I needed to change the subject. I held my breath.

'Oh, for fuck's sake. Why? What the hell did you have to do that for? What did I tell you? Shit, Stacey. Your mum didn't like the fact that I was with Emma. She tolerated me most of the time. She most certainly won't be impressed that we're together.' He glanced at my expanding tummy. 'Did you tell her about the –?'

I nodded. 'I threw up.' It was true. I had actually thrown up all over the place. I felt slightly guilty that I had also left my poor mum to clear it up, Eva already awaking to a nasty whiff of the putrid contents my stomach seemed entirely incapable of keeping to itself, as I left the house in a hurry. I had gone to my mum's with the intention of telling her everything about Jason and me, about the baby I was carrying, about the new life we were beginning. The subsequent revelations I'd received in the process were entirely unfortunate.

'Christ, Stacey.' He looked towards the ceiling for a moment as if trying to converse with the Almighty for answers none of us knew how to find.

'So you didn't cheat on Emma? Before we got together, I mean?' The fact I even had to ask made me feel sick. The simple truth that he had indeed cheated on my sister with me did not in any way reach my brain matter at that point. I couldn't believe that he would ever consider cheating on *me*. Why would he? I gave him everything he would ever need. The past was the past. It was gone, nothing more to be done about it. I could barely comprehend the notion that I was even asking the question.

Jason sighed, unwilling for things to remain unsaid between us any longer. 'Once. Maybe twice,' he muttered. *Shit.* I wasn't expecting such an impulsive response. He ran a hand through his hair, holding his free one towards me, hoping I'd embrace him, needing to explain. 'We were unhappy, Stacey. You know that more than anyone.' I did indeed know that truth. It was the reason I needed to save him, the very reason I did what I did. Everything was for him. *For us.*

I walked willingly into his open arms then, allowing him to hold me, embrace me, to protect me always. I recalled our first frantic lovemaking moment — my half-forgotten balcony now feeling so long ago, my sister's drunken and drugged body lying weak and pathetic in my front room. He had been unhappy that night. I could see it in his eyes, feel it in the urgency of his thrusts. I had saved him that evening. I knew from that moment on, I would always make it my duty to save him. To protect him. Forever.

Jason began to cry. I couldn't help bursting into tears too. When he kissed me, I didn't hold back. I felt terrible at having accused him of such irrational crimes I now knew were not entirely his fault. He had been unhappy in his marriage. It was completely understandable that he would find solace elsewhere. He pulled me to the kitchen floor, and we had sex right on top of those bloody debt letters, telling the entire world that we did not care about such trivial items. Those poor sheets of paper did not stand a chance amid body fluids and eager desire, the subsequent tearing and crumpling sounds below us rather amusing to my ears.

We were both desperate for love, desperate for each other. He didn't even bother to remove my clothing, opting to keenly penetrate me between roughly separated knickers that tore easily within the grasp of wandering fingers. The jeggings that would now need to go into the bin. It was okay, though. This was how we displayed our love — fast, keen, desperate. I hadn't known much else from Jason, those lovemaking scenes in movies stupid and fake to me. They were too slow, weirdly gentle; too obviously manifested for viewing purposes, or simply so the actors involved did not get hurt.

***

My mum called me that afternoon to check on me after

I'd run out on her a little too swiftly. She had been unable to settle the nerves that had grown in her belly ever since I left, especially as I had told her I would be no longer than an hour.

'I'm fine, Mum,' I breathed. Her earlier somewhat twisted words were still loud and clear in my ears, and my inability to trust my own man now added to my growing irritation. I could still see the look in his poor, saddened eyes, the lost stare he gave me, a grown man hurt, consumed by a single thought that his girlfriend did not trust him. *I would not be listening to idle gossip again.* 'Thank you for having Eva for me, Mum. Are you okay to keep her until tomorrow?' I needed to keep our chat light, unable to ponder words I no longer believed held any merit. I did not need to fall out with my grieving mum over any of this.

'Stacey, Eva is not your responsibility,' Mum took a breath, probably realising it would make no difference what she said to me now. I was in love with the man. Of course I would assume that Eva was my responsibility. By the time I got off the phone, I was in no mood for further interaction with anyone, my mother especially.

Jason had reluctantly returned to work after our lascivious sex act was complete, his lame excuse for leaving the office in such a hurry made because of a pregnant girlfriend he hadn't yet told a soul about. He would be working late tonight to make up for his unappreciated and rather sudden dash out of the office, an important meeting now overrunning, deadlines looming. My fault, I knew.

It was okay. I would sit at home and ponder my

unfathomable stupidity. How could I have ever believed that a lifestyle such as this could be achieved without a few unavoidable overdue payments, credit cards, or loans? This house cost a fortune, as did everything in it. Had I honestly believed them to be millionaires? The longer I sat with time to think, the more I began to assume that my mum had blown everything out of proportion. Of course, they had debt. *I had debt.* Nobody lives without some kind of arrears, no matter what level of income your life resides at. *Welcome to the real world, Stacey.*

I tidied my mess, carefully folding every red-inked stamped letter and placing them into a neat little pile. Actually, quite a large pile. No matter. We would sit down and go through things together when Jason came home, like a proper couple — like grown-ups having an actual grown-up relationship. We could check what needed paying first, how I could help. I couldn't live with my head in the clouds anymore. This was the real world now — time for me to take my head out of my arse and get a grip.

As for Jason's apparent infidelity, I wondered if the true connotations behind my mum's conclusion had been merely due to my sister's bitter tendencies, lying to our parents about the actual state of her marriage, making Jason look far worse than he was. Poor guy. He had openly admitted a couple of mistakes to me, cried, confessed to events he had no genuine control of, my sister and him not well suited in the first place. He was bound to look for love elsewhere eventually. It was inevitable. I was just so grateful that, in the end, it was me who had been able to help him escape. To show him what real love was meant to feel like.

Eva, of course, was another matter. Jason had simply assumed I already knew about her autism. Why wouldn't he? He innocently believed that Emma and I were close. Despite the outward dislike we often expressed in public, he had no doubt assumed we loved each other. We were sisters, after all. He would have thought that, deep down, our irksome attitude towards each other was nothing more than simple sibling banter, healthy sibling rivalry. As for the money in a secret bank account, I had no idea how to begin to process such a discovery. The mere notion gave me a headache I couldn't dispel.

I lay in bed and messaged Jason, feeling terrible for having caused such undue stress. I keyed 'Love you' into the phone's brightly lit screen, the darkness around me feeling overwhelming, oppressive, wishing he was here now, on top of me, inside me.

'Love you too,' he replied. 'Stop stressing.' I smiled. I would. I would stop stressing. He loved me. That was honestly the only thing that mattered.

37

I could not believe that I had absorbed my mum's words in such a dramatic way. The only thing my conversation with her had achieved was to make me look a complete and utter fool. To wholly appear as if I couldn't trust my man. I was busy throwing up in the bathroom, bitter thoughts and words twisting my gut along with a baby growing fast. I had cried off work for the last couple of weeks, my pregnancy the perfect opportunity for me to now become a kept, wealthy woman. I shook my head. How stupid of me to assume such a status. How pathetic did that now make me look? I needed to step up, help out. Act the responsible partner and adult that Jason needed me to be.

I opened the bathroom cabinet, searching for aspirin, paracetamol. Anything, in fact, that would help ease my relentless morning sickness. I didn't even bother to check that any of those medications were safe for a pregnant woman to consume, my mind flitting from thought to thought, no place in my head for such trivial details. I discovered a little box tucked away at the back of the cupboard, half-empty, and seemingly hidden. Citalopram. *Antidepressants?* Who in this house would need such medication? Certainly not Jason. Emma? Thoughts of my sister's lifeless, dead body popped into my head, and I threw up again, almost missing the toilet bowl completely.

***

I ventured downstairs and picked up the mail from the hallway floor, noticing more angry red stamps across several white envelopes, as well as a couple of brown ones I did not wish to think about. How much debt was Jason actually in? I hadn't yet been able to bring myself to collect Eva, my mum insisting she stay with them for a few days while I *sort things out*. I knew what she meant. She assumed I would be going back to my flat now I knew the truth. She had no idea that I had already severed my tenancy agreement, rent overdue, the landlord unforgiving. The idea of leaving her granddaughter in the hands of a man she didn't trust was something that didn't sit well with her at all. I fully expected her to request that Eva go and live with them for a while — to take responsibility for his daughter out of my man's hands. I was waiting for the conversation. I was expecting Jason's response.

It was rather ironic that Jason hadn't minded the fact that his daughter was currently being looked after by the grandparents he knew she adored yet apparently retained a fundamental dislike for himself. His child's absence gave him the morning, in his words, to indulge in uninterrupted sex with me, no distractions, our morning routine taking on a new, exciting existence — even if it would only be for a short while. More panting, swift pumping, then he was gone.

It wasn't lost on me that, in a few months, we would have a second needy human in the house. Two young children to clothe and feed. Both requiring time I wasn't entirely convinced Jason had in him. The thought dawned on me that I was about to bring a life into the world with almost no money to support us with, my job hanging by a metaphorical thread, my inability to give an actual shit something my boss had recently grown somewhat weary of.

I sat at the kitchen table, debt letters spread in front of me, dotted now with dried semen and body fluids telling of yesterday's panicked passion. Why did Jason always have to be so hurried in our lovemaking efforts? It weirdly felt as if he always had something else to do once he'd finished with me. His urgency and desperation were what I had loved once. Yet, I now wondered if they were enough. I rarely reached orgasm — an undesirable state of affairs that had been made worse since Emma's death.

I had equated it to nothing more than a little stress, although it wasn't lost on me that Jason no longer seemed to touch me in the way he had done when she was alive. It was almost as if, now that he had me all to himself, I wasn't quite enough anymore, my needs no longer factoring highly enough in his frantic, fast-paced action. He often simply fucked me and left. The idea made me cringe, and I threw up again in the kitchen sink. No one had told me how bad morning sickness could get. No one had warned me.

Jason had advised me that I shouldn't eat too much, yet I was hungry all the time now, my baby needing sustenance twenty-four-seven, dissatisfied, needy. He told me quite firmly that he didn't want me to get fat. Apparently, pregnancy could turn an otherwise beautiful woman into something rather undesirable. He had even expressed a rather odd affection for his deceased wife, a woman who ate only healthy food and looked after herself, in his opinion, better than I seemed to. I sat at the kitchen table staring at a piece of toast dripping with butter, hoping he wouldn't go off me if I became fat and bloated, his desire for me wavering due to a pregnancy that he had created. I had already given up wine and coffee. What more did he want from me?

By the time I had organised Jason's out-of-control outgoings, adding up the total amount of debt he and my sister seemed to have found themselves in, the morning had slipped by. Emma's Mercedes wasn't yet paid for. Repayments were two months overdue already, and bailiffs would have been repossessing it any day had it not already been written off, sitting in some scrap yard, waiting to be crushed, no longer worth a damned thing. I was glad that this was at least one debt we could write off. The car itself was already long gone, and their GAP insurance would now cover the difference.

I wondered if Jason had cancelled the direct debit after Emma's death, her vehicle of no consequence to him now, his mind elsewhere, not fully able to deal with such things in his grieving state of mind. The mortgage was now five months in arrears. *Jesus Christ.* According to several bank letters I found, Emma had already requested a payment break for three of those months, including an application for an interest-only scheme to further reduce the monthly amount, apparently until she could sort things out. They had already received letters of potential repossession. Shit. They owed over six hundred thousand pounds.

I found five credit card statements, all of which had been maxed out several months ago. Mostly on designer products, luxury restaurants, trainers, gym equipment, lavish hotels. I was quite troubled to presume these debts might have belonged to Jason. Nothing at all, in fact, to indicate my sister was a crazed spendaholic, her own credit card bill consisting of nothing more than some unavoidable book printing costs, a few items for Eva, some private health assessments she had attended a couple of times, a cash withdrawal to pay a gas bill, and her book celebration meal total. Which I was mortified to realise I'd significantly contributed to.

Phone bills had racked up, as had costly gym memberships and invoices from expensive personal trainers. I knew Jason liked to look good. I loved how he felt against my skin, how he smelled. It simply added to the allure, the mystique. I now wondered why a nice little jog around the neighbourhood wouldn't have kept him in shape just as well. *And for free.*

I then found a phone bill statement printed on Emma's nutrition business headed paper.

THE NATURAL EATER - THE PERFECT DIET FOR A

LIFETIME OF HEALTH AND WELLBEING.

It was typical of my sister to create such a well-worded catchphrase. I thought about her slim frame, bones that seemed to protrude from skin stretching too thinly over her somewhat emaciated body. *Healthy eating?* If that was the result of such efforts, you could keep it.

I returned my attention to the phone bill, merely a screenshot from an email that had been printed out for reference. There appeared to be several messages to the same number—all within the last month. That couldn't be right. I stared at the number in front of me. Sometimes it had been called early in the morning, sometimes around midnight. Some were actual calls, but most were text messages, sometimes several in one day. I didn't mean for my thoughts to go into overdrive, the assumption that my mum had exaggerated Jason's infidelity still firmly in my thoughts. But I also did not understand why the guy would need to call any mobile number at twenty past midnight, four nights in a row, some lasting around forty minutes each, including text messages he had sent when he should have been at work.

My heart began to pump as I thought of my mum, sitting innocently in her kitchen, explaining how Jason had cheated on Emma so many times in the past, her nonchalant facial expression slowly welding itself to my surprised, unsuspecting eyeballs. I shook my head. No. He wouldn't do that to me. Emma was entirely different. She wasn't a nice person, she didn't treat him well, and Jason did not love her in the way he loved me. Jason was amazing. He adored me. I thought about an innocent bank account full of my sister's money that she had saved for me, and threw up again.

***

I rarely used Jason's landline, mobile phones now all anyone needed to get by, primarily used for searching the internet, ordering items online, sending text messages, checking social media to see how many people had a better existence than the rest of us mere mortals. I knew I needed now to hide my identity, a secret desire to uncover this mystery number growing steadily and uncomfortably in my belly. I assumed my ridiculous ideas would shortly be sedated, my mind set at ease. After all, Jason had explained his past mistakes, cried while he fucked me, expressing keen suffering we both knew he could not have avoided — Emma's presence in our lives the cause of many troubles.

I sat listening to a dialling tone purring in my ears. It reminded me of Sylvester. I took a breath, closed my eyes. A click. A woman's voice. 'Hey you, sexy bum,' she purred down the phone to my unsuspecting eardrum. 'I assumed you would be at work today. When can you get away? I need to see you before I burst something.' She used the same voice I had adopted when Jason and I first got together. The same sultry, *fuck me* voice that I still used daily on him, in fact. When I wanted something.

I swallowed. 'Sorry? Who are you?' I asked, my voice wobbling. A click. A drawn-out, loud buzz against my ear. She had hung up. *Who the hell was that?* I redialled the number, anger and fear building in my lungs that I had nowhere to place. It rang out several times, the woman behind the mystery number remaining elusive. I tried a few more times, frustration developing each time I was left ignored. *Answer the phone, bitch.* My breathing had turned shallow, my head about to explode, my belly churning my breakfast to pulp that would no doubt show itself to me at some point if my phone call remained unanswered for much longer.

Jason wouldn't cheat on me. He wouldn't do that to me. I knew him. I knew him better than anyone. Yet, if I stopped to think about it, I didn't really know him at all. I knew only what I wanted to know, what I felt I needed to know — the almost three-quarters of a million pounds worth of debt he was in testimony to that painful truth. *Shit.*

38

Panicking, I called Jason. Thought better of it. Hung up.
He would only deny it all, anyway. I had to have solid
proof. Why hadn't that woman simply explained who
she was and prevented the enraged emotions now
swilling in my gut? Why was I sitting having wild
thoughts I shouldn't be having? *Why was she calling my
man, sexy bum, and why the hell was she telling him that she
needed to see him before she burst?* She sounded like *me*. I
called my mum, on the brink of tears, unsure what else
to do for the best.

'Stacey?' Mum sounded genuinely worried.

'Tell me about Emma, Mum.' I couldn't believe I
actually wanted to understand my sister's life for the
very first time, my own now looking a complete fallacy.
A sham. I was nothing more than a charlatan, in fact, a
fake — a murdering psychopathic freak who seemed to
have got everything so very wrong. I was crying.

'What do you want to know?' Mum sounded tired, as
if Eva had kept her awake all night. I felt guilty. I had
been lying flat on my back for most of mine, or bent over

Green Monsters

on all fours, Jason inside me, my thoughts anywhere but with a little girl who needed me. It was our thing. Our selfish, deluded thing.

'I want to understand my sister.' I realised with a sudden sharp jolt that I didn't really know her at all.

'Oh gosh, where do I start?' Mum took a breath. 'Well, she had been on antidepressants for a while.' Shit. That explained the box of Citalopram I'd found this morning. I closed my eyes, tears stinging the corners, threatening to burn them out of my head.

'Why?' *Did I need to ask?* With Eva's problems, insurmountable debt, and Jason's infidelity that I now wondered might be true, I would have been on several antidepressants myself. I probably would have committed murder. *Oh, wait. I already had.*

Mum sighed. 'Her business wasn't doing that great. She had far too many other things to focus on in her life, unable to give her fledgling company the attention it needed. She couldn't afford to pay employees, so did most, if not all, the work herself. She packed those cute little healthy nutrition boxes as the orders came in, sometimes working late into the night after she had put Eva to bed. She paid the invoices, ordered ingredients, spoke to the customers directly.' Mum managed a little laugh at the thought of her daughter's creative business idea, monthly nutrition meal boxes that she sent to clients in need of help and support with weight loss and health management, among other things. It was, in fact, an idea that I had taken very little notice of until now. I hadn't cared about such things at the time, Emma's enthusiasm going entirely over my head. 'I am surprised

312

she even had time to write her book,' Mum added with a sniff that made me wonder if she was wiping away a stray tear.

'Eva had just been diagnosed as autistic,' she continued, seemingly composing herself again. 'Jason was always at work, spending money they didn't have, working late hours he didn't need to be working. *Or, so he said.* The debt was mounting.'

I stared at the letters around me, ashamed that I had allowed Jason to fuck me unrelentingly on top of them all, their presence nothing more than an inconvenience I'd assumed we could somehow magically fix. I had forgiven nothing because, in my mind, he had done nothing wrong. Now I wondered, questioning my ability to understand a damned thing.

Mum continued to speak as if she needed no interruption during such a cherished memory of her eldest child. 'She asked Dad and me to help a couple of times. I told her to use your money, but she refused. She said it wasn't your fault that she was in such a mess. She had been saving that money for a while and had made me promise to tell nobody. Besides, sixteen grand wouldn't have covered a fraction of what they owed.' Mum sounded as if she was drinking a cup of tea as she spoke. Mum loved her tea.

'Your sister was always on a diet too. She often claimed she was too busy to eat. Joked about it, even. But the stress was getting to her, Stacey. I discovered she had been vomiting her meals back up after catching her in our bathroom one Sunday afternoon. She cried. I cried. Bulimia, apparently. The irony wasn't lost on either of us, considering she spent most of her time helping others to eat better, her young daughter included. She was getting help, she said. But it wasn't enough. She was losing weight fast. I was terrified of what might happen to her.'

I recalled the amount of food Emma had consumed during her book celebration dinner and the meal I had cooked the following evening, memories of my sister's plentiful bathroom trips, including the one after eating a double helping of chocolate pudding, now firmly threatening my sanity. I thought of Jason's earlier request that I eat less, a demonic idea forming in my head that Emma's eating disorder might have had more to do with the insatiable demands of her husband than what she had once uncomfortably shared with my mum. I found it ironic that my sister's ill health did not match the words on her company strapline. I could never have predicted she was suffering from Bulimia. *How the hell did I not see any of this?*

I took a breath. *Jesus Christ.* Could this day get any worse? 'I found a number on Jason's phone bill statement, Mum. I think he's been seeing someone else.' I paused, waiting for her reaction.

Mum took a deep breath of her own. Eva, in the background, threatened to burst my heart into pieces with her self-activated chatter, her innocence so heart-warming. *God, how I loved that little girl.* 'Jesus Christ, Stacey. Go home. Get your head straight. You don't need to deal with Jason's shit.' It wasn't a request. I hadn't even responded to my mum's revelations about my sister's Bulimia or the amount of stress she was under.

Up until today, I had assumed that Jason's shit was my shit. That we were a couple. Loved up. Eager to start our new life together. It was the very reason I had been forced to kill my –

I closed my eyes. *Shit.* Emma was dead. It was all my fault.

'Stacey?' Mum's worried voice filtered into my own anxious head. 'Are you still there?'

I nodded. 'Yes, Mum, I'm here.' What if I had this all wrong? What if Jason wasn't cheating on me at all? What if those phone calls at midnight had been merely an innocent event? Then I thought about how that woman had called him *sexy bum*. 'I have to go, Mum.' I was crying now. 'I'll collect Eva later. I promise.' I hung up before she was able to say anything more.

***

I stared at the phone statement for several minutes — that single number one of only three on the entire printed inventory. *Three numbers?* That couldn't be right. Jason was always using his mobile for work. He probably spoke to dozens of clients in a single day, his mobile permanently welded to his ear. Something impossible dawned on me. It was nothing more than a simple thought yet held the capacity to rip my world into pieces. Jason had two phones. One he used daily — the one he openly left on the side in full view, so I could see any call or text that came through, trusting me, nothing at all to hide. The other hidden somewhere far away from me.

315

I grabbed my phone, searching the list of stored numbers until I reached Jason's. His number did not match the one at the top of the phone statement in front of me, and neither did my sister's. This was a different number altogether. Panicking, I raced upstairs, searching Jason's bedside cabinet, pulling out drawers and ransacking his wardrobe until I pulled out a small, black smartphone tucked away in an old shoebox, inside a sock. A cheap one. Not the latest iPhone he couldn't live without. I turned it on, shocked to see the volume of messages swarming the home screen in frantic pursuit of attention. The bloody thing didn't even have a passcode requirement to prevent my impromptu search.

'Missing you.'
'Loved what you did to me last night.'
'Can't wait to see you again.'
'Let me know when you can get away.'
'Need your cock inside me right now.'
Lots of aubergine emoji texts, love hearts, kissing face icons.

There were other messages that actually made me feel quite ill, their explicit nature creating a glow to my cheeks that had nothing to do with embarrassment: photographs of naked women, breasts, body parts I struggled to recognise until I took a closer look. *Yuk.* Each message had been replied to, encouraged, confirmed. And all within the last three weeks. *Three weeks?* No. That had to be wrong. This phone must have been sitting in this sock for over a year, surely? Sitting unused for a long time, forgotten about, no longer required, my sudden intrusion creating an entirely unrequired panic. I flicked through the phone, noticing two other numbers that matched the ones on the statement. These were from a mere two days ago. The dates were current. I double-checked. Bloody hell. *Two additional women?* Wow. Surely I was getting this completely wrong?

One of the messages actually sounded as if it had come from a prostitute, the solitary conversation stored in the memory talking of payment and timings she would be available to book him in for his hourly session. She was busy, apparently, her client list growing. He told her that he couldn't wait to see her. She told him that she would offer whatever sex act he so desired. Nothing was off the menu, as long as he had the funds. He told her she was exactly what he was looking for. She told him exactly how far she was willing to go. She allowed a little piquerism but drew the line at breath play. *What the fuck is piquerism?* I couldn't help searching online, not entirely convinced I wanted the answer.

PIQUERISM: Blood kink. Sexual cutting. To some people, the act of cutting another person during sex is gratifying and thrilling. It may be part of a power dynamic.

Jesus fucking Christ. What kind of prostitute was this woman? The last message was from a girl who worked in Jason's office. She was looking forward to arranging their dinner date, apparently, keen to get to know him better, her short time in the office made all the better by his presence. She had been enjoying working alongside him and was looking forward to their date. Jenny. *The young girl I had met a couple of months ago in his office.* The girl I'd felt might have been better off going back to school. She had made me a cup of tea. I vomited on the bedroom floor, not even bothering to clean it up, simply glad it was on Jason's side of the bed. What was a puke stain when my man was sleeping with other women behind my back and visiting the type of prostitute that made inflicting pain sound entirely normal? I thought of Emma again, and the first pang of genuine sorrow for what I had done to my poor sister crept into my conscience.

39

I couldn't simply sit around and wait for Jason to arrive home. I needed to confront him while I had enough anger inside me to wake the dead, my sister's corpse included. I took his *spare* phone and headed out of the door, ignoring my mum's warnings to leave it and simply go home to the flat she wasn't even aware I no longer possessed. I didn't need the stress, she said. Although she might have been right about the stress, I wasn't about to sit in that house and do nothing. It reminded me of a sister now dead.

Jason had made a fool of me. He had made me do things I would have never at one time considered undertaking. To cheat with my sister's husband was bad enough. To get myself deliberately pregnant so he would willingly leave her for me, a horrible situation to find myself in. But murder? How could I have allowed myself the notion that murdering Emma would fix every problem I'd ever had? To save Jason? To save him from what? *From himself*

***

I called his mobile. The one he knew I knew of. The one that neither of us usually thought a damned thing about. 'Hey, you. Everything okay, honey?' His casual tone cut through the air like a hot knife through melting butter. I hated it.

'No,' I replied sharply, not entirely sure what I was going to say once able to express my emotions freely. I was standing in the middle of the high street, too far from Jason's work to get there on foot, and I had forgotten my purse, so ordering a taxi wasn't an option. I felt sick, but it was no longer the baby that was causing it. 'I don't know what I'm doing,' I cried, my words echoing around me. It was true. I had no idea. My actions over the last few weeks now seemed ludicrous, unhinged, psychotic. Maybe I was nothing more than a crazed nutcase who needed locking away for the sake of everyone around me?

'Stacey, where are you?' He sounded worried. It made me wish all the more that my thoughts about him were incorrect, brought about by misinformation.

'How could you do this to me?' He would deny it all but on the other end of a phone he couldn't kiss away my troubled words, touch me, distract me, make me believe everything was okay.

'Stacey, what exactly am I meant to have done this time?' I could not dislodge his condescending tone, his irritation my apparent inability to stop accusing him of random acts.

'Who the *fuck* is Olivia?' I spat into the phone, unable

320

to hide the anger building in my belly. Those messages were disgusting and, considering how my mind worked, that was saying something.

'I have no idea what you are –'

'Don't lie to me.' I was beyond angry. His sultry voice meant nothing to me now. His lies could no longer convince me that everything was inside my head or that my mum possessed the vicious tongue he had invented for her. 'Don't you *dare* lie to me!' My teeth were clenched so tightly, I almost wet myself with fury. If he had been standing in front of me, I probably would have punched him.

Jason sighed. 'She's no one. I don't know anyone called –'

He had totally contradicted his own sentence. 'Jason, I swear, if you lie to me again, I will not be responsible for my actions.' I had killed my sister in cool temperament, calm, calculating — utterly prepared for what lay ahead. Jason was not immune from my wrath now. His murder would not be so easy to cover, his blood literally on my hands and my inability to hide my temper would see me rotting in a jail cell without remorse or apology.

'Where are you?'

'I was on my way to see you.'

'Stay at home. I'm on my way.' He sighed, hanging up before I could tell him where I actually was, leaving me standing in the middle of town, deranged, wondering what to do for the best. Was he planning on talking his way out of this situation? Had he treated Emma this way? Had she too been pregnant when he

321

had started chasing other women?

***

I arrived home to find Jason's car already on the driveway ahead of me. He ran from the house when he saw my approach, his face contorted, hair unkempt. 'Stacey, for Christ's sake, I was worried about you.' My phone had died en-route home, my consistent bouts of vomiting making my journey longer than it should have taken.

I held Jason's cheap, black smartphone in front of me, the screen displaying messages I couldn't bring myself to reread. 'I found this.' I laughed, not intending to sound as if I was enjoying myself. I wasn't. 'It was quite by accident. I was looking for a phone charger.' That was a lie. If necessary, I would have searched the entire place. The recently printed mobile phone statement was still on the kitchen table, exposing what he had done. 'And I was looking for something to help with this bloody morning sickness.' Jason's face appeared as ashen as mine, his words failing him now he was confronted with the truth.

'Stacey, come inside.' He obviously didn't wish the neighbours to hear what I was about to say to him so openly.

I shook my head. 'Why, Jason? Three weeks ago? Two days ago? Are you serious?' I scrolled down to the last message. 'Last night?' He had fucked me harder than a woodpecker going at a tree stump last night. Twice, in fact. I had fallen asleep almost immediately, feeling content, slightly sore admittedly, but content nonetheless. He must have swiftly disappeared downstairs to call *her*. 'What the hell are you doing to me?'

Jason sighed, motioning me into the house. I followed, crying, unable to disguise the fact that he had broken my heart. Broken both sisters' hearts, it seemed. Killed one.

Once inside, Jason closed the door before walking up to me and placing a hand on my shoulder. I pulled away. He couldn't fuck his way out of this. Not this time. I thought of all the times my mum had told me Emma had forgiven him. He had a way of making me melt into his arms. He must have used the same charm on my sister, too.

'Stacey, please.'

'Tell me. Why do you do it? What do you get out of chasing women around?' He had indeed chased me, right into my willing underwear. How pathetic was I? How pathetic did I now sound, asking this very question? *What right did I have?* 'Why would you need to see a prostitute?' I felt sick. The idea of what she was willing to allow as long as he paid for her services still uncomfortable in my mind.

'I can't help it.' He sounded sorry, saddened, his words coming from a place of apparent pain. 'I have a problem.'

You're not kidding you have a fucking problem. You will have a bigger one too soon if you don't start making sense. 'Am I not enough for you?' I simply could not comprehend the idea of him being with any other woman, my attention the only thing I ever felt he needed to exist. I had even stupidly convinced myself that he hadn't slept with Emma for months before we got together. Before Eva was born, actually. In my twisted logic, Jason had merely been waiting for me. Waiting for what I could offer him. My wayward thoughts set only on getting what she had, having some wonderful life I once believed she lived.

'Of course you are, honey,' he whispered, grabbing my neck with both hands and pulling me roughly towards him. I knew what this was. He was going to try and have sex with me, his cock pumping wildly into me as if my cries of apparent joy would make everything better, then leave me spent and dissatisfied on the floor of my sister's soon-to-be-repossessed house. It wasn't going to happen. Not today. I couldn't believe how stupid I had been. Everything I had told myself had been a lie. Everything. Jason's love for me. My sister's hatred. Nothing was real.

It seemed that Emma had been struggling for a long time. She needed a sister to support her — a sister who had hated her merely for having a life that wasn't my own. I had callously allowed my jealousy to cloud everything I was. I had even murdered my poor innocent cat in pursuit of Jason's attention. I was nothing more than a stain on life — a liar, a coward. I didn't deserve anything now.

'If I'm all you need, Jason, tell me why you have been messaging three women this last month? We haven't been together all that long. Surely you're not bored with me already? I met Jenny, for fuck's sake. She's just a kid.' I pushed him away, my words no more hitting Jason's conscience than my own thoughts once had about killing my sister or my cat.

Jason groaned. He didn't want to answer my questions. Instead, he was kissing me, opening my lips, his eager tongue searching, probing. I pulled away. 'No, Jason. We can't do this until I understand why you would ever cheat on me? Why you would ever cheat on my sister?' I felt sickened by the concept. Now, I just wanted the truth — for two sisters no longer together. He grabbed my arm, pressing me against the wall, forcing my legs open with his free hand, pulling at my underwear, searching for what lay beneath. I regretted wearing a dress today, access to my body now seemingly effortless.

'No!' I yelled, kicking out, catching him between the legs and momentarily forcing him to let go. I simply wanted to talk. Properly. Like the adults I wrongly believed we were.

'Bitch.' He brought his hand up, slapping me hard across the face, causing me to reel backwards into the side of the fridge. My loving and supportive man had become violent, my probing questions too much for his ego to take. I thought of all the times Emma seemed to wear too much make-up. I had often secretly called her a whore, believing she only wanted to claim as much attention for herself as she could find. I thought back to the night of her book launch celebration dinner. A book I realised would now never be fully appreciated, never read by her customers. How tarty I had thought she appeared. Dark smoky eyes, potentially disguising a black eye, that I had taken for overcompensation for an otherwise less than perfect appearance. I wondered how many times my sister had covered bruises.

My pregnant belly meant nothing to Jason it seemed. He came in for a second attempt, ripping open my dress and digging nails deep into my bra. I heard something snap. I thought for a moment that Jason was going to rape me. Should I lie on my back and let him get it over with? Our previous sex acts were little more than frantic thrusts anyway, merely rape disguised, a forceful step further than the fierce need I had always seen in him and had allowed freely. Would this moment honestly be different to any of the others? Jason always took precisely what he wanted, when he wanted it. Why should today be any different?

40

I did not choose to lie back and take it. Instead, I decided to fight, kicking my man for a second time, punching him in the face, creating deep nail marks to the side of a cheek and neck I had once considered beautiful. He swore, slapping me firmly across my cheekbone before bringing his face close to mine, kissing me, telling me he loved me, crying for the pain he had caused us, physically, morally, hating what I had turned him into. He would never hurt me again, he said, tearing at my underwear, leaving unforgiving welts on the insides of my thighs where his fingers dug in too hard.

I was pressed against the fridge now, between a cold, unfeeling kitchen appliance and a cold, unfeeling man, both slowly becoming unhinged — a quiet, unseeing hum behind me telling of a romantic meal waiting. A rather expensive T-bone steak, a bottle of dry white wine for him, and for dessert chocolate pudding that I had wanted to lick off his—

Jason ate his dessert in one go now, thrusting himself relentlessly inside me as he shoved me hard against the outer casing of the purring fridge. His thrusts were violent, his grunting angry. I no longer deluded myself than this man was either loving or caring. He had no gentler side unless it was to get his own way about something. Our previous sexual encounters now equated to nothing more than volatile and probable rape — a terrible, all-consuming relationship that I had freely enabled. Unhealthy, immoral, downright wrong.

I had always believed that sex was love. The more frantic our lovemaking, the more it meant he loved me. I couldn't have got this more wrong. Jason did not love me. His urgency and keen desire did not equate to *love*. Not that I even honestly understood what love was. Jason merely wanted an easy life, a life that allowed him to behave like the cruel animal he actually was. It was as simple as that.

Emma had initially provided something that I never could. Money. A way for him to live a life that was better than the one he assumed he might otherwise have had without her. His job wasn't what I had thought it to be, his earnings far less than I expected. My sister had also given him a daughter, an innocent child, not unlike the one that now grew inside me.

Hovering painfully between my man and the air I needed to breathe, legs forced open, crushed against a refrigerator that creaked and groaned beneath the magnitude of Jason's rage – experiencing pain that Jason seemed unaware that he was inflicting – I wondered if he had ever possessed any genuine feelings for me at all. I could no longer tell. He was kissing me, his tongue deep inside my mouth, choking my thoughts, words of love that were not true spilling from his lying, cheating tongue.

Of all the, short-lived sex acts Jason had performed on me, often leaving me gagging for more purely because of his inability to perform long enough to help me achieve climax, this was by far the longest I had to endure him inside me. But now I did not want him anywhere near me. It was as if, without warning, something in my brain had shifted, shut off, silenced. I could finally see him for what he was — nothing more than a cheat, a liar who strutted around as if he was untouchable. Designer clothing, personal trainers, and expensive restaurants he couldn't afford, creating a falsehood of a life I now realised simply did not exist.

Now I only wanted him to complete his mission and leave me alone. I didn't kiss him back. I didn't moan or create any impression that he was in any way providing me with pleasure. He grunted and thrust his way to an orgasm that, for a moment, I wondered might evade us both, forever. Maybe I was destined to be pinned to this fridge for eternity, my clothing in shreds, my skin red with welts of desire that appeared now more of anger than anything else, naked and exposed for the pathetic fake I was?

Or perhaps this was simply my justice. I deserved everything coming to me. I deserved to be raped and attacked under the disguise of lust, my man knowing nothing of real love, honest passion or how to treat women. His only genuine abilities were limited to achieving erections that now felt inadequate, entirely pathetic. Eventually, he came inside me, his once adored love juice now feeling as if I had been forcibly injected with alien goo. He may as well have pissed inside me for how disgusted it made me feel. Finally, he pulled out, panting. My torn clothing hung from my trembling body, my naked skin nothing more now than a cause of shame and repulsion.

'Wow, girl, you seriously know how to turn me on,' he whispered, breathing hard, sliding a tongue inside my ear, utterly oblivious to the state of me, the look on my face, the injuries on my body. They meant nothing to him at all.

I thought of the baby growing inside me. I never wanted any child of mine to suffer what I had been forced to endure today. My daughter would know of a better existence; my son would be taught how to treat a woman properly. Turn him on, had I? *Was he completely insane?* I pulled my tattered clothing around my body as best I could, ignoring the slap Jason gave me on my bare backside. It was the second time I had genuinely felt violated by this man, a man I once thought adored me. He wrapped his arms around me, my back to his sweat-covered belly, unable or unwilling to look me in the eyes.

'No one makes me feel like you do, Stacey. I promise.' What he actually meant was, no one allowed him to do the things that I allowed. I repulsed myself. He kissed my neck, still assuming we were completely fine, loved up, happy. Nothing had happened here today that hadn't already happened many times — in his head, at least. Nothing that I hadn't encouraged and confirmed as normal in the responses I had once willingly provided him. I'd made him believe that his actions were acceptable.

'Those other women don't mean anything to me,' he muttered. 'I guess I'm a sex addict. I can't help it.' I turned around, allowing my tear-filled eyes to fall onto the face of a man I once would have done anything for. *Committed murder for.*

'A sex addict?' *Was he fucking kidding me?*

Jason nodded, cupping a demonic hand around a breast that I realised felt somewhat painful, sore. I flinched. Jason did not notice. 'Emma did not understand me, Stace. When you and I got together that first night, when you let me fuck you so hard on your balcony without telling me I was too rough or reminding me to wear a condom, I realised what I had been missing with your sister.' Wow, shit, he genuinely believed his actions were acceptable. Saying that, though, so did I at one time. I had been as needy as him in those early days. Even last night, in fact, still believing this was all completely normal.

'She would never allow my fantasies to play out so willingly and with such aggression. The bloody woman could be quite frigid sometimes.' He laughed, seemingly recalling a time I wasn't comfortable musing over. 'I was shocked that you seemed to love forceful and urgent sex almost as much as I did.' He was giggling now, pulling me towards him as if readying himself for another session. Shit. *What had I done?*

I pulled away, ashamed, embarrassed to have ever allowed any of this to happen. To let things get this far. 'I love you, Stacey. I really love you,' he whispered. 'No one else understands my needs as you do. My urgency.

My passion.' He cupped my hands in his, unaware of the rape he had just performed. In his mind, this was merely the way of things for us. Acceptable. Normal. 'Olivia is a woman who lets me fuck her sometimes. She likes it rough too, although not in the way you do.' He squeezed my breasts. 'We met in a bar a while back. She is married. She hates her life. We get together a few times a month to release our pent-up frustration.

'But I could never love anyone the way I love you, Stacey. You have to know that. She can't go home to her husband with torn clothes, bruises on her body that I just want to trace with my fingers and watch for hours as I do yours.' He pressed his hot hands over my bare belly, tracing a fingertip across a freshly created welt, his eyes delighted by what I had allowed, by what he had lustfully, repeatedly, created. 'With Olivia, I have to let my cock do the talking. It wouldn't be right to leave my *mark* on another man's wife. Things are different with you. I can do to you pretty much what I like, and you never complain.'

He laughed at the magnitude of his words, unable, it seemed, to get over the idea that someone like me existed. He genuinely believed, as I once had, that sex equalled love. The harder and faster it was performed, the more we both assumed it meant we loved each other. To Jason, he couldn't *love* Olivia in the way he loved me because he couldn't leave physical marks and proof of his lust. His so-called *mark* the power he honestly believed he held over women. The influence he felt he could impart. *Bollocks*.

Jason tipped his head back, his eyes becoming darker,

sullen, almost cold. 'However, with a baby growing inside you, I won't be able to fuck you in the way I need for much longer, will I? I will have to be gentle with you. *Take my time.*' He did not sound happy about this. He shook his head. 'I don't think I can do that. I have my needs, Stacey. But I know for a fact that out of everyone in this world, you will understand what I will need to do occasionally. You know me better than anyone ever has. Better than Emma ever did. That much was evident the night you allowed me to tear your underwear from your body without expressing any disgust or concern at all for my keen urgency. I kept them as a trophy, you know, your black lingerie. I never told you that, did I? I keep them tucked away in my sock drawer as a reminder of our first incredible night together. I was in awe of you that day, Stacey Adams. I have been ever since.'

I realised then why I had never found the damned things — *bloody hell.*

He sighed, unaware of the vomit rising to the back of my throat. 'That's also why I booked a few sessions with Amy. The professional escort you so eloquently reminded me about. She is willing to let me do things that I need to do. Things I have to do in order to feel complete, sane.'

I stared at his twisted face as words spilling from lips that held no concept of love in them at all. I felt terrible for the number of times I'd openly laughed while he tore my clothes and underwear from my body as if they were nothing more than discarded tissue paper he assumed I no longer needed — merely packaging around my awaiting body that he could eagerly tear off, like a child on Christmas morning, ready to feel his urgent thrusts into my naked figure desperate for his urgency as he had been for mine.

I had genuinely believed that Jason's frantic need meant that he loved me so very much. That it was because he was so unhappy with my sister that he needed to play out such keen desire with me, out of pure frustration more than anything else. Now I knew better. *Maybe I was the sick one?* A sick, deranged psychopath who had enabled her very own rapist? I leaned over and vomited on the floor.

41

Jason stood at the kitchen sink, singing a tune he had heard on the radio earlier that morning, quite unprepared to speak to me about what had just happened. But I was not about to let go his shameless acknowledgement of his infidelity. I had taken a shower and was wrapped now in Emma's beautiful cream robe, my hair wet, my body aching, my mood in tatters, my clothes once again in the dustbin.

'Do you want a cup of tea, honey?' he asked, turning around with a smile that I would have at one time given anything to see, wiping his hands on a tea towel that I wished I had the guts to wrap around his goddamned throat. Tea? *Seriously?* Did he think he could buy me so easily?

I'd thought I loved him so much. Everything I had done had been for him and the life I believed we could build together. Why he couldn't see what I had sacrificed for him, I do not know.

'No. I don't want any tea,' I replied, the glare I gave him seemingly missing its mark entirely.

He shrugged, turning around to continue what he considered to be his share of the chores. Drying a wine glass that he had enjoyed without me, my pregnancy apparently now meaning that I was *boring*.

'Did you ever —?' I paused, unable to bring myself to utter the words I needed to say, words I had to get out of my head while I was in the right frame of mind to express them.

'Did I ever what?' Jason grinned, offering me a wink, still singing that bloody annoying tune.

How could I phrase this without making him angry again? 'Did you ever? I mean, did Emma enjoy it fast, urgent? Sex, I mean.' Shit, did I really want to know? What I really wanted to ask was, did he ever *hurt* Emma? Sexually?

Jason sighed, seemingly no longer in the mood to sing. 'Emma wasn't like you, Stacey. She wasn't as much fun.' I swallowed, suddenly feeling like the cheap whore I had once accused my sister of being. 'Emma was my first real long-term girlfriend. Before her, I played the game, slept around,' he laughed, obviously recalling some earlier time in his life I wondered if he had recently needed to reaffirm. 'But I knew I needed to settle down at some point. I wanted to settle down. I really did. And I loved your sister. I hope you know that.'

Yeah, sure, like you love Ready Salted Crisps, no doubt. They are great for a while. But then you fancy something else. Prawn Cocktail. Salt and Vinegar. Plus, Emma was already doing well in life when you met her. So that must have swayed your decision a little. I clenched my fists together by my sides, not entirely wanting answers

336

to the question I'd already raised.

'But shit, she would never let me bite her, slap her or act out any of my sexual fantasies like you do.' Jason shook his head, remembering his relationship with a woman now dead. He turned to face the sink again, chuckling under his breath.

'And what about Olivia?' I asked the back of his head, my fists raw with fury as I squeezed my fingers together, twisting with the thoughts in my mind, a blackened disease that had become my normality.

'Shit, Stacey, I wish you would just drop that. I thought I had already explained.'

'You haven't really explained anything.' I was developing a palpitation I didn't know how to appease, my lungs struggling to cope with the oxygen that failed to reach my mind. 'All you did was attack me.'

'*Attack you?* Jesus Christ, are you serious?' Jason looked genuinely confused.

I nodded my head. *Deadly.* I lifted my sleeve, an angry welt snaking up my arm, coupled with finger marks where he had recently held me against the fridge door. I didn't dare undo my robe in case it kick-started round two. 'What do you call that?'

Jason scoffed again, chuckling to himself as if he could not believe my words. 'You usually laugh about our passion wounds,' he began walking towards me, but I backed away. Jason stopped, and we stood, staring at each other for a moment, neither of us knowing what to say or do next. *Passion wounds.* That is what I had comically nicknamed the marks left behind from Jason's apparent lovemaking. How stupid was I? How weak?

How did that now make me look? There was nothing passionate about what Jason had done to me.

'For fuck's sake, you stupid bitch.' Jason lunged forward, grabbing my arm before I could stop him. 'Come on, Stacey. I thought you were different. You always acted differently. You made me believe you could be the one to change everything.' Jason was staring at me, cold, unseeing, something in his eyes that appeared as dead as his wife's corpse. What exactly did he believe I could change?

Fresh tears lingered in eyes that to me now looked unfeeling, blank, as if Jason had left the room some time ago, leaving behind nothing more than a demonic entity I had no idea how to appease. 'You let me do things to you that Emma hated. She would run to Mummy whenever I *hurt* her.' He emphasised the word *hurt* as if he had never actually laid a finger on her, that his furious sex acts were purely a way for him to release his otherwise pent-up frustrations, something he assumed his wife, of all people, would understand.

'I thought you would be the one to make everything better.' He whispered, stroking my hair, reminding me of how things had been when we first got together. 'Don't be like your fucking sister.' He grabbed my hair then, his tone changing, yanking my head back so that my face was aligned with his, kissing my neck, sucking my flesh. The love bite he wanted to leave on my skin now feeling as if he was going to bite a chunk out of my soul, leaving a scar so deep I would never forget what I was to him. *His whore.* 'I want you. I need you. I can't fuck other women the way I can fuck you.' Shit, Jason honestly felt as if I was saving him. I had thought that too, a while back. *Jesus Christ.*

'Tell me more about Olivia,' I spat, needing the truth I felt would not be forthcoming.

Jason grunted, shoving me against the kitchen table before releasing his grip on me. My neck hurt. I tasted blood from an earlier slap, my swelling lip still throbbing. 'She is nobody. Okay? Happy now? I fuck her sometimes when I can't have you.' He stared at my expanding belly. 'Or when you are too busy throwing up into the goddamned toilet.' I seriously hoped he wasn't planning on blaming my pregnancy for his cheating. 'There. I've said it.' He continued, oblivious to the look I gave him. 'I have tried to explain that I am a sex addict, but you have to keep picking at it, don't you? You just couldn't let me love you, make it up to you. I can't screw other women as I can you, Stacey. They won't *fucking* let me.' He laughed then as if his words were as ridiculous as the accusations I'd inflicted on him. How dare those other women not allow his violent acts of passion? Slamming his fist into the table, he lunged towards me again, grabbing me, his face contorting in anger, unseeing, uncaring. *Jason had well and truly left the building.*

'What are you going to do? Rape me again?' I actually sounded a little frightened. I couldn't believe I was expressing such fear.

'There you go again with that *attack, rape* bullshit? What the fuck are you talking about, Stacey? When have I ever hurt you? You usually love it. You can't get enough of me. You tell me that much all the time.'

He was right. I had said as much, many times. I had usually desperately wanted him inside me, thrusting away as if his life depended on it. I had created a monster. No. The monster was already lying in wait. We were both monsters, in fact, waiting to get precisely what we deserved. He had hurt me today. Hurt me on more than one occasion if I was honest enough to admit it.

'Do you love me, Jason?' Why I felt I needed to ask such a question, I have no idea. Of course, he didn't love me. Jason loved only himself.

'Stacey, I need you. Without you, I don't know what I might be capable of.' He smoothed my hair. He looked deranged.

I swallowed, terrified that, without me to suppress his needs, absorbing his wrath, he might go out and rape women simply to get his kicks. He hadn't answered my question about love. I no longer wanted the answer. He confirmed he needed me, yet his need was purely selfish. There was no love in that assumption.

'And the prostitute?' I was on shaky ground, I knew. But I asked anyway.

Jason scoffed. 'Amy lets me do things. Tie her up. Fuck her hard, sometimes until she bleeds.' Shit. He was still utterly incapable of admitting that his acts equated to rape, nothing more. In his head, his actions were totally acceptable as long as the women allowed them, if he paid enough for services rendered. He had undoubtedly paid enough for mine.

'How often have you seen her?' I closed my eyes, terrified of the answer, trying not to choke on my own thoughts. I recalled that single phone message conversation. In my mind, it didn't appear that they had met at all.

'Only twice, so far,' Jason licked his lips as if recalling their latest encounter. 'She doesn't mind. I pay her well. In fact, I pay her *really* well.' He grinned. I felt sick, realising that Jason was an actual serial rapist. A rapist that I had, in some unhealthy way, helped create, helped enable. He was deluded, convinced that he was well within his right to express himself, as long as he believed he had a willing partner to share his requirements.

'And Jenny?'

Jason shook his head. 'Jesus, you're obsessed, woman. I haven't done anything with Jenny. I offered to take her out to dinner, that's all.'

'Why?'

'Because she's a new girl at the office –'

'But you intend to fuck her at some point?'

Jason fell silent, seeing for the first time the hurt in my eyes. He didn't answer me, instead choosing to stroke my cheek. It was merely as if my constant questioning had triggered an automatic non-verbal response. He smiled then, pulling open my bathrobe, ready to act out some twisted fantasy that had popped into his head, assuming this was all completely normal. My statement about what I assumed he wanted to do to young Jenny altogether creating a twisted reaction in his already deranged brain.

'Jesus, Stacey, you are bloody incredible, you know that?' He was pressing his fingers between my legs, searching, readying himself for a session to end all sessions. At one point, I would have killed to hear him say such words to me, happy to lie on the floor, legs held akimbo, allow him to penetrate me in a rage I honestly believed signalled an authentic and genuine urgency to love me. I had wanted his *love*. I had needed it.

'What are you talking about? Why am I so incredible?'

'Because I know that once we have had this conversation and you understand why I do what I do, what makes me tick, you'll understand me better than any of the others.' He stroked my hair. 'I've never had that before.'

I laughed, straight into his face, a mocking laugh I could no longer hide, his grabbing fingers things I no longer felt anything for. It was as if my body had turned to stone, nothing more than a slab of cold meat I was no longer willing to offer him freely. His hot breath against my cheek felt like acid, poisoning my mind and allowing a truth I had failed to acknowledge until this very moment.

'Get the fuck away from me,' I screamed, biting his top lip, making him wince. I pushed him in the chest, causing him to reel backwards in pain, the obvious erection in his boxer shorts nothing more to me now than a thing I wished I had the guts to chop off.

'God, I love it when you act your part,' he breathed, rushing towards me again, his face stretched into a vile grin, nothing behind cold eyes but hatred for women he felt did not understand him. He was planning on hurting me — the baby in my belly nothing more to him than a by-product of our supposed love. I understood why condoms had never factored in our sex acts. Rapists do not care for such items. To them, it is all about the power and control they can possess over others. I had incorrectly assumed it meant he wanted to give me his child, to share himself freely with me, to feel every inch of me uncovered. *What an idiot I was.*

He tore my sister's lovely robe, more clothing ready for the bin. I was crying. He thought it was all part of our fun. How could he be so vile to me? He dragged me across the kitchen table, bending me over, opening my legs while whispering that this was going to be a performance of a lifetime, something I would never forget. My tears blurred my vision, but I needed to protect my unborn child because Jason was readying himself for frantic entry.

Without thinking, I picked up the half-consumed wine bottle from Jason's earlier solo drinking session, slamming it into the side of his face before I could change my mind. I heard the crunch as he cried out in pain, releasing his grip on me, staggering backwards, his cheek exploding. I turned, away, my hand shaking, blood dripping from it. He spat blood onto the floor, displaying teeth now red and angry.

'What the hell are you doing, you idiot?' he yelled, his boxer shorts already around his ankles, his exposed penis creating a repulsion I had nowhere to place. I could not even bring myself to look at it. He lunged at me again: he needed that bottle out of my hand so he could continue his quest. 'I love it when you put up a fight, but bloody hell, girl, calm down.'

He honestly thought this was a game. A game I had willingly helped create. We had invented many fantasies,

Jason and I. I was always his slave girl, his bitch, his *whore*. He was my kidnapper, forcing himself upon me, acting out many frantic indulgences. I didn't want to play Jason's games anymore. 'Get away from me, you freak,' I yelled, nothing in my mind now but to escape Jason's grip unhurt, although not entirely unaffected by this impossible day.

'Yeah, go girl,' he chided, spitting blood onto the floor. *What the hell was wrong with this man?* Jason was laughing now, his erection in one hand, our apparent game turning him on.

I swung the now broken bottle towards him, uncaring that I was spilling what was left of fairly decent wine onto the floor. 'Get away from me, Jason.' I stared into dead eyes that I hadn't noticed before. 'I'm not kidding around.'

Still laughing, Jason grabbed my hand, forcing the bottle from my grip, his strength and determination too much for my weak, pathetic attempts. I had never felt so pitiful in my life. The only thing I knew to be true at that moment was that Jason was *not* going to rape me again. Not today. Not ever. Summoning every ounce of strength I could muster, I kicked him directly between the legs, scrambling off the kitchen table and out into the hallway. I was half-naked, covered in bruises, tears falling unforgiving, and I was running.

I attempted to open the front door, uncaring of how I looked or how the neighbours would react, not entirely surprised when Jason grabbed me from behind. He pinned me to the door, still grabbing between my now trembling legs, kissing my neck, the feel of his breath against my skin more than I could stand. I honestly felt that he might kill me, his need too strong, his desire too much. I cried, but he wasn't listening, intent only on releasing the orgasm he felt I was not giving freely. He didn't care how much he had to hurt me in the process of achieving total satisfaction. My face was pressed against the stained-glass panel of the front door, seconds from further terrifying endurance. My once adored man now so cold, so terrifying.

I turned my head sideways, noticing a set of discarded golf clubs propped against the hallway cupboard. It was a simple idea, not unlike the one that had formed before callously taking my sister's life. I reached out a free hand, relieved that my fingers were able to wrap around the handle of the nearest club, grateful for its cool metal in my grip, close enough to become my willing assistant. I momentarily thought back to an unassuming pair of scissors probably still sitting in the pocket of my since unworn, now forgotten, fake leather jacket.

I craned my neck to see Jason offering a brief smile, penis in hand, already probing between my unwilling clenched cheeks, caught within private delusions, totally unaware of the thing I held in my own hand. It allowed me the precious few seconds I needed to bring that golf club over my head and slam it full force into the side of his head. I heard a dull thud as Jason dropped to the floor, his crumpled body a pathetic sight in front of me.

'Fucking hell Stacey, we are only playing,' he scolded, ready to get to his feet again.

The sight of his bare backside upended made me

want to vomit. *What the hell was wrong with this guy?*

I shook my head. 'No,' I whispered, unable to believe that things had come to this. 'I'm done playing your games.' I bought the club up again, slamming it against the side of my man's head and neck as hard as I could. I kept on beating him until I could see no more movement from his demonic form, the unassuming weapon in my hands a bloodied mess, an otherwise innocent metal pole indistinguishable from the fingers that held it.

I hit him seven times – I counted – blood unapologetically splattering over the walls, the front door, my permanently damaged body. I was screaming as I hit him, yelling into the void of this once prized property. He had taken everything from me, my independence, my sister, my sanity. My desire for him had been nothing more than a sick indulgence that had allowed this man's disgusting innermost fantasies to become a reality. What I once assumed was Jason's desperate love for me was nothing more than his own deluded need for power.

42

He was dead. I knew that to be true — nothing left of his face that the police might have used to identify him, dental records potentially their only way forward. By all accounts, Jason had turned me into a killer, a serial killer — two dead humans and a poor dead cat proof of what I had become. I had nothing left inside me except a growing baby who was my only hope for redemption, for potential salvation I did not believe I deserved.

I checked for a pulse, unsurprised to find none as I sat on the floor shivering, the stench of blood in my nostrils that might never leave me again. This was such a different experience compared to how I had felt during and after killing Emma. Although both murders had been carried out with cruel intention, this act was pure self-defence. It did not sit well with me that both acts had been achieved from self-deluded self-preservation. I dreaded to think what Jason might have done if left to his own devices. What he might have done to someone else had I left him alive. I thought about our baby, about Eva. She deserved so much better than a father like that.

They both did. I thought of my sister, dead and gone. *What the hell had I done?*

***

I winced at the pain in my arm as I dabbed foundation around the dark shape under my eye. I shoved on some lippy, a tear welling. I looked a bloody mess. Pushing the last of my unwanted belongings into a plastic bag, I straightened Jason's bed, tucking his brand new trainers under my arm, ready to throw them in the bin. He would have hated that, considering how much they had cost. Still, there was nothing he could do about that now, already covered in blood that would never wash off: a broken wine bottle and blood-soaked parquet flooring, a devastating reminder of the night before. I closed my eyes, holding my breath as I closed the bedroom door behind me.

I laid a suitcase, two carrier bags, and a box of belongings that I fully intended to donate to charity at some point, onto the front step of the porch, slamming the front door behind me, Jason's body still cold, bloodied and dead in the hallway beyond. I stood clutching Emma's set of keys that I had once been so excited to possess. It was finally over. Weeks of slow deterioration, putrid hatred, my mother's words lingering in my mind, Emma's cold dead stare that now matched her husband's. Taking a breath, I posted the keys through the letterbox, allowing one last glance at a house I had convinced myself I could make my home. I wondered if husband and wife would now be reunited on the other side. *Would Emma even want him?*

Jason had pushed me further than I was willing to go. Convinced I wanted my sister's life, I had thrown myself unsuspectingly into a daunting existence. A downward spiral that I had willingly instigated, willingly conspired for, irrefutably invented. I wondered how Emma had put up with his behaviour for so long. The cheating. The abuse. Jason Cole – kind, loving, capable of turning every woman's head without trying. *What a bloody joke.* Emma had kept this part of her life hidden so well that it had fooled everyone. It had fooled me. I felt sorry for her, the first genuine pang of guilt twisting my gut into a knot. Had I ever done anything nice for my sister? I hated the answer.

Hands trembling, I loaded my belongings into a taxi, the driver offering sympathetic glances. He knew I was an abused woman, the angry bruising on my neck and face testimony to that. I could tell the poor guy felt sorry for me, fleeing her home without looking back. He was utterly unaware of the dead man a mere ten feet away, lying cold in his own hallway, penis still slightly erect, mocking everything I once believed he stood for.

I wasn't getting away with what I had done here today, fingerprints everywhere, a murderous deed unforgivable. No one would have believed self-defence was a sufficient motive. Still, I needed to buy some time for one last trip. A trip I should never have had to make, my actions bringing me to this very moment. I stared at the house as the taxi drove away. *Goodbye, Jason Cole. Goodbye, once assumed beautiful life.* This simple journey signalled the end of so much, the beginning of something much worse to come.

***

The look on my mum's face was priceless. She didn't need to acknowledge the bruising on mine, both of us knowing exactly where they had come from, who had done this to me — the reason behind tears that welled inside dark eyes, something I could never adequately explain. She knew what had happened. The way things would have ended. I stood in her hallway, suitcase and carrier bags the only evidence of a life now over, a deadly poison slowly devouring the very soul she once considered beautiful. My soul. *My ugly, condemned soul.*

Although she was initially pleased to see me, just one look was all she needed to confirm her daughter's suffering. Both daughters' suffering. She couldn't help the gasp that left her lips as she opened her front door. She was surprised by the state of me, of course. Shocked, most definitely. But pleased to see me, all the same, pleased I had left him, knowing what Jason was and failing to get through to either of her daughters until it was too late. I didn't wish for my dad to get involved. He was an ageing man. He didn't need the stress, his time now primarily spent in the garden, pruning bushes, removing weeds. Mum said it kept his mind busy. I knew it kept his sanity.

'I'm so sorry, Mum,' I breathed, unable to offer any further explanation as we stood, eyes locked, unsure whether to embrace each other or simply leave things unsaid. She had absolutely no idea what I was apologising for. *How could she?* How could anyone presume to know what I had become? 'I had nowhere else to go,' I sobbed, my voice no more than a whisper.

Mum nodded. She didn't need to ask why. She already knew what Jason was, what I had failed to understand about the man my sister had never spoken the truth to me about until it was too late — until I was already entangled in his venomous net. Too caught up in fake emotions to ever see the truth.

'Eva could do with some fresh air if you're up to it?' It was a kind offer, made with the single intention of helping me escape what she no doubt assumed was Jason's fathomless wrath. My poor mum didn't know the half of it.

I smiled, my swollen lip too much for my face to create any natural shape, my black eye unable to hide beneath the make-up I had painfully applied. Mum turned, collected her granddaughter from the kitchen floor and popped her into her buggy. If she understood anything of what I had done, she would have never made such a thoughtful offer.

'Are you okay, sweetheart?' Mum asked, utterly unaware of the vile, toxic murderer standing right in front of her. She was holding a tea towel. I just wanted to fling my arms around her neck and cry like a baby. Like the little girl I had once been to her. Innocent again. Her loving child.

Instead, I shook my head, unable to speak another word as I turned and left the house, Eva's gentle chatter the only sound remaining as we ventured out into fresh air together and freedom I knew was only temporary. I would never be okay again. It was a simple truth, an unfortunate reality that I literally had no place for. There was so much I wanted to tell my mum, to confess, elaborate on, share my experiences of. It was such a shame she would now only ever see what I became in the end.

***

I found myself standing by my sister's grave. It was the first time I had returned to this location since the funeral. I had vowed never to come here again, convinced I could avoid acknowledging actions no longer changeable. I was covered in bruises, my hips, arms, and legs aching from a rape I could never have anticipated, soreness apparent each time I tried to pee. I could not tell my parents the truth. My stupid inability to register what Jason was doing to me ultimately became the very thing that had enabled events now complete. I had attempted to cover my so-called *passion wounds* with make-up, precisely how Emma had done once, packing a suitcase amid the silence of a home I no longer wanted. I'd received no genuine explanation or apology for his actions, cheating and raping ways. There would be no closure, it seemed, to this short chapter in my life.

He had simply kissed me and told me he loved me, the angry marks on my skin meaning nothing to him at all, his actions merely part of a game that turned him on. I had welcomed his forcefulness at one point, bruises simply a by-product of our now incomprehensible, so-called fun. *Fun.* How fun was I finding all this now? I had utterly deluded myself that it meant he loved me.

The police would arrest me soon enough, my parents uncovering a terrible truth about their eldest daughter and the vile, violent murderer their youngest had become. They would take one look at me and see a horror once hidden. I had, of course, brought this entire thing upon myself. I was as sick and twisted as Jason, deserving of everything coming to me now.

I laid flowers on Emma's headstone, her cold dead body lying a mere six feet beneath my own. My pregnant belly was swelling, a bubbling sensation inside telling of an innocent child yet to be born. Eva was asleep in her pram, the sun shining. I had refused the bank card that my mum had been holding for me, my sister's excited instruction now a fitting irony to the life I had callously taken from her. It would have been a terrible thing to do anyway, an act of evil calculation. That money should be saved for Eva. I would transfer the funds when needed, give my niece a chance. Tell her I was sorry. My thoughts made me choke. Who was I kidding? *I was evil. I was calculating.* I had only deluded myself that I could be anything else.

'I don't know if you can hear me,' I whispered, more to myself than to the sister I wished, more than anything, could hear me. I was sitting before loving words carved forever in stone, thoughtfully adorned by parents grieving for the loss of a daughter never to be forgotten. 'But I want you to know that I got this thing all so very wrong.' There was a light breeze in the air. I pretended it was Emma. Swirling around me, hearing my words, listening, forgiving unforgivable deeds. I needed her forgiveness that I had no right to ask for.

I traced a trembling finger across my sister's name, quite unable to stop myself from releasing honest and heartfelt tears I had no right to express. 'I always believed that you hated me.' I laughed, an awkward sound erupting from my throat, causing Eva to stir. 'Because I hated you. I really did. I thought you had it all, and I detested what you stood for.' I closed my eyes, unable to comprehend how wrong I had got everything, how wrong I had got my sister, how jealous I had become.

My parents would soon know exactly what I had done. They would disown me, cut me off, forget my existence. They would take Eva away, never let me see her again, this child I needed to care for and love for the sake of my sister. She was all that was left of the beautiful woman who had sacrificed her already fragile financial status and equally fragile relationship to help her undeserving sister.

Jason would not care if his daughter was raised by someone else. He barely had time for her anyway, his fatherly devotion on display only when in company of those he needed approval from. *Fast Dad* was someone I no longer wished to think too long about. I simply didn't know what would happen now. Nothing in my life seemed real at all.

I lost track of how long I sat by Emma's grave, Eva asleep, my own child kicking for attention I wasn't yet fully able to provide. I felt lost, utterly lost. I had wanted so much from life, but there had been so many thoughts in my head that shouldn't have been there. I did not know what love was. I did not understand. The simple truth was Emma had loved me more than I could have ever appreciated. She had wanted to be there for me, to look out for her little sis. She had included me in her life whenever possible, sharing her goodness, her selflessness, her experiences. She had wanted me to be happy for her, happy for myself. Yet, I merely took it as her way of rubbing my face in the success I believed she had. Her money. Her marriage. All of it lies. I knew that now.

I would never be able to put Jason behind me, his child a permanent reminder of a past I could no longer change. I would have loved to help my parents raise Eva, God willing, take her on as my own, had things turned out differently. It mattered little. The police would arrest me soon though Jason's dead body still lay undiscovered. A cleaner would eventually arrive at the house, her screams revealing such a vile truth.

I stared at my hands, still trembling from a previous moment of terror, Jason's hands around my throat, uncaring, unfeeling. Traces of blood left behind that I felt might never wash off. I was a murderer — nothing more, nothing less. No self-created delusions could ever refute that fact. I fully intended on going quietly, already guiding the police to the house with its secret. My sister's once cherished cleaner had been unrequired until today, no money available to pay her until I made a call this morning. Her help needed once more, my needs appearing genuine, Janet would not have considered my phone call suspicious, neither could she have expected such an abysmal scene to await her. For that, I was sorry.

It couldn't be helped.

I would willingly tell them all that I had murdered Jason, Emma too, should they ask, my life equating to nothing more than a collection of painful memories I no longer wished to endure alone. I thought about the baby inside me. The child did not deserve to go through such pain, being born into a system that would take them away from me. I understood that I needed to give my baby a chance. I owed it that much, at least. I needed to give Eva a chance at a happy life, too, with my parents who were so desperate for closure on what had happened to their own child. I closed my eyes for a moment, needing a break from my impossible thoughts.

A sensation crept across my cheek then, as if I'd been touched. Gentle, caring, soothing. I opened my eyes, the light breeze becoming stronger, Eva's buggy rocking gently. It was as if Emma was checking in on her baby. I sat up, tears still stinging, bruising still mocking. I had got precisely what I deserved. I would suffer my own pain now, probably forever, as Eva grew into the woman her mother would never know, and my child would grow up in this dangerous world without me.

'I am so sorry for what I did to you, sis. Truly I am.' For the first time in my life, I genuinely was sorry. I didn't have to fake it, pretend that everything was as it should be, verify deluded emotions. This time my pain was real, honest. So different from how I'd acted when I sickeningly lured my sister to her untimely death. 'I love you, Emma,' I whispered into the breeze, feeling for the first time in my life a connection to a sister I didn't entirely know. A sister I should have loved with everything I had inside me, unconditionally. She was, after all, family. 'I love you so much.' My words disappeared amongst the rustling trees as Eva opened her eyes.

'Mama,' she cooed, inside her pram, her arms reaching towards a space somewhere between this world and the next. 'Mama.' It was the first real word she had ever spoken. Upon hearing it, I burst into tears. I told myself that Emma was here, that she had clearly heard her daughter's first words. I hoped that she was able, from wherever she was now, to watch her grow up, to watch over us both. And to even forgive her sister once so bitter and *deluded*, someday maybe. I could only wish for that. I could only hope.

I remained seated by my sister's grave as the sound of sirens surrounded me. My mother had probably confirmed my intended whereabouts, confusion no doubt developing about a daughter she had once adored, once believed in. Car doors slammed, footsteps grew closer. I closed my eyes. They might understand my delusion, appreciate that the green monster living inside me was simply a confused young woman who did not understand love. It was my inability to truly appreciate what love was that had brought me here now. I would go quietly, no cause for concern. No need for dramatics.

I had nothing now to live for other than a baby yet to be born, an apology still to be acknowledged, although probably never accepted. When firm hands pressed against my shoulders, the voice of an officer asking me to confirm my name, verifying the reasons they were here, I was almost relieved. This was the end of the way of things for me, the end of my delusion, my path of unfathomable destruction. I wondered if I would ever receive the help I needed to become a sane, normal human being. *Maybe not.* I was probably beyond saving. For the first time in my life, I wished I could have been more like my sister. Life might have turned out very differently for both of us.

ACKNOWLEDGEMENTS

Thank you to all the narcissists out there who made the main character possible to achieve so effortlessly. You know who you are.

Thank you, as always, to my incredible husband for his unwavering support, and to SRL Publishing who see beyond traditional story-telling methods, searching for stories that delve deep into the human psyche and beyond.

SRL Publishing don't just publish books, we also do our best in keeping this world sustainable. In the UK alone, over 77 million books are destroyed each year, unsold and unread, due to overproduction and bigger profit margins.

Our business model is inherently sustainable by only printing what we sell. While this means our cost price is much higher, it means we have minimum waste and zero returns. We made a public promise in 2020 to never overprint our books just for the sake of profit.

We give back to our planet by calculating the number of trees used for our products so we can then replace. We also calculate our carbon emissions and support projects which reduce CO_2. These same projects also support the United Nations Sustainable Development Goals.

The way we operate means we knowingly waive our profit margins for the sake of the environment. Every book sold via the SRL website plants at least one tree.

To find out more, please visit
www.srlpublishing.co.uk/responsibility

Nicky Shearsby returns with…

BLACK WIDOW

Coming March 2023

Available to order

SRL Publishing Ltd